Born in Tynemouth in 1919, C. L. Skelton's varied career has included stage and film acting, war service in the RAF, seven years as a lay brother with a religious order, hunting the Loch Ness monster and selling insurance and brushes door-to-door in the Scottish Highlands.

Other novels by C. L. Skelton in Grafton Paperbacks are *Hardacre*, *Hardacre's Luck*, *The Maclarens* and *Beloved Soldiers*.

By the same author

Hardacre
Hardacre's Luck

The Maclarens
Beloved Soldiers

C. L. SKELTON

Sweethearts and Wives

This edition published 1994 by
Diamond Books
77–85 Fulham Palace Road
Hammersmith, London W6 8JB

Published by Panther Books 1980
Reprinted in Grafton Books 1986, 1989

First published in Great Britain by
Granada Publishing Ltd 1979

Printed and bound in Great Britain

Set in Times

Author's Note

In this sequel to *The Maclarens,* I have again taken liberties with the actual details of various campaigns. Several of the exploits of the Maclaren Highlanders, a fictional regiment, which are detailed were based on actions fought by some of the great Scottish regiments. Them I salute as the great soldiers they are and always have been.

I want again to thank Major Hugo Macdonald-Haig, M.C., Captain Gordon Mackintosh, and Doctors Peter Sutherland and Edgar Abbas, for the advice and assistance they have given me in the writing of this book. The accuracies are theirs, the errors my own.

Finally I want to dedicate this volume to my friend and comrade of more years than it is good for a man to remember, Barry Gray.

C. L. Skelton
Scotland
1978

Sweethearts and Wives

1
The Imperial Wars

1

The north-east wind had brought with it the *haar*; that mist which is nearly rain, that fills the air with droplets of water so fine as to be near invisible, but which will cut through a man's thick woollen doublet and give his shirt a clammy dampness that lies cold and cloying on his skin.

The barrack square was deserted and silent and miserable in that cold, grey, near dawn. It was surrounded by the shadowy piles of the barrack blocks, which glistened pink from the Moray sandstone of their building whenever the sun struck them, but now, in the gloom, were grey and damp. Here and there little rivulets ran half-heartedly down the walls where some imperfection in the guttering allowed the water which had oozed down the Ballachulish slates of the roofs to escape to the earth whence it came.

The square itself, upon which a thousand boots had stamped a million times, was scattered with little pools where the water had gathered wherever there was an indentation in the pounded surface. Here and there a yellow light was reflected fitfully in a pool, a light which gleamed pathetically through a window as it awaited the approaching dawn. But there was no one there, no single person in sight; it was a world damp, deserted, and dead.

It was November, 1883, and the first battalion the Maclaren Highlanders, until recently the 148th Regiment of Foot, were parading at their home barracks just south of Beauly, some nine miles north of Inverness. They were not on the parade ground, for the work they were to do that morning was not a deed that could be performed in an area cocooned among tall buildings of pink Moray sandstone.

They were standing easy, grim faced, on the east side of the buildings which comprised their home. They had formed three sides of a hollow square, the open side of which led down to the mud flats of the Beauly Firth. In the centre of this gap, standing like a grim sentinel, was a single raw, rough wooden post some six inches in diameter, driven into the sandy ground.

They had put it there last night, four of them. They had gone out, stern faced and solemn, to the scrub birch which grew, like a weed, in profusion around the Beauly Firth. There they had felled a young tree. They had stripped it of its bark so that it was slimy to the touch. Then they had adzed a point at one end. They had carried it to the barracks and hammered it firmly into the sandy ground. All of this they had done in total silence, for, rough soldiers though they were, they did not talk of the purpose of their task.

Facing the post the battalion were dressed in review order, kilts, spats, red doublets, crossbelts, and feather bonnets. They carried no packs but leaned silently on their Snider rifles, without even an attempt at an illegal whispered conversation when their pacing N.C.O.s were out of earshot.

Behind the waiting men and out of their sight, shielded by the tall barrack buildings, a small squad of men marched from the armoury towards the guardroom. At the guardroom, Lieutenant Donald Bruce was pacing nervously as the squad halted facing the open doorway. These twelve men had been drawn by lot from the various companies in the battalion, three from each. They stood in open order, six to a file, rifles at the slope, as Donald walked quickly through the ranks in a cursory inspection. Lieutenant Bruce was tall; even taller than his father who commanded the regiment, and Willie was all of six feet. Donald had his father's looks, reddish-blond hair and blue eyes, but lacked something of the colonel's ruggedness, the squareness of jaw, and the set of his shoulders. Of course, he was barely twenty and would fill out as he grew older, but his features were more finely etched, gentler. Gentleness was probably his most outstanding characteristic. Willie Bruce had been brought up on a small croft and then in the rough, tough world of the barrack room. Donald Bruce had known none of that, he had always been treated as a gentleman and a gentle man he had become. The eyes of father and son, which were so alike at first glance, were different in reality. The colonel's seized you with their power and held you until they were ready to allow your release; the colonel's commanded. Donald's did not. His eyes welcomed you and inspected you almost with deference. They were the same blue as his father's, the same blue as all of the Bruces and the Maclarens, but they were not the same eyes.

Donald had a habit, whenever questioned, of drawing the three middle fingers of his right hand slowly down the line of his jaw-bone and stopping at the point of his chin. Then he would rub his lips together and, having made his consideration, give you his reply in a softly modulated tone. He was slow to talk, as if words were important to him, but he was quick to listen, ever willing to hear the other point of view. Those who met him in civilian clothes were always surprised to discover that he was a soldier. A cleric or a doctor, yes, but Donald Bruce did not give the impression of being the military type. However this was not quite a fair assessment, for he had studied at the Royal Military College at Sandhurst with rare distinction, winning that august establishment's highest award, the Sword of Honour. He had joined the regiment flushed with success, only to have his father make it abundantly clear to him that academic prowess and the Sword of Honour were no guarantee of a good regimental officer.

The inspection over, he stood the men at ease and continued his fretful pacing, expressionless. He glanced quickly at the other party which stood waiting in front of the guardroom; four men, two on either side of a long box of rough pine, painted black. Then with equal haste he averted his gaze. Donald glanced at his watch. It still wanted ten minutes until nine o'clock; that would be dawn, officially. He tried with no success to keep his mind off that which he knew was taking place beyond the door of the guardroom, and what he would have to do during the next fifteen minutes. In his mind's eye he could see his father reading out the sentence of the court martial and the warrant for the execution of that sentence. It had been the only possible verdict. But it had had to go to the office of the Commander-in-Chief Scotland, in Edinburgh, for confirmation. So the condemned man had lived on a few more days waiting for the inevitable return of his sentence of death. It had arrived the previous afternoon and now Jimmy Grigor would be listening to Willie Bruce as he read it.

The formalities over, the colonel would leave the cell and Jimmy Grigor would be alone with the chaplain. The Maclarens did not boast a chaplain of their own. Mr Campbell, grey haired and a little bent from years of devoted service to his parish, was the minister at Beauly within which parish the Maclarens's barracks fell.

Mr Campbell had seen many people die and he knew that he had in nearly every case been able to ease the passage of the soul out of this life. But this was the first time that he had been in the company of a man so obviously full of life and so obviously to be dead within the next half hour. It was no easy task. He had visited Grigor on several occasions since sentence had been passed and he had mildly accepted the oaths and blasphemies which had been flung at him. It saddened him that he could find no way of reaching this man. He hated the whole business, or he would have done had he been capable of hate. The brutality of it all was so foreign to his nature and now they were alone together. He looked down at his own thin bony hands which clutched at his Bible, searching for words and wishing that this useless time would pass. And then he condemned himself for wishing a man's life away. But it was only for a moment or two and then they would come out, the prisoner, the minister and two guards, and then Donald Bruce would take Jimmy Grigor out before the assembled battalion and kill him. He would not kill him with his own hands, but he would say the word upon which the twelve men in his party would send Jimmy's soul speeding to Eternity.

Earlier Donald had superintended the loading of the rifles, ten with ball and two with blank according to the regulations, so that no man in the firing party could ever know for certain that it was he who had fired the fatal bullet. The rifles had been drawn at random from the armoury and now all was ready for the grim ritual of killing Jimmy Grigor.

Donald was fighting back the feeling of nausea that was welling within him. He kept telling himself that it was wrong to feel sympathy for Jimmy Grigor and that his punishment was well earned. The crime for which he was now about to suffer was one of brutal and deliberate murder. Lance-Sergeant Murdoch, young and recently promoted, had caught Grigor and three others gambling in the barrack room and as was his duty had immediately placed them under open arrest. Grigor, a one-time corporal who had lost his stripes for losing his temper, had flown into a violent rage, seized a bayonet, and before anyone could move to stop him, had stabbed the unfortunate Murdoch half a dozen times. Murdoch had died the next day in the regimental sick bay. Sergeant Murdoch had been a good man. He had only been with the regiment for five and a half years, and in those days of slow promotion had risen dramatically once his training period was over. He had had all the markings of a good soldier, a man who might even have emulated his commanding officer's feat and risen from the ranks. He had been respected by officers and men alike. Lance-Sergeant Murdoch had had that rare ability of being able to command men without causing rancour or resentment. Had he been permitted to live he would have commanded. But it was not to be, for at the age of only twenty-four he had been savagely cut down by a drunken oaf.

Frankie Gibson, sometime ghillie, sometime poacher, and now Colour Sergeant of C Company, a position once held by the commanding officer himself, walked slowly round the ranks assembled at the bottom of the hollow square and facing the stark, solitary post. He was a small man, dark, and with a lined, weather-beaten face. A man of great humour, whom old Colonel Sir Henry Maclaren had accepted into the regiment with the words: 'Your wages will be more than covered by the salmon I save.' But there was nothing to laugh at today.

'Frankie.' It was Corporal Munroe standing at the rear of C Company who hissed his name.

'What is it, Johnny?'

'When are we going to get this bloody business over wi'?'

'Bide yoursel',' replied Frankie. 'Jimmy Grigor's in nae

hurry.' And then turning on a young private in the rear rank, 'Pull yoursel' taegether, sodger.'

Frankie had recognized the signs. The man was swaying and clutching on to his rifle for support. It was young Peter Leinie, C Company's newest recruit, a man who looked considerably less than the eighteen years he claimed.

'Ye'll see a damned sight worse than this when we get to Egypt.' And he spat upon the ground. He hated this business as much as any man in the regiment.

'Squad! Squad, attention! Present arms!' called Lieutenant Bruce, drawing his broadsword and holding it at the salute. It was that same broadsword that he had so proudly received from the hands of the Prince of Wales at the passing-out parade at Sandhurst. A beautiful thing it was too with the blade finely chased and his name engraved upon it and the little splash of red velvet peering through the intricate workings of the basket hilt. He stood there, tight lipped, as his father Colonel Bruce emerged from the guardroom.

Willie Bruce returned the salute. Donald was looking at a point somewhere over Willie's head and Willie fixed his gaze on the top button of his son's doublet. It was not a time for looking a man in the eye. His left hand tightened on the crumpled piece of paper which he had just read to the condemned man.

'Carry on, Mr Bruce,' he snapped, and turned away in the direction of the battalion.

Willie's leathery face, the legacy of many campaigns and long service under the hot suns of the Empire, was expressionless as he strode away, concealing the emotion which he felt within himself. He hated the fact that it had fallen to his son to do this filthy job. 'What a bloody awful way to blood a man,' he had said the previous day when he had lunched with Andrew Maclaren over at Culbrech House, ancestral home of the founders of the regiment. Andrew Maclaren, who had commanded the regiment before him until a burst of fire from a Gatling gun, their own, in India had shot away the lower part of his right leg, was sympathetic towards his old friend. They had been boys together, served together all of their adult lives, loved the same woman, and they were half-brothers.

'Bring the whole family over to dinner tomorrow,' Andrew had said. 'I'll try and lay something on to take Donald's mind off it.'

Willie carried on between the barrack blocks to where the men were waiting. It was Frankie Gibson who spotted him.

'Ser'nt-Major,' he called. 'C.O.'s coming.'

Regimental-Sergeant-Major Macmillan took up his position at the rear of C Company and called the parade to attention.

At the guardroom Lieutenant Bruce gave the order:

'Reverse arms, left turn.'

They made the turn almost with gratitude, for the command meant that they would not have to face their victim. There were two drummers and a piper about three paces ahead of them and they too turned with them. They were all looking intently ahead. All brutally conscious in that silence so intense that every creak, every breath they took, every drip of water which slid from the guardroom roof into a little puddle below registered on their minds. Their minds were numbed, insulated against the act that they were about to perform. They tried to think only of what they could see, and what they could see was the back of the neck of the man in front of them. Some of them tried to count the hairs. Private Wilkie, standing behind Billy Anderson, intently studied a burgeoning boil on the back of his thick, red, pock-marked neck.

In all of them there was a terrible desire to get the damned business over with and yet every one of them realized that each minute they prolonged their duty was another lifetime to Jimmy Grigor.

It was only a moment in actual time after the command to turn had been given that the drummers, their instruments muffled in black cloth, raised their sticks, while the piper inflated his bag and the first plaintive notes escaped from the drones.

A moment later the minister emerged, followed by Grigor, flanked by two guards holding him under the arms. He was wearing fatigue dress, the buttons stripped from his tunic, and his pinched and pointed face was grey.

'Tak' your fucking hands off me,' he yelled at his guards. 'Dae ye think I canna walk?'

No one took any notice of him.

'By the right slow march,' commanded Donald, and the piper struck up a lament and the drums beat a solemn tattoo as they started towards the battalion.

Among the execution detail there was one man alone who hoped that he had not drawn a blank. Billy Anderson was Jimmy Grigor's *marra*, his friend and drinking partner, a man as hot tempered and violent as Grigor himself; a man who, had he believed in God, would have realized that 'there but for the grace of God . . .'

Anderson had already made up his mind to disobey the order to aim at the victim's heart. He was a good shot and he was determined to shoot poor Jimmy right between the eyes. It would be quicker that way. It was the last favour he would be able to do for him.

Though it could not have been more than a couple of minutes, it seemed an eternity to Donald Bruce before the regiment came into sight. He wanted to run, get the damned business over with, but like everything else in the bloody army, it had to be according to regulations. So the procession crept in slow time towards the battalion. First the piper, followed by the drums draped in black. Then the firing party, twelve men and Donald Bruce. Then the coffin and last the prisoner with his guards and the minister who was murmuring all the while in a low monotone.

Grigor, as the battalion hove in sight, seemed determined to put on a show. 'Hald ya gob, ye psalmy bastard,' he shouted at the minister, and then to all in general and to no one in particular: 'Can ye no hurry? It's fucking cald and youse'll all be late for breakfast. I've had mine.' He laughed, and there was just a touch of hysteria in his laughter. 'Will somebody tak' this bloody Bible puncher awa'? I'll see ye in hell, minister.' He paused and looked at the assembled men, men that he had lived with for ten years and more. He spoke again, but now his voice was calm as he looked at them all. ' 'Tis a bonny sight ye are for a mannie's last look. Hurrah for the fighting hundred and forty-eighth!'

That was when the first man fainted. Peter Leinie slumped forward over his rifle.

'Leave him,' growled Sergeant Gibson as the man on each

side of him moved to pick him up. Frankie was sympathetic towards the youth; better to leave him where he was until it was all over.

Donald marched his men to a line which had been marked twelve paces from the execution post, and there he halted them. The drums and pipes stopped and the instrumentalists marched off in quick time to the rear of the battalion. In the silence which followed, the coffin was taken to a wooden marker a few paces beyond the post.

Then came Grigor. Quickly the two guards strapped his hands and ankles to the post with a coarse hempen rope and then stood aside while the minister said a few last words to him. Private Anderson was watching Grigor intently, trying to catch his eye, but Grigor looked neither at him nor at the minister, and his lips never moved. Then the minister, his head bowed and shaking sadly in recognition of a task undone, moved away. The two guards placed a white bandage over Grigor's eyes and stepped aside.

Colonel Willie Bruce, standing to the right of the firing squad, looked at his watch. It was exactly nine o'clock. 'Carry on, Mr Bruce,' he said quietly.

Donald ran his tongue over his dry lips. The wind had dropped but the air was still heavy and damp and the only sound he could hear was the heavy breathing of his men. Five words now stood between Jimmy Grigor and Eternity, and Donald Bruce had to say them.

'Mr Bruce,' the colonel spoke again, and there was a note of censure in his voice.

'Squad!' Four words left. 'Present!'

The rifles came to the men's shoulders. Three.

'Load.'

There was a ragged clicking as the men cocked the hammers of their Snider-Enfields. Two words left.

A longer pause this time, then . . . 'Aim.'

A single word now and it would all be over. A second man in the ranks fell, but no one else moved. Their face muscles were tense as they stared compulsively, but unwillingly, at the drama before them. Twice Donald opened his mouth to utter the fatal word. Twice no sound came from his lips. It was too long. Men tried not to look, screwed up their faces, tried to close their eyes or look down at their boots. The pause went on and on until . . .

'Fuck you! FIRE!'

It was Jimmy Grigor who gave the order. There was a flash, a line of curling smoke, and a single ragged craaack which killed Jimmy Grigor and brought Donald Bruce back to reality. He looked towards the dead man. There was a mass of blood on his chest, and one neat round hole between his eyes.

It was in that moment that the wind blew. A fierce gust cutting in across the Beauly Firth taking the *haar* with it and revealing the red disc of the rising sun to flood the parade with light, picking out the yellow brasswork and the silvery burnished bayonets of the men. They were standing there transfixed by the horror of the ritual killing and waiting for the next command which would free them from their ordeal.

Two men helped Peter Leinie to his feet.

'What happened?' he whispered.

'It's over,' said Frankie Gibson. He eyed the lad with some concern. He was young, probably too young and sensitive, though that apart he had the makings of a good soldier.

'Firing party, slope arms. Right turn. Quick march.' Donald called out the orders in rapid succession. He marched them back to the parade ground where the cold grey light was gleaming off the pink of the tall barrack blocks.

'Firing party, halt! To the left, dismiss.' He did not even pause to return the men's salute as they fell out, but ran directly to the toilets in the officers' mess where he was violently sick.

Slowly he returned to his room in the mess. There he sat down at his plain wooden desk and took pen and paper. Then he stopped.

More than anything he wanted to forget the horror that he had just witnessed. He had not observed the actual moment when Jimmy Grigor's body slumped at the post, the life torn from it. His eyes had been shut, his facial muscles tensed as he tried to screw up the courage to utter the fateful word. He sat there with the pen clutched in his hand pressed hard upon the surface of the desk. He could not think of anything else, strain though he might. If this was soldiering he knew that he wanted no part of it. He had hated the cold brutality, as cold and bitter as that November morning, more than he had ever hated anything in his life. It was more than he could bear. Desperately he tried to banish the brutal memory from his mind. But it was no good. Over and over again he heard the crackle of the rifles and almost felt the bullets tearing into his own body as they had ripped the life out of Jimmy Grigor.

He sat staring for what must have been several minutes at his blurred and unreal surroundings.

Finally, with an effort, he dipped his pen into the inkwell and started to write. When he did his mind was made up. He wrote rapidly and firmly in his neat precise hand. The letter was addressed to his commanding officer, requesting permission to surrender his commission. He read it through and placed it in an envelope; at that moment Donald had no stomach for the army. He wanted to be out.

As he was sealing the envelope, there was a tap at his door. He looked towards the door, irritated at the interruption. The knock was repeated.

'Come in.'

Captain Farquhar entered. Farquhar, probably the wealthiest man in the battalion, who loved horses, thoroughbreds, of course, and had been given command of the battalion mules as a consequence, was also commander of C Company and the Gatling gun which went with that honour.

Farquhar in his own way was as much an anomaly in an infantry regiment of the 1880s as was his commanding officer Willie Bruce. Tall, wealthy, and extremely handsome, he was the type of officer that you would have expected to find in one of the crack cavalry regiments. He had a capacity, however, for action which was well hidden under his indolent façade. He was one of those people who could take part in a violent skirmish with the same casual ease with which he would take his after-dinner brandy and cigar in the mess. He had been several years with the regiment. In a way he was responsible for Willie Bruce getting command, for he had fired the Gatling gun which had cut down Andrew Maclaren and caused the loss of his leg. It had been an unfortunate accident and he knew that he himself was in no way blameworthy. He was sorry of course, but guilt had never entered his mind. He did not brood and he did not dwell on the incident, it was a pure mischance and, as far as Alex Farquhar was concerned, that was an end to the matter. Not that he lacked feelings. When he walked into that room, he knew full well the torment that Donald Bruce was experiencing. It would not have happened to him but he could understand it happening to someone else.

He stood just inside the door, his neatly drawn, delicate features moulded in an expression of sympathy for the suffering of his brother officer.

'Donald,' he said, 'the old man wants to see you now.'

'I can guess why,' replied Donald, chewing at his bottom lip. 'It wasn't a very good show, was it?'

'My dear chap,' Farquhar was sympathetic, 'I can only say thank God it wasn't me.' Then as Donald made no move, 'I shouldn't keep the old boy waiting if I were you. He didn't seem very happy.'

'Thanks, Alex,' replied Donald, getting to his feet. 'I'll go now.'

'Look, Donald,' said Farquhar, 'I know what you must be feeling. I've been through it too, I shot one of my own men once. You've just got to learn to live with it.'

'That was in India, an accident, in action; this is different.'

'I suppose so. You'd better go and see the C.O. Like me to walk over with you?'

'No, no. I'm all right, honestly.'

Farquhar left him and Donald picked up his note, put on his feather bonnet, and went out through the pillared portico of the officers' quarters. The day was brightening and the winter sun was beginning, fitfully, to break through, gleaming off the little puddles, and here and there sparkling on the wet walls of the barrack blocks. There was a chill in the air and there was no one about, and for this Donald was grateful. The men would have been given a stand-down until after the midday meal. He could visualize them sitting around in their bare, strictly functional barrack rooms. Each of them exactly like its neighbour. The walls painted brown to a height of exactly four feet and six inches, topped by a line of black one inch wide and then yellow up to the white ceiling. The two rows of iron cots, twelve a side, with their straw palliasses and blankets neatly folded. Above each bed a green painted tin locker with the owner's kit neatly stacked according to regulations. A spotless rifle would be standing by each bed and just in front of it a scrubbed wooden bedside locker. The centre of the room would be dominated by a cylindrical iron stove. Though the day was cold, the stove would be unlit, for the rules demanded that fires should not be ignited before four o'clock in the afternoon. Beside the stove a burnished coal bucket, gleaming in the gloom, filled twice a week by the barrack orderly from the regimental coal dump.

At least there would not be the smell of stale food so common to army barracks. The Maclaren Highlanders were modern; by current standards, innovators. They had built a proper mess hall for the men where all meals were taken, something unheard of in most regiments, where the men ate sitting on their beds in the same room in which they slept.

The men themselves would be sitting around on the ends of their beds in tight little groups, and if they said anything, it would be to the effect that at least there would be no kit inspection that morning. Of what they had witnessed, they would say not a word.

They would talk about it eventually of course. In a week or two it would become a coarse soldier's joke and Donald Bruce would be the butt. Donald's lips tightened as he looked round the familiar square, gripping his letter. He hurried to the front of Headquarters Block and went in through the main entrance, returning the salute of the sentry as he passed.

He walked on down the long corridor – it was painted in exactly the same brown and black and yellow as the barrack rooms – his boots echoing in its bare emptiness. Offices flanked him as he passed: the regimental sergeant-major, the Orderly Room where they did the paper work, the adjutant, and the second-in-command. But always facing him, almost threatening in its heavy dark polished oak, was the door to his father's office, bearing the legend picked out in gold: Commanding Officer the Maclaren Highlanders, and beneath this an embossed plaque of the regimental crest, a snarling Highland wildcat's head and their motto: *Si Vis Pacem Para Bellum.* He tapped on the door and went in.

Colonel Bruce glanced up from behind the desk which was a legacy of the man who had founded the 148th Regiment of Foot, eighty years ago on the twenty-second of January. Sir Godfrey Maclaren, great-grandfather of the current holder of the title, Sir Andrew Maclaren, gazed disapprovingly down from his gilt frame on the wall flanked by similar portraits of his successors including Sir Henry Maclaren, father of both Andrew and Willie – Andrew from the marriage bed and Willie from an idyllic moment in the heather. The wall was getting a little crowded and Willie was determined, if he could persuade the mess committee to accept, to present them with the portraits. Also on the wall, framed, was Willie's personal indulgence, the badge of every rank which he had held throughout his military career, from the single stripe of a lance-corporal, through regimental sergeant-major, to the crown and single pip of lieutenant-colonel. There were also a few, a very few, personal trophies and mementos. There was a spear (or was it an assegai? Donald was never sure), a leather shield from Africa, a boomerang from Australia, a carved ivory elephant from India, and a daguerreotype of Donald's mother, Maud Bruce.

Donald approached the man at the desk, saluted, and stood to attention. For some moments Willie Bruce regarded his son from under his bushy, ginger eyebrows which seemed to grow more out than across. There was a sympathy and a gentleness in his father's expression which was the last thing Donald had expected to find.

'All right, Donald,' said Willie. 'Tak' your hat off and sit ye doon.' Willie still spoke with the distinct accent which he had acquired during his childhood which had been spent with his mother and stepfather in the little whitewashed cottage which nestled in the south face of the hill behind Culbrech House.

'Sir,' said Donald formally without moving, 'before you say any more, I want to apologize for what happened this morning. I am sorry, sir, I know I behaved in an unsoldierly manner, but I couldn't do it. I just couldn't bring myself to say that word. And that is the reason why I have brought you this.'

Donald held the letter out and towards his father, and when Willie made no move to take it from him, he placed it on the desk in front of him.

Willie had not taken his eyes off his son for a moment.

'I told ye to sit doon.'

'Sorry, sir,' replied Donald, obeying. He took off his feather bonnet and placed it on the floor beside the plain straight-backed wooden chair across from his father and sat there waiting as Willie slowly picked up the envelope.

'I think,' Willie said, very slowly, 'I think I ken what is in here.' He tapped the envelope against the tips of the fingers of his left hand. 'I think you should take it back and tear it up.'

'No, sir.' Donald looked down, not wanting to meet his father's gaze. 'No, sir, my mind is made up. I'll never be a soldier, sir.'

'Wait a bittie,' said Willie. 'Before you say any more, there are two things I want you to know. First, you're a Bruce. You're my son. And secondly – I had intended it as a surprise, but in the circumstances, I shall have to tell you now – young Gordon will be joining the regiment next week.'

Donald looked up sharply and met his father's gaze. There was no vestige of expression there. The leathery weatherbeaten skin, creased with long service and increasing age, was immobile. The eyes were neither hard nor gentle, neither cruel nor compassionate; they just looked, and they seemed to look right into his mind.

Willie Bruce waited as he looked into the young man opposite him, waited to see what sort of effect his pronouncement would have. He saw the uncertainty in his son's eyes and he thought he saw the torment there too at the mention of Gordon's name. Donald's mouth was half open as if he was wanting to reply and could not find the words. The announcement had certainly come as a surprise to him, though he should have known. Young Gordon, who had gone to Sandhurst during Donald's last term there, had aped his elder brother in fervent adulation of everything that he did. Not without cause, for Donald was one of those people who did everything well. Everything until today. Today he had failed, completely.

Naturally Gordon would know nothing of this, but he would find out. Donald was Gordon's god and the knowledge of what this would do to their relationship weighed heavily upon Donald, for he had a very great affection for his younger brother.

'I see, sir,' replied Donald after a long pause.

'What do you see, Donald?'

'Well, sir . . . I'm not sure.'

'Do you not think that it might be a terrible thing for a

young man to join his regiment on the day that his brother ran away?' He stressed the words 'ran away'.

'But I'm not running away, sir.'

'Are you quite sure, Donald?'

'Yes.'

'Then I tell you that you are wrong. You are running away, my son,' said Willie. 'The job that you were given to do today was probably the worst job that you will ever be given in the whole of your career, unless you get command and have to order good men to what you ken well will be their deaths. This morning, there was not a man in the battalion who would have willingly changed places with you.'

'But they would have done it, sir.'

'I have not yet finished, Donald. There was a time, it happened only once, but I mind fine there was a time when I too would have left the regiment. I did not, through no virtue of my own, but I bless the day that I did not.'

'You, sir?' Donald was amazed.

'Aye, laddie. I'll tell you aboot it, though the telling of it still hurts. It happened thousands of miles from here in China at a place called Taku. We had just fought an action. I was in C Company. We lost a third of our men. It was a hard day. There was a wee drummer boy, Wee Alex we used to call him. I had recruited him myself. Alex came through the action untouched; we had taken the fort and he was standing on a heap of rubble cheering and shouting when he was killed by a falling rock. I remember picking up that wee body and holding him in ma arms and cursing the army which had done that to him. I tell you, Donald, if I had been an officer, I would have been out the very next day. But I was only a sergeant at the time and it is no so easy if you are in the ranks.'

'But, sir, that was in the heat of an engagement. This morning was just blind violence.' He paused. 'I couldn't take it, sir.'

'Did Grigor deserve what he got?'

'Yes, sir, I don't dispute that.'

'Donald, listen carefully to what I have to say. It is important to any soldier. I am not a violent man and I know fine that you are not, either. Do you think that the army wants violent men? They do not! The man who died this morning was a violent man, that was why he died, and it was why Sergeant Murdoch died; and Sergeant Murdoch was a good N.C.O., he was not a violent man. You know, Donald, violence never made a good soldier, but a man like you could, and that is why I want you to stay in the regiment.' He picked up the letter and looked at his son.

'What shall we do with this, Donald? Until I open it, it does not exist, but once I do, I am bound to act upon its contents . . . Well?'

'Sir, I think you had better tear it up.' He watched as his father ripped the letter deliberately and slowly into fragments and dropped it into the wastepaper basket. 'I am not fully convinced, sir, but it may be a mistake. You will understand when I tell you that I cannot promise that I shall not resubmit it.'

'Thank you, Donald, I understand.' His tone changed: 'And now, Mr Bruce.'

'Sir,' replied Donald, getting to his feet and standing at attention, his feather bonnet under his left arm.

'This morning you performed your duties in a most unsoldierly manner. You will report to the adjutant and request that he give you three extra orderly officers.'

'Yes, sir.'

'You may go now' – and as Donald turned to leave him – 'Tell the adjutant, not tonight. We're dining with Sir Andrew.'

2

Ian Maclaren, the eldest son of the laird, stood at the window of his room on the second floor of the west tower at Culbrech House. Culbrech House was one of those houses peculiar to the Highlands of Scotland. It was a fortified house, neither a castle nor merely a dwelling place but something between the two. It was certainly a home. It had been built several centuries previously by a Maclaren, for the Maclarens, in the days when the clans still raided and fought one another. It had never passed out of their hands, which was a credit both to its builder and to the fortitude of those who for generations had occupied it. It was built of the same Moray sandstone that had been used only a few years ago to build the barracks of the regiment which bore their name.

Ian's Aunt Maud had once described Culbrech as an upside-down house and this was probably fair comment, coming as it did from an English lady. The house consisted of a large rectangular block, taller than it was long, flanked by two towers. The banqueting hall occupied the whole of the top storey of the centre block. The ground floor, with its six-foot-thick walls, contained the kitchens and the servants' quarters. The huge iron-studded oak door which stood in the centre of the front of the house led directly into these departments, while the entrance used by the family and guests was a much less imposing affair around the side of the west tower and at the top of a flight of stone steps. The ground-floor windows had been designed with defence in view: they were elongated slits through which a man might fire an arrow or a musket without being seen. As a result there was very little light in the domestic quarters and the gas lamps were always lit. Just above the kitchens and on the first floor was the dining room with its long, polished mahogany table which could seat twenty; the library, which had served the lairds also as a study for the last three generations; the gun room; and in the east tower, or more accurately the south-east tower, the morning room. The towers themselves each contained a narrow stone, spiral staircase which wound its way upward to the bedrooms, piled one on top of the other. Each one of these had a little alcove containing a huge copper bathtub. These tubs now boasted piped water and no longer was a bath something which required an hour's warning for the servants to clamber up the stairs carrying buckets of steaming water. Above the dining room, the whole of the area of the main block was occupied by the large withdrawing room. Above that and just below the banqueting hall were the two master-bedroom suites consisting of bedroom, dressing room, and a small sitting room. One was occupied by Sir Andrew, Ian's father, and the other by his grandmother Lady Maclaren.

During the years since the regiment had been formed, the house had acquired a mass of militaria. Everywhere there were old swords and guns and portraits of men in uniform and even children in Highland military dress. There were sketches of actions in which the regiment had taken part and of course the inevitable profusion of ancestors in oils.

The Maclaren estates covered several thousand acres and the people who lived upon them were utterly dependent upon their laird, for that was how it always had been. But Sir Andrew always maintained that the laird was equally dependent upon the people. Not that Sir Andrew did much about the running of the estate; this was all handled very efficiently by Ian's uncle by marriage, Richard Simpson. The estate was important to Andrew in another way, for almost every family had one or more of their men serving in the regiment and as far as Andrew was concerned, it was the regiment that mattered.

The only part of the estate which really interested Andrew was the four acres which immediately surrounded the house. This area was kept in what must have been one of the finest lawns in the whole of Scotland, bisected by a long, straight, gravelled drive which scythed its way down to the main Beauly road.

It was down this road that Ian was looking to catch the first possible glimpse of the Bruces' carriage.

He had already changed for dinner into the new and fashionable mess kit only recently authorized by the Queen. Trews in the regimental tartan of blue and green, over-checked with red and yellow, the short red open jacket with twisted epaulettes and yellow facings over a tartan waistcoat, and an uncomfortably stiff starched shirt and high collar.

Ian stood there gazing out of his window, ready to be the first to greet his father's guests at the door. Lieutenant Maclaren's keenness did not spring from the very genuine affection in which he held his uncle and C.O., Willie Bruce, but from a strong desire to monopolize the company of Willie's daughter Naomi, several years his senior, but none the less in Ian's opinion the most beautiful and charming of God's creations. What added to her fascination was the mystery that surrounded her.

To start with, the Maclarens and the Bruces all looked alike. They were tall, lean, red or fair in colouring, and with faces that were destined to become craggy and stern as the years took their toll. There were only two exceptions to this; Ian's grandmother, who was small and round, but fair eyed and, before she had become grey, blonde haired. Naomi, however, was quite different. Her hair was black, not just very dark but black and shining. Her eyes, which should have been blue, were of the deepest brown. Her skin, which should have been white, and sometimes appeared so against the black of her hair, was more the colour of thick Jersey cream, smooth; and though he had never dared to investigate the fact, Ian was sure that it was deliciously soft to the touch. But above all it was her hands. Slender yet full fleshed so that the creases over her knuckles were barely visible. Long tapering fingers accentuated by the smallness of the hands themselves and always they seemed to be in repose for they always moved with slowness and grace.

Once only had Ian mentioned Naomi to his grandmother, who had replied, 'Don't talk about the child.' And whenever it had appeared that there was a chance to discuss her with his father, Sir Andrew had changed the subject with a complete lack of subtlety. So Ian was left wondering. If it had been his father's intention to still any interest that he might have had in the lady, he had failed, succeeding only in making her all the more fascinating.

Ian had never known his mother. She had died in India shortly after the birth of his younger brother, Robert, and his father would seldom discuss her. He knew her only from the large portrait which hung in the dining room, a tall, fair, beautiful girl with sad blue eyes. It was strange that he knew so little of her; his father, who was a good friend and affectionate towards his sons, was curiously guarded about her, and Ian always had the feeling that Sir Andrew had a guilty feeling about his late wife.

As for the Bruces, they were family. The colonel had always been Uncle Willie until he became Ian's commanding officer, and his wife was still Aunt Maud, though he was sure that there was no blood relationship there and the Bruces were uncle and aunt by adoption.

Ian was enjoying the last of a few days' leave. He had been with his father down to Sandhurst where they had taken young Robert to start his official studies prior to his being accepted into the regiment. Robert would enjoy Sandhurst. He was not a deep thinker like his brother, and would happily comply with all the restrictions that would be placed upon him at that august establishment. The brothers Maclaren and the brothers Bruce had, of course, gone into the regiment. Any other course would have been unthinkable. The regiment was theirs and they were the regiment's, just as though it had been ordained thus from the beginning of time.

A carriage was turning into the main drive. It was closed against the November cold, but Ian spotted the twin lamps and could visualize the pair of black hackneys which drew it. It was the Bruces' party. He left his room and went downstairs, timing his move so that he would 'accidentally' arrive in the small hall inside the door just as they entered. He could not pre-empt his father's position as host and be waiting for them at the door.

Sir Andrew Maclaren was in the library on the first floor awaiting the arrival of his guests. He was seated in a wing-backed leather armchair facing the fire, with his pegleg propped on a small tapestry-topped stool. Andrew was surrounded by shelf upon shelf of leather-bound volumes most of which had never, to his knowledge, been read; indeed many of them still remained with their pages uncut. The Maclarens were not great readers. There was, though, one well-thumbed section, the medical section, which consisted of about thirty volumes. This, army medicine, had been Andrew's father's abiding interest. He had spent many years, especially towards the end of his life, working for the cause of army medicine even to the extent of enlisting the aid of the Prince of Wales who himself supported that cause. The medical books were all together on the third shelf behind the big leather-topped desk, his father's books, and his father's desk. Andrew often wondered if his father also always thought of that desk as belonging to his own father. Ownership was a strange thing, more a state of mind than anything else.

As in all of the occupied rooms in the house there was a log fire burning in the grate, the logs balanced across a pair of wrought-iron dogs, spluttering away and falling as ash into the bed of ashes which lay six inches deep beneath them. On the sideboard there was a decanter of whisky and four crystal glasses. The decanter was topped up every morning by MacKay, Andrew's butler. Not that Andrew drank much; apart from anything else, it was too much damned trouble to heave himself out of his chair and stomp over to the sideboard.

He could get around all right, with an effort, but too much standing made his non-existent foot hurt where he had lost his leg just below the knee. As a result he had, during the last few years, lived a rather sedentary life, and had put on quite a bit of weight in the process. He still tried to stalk; he had got a fine stag, a ten pointer, only two days ago. But it was really his ghillie who did it all during the hunts. They would put him on a small Highland pony and he would follow the ghillie until beasts were near. Then he would dismount and crawl the last few yards to take his shot. But that last stag had been a good one, right through the heart, and he had told the ghillie to help himself to a haunch when he butchered it.

He had, when he lost his leg, left the regiment which he had commanded. The Maclarens were a kilted Highland regiment and his pride would not allow him to wear the kilt with a pegleg.

Andrew had had a protracted youth which really ended on that day on the North-west Frontier when his leg had been shot off during his successful rescue of Willie Bruce from the Pathans who were holding him captive. But as he said himself, 'There was only one place that a Maclaren could serve.'

Now he sat nursing a glass of Glenlivet and awaiting the arrival of his guests. Not that he really regarded Willie Bruce as a guest. In a way he considered Culbrech House as much Willie's home as it was his own. Maud would be with him, Maud whom he had loved once after he had rescued her in 'fifty-seven at Cawnpore; and who had finally chosen Willie, and in doing so earned Andrew's respect and eternal friendship. He now felt more at ease with her than he did with his own sister Margaret who with her husband, the factor, really ran the estate.

MacKay, their butler, came into the room. MacKay was getting quite old; Andrew did not know how old, but certainly he must be over seventy. Like nearly all of the men who served in the house, MacKay was a retired Maclaren. He had been senior mess steward with the rank of sergeant when he left the army to go into service. A man proud of his past, straight backed and smart of bearing as befitted an old soldier, he wore his morning coat and striped waistcoat as if it were a military uniform. Indeed all of his buttons were regimental buttons embossed with the head of the wildcat emblem of the Maclaren Highlanders. But age was beginning to tell and, sadly, he would soon have to be pensioned off. One of his buttons was missing and there was a slight dusting of tobacco on his collar.

'Colonel, sir, I think your guests' carriage has just pulled into the drive.'

'Thank you, MacKay,' replied Andrew, and then, as the older man moved to help him, 'No, dammit, I can get up by myself.'

'Of course, sir,' said MacKay, and stood aside as his master stepped out of the library.

Inside the main door was a small hall or large landing, and it was to this spot Sir Andrew stomped to greet his guests.

Andrew's second footman, a time-expired Maclaren Highlander, opened the door, and the Bruces came into the house.

Naomi was first. She ran up the stairs and planted a kiss firmly on Andrew's cheek.

'Uncle Andrew, lovely to see you, but you shouldn't have bothered to come to the door. Oh, hello, Ian.'

'Dammit, I'm not a cripple,' grunted Andrew as Naomi swept past him.

Then came Maud. Andrew could never look at her without a feeling of nostalgia. She was over forty now but still beautiful. That golden fair hair which he had first seen matted and torn in a cellar at Cawnpore all those years ago; perhaps it was a little less lustrous now but not a lot and still beautiful enough to make any man turn his head. They had been lovers many years ago, even after she had married Willie Bruce. It had been a mad, mad time, but Andrew still found it difficult to regret the memory of it. Once, he could have let Willie die and had her for himself just after his own wife had died; thank God that he had not succumbed to that temptation. Now it was all different, the years had softened passion and turned it into an affection much more deep and more real than youthful lust. It was an affection which had flowed across both of their families and, Andrew liked to think, made them as one, as the regiment was one.

She was wearing dark-green velvet. Somehow she always looked best in green and Andrew always thought of it as Maud's colour. Strange, he thought, looking at her, that they might have been married but for the social dictates of society. He often wondered what things would have been like now if that had happened. But now she was coming towards him, assured and calm as ever.

'Thank you for asking us, Andrew,' she said, brushing his cheek. 'You won't mention this morning?'

'Think I'm a fool?' And they smiled at each other and there was understanding in their smiles. 'Just go through to the drawing room, I'll come up with Willie. Donald, you and Ian take the ladies through,' he said to the solemn-faced young man who was approaching him, followed by his father.

Willie grinned at Andrew as he followed his son up the stairs. He knew that Andrew needed help to get upstairs and the drawing room was on the second floor. But he also knew that Andrew carried on a fiction that aid was unnecessary, and only Willie or MacKay were ever allowed to help him.

'How did it go?' asked Andrew as the others disappeared up the curving staircase.

'Not too well. The lad made a mess of it.'

'Don't be hard on him, Willie. I think I would have made a mess of it at his age.'

'Och, no,' replied Willie. 'Three orderly officers. But he was quite ready to resign his commission.'

'Not really. I don't believe that. I was ready to do that once, but I don't think I meant it, and I'm sure Donald didn't. It was just the moment.'

'I wish I could be sure. He hasna spoken a word since he got home.'

'Well, I'll put him next to my mother at dinner. She'll soon sort him out.' Andrew put his hand on Willie's arm. 'Well, are we going up or not?'

They went up to the drawing room. Lady Maclaren had recently had the whole of this room redecorated. Gone were the dark oak panels and in their place she had had the walls plastered and painted in cream and gilt. It was now furnished with occasional chairs, gilt-framed with light brocade seats and backs. Chintz covered the dark velvet of the easy chairs and the two sofas. All of this combined with the flickering fantailed gas jets recently installed, and the two large crystal chandeliers carrying twenty-five candles each, reflecting the facets of the cut glass surrounding them, gave a bright and airy atmosphere to the room.

As they came in, Andrew glanced around at his guests. His son Ian was standing in a corner very close to Naomi Bruce, who was holding a glass of sherry in her delicate hand and sipping at it. Well, he could not blame him, she was a damned attractive woman, though he hoped that the lad was not taking things too seriously. Possibly he would have to have a chat with his son about her.

His mother, Lady Maclaren, was sitting in one of the chintz-covered settees with Maud. Her Ladyship was talking away as if she was afraid to let Maud either escape or get a word in edgeways. Funny how she always behaved like that with Maud. It was as if she was trying to prevent conversation by dominating it. But how on earth could his mother have anything to hide or be ashamed of? Anyhow none of these thoughts really mattered, because the purpose of the evening was to take Donald Bruce's mind off the happenings of that morning. And there he was, standing alone near the sideboard, nursing a whisky. This was not what Andrew had intended. He did not want Donald left alone to brood. He stomped over in the boy's direction, clearing his throat in order to draw the young man's attention.

'Let me top up your glass, Donald,' said Andrew.

'No thank you, sir, I have more than enough,' replied Donald in a flat, toneless voice.

'Your father tells me that Gordon's coming back at the end of the week.'

'Yes, sir, I know,' said Donald, looking down at his boots.

'Hrrumph,' said Andrew. He was not having much success. 'I suppose that you'll be looking forward to that, eh?'

'I suppose so, sir,' said Donald without enthusiasm.

'Well, I know that Gordon is. We saw him last week when I took Robert down to Sandhurst. He can't wait to join the regiment, especially with Egypt coming up. You must be looking forward to that as well.'

'Oh, yes, of course.'

Andrew resolved to try a different tack.

'Donald, I know what happened this morning. Your father was in a dreadful position. Circumstances dictated that you had to do that job. But you ought to remember that it was the army that did it, not you.'

'But I failed.'

'That is as may be, but remember that you would have been every bit as responsible for what happened even if you had been on leave at the time.'

'Would you mind very much if I did not stay to dinner, sir?'

'I would mind very much indeed, Donald, and my mother, who knows nothing of this, would be most insulted. You're a soldier, and soldiers do not run away, especially if their father is Willie Bruce.'

'Yes, sir. I'm sorry.'

'All right, lad, we won't talk about it any more.'

MacKay opened the double polished-mahogany doors.

'Ladies and gentlemen, dinner is served.'

Lady Maclaren had protested to her son when she was shown the guest list for dinner.

'Seven is a ridiculous number,' she had said. 'Almost as bad as eight. Can't we invite three more and make it ten?'

'No, mother,' Andrew had replied. 'This is just us and the Bruces.' And there the matter had rested.

Andrew took his place at the head of the table with Maud on his right and Naomi on his left. Ian Maclaren sat between Naomi and Donald Bruce who was on Lady Maclaren's right, while Willie on her left had to sit next to his wife.

They dined in the small dining room; the great banqueting hall was used only when there were more than twelve at table. Dinner in the banqueting hall was always a difficult proceeding as it was situated on the top floor, right beneath the black oak trusses of the roof. The small dining room was much more intimate, made warm by the heavy oak panelling and the candlelight flickering from the twin candelabra which stood on the table. The meal was served by MacKay and a footman, dim shadowy figures who emerged from the gloom at the edges of the room to deliver plates of cock-o-leekie soup, venison, and a selection of desserts. And MacKay, ever watchful, kept their glasses topped up with Andrew's excellent claret.

The meal was not a success. Conversation was desultory and confined to small talk. Lady Maclaren tried hard with Donald but he refused to be drawn, limiting himself to monosyllabic replies. At last the ladies went into the withdrawing room for coffee and the men moved up the table around their host. MacKay placed the port and cigars in front of Andrew.

'Will there be anything else, sir?'

'No, thank you, MacKay. We'll ring when we join the ladies so you can get cleared up.'

The servants withdrew and as soon as the men were alone, Willie went off on a different tack.

'Well, Andrew,' he said, 'I suppose that I ought to bring you up to date with the news.'

'If you don't, no one else will,' was the reply.

'We're re-equipping.'

'With what?'

'Rifles. We're getting the Martini-Henry at last.'

'I didn't know that, sir,' interjected Ian.

'You're not supposed to,' said Willie. 'A second lieutenant is the lowest form of animal life in the British army.' But he smiled as he said it.

'It's not before time,' said Andrew. 'Some regiments have had it for over ten years. Mind you, the Snider-Enfield is a pretty accurate weapon.'

'But the Martini is much quicker to handle,' said Willie. 'And then, after that, we're off. I suppose that neither of you two young gentlemen would care to tell us where?'

'Why, yes, sir,' replied Donald. 'I think I can. My platoon sergeant told me a week ago that we were going to Egypt.'

'The devil he did,' said Andrew. 'Is that right, Willie?'

'Aye, it's right enough. But it beats me how they get the information. We are going to join Graham in the Sudan. He has been given a couple of brigades to sort out the Mahdi.'

'Who's the Mahdi, sir?' asked Donald.

'Really,' said Andrew, 'Lieutenant Bruce, you ought to read the papers. The Mahdi is a very dangerous character. Ever since about 1880 he's been whipping up the Sudanese tribesmen. Calls himself the successor of the Prophet. The Egyptians can't do anything about it, that's for sure. They've got garrisons down in the south at Berber, Suakim, and Khartoum, and a few other minor ones scattered about, but nothing much. Certainly nothing that would be able to contain the sort of mob that the Mahdi is getting together.'

'Isn't General Gordon in charge out there?' asked Ian.

'Yes,' continued Andrew, 'Chinese Gordon has gone back, Bible and all. He resigned as governor of Egypt about three years ago. What the devil he's going to do now I don't know – he hasn't got any troops to speak of. Anyhow there's one thing I'd be willing to bet and that is that if you see action it will be south, in the Sudan, not in Egypt. How do you two youngsters feel about that?'

'I suppose that it's just part of the job,' said Ian.

'I'm not so sure,' said Donald quietly, 'I always feel that a soldier's job is to keep the peace; fighting should always be a last resort.'

'Will we be under Gordon?' asked Ian.

'No, I told you you're under Graham.'

'And who are the brigade commanders, sir?' asked Ian.

'Ours will be commanded by Major General Buller,' said Willie. 'Have you heard of him?'

'Yes, sir,' said Donald. 'He's a V.C. They say he is one of our best generals.'

'Well,' replied Willie noncommittally. 'The troops certainly love him.'

'But that's jolly important, isn't it, sir?' said Donald.

'Aye, I suppose it might be,' said Willie.

Andrew allowed himself a smile. Donald was beginning to enter into the conversation. Maybe this evening would be a success after all. 'Well, gentlemen,' he said, 'this is a family party, so I don't think we should keep the ladies waiting too long, and besides, I can't abide lukewarm coffee.' Which last remark even got a smile out of Donald.

'Shall we?' said Andrew, rising from his place.

When they did join the ladies, and Lady Maclaren with Maud's help had finished fussing with the coffee, the evening became more relaxed. Ian had eyes only for Naomi. Her pure white silk gown set off the creamy gold of her skin to perfection. Within a very few moments he had sought her out and managed to steer her to a corner of the room where they could talk quietly without being overheard.

'Naomi,' he said, 'I have just heard that we will be off to Egypt soon.'

'Oh, yes, I already knew that,' she replied. 'Daddy told me this morning. I do hope you will like it there. It must be wonderful to be able to travel the world as soldiers do. Sometimes I wish that I had been born a man.'

'Naomi, I know that we are very young . . .'

'Well,' she replied, laughing as he hesitated, 'you are younger than I am.'

'Yes, I know,' said Ian. 'But . . . do you think that that is terribly important? I don't.'

'I agree. Why should it be important? Everybody must be younger than somebody, unless you happen to be the oldest person in the world.'

'Yes, but don't you understand, I'm talking about you and me.'

Suddenly those beautiful, big, dark brown eyes of hers became solemn and fixed him with a disconcerting attention. 'Ian, what are you trying to say to me?'

'It's like this. If we are going overseas, God knows when we will be back. Naomi, do you think that I could possibly see you alone?' he blurted out.

'That would hardly be proper – but I think it could be arranged. Can you not tell me what it is that you want to see me alone about?'

'Well . . . it's terribly important . . . and . . . do you think I should ask your father if I can see you alone?'

'You can if you want to, but you needn't worry about Daddy. He won't object. The only thing I must say is that I do hope that you are not thinking too seriously about me.'

'I could never think *too* seriously about you, Naomi.'

'Because it's no good, you know.'

'Just because you are a little older than I am?'

'No. No, if that was the only reason it wouldn't be important. Speak to your father, Ian. He knows.'

She looked sad.

'Naomi, I . . .'

'Enough for now, Ian.' And she placed the tips of her fingers on his lips. 'The others are watching us.'

Willie Bruce was certainly watching them. He watched them with an intensity and a feeling of near pain. They were a beautiful couple. Ian tall and lithe, with his Maclaren red hair and blue eyes, broad shouldered and narrow hipped. And Naomi, so much a perfection of young womanhood, the sort of creature that most men know only in their private fantasies. He watched his stepdaughter put that delicate hand to Ian's lips, he saw her mouth move slowly as she said something to him and he felt a pang, a twinge of sorrow for the pair of them. For Willie knew that just as Naomi's mother could never have had Ian's father, neither could this pair ever fulfil the promise that was so apparent in them as they stood there. It was a damned shame, they looked so right, so perfect for one another and so much in love.

Willie watched as Naomi slowly drew her hand away from Ian's mouth, the whole movement so intimate and so sensual. Then she walked away from him in the direction of Donald her brother, leaving Ian standing there, his own hand upon his lips where she had touched him.

'I suppose that you will soon be off to Egypt with your husband, Mrs Bruce?'

Lady Maclaren and Maud Bruce were sitting together on one of the large chintz-covered sofas, sipping their coffee. Maud smiled at Lady Maclaren's remark and the formality with which Lady Maclaren always addressed her. After all, Culbrech House had been, for a short while, her home, when Andrew had brought her there from India after the mutiny at Cawnpore. She had left Culbrech House because Andrew had started paying court to her. Not that she personally objected to his attentions, but because she knew that it met with the disapproval of both of his parents. It was a long time before she returned to Culbrech House; not until the regiment had returned from India four years ago. Andrew, since she had met him, had been her saviour, her lover, and now he was her friend. Somehow she always felt that Lady Maclaren was afraid of her, even though she was now happy and contented in her marriage and a threat to no one. But Maud Bruce was still a very beautiful woman, tall and slender, with the skin of someone fifteen years her junior, and not a trace of grey in her golden-yellow hair.

'No, Lady Maclaren, I shall not be going to Egypt,' Maud replied. 'And as far as I know, Willie won't be going, either.'

'But isn't the whole regiment going?' said Lady Maclaren.

'No, it's rather more complicated than that. I understand that the second battalion are being withdrawn from India and Colonel Mackinnon will stop off in Egypt with his headquarters company. We are sending out three companies to replace the men that he is sending directly home.'

'Will your boys be going?'

'Donald certainly. Gordon, I'm not sure, but I imagine that he will be going as well.' She glanced over to where Donald was standing alone and smiled as she saw Naomi go up to him. 'I'm not very happy about them leaving, and I wish that I could be there with them. But it's not to be. Even if Willie was going, it would all be active service and wives would only be an encumbrance. So I shall sit at home and watch for the postman.'

Lady Maclaren patted her knee in an unusual display of affection. 'Well, my dear,' she said, 'that is what comes from marrying a soldier, as I know only too well.'

'I'm not sure that marrying a soldier is such a bad thing,' said Maud. 'But I seem to have married the regiment.'

'One always does.'

'It might have been easier if I had had another daughter. Naomi is a great comfort.'

At the mention of Naomi, Lady Maclaren withdrew her hand. 'I'm sure she is,' she said coldly. 'Did you notice just now?'

'Notice what?'

'She and Ian were talking very earnestly. I do hope that they're not . . . well, you know what I mean. After all, she is so much older than Ian.'

'Not so much as to matter,' said Maud. 'But I understand exactly what you mean, Lady Maclaren.' She paused. 'I went through it myself, I'm sure that you will remember.'

'Let me get you some more coffee,' said Lady Maclaren, deeply embarrassed at the turn that the conversation had taken.

Maud watched the dumpy little figure of Lady Maclaren as she waddled off to the sideboard in search of more coffee, and allowed herself a wry smile. It was an open secret in the glen that Naomi was not Willie Bruce's child; how could she be with her looks? Among Maud's more intimate circle, it was known that Naomi was in fact a Eurasian. For Maud had been raped during the Mutiny, and the sepoy who had violated her had fathered this beautiful woman. It was her knowledge of this, when the pregnant Maud had first arrived at Culbrech House and Andrew had started paying her undue attention, that had made Lady Maclaren regard Maud as a threat. Strange, thought Maud, how history was repeating itself. Now Naomi was the threat. She looked around the room for her daughter and caught sight of her chatting with Donald. Poor Donald, he was not enjoying this at all. Maud knew her son, how sensitive he was, how fundamentally gentle. It would take him a long time to get over the chance events of this day.

Naomi noticed her mother looking at her and came over.

'Mummy,' she said, 'I think we should go home. Donald is utterly miserable.'

'I can see he is,' replied Maud, 'but I very much fear that he would be utterly miserable wherever he was. I don't think that going home is going to help.'

'But, Mummy —'

'All right, I'll speak to your father. You go back to Donald.'

Maud went over to where Willie was deep in conversation with Andrew. 'Excuse me,' she said to Andrew, and then she told Willie what Naomi had told her.

'What dae you think, Andrew?' he asked.

'I dunno,' Andrew replied. 'It's a difficult one. Maybe this party was a little hasty. Perhaps after a good night's sleep, he'll see things better in the morning.'

'If he sleeps,' said Willie, glancing towards his son. He turned to Maud. 'All right, my dear, you can get your wraps and we'll be awa'.'

Lady Maclaren rang for MacKay and told him that their guests were leaving. When the ladies had their wraps and Willie and Donald their greatcoats, the Maclarens accompanied them to the hallway to make their farewells.

'Don't ye come any further,' said Willie to Andrew. 'You've nae coat and it's a cold night.' Though what he really meant was that Andrew would have a devil of a job stomping up and down the stone steps.

Andrew stopped. For a moment, and it was only for a moment, he thought of himself whole and entire, walking down those steps with Maud. He was looking at her so intently, remembering, until he suddenly caught Willie's eye. There was compassion on his half-brother's face, not jealousy or anger; Willie did not need that now, he was too secure in his own happiness. Just as suddenly as it had come, the feeling passed.

'Aye, Andrew,' said Willie breaking into a large grin, 'A lot o' water's gone under the bridge since then. Good night to ye all and thank ye.'

Ian had accompanied his parents to the hall and now hurried down the steps to hold open the door. As she passed him, Naomi offered Ian her hand.

'Good night, Ian,' she murmured softly, 'I have enjoyed this evening.'

'Good night, Naomi,' said Ian, taking her hand, and then he

stopped as he felt the hardness of a piece of paper against the softness of her flesh. Naomi smiled at him as the colour rose in his cheeks while he withdrew his hand clutching tight at the precious document.

It seemed an age to Ian before they were all in their carriage and he was free to run upstairs to his room where he shut the door and reverently spread the piece of paper, smoothing it carefully, under the light of a candle.

It was written in pencil, the hand was rounded and voluptuous, each letter as perfectly formed as the hand that had written it. It read: *Tuesday, three o'clock, the Priory Inn.*

And it was signed with a single letter *N.*

3

'Battalion! General Salute! Present ARMS!'

There was a clap as a thousand hands hit the stocks of their rifles. A pause and then a rattle as the rifles were brought forward and held out before their owners. Finally a crash as the rifles were drawn into the body and lowered and a thousand boots thumped the parade ground, the right instep up against the heel of the left boot.

Gordon Bruce stood proudly in front of number two platoon of C Company, his drawn broadsword motionless and pointed up with the hilt brushing his lips. Behind him and a little to his left stood his platoon senior N.C.O., Lance-Sergeant Smith.

Smith stood proudly to attention. It was an ill wind . . . and he had been promoted after the tragic death of Lance-Sergeant Murdoch. Like so many of the men around him he too came from the glen and held a proprietary interest in the battalion. Chin drawn in, chest out, his eyes staring straight in front of him past the glitter of his bayonet towards the backs of C Company. Smith now had a platoon of his own. In common with so many when they were newly arrived in the sergeants' mess, he was the proverbial 'new broom'. He determined that C Company and in particular number two platoon, would be the finest in the regiment. Of course, like every long-serving soldier – he had been in the army ten years – he knew that he would have to nurse his young officer along. But that would not be difficult. Young officers expected to be nursed. His was a Bruce, the younger son of the C.O. himself, and no soldier, whatever his rank, could have a finer example than Colonel Willie. Gordon Bruce would be all right, Smith was sure of that.

The colours broke at the mast and the bugler sounded the general salute. It was a long bugle call and all the while the regiment stood there motionless, their burnished bayonets glinting in the early morning sunlight, the white blancoed webbing of their rifle slings bisecting each man from his chin almost to the bottom of his kilt.

'Battalion will slope arms. Sloooope arms!!'

Colonel Bruce turned to face his men as Gordon sheathed his sword, trying hard not to glance down at the scabbard as he fumbled the point into the aperture. Out of the corner of his eye he could just see his brother Donald standing in front of number one platoon. Donald did everything so perfectly, his sword slipped easily into its place. Donald, of whom Gordon was so proud, and who had hardly said a word to him since he had joined the regiment four days ago.

'Fall out the officers,' called Colonel Bruce.

Jimmy Taylor, standing in the rear rank of C Company, made a grimace. They should by rights have marched past the C.O. and then off to breakfast. Falling out the officers now could mean anything, but it was probably work and Jimmy had had a skinful of whisky last night, had puked up all of his dinner, and as a result was suffering from a sick headache and the gnawing pangs of hunger. It was Tuesday, but Jimmy had been on guard duty over the weekend and still had his pay intact on Monday evening. The seven shillings less one shilling and twopence for barrack damages had left him a total of five shillings and tenpence; this he had converted into whisky as soon as he could get away from camp on Monday. For Jimmy the army was a damned sight easier life than sweating your guts out on the land but, like everything else, it had its drawbacks. The officers and senior N.C.O.s existed, in Jimmy's mind, solely for the purpose of plaguing the private soldier and Jimmy could well recognize the signs of some new evil. Any break in routine, and this was one, spelt some new form of devilment. However there was plenty of time off and the lassies liked a braw soldier laddie in his kilt and feather bonnet. Maybe one day he'd get down to it and become an officer himself just like the colonel had done.

As Second Lieutenant Gordon Bruce hesitated, Lance-Sergeant Smith hissed, 'Awa' and get yer breakfast, sirr.'

'Oh yes, thank you,' Gordon whispered, and he turned to his left, saluted the C.O. somewhat tardily as his brother officers were already moving off, and marched away in the direction of the mess.

'Carry on, Sergeant-Major,' called the colonel.

'Sirrr!' roared R.S.M. Macmillan, thumping the ground with his right boot as if he hated it, throwing up a quivering salute, and marching round to the front of the battalion.

Every man there tensed himself as the R.S.M. assumed command. The officers, the amateurs, had gone and the professional had taken over. Now they were going to find out what all this was about. Macmillan glared at them disapprovingly.

He was a great bull of a man, six feet two in height, with close-cropped sandy hair and a head that dissolved straight into his neck which carried down the ramrod of his back to his rather prominent buttocks, giving his kilt a sway when he walked that was the envy of every man in the battalion and the delight of the ladies upon whom he bestowed his liberal favours. His pale blue eyes always seemed without expression, but it was said that he could spot a misdemeanour at a mile, and woe betide the man who fell foul of R.S.M. Macmillan. By sheer effort and perfection, he had risen from the rank of corporal to his present exalted post in a little over five years. Younger than most of his senior N.C.O.s, he was an object not of their envy but of their admiration. Hamish Macmillan was the complete fighting machine and there was not a man in the battalion who would not have volunteered to stand at his side on the battlefield.

Now he stood firmly at attention facing the battalion.

'Battalion, stand at ease! Stand easy! No talking in the ranks.' He eyed them balefully. 'Now, whist ye tae what I am going to say for I shall only say it once and anyone who fails to comply with these orders is for the high jump. When you are dismissed, you will return immediately to your barrack rooms and from there you will go and get your breakfast.

'At oh eight hundred hours, you will parade by companies at the armoury with your rifles, cleaned and unloaded, and without rifle slings. There each man will be issued with a shining new rifle. It is an improved design and it is in perfect condition, and it will remain in perfect condition, and it will remain clean and spotless or I shall want to know the reason why. You will then return to your barrack rooms, make a note of the number of your rifle, after which you will parade again. This time you will fall in at the quartermaster's stores with your feather bonnets in their canvas cases. There, in exchange for your feather bonnet, you will receive a shining new white helmet and a roll of cloth. This roll of cloth is called a pugaree. Anderson, what are you laughin' at?'

'Nothing, sir, it sounded daft what you said it was called.'

'Maybe ye'll no think it's sae daft after you finish peeling tatties at the cookhouse this afternoon. See to it, Sergeant Gibson.'

'Sir,' replied Frankie as Anderson relapsed into sullen silence.

'The pugaree is to be bound around the helmet in the prescribed manner which will be demonstrated to each barrack room by an N.C.O. who has already learned how to do it. Your white helmet will remain white as snow. It can be cleaned with the same blanco as you use for your webbing, so see to it.

'Now,' he said, 'these instructions apply to every one of you excepting Headquarters Company who will not be issued with white helmets or pugarees, but will retain their feather bonnets.

'Any questions, no, right,' he said all in one breath. 'Parade tae the right dismiss!'

The men sprang to attention, turned right and then broke ranks.

When Sir Henry Maclaren, Andrew's father, had designed the barracks which were to become the permanent home for his regiment, he had introduced what was then a revolutionary concept to the army. Instead of having the men eating in their barrack rooms, as they did throughout most of the service, off tables laid down the centre aisle, each man sitting on the end of his bed, he had built a complete mess hall for the private soldier. Here, seated on forms, the men could eat off scrubbed wooden tables after receiving their rations from the serving counter.

It was to this building that the men went after their dismissal from parade, pausing only to dash into their billets and pick up a tin plate, a spoon, and a tin mug from their kit. Inside the mess hall the cooks stood behind the serving counter of scrubbed pine, framed in a brick rectangle which separated the mess deck from the cookhouse. Before them was a huge black cauldron full of steaming oatmeal porridge. The men lined up in an orderly, if rather noisy, queue and received their ration of one and a half ladles of porridge and three-quarters of a pint of strong sweet tea. Then they went and sat on the forms at the scrubbed wooden tables and, with a great deal of clatter and loud talk, had breakfast. Most of them ate quickly, for there was always the chance of 'seconds'. If, after all had been served, there was anything left, it was first come, first served. Jimmy Taylor managed to get to the counter, plate in hand, just as the huge pot was carried away into the cookhouse, empty.

'Fuck them,' he said. 'Just like the bloody army. Work oot hoo much yer needin' and then gi' ye half.'

After breakfast they returned to their barrack rooms, from where they would take their rifles to the armoury at eight o'clock when summoned by the bugle.

The sergeant-major's announcement had, of course, given rise to a great deal of speculation and rumour. When Colour-Sergeant Frankie Gibson returned to his little room at the end of number two barrack in C Block, the argument was in full swing.

'I tell yees, yees are going tae war,' Anderson was saying with all the authority of his eighteen years' service.

'Ye'll be going too, will ye no?' replied Peter Leinie, who had never been more than ten miles away from his village in his whole life, and was feeling nervous and overawed at the mere thought of having to travel across the world to the outposts of Empire.

'Och, aye,' said Anderson, 'I'll be going, but I'll be coming back. There'll be fechting, plenty of it. How are ye goin' tae like it, laddie?' he said, getting up and lumbering past a couple of bedspaces to where the boy was sitting. Anderson was a great brute of a man. When Wellington said that 'the British soldier was the scum of the earth', he must have had someone like Anderson in mind. He was a bully who would always pick on the weakest and try to terrorize the innocent. He was not a Highlander. He came from somewhere in the south, though no one knew quite where. He had got into the army after being given the alternative of prison or service with the colours. Having got in, he had discovered, with a certain brute cunning, that if you had a strong arm and little conscience, you could avoid most of the work that was going. He stuck his face close to Peter Leinie so that Leinie could see the little purple blackheads which pockmarked his skin, and he grinned, revealing a set of yellowing teeth and stale beery breath. Leinie tried to turn his head away to avoid the stench.

'Yees are scairt, are ye,' rumbled Anderson. 'Youse'll be a fuckin' sight mair scairt when a fuzzy-wuzzy or a Pathan sticks his wee spear intae your guts and ye sit there and watch them all fall oot and spread oot in front o' ye.'

'Leave the laddie alone.' The speaker was Private James MacTavish.

'And just who the hell de ye think youse is talking tae, sodger?' replied Anderson, turning on him belligerently.

MacTavish was a big, quiet man whose father had been killed when the regiment had stormed the forts at Taku in China and whose mother had died in his infancy. He had been brought up 'on the Parish', serving as potboy in the manse with only two days off a year and sixpence a week for his pocket. The restriction had been too much for him and, as soon as he was old enough, he had joined the army. It was probably because of these experiences that MacTavish was always likely to side with the underdog in any dispute. Besides, he was essentially a peace-loving man, slow to rouse, but, when roused, quick to deal with whatever trouble was offered; and James MacTavish was one of the toughest men in the regiment.

He had been sitting on the end of his cot, cleaning his rifle, but now he put down his gun and rose to face Anderson. 'Ye dinna mak' me scairt,' he said. 'But yon laddie there doesna ken oot aboot it. If ye want tae pick on anybody, try me.'

'Youse fuckin' keep oot o' this,' snarled Anderson.

The conversation in the barrack room stopped at the prospect of a fight. The two men stood looking at each other, eyeball to eyeball, and it was Anderson who backed down. 'Och awa', mannie. Ye canna take a joke.'

'I can, Anderson; but yon laddie canna. So just tak' it easy when ye ta'k tae him. He'll find oot soon enough aboot fechting.'

'Watch it, mister,' said Anderson, unable to take reprimand in front of the whole barrack room and folding up his huge hamlike fist. 'Just ye watch yoursel'.'

The other man did not move but just stood there with his arms hanging loosely by his sides. 'You're no gonna tak' a skelp at me, Anderson. For ye ken fine that I can tak' care o' you.'

Anderson drew back his fist, but before the blow was struck MacTavish had hit him hard in the solar plexus. He staggered back gasping for breath right into the arms of Frankie Gibson, who had just entered the room.

'Attention!' bellowed Frankie, reeling under the impact of Anderson's huge body. 'Stand where you are, the lot of ye. Stand up, Anderson. All right, now, what's going on here?'

'Nothing, sarge,' said Anderson, glowering.

'It better not be. Fechtin' in the barrack rooms will cost ye twenty-eight days jankers.'

'Please, sergeant,' said Leinie, 'we was wondering where we was going.'

'We're going east. That's all I can tell youse. Now get yourselves fell in ootside wi' your rifles. Nae slings.'

'But, sarge,' protested Leinie, 'the bugles hasn't gone yet.'

'The bugler's changing his rifle. Oot wi' the lot o' ye.'

Ian Maclaren hurried over to the officers' mess. It being Tuesday, he had to seek out his company commander Alex Farquhar. He went through the pillared portico into the main entrance hall. The mess was set back some distance from Headquarters Block. It was fronted by a beautifully kept green lawn which had two circular patches of brown earth. One of these was in front of the dining room and one in front of the main anteroom. These contained the skeletal stumps of rose bushes recently pruned. The whole of the lawn area was surrounded by a gravelled drive so that carriages could drive up under the canopy of the entrance and disgorge their passengers without submitting them to the elements. The entrance hall itself was oak panelled, and facing Ian as he entered was a wide, sweeping staircase, the treads covered with thick-pile brown carpeting, which led to the upper stories. The first of these contained the library, writing room, and billiard room, and above them were the officers' quarters. To his left as he entered was the heavy oak door which led to the regimental dining room where the colours were kept, the Queen's Colour and the Regimental Colour crossed on their brass-topped poles and, behind, the chair which was occupied by the colonel when he chose to dine with his officers. On his right just beyond the stuffed wildcat was the anteroom where most of the drinking and horseplay took place among the younger officers. He went into the anteroom, surveying its comfortable deep leather armchairs, the trophies on the walls, and the prints and citations, one of which was to his grandfather Sir Henry Maclaren, praising his gallantry at the battle of Balaclava. He saw Alex Farquhar lounging, completely relaxed, in one of the leather armchairs by the fire. Ian went over to him.

'Hello, Ian, can I get you a drink? I'm just going to have one myself.'

'No thanks, Alex,' replied Ian. 'It's a bit too early for me.'

'Suit yourself,' said Farquhar. 'Steward.'

'Alex, I want to ask a favour,' said Ian as Alex was ordering his drink.

'Ask away, old boy. It shall be granted if it is within my power.'

Ian took a deep breath. This was too important to be flippant about. 'May I take the afternoon off?' he asked.

'What, today?'

'Yes, please, Alex.'

Farquhar cocked his head on one side and gazed at the young man quizzically with raised eyebrows. 'For God's sake, Ian, you know what we've got on today. The men are being issued new rifles this morning and we've got musketry all afternoon. How the hell do you think I can give you the day off?'

'Not the day, only half, sir.'

'Sorry, old boy, it's just not on.' And then, seeing the crest-fallen look on the younger man's face: 'What is it? A woman?'

'Really, sir —' and Ian blushed. He felt the colour rise in his face and wished he could run away.

'So it is a woman. I see. Is she very important?'

'Yes, sir, very, but I can't discuss it,' Ian replied formally, resenting the mocking tone in his company commander's voice.

'Listen, Ian, there's no way I can give you this afternoon off. The colonel would have my guts for garters if I did. Why don't you ask him? If he says yes, I won't raise any objection. I'm damned sure that he'll say the same as I did. But —'

'But what, Alex?' said Ian eagerly, sensing a chance.

'But,' repeated Farquhar grinning slightly, 'if it is in the interest of true love —'

He paused, and Ian would willingly have hit him.

'—and you didn't happen to appear this afternoon,' he continued, 'I wouldn't notice. But you must understand that I'm not giving you the afternoon off. If the colonel notices that you are missing, there'll be no backup from me. Now if you want to take that chance, you can.'

'Oh, thanks, Alex, thanks a lot.'

'Don't thank me. Just cut along and hope that no one notices.' And as Ian turned to go, 'And good luck with the lady.'

Alex Farquhar grinned as he saw the colour begin to rise in Ian's cheeks. 'Go on,' he said, 'it happens to the best of us.'

Ian left the mess and Farquhar turned his attention to his drink. Ah well, he thought, things didn't change. Perhaps he should not have mocked the lad. He remembered his first love, the daughter of a bishop; that had ended up in a haystack somewhere in Perthshire. Things didn't change, he was right; it was only the participants who thought that their own case was unique. He turned his attention back to more important matters and ordered another whisky.

Beauly Priory, founded in 1230 by Sir John Bisset of the Aird to house a community of the Valliscaulian monks, and destroyed just over four hundred years later by Cromwell in order to provide stone for his fort at Inverness, stood on the north corner of the market square in Beauly. Outside the grey stone walls, which surrounded the still beautiful remnants of the

Priory, even though it was but an empty, roofless shell, stood the Priory Inn. It had once been the guest house but was now fully secularized.

Ian had never been inside the building before, which was surprising, as the inn was used by most of the big houses in the area for overflow guests. It would be crowded during such times as the opening of the shooting season on the 'glorious' twelfth of August, when the first of the season's grouse fell to the guns, and in the autumn, when large stalking parties came up from the south for the annual cull of red deer.

He arrived just before two-thirty and went in through the arched stone doorway and turned to his left. He found himself in a large, well furnished lounge, amply supplied with leather armchairs and a large wood fire burning in a massive grate at the far end.

It was a room in which middle-class matrons from the surrounding area would gather for afternoon tea and gossip and ensure that their figures were a threat to no one by consuming vast quantities of the delicious cream cakes for which the inn was justly famous. Over the fireplace hung a burnished post horn, a recent relic, for the Priory had been a coaching inn until the coming of the railways. That trade having all but vanished, the proprietors had refurbished the whole building to a much higher standard of comfort and succeeded where so many had failed, in attracting a new clientele from the middle and upper classes. Ian was struck by the sameness of all institutionalized buildings as he walked into the lounge. This might have been theanteroom of the mess except for the fact that, unlike that all-male establishment, this was populated almost exclusively by females. They all had leather armchairs and sofas, they all had large log fires, they all had half-panelled walls, and they all had heavy velvet curtains hanging from brass curtain poles.

Ian made his way among the small tables and the large ladies and the hunting prints with their unnatural horses frozen into immobility and found himself a recently vacated place near the fire where someone had left a copy of the *Inverness Courier*. He sat down and picked up the paper and pretended to read.

His mind was a mass of conflicting thoughts as he stared unseeing at the print in front of him. He was not thinking about the battalion, nor indeed about the wrath which would await him should his absence be noted. He was thinking only of her, the woman he was supposed to be meeting.

Supposing she did not come? Not a word had passed between them since she had pressed that note into his hand. Supposing circumstances had changed and she could not come? Why did she choose this day and this time and this place? What could it be that had made her act in so unladylike a fashion as to instigate their meeting? Perhaps she did not mean it at all. Perhaps she wanted merely to make a fool of him. No, he could not believe that, not of her. For if she did that, he would never be able to approach her again; but then, that might be what she wanted.

So Ian sat and worried away his half hour until the clock in the market square chimed three, and just on the third stroke Naomi came into the lounge.

He saw her before she saw him. She was standing framed in the stone arch of the doorway. She wore a gown of orange silk scattered with black polka dots. Her skirt fell straight down in front of her in horizontal folds, emphasizing the smallness of her waist. Her bodice covered the entire top of her body, ending in a tight little ruffle around her neck tied with a single piece of narrow, black velvet ribbon, which accentuated her creamy skin. She was wearing a bustle, still considered rather shocking in the Highlands, but all the rage in the more fashionable society of Edinburgh and London. The silk of her gown fell down over the bustle to form a tiny train which just swept the floor behind her.

Ian was surprised to see that she was wearing neither cape nor gloves nor hat. She caught his eye as he rose from his chair and smiled a greeting as she came towards him with her hand extended. He took her hand and brushed the tips of her fingers with his lips, astonished as ever at how tiny she was; she to whom he had always to look up to see her face in his dreams.

'I'm so glad that you were able to come,' she said in her low, soft voice.

'There is no power in this world which would have kept me away from here this afternoon,' he replied gravely, releasing her hand.

She looked hard at him, for she knew that what he had said

was true. 'Yes, Ian, but first let us have tea and then we can talk. If you will ring that little bell there, someone will come and serve us.'

She sat down and Ian seated himself opposite her, gazing at her across the table in dumb admiration while she ordered tea and hot scones from the waitress. A thousand phrases flooded his mind, phrases of endearment and longing and worship. But when he finally found his tongue and broke the silence, it was only to say, 'Thank you, no sugar.'

'I didn't see you arrive,' he said at length, watching her as she sat calmly sipping her tea and nibbling at a scone.

'No, I arrived this morning,' she replied.

'This morning? But how did you do that?'

'It's quite simple. Mummy's down in Edinburgh on a shopping expedition, and Papa has decided to stay in his quarters in camp for the next few days. It seems that they have so much on, I was quite surprised that you managed to get away. Anyhow, rather than be left in the house alone with only the servants for company, I've taken rooms here.'

'Oh,' replied Ian, 'I see. So you're —' He stopped abruptly.

'Very vulnerable?' she said. 'Yes, I am.' She looked him straight in the eye.

'I didn't mean that,' he protested.

'Yes you did,' she replied. 'But before we talk about me, why don't we talk about you. I am sure that you must have a great deal to say and that it must be most important.'

'It is important, but there's not very much to say, not really. It's very simple, only it's not easy to say. The words, I mean. Do you understand?'

'I know exactly what you mean, Ian,' replied Naomi, and she looked a little sad.

'Would you rather I didn't say them, then?' he asked.

'I don't think it matters since we both know. Perhaps it would be easier if I were to say them for you. Shall I?'

Slowly he ran the tip of his tongue around his dry lips and looked down into his teacup, avoiding her steady gaze. 'It's not easy,' he said at length.

'You think you have fallen in love with me, Ian, is that not what you wanted to say?'

He looked up at her. 'I don't *think*,' he said quickly, 'I know.'

'Have you stopped to consider that I am five years older than you are?'

'What does that matter?'

'Doesn't it? Then let me put it this way. Most women are married long before they reach my age. Do you think that your family would approve? Of me, I mean?' She waited for his answer.

'Why shouldn't they approve? Five years is not all that much.'

'Ian,' she spoke very deliberately, 'I want you to understand this, and it has nothing to do with age. Your father would never, under any circumstances, approve of me.'

'My father? But that's ridiculous. He and Colonel Bruce are the greatest of friends. I should think he would be delighted.'

'I am quite sure that he would be delighted,' said Naomi, 'if I were Colonel Bruce's daughter.'

'Naomi! What are you saying? I don't understand. If you were Colonel Bruce's daughter? Who else's daughter could you be?'

'I don't know,' she replied. 'I only know that Willie Bruce is not my father and that I was born before he married my mother. None of us knows who my father was. We know that he was not British, not even European. He was someone over there in India, a sepoy. He – raped my mother – your father knows this. Can you imagine Sir Andrew approving of his son marrying a half-caste? A bastard?'

Ian's world disintegrated. His shoulders sagged as it collapsed around him with her words. He was only too aware of the social implications of what she said and he knew full well that she spoke the truth. You only had to look at her to see that. However, he was not willing to give her up. He said, 'Why should it make any difference who your father was?'

'Probably it shouldn't, but it does.'

'Anyhow, what's it got to do with my father? If your fa – if Colonel Bruce was to give his permission, I could marry you tomorrow. I *would* marry you tomorrow. My father would have no say in the matter.'

'Oh, Ian, my dear, dear Ian, you know that that is not true.' She paused. 'Well, don't you?' she said softly.

Gazing at this beautiful creature, Ian had never felt so

miserable in his life. 'But I want you so much. I just don't want to go on without you. I love you, Naomi.'

'Yes, my dear. I know that you love me. I know that you want me, and that at least I shall not deny to you.'

He looked up at her solemn face, not able for a moment to fully realize what it was that she was saying to him.

'I mean,' she replied, 'that I cannot be your wife, but no power on earth will stop me from fulfilling my heart's desire and becoming your lover.'

'But how . . . ?' he asked.

'If you wish it, my darling, it is very simple,' she replied. 'There is only one condition.' Her voice was low and her smile was gentle.

'Anything.'

'There must be no more talk of marriage. I, too, for a little while dreamed dreams, but I know that it cannot be. Do I have your word?'

'You have my word in so far as I am able to give it.'

'You will be gentle with me?'

'I swear it,' said Ian.

'Come then,' she whispered. And led him up the stairs.

4

Willie Bruce was not a man given to hating, but if he had been he would have hated his lords and masters at the War Office. He had been there only twice in his life and what he had seen had confirmed his contempt for the establishment. Smooth-cheeked young cavalry officers, whose regiments had never heard of them, in tight-fitting strapped trousers with tiny silver spurs that had never been thrust into a horse's side in a charge. They walked around carrying pieces of paper in hands that had never carried a rifle and smiling benignly at each other with eyes that had never seen a shot fired in anger. They were gorgeous and useless, almost as useless as the generals who inhabited palatial offices and sat over their port after dinner and said it would be a 'jolly good idea' to send suchandsuch a regiment to suchandsuch a place. Not because they were needed there but because, somehow, these old men had to justify their existence. They justified it by using the Empire like a giant chessboard and the regiments which fell under their command were the pawns in their game to be moved about at will.

Willie remembered, with bitterness, how the Maclarens (they had been the 148th Foot then and he a senior N.C.O.) had been shunted about the oceans. To China and then to New Zealand and then away from New Zealand and then back to

New Zealand. And all because somebody in Whitehall was trying to hang on to his job.

It was two weeks since Ian had gone up the stairs of the Priory Inn with Naomi and they had just had the first light snowfall of the winter. A package had arrived on Willie's desk bearing the War Office seal. It contained orders for the embarkation of the Maclaren Highlanders. At least, thought Willie, they had got it to the right address.

Willie sat in his office glaring at the documents in front of him, surprised at the unusual amount of information that they contained and furious that they were daring to send *his* regiment overseas without himself. God, he hoped that this did not mean a staff appointment. He knew that if it did, he would have to accept. Willie was not a rich man. He lived on his pay and the three hundred pounds a year that had been bequeathed him by Sir Henry Maclaren, Andrew's father, and his own father for that matter.

He thought of the men who would be leaving. They would not all come back, they never did. He thought of the rank and file first because he had been one of them and because so many of them had spent their childhood on the estate in the glen and been brought up in a little but-and-ben just as he had been. He saw them all as individuals like Frankie Gibson. There was the best soldier in the battalion. If Britain had had an army of Frankie Gibsons a hundred years ago they would not have lost the American colonies. But they hadn't, the Frankies had all been on the other side. And MacTavish, the backbone of the army, his type, a good soldier, not very bright but solid and reliable. He really ought to see about promoting MacTavish. The MacTavishes were so often ignored. Of course they were not all good; there were men like Anderson, mind he was not a Highlander, but he was another Grigor, dangerous. Willie would like to find an excuse to discharge that one. But all of this reminiscing was not getting the job done. He looked back at his orders.

He was to bring three companies up to full establishment and dispatch them, under the command of an officer of field rank, to Liverpool. There they would embark on Her Majesty's Troopship *Avonside* for active service in the Middle East.

They were to sail December 20, 1883; their port of arrival would be announced to them later, but it would be somewhere to the south of the Suez Canal.

They had had a busy couple of weeks and by now the men were becoming quite proficient with their new Martini-Henry rifles. A, B, and C Companies had been made up to establishment at the expense of H.Q. Company, and Willie had no doubt that they would acquit themselves well and in the best traditions of a Highland Regiment.

The question of an officer of field rank was one to which he had given much thought. He had two majors, Macadam and Scott. Macadam was the adjutant – he did not want to lose him as there would be a great deal of administration here especially when the replacement companies arrived from the second battalion. Besides, Major Macadam was a very efficient administrator. He came from a comparatively well-to-do family that had a small estate a little north of Strathglass. He had spent his years at school studying, rather than enjoying himself and playing games. He was a man who was happier with a pen than a sword. It was highly unlikely that he had the dash which was needed for a command in the field.

Then there was Major Scott. He commanded Headquarters Company. H.Q. Company would be staying of course, not that that would be any barrier; Scotty was about the same age as Willie but he acted ten years older. He was a heavy man – he must have been sixteen stone – and he tired easily. Willie doubted that Scotty could stand the rigours of another campaign. He would never rise beyond his present rank; he was aware of this and was content in that knowledge and moreover he had recently been giving out broad hints that he was contemplating an early retirement. It was the best thing for him, Willie realized that. He lacked either the drive or the family background that would have taken him beyond his present position. Middle-class generals were very rare. No, Scott was not the right man either.

This meant that the obvious thing Willie would have to do was to promote his senior company commander. Unfortunately he did not have a senior company commander apart from Scotty. His three captains, Grant, Farquhar, and Murray, who commanded A, C, and B Companies respectively, had all joined the regiment on the same day. They were all first-class line officers. None of them lacked courage, though this issue alone helped him in his decision, for Hugh Grant was a man who carried courage to the point of foolhardiness. Tall and dark with a moustache which he tended with loving care, he was a Highlander whose family had probably inhabited these parts since the mountains which surrounded them were formed. The Grants were one of the major clans of the area and Hugh came from one of the minor establishment families which they had spawned. He was made of the stuff that in times gone by had necessitated the building of the forts and fortified houses in which less daring and aggressive mortals could barricade themselves. Hugh would enjoy action just for the fun of it. He would always make a wonderful number two, but command? Perhaps he needed a few more years.

Willie's first reaction was that the job should go to Farquhar, but Alex's inability to take anything seriously forced him to consider Murray. Murray, Willie considered, was a reflection of the changing army. He was not a spectacular man, not in the mould of either Grant or Farquhar. Quiet and unassuming, he was the son of an Edinburgh doctor. He had done well at Sandhurst and from the moment of his arrival at Strathglass had taken a professional interest in all that pertained to his duties as a regimental officer. He was the thing that Willie admired most, a true professional, like himself. He was of average height, dark, and with a beard that needed shaving twice a day. His eyes were blue and intense and he would listen solemnly to anything that even the lowest private in his company had to say. On top of all of that he was almost fanatically honest, never ran up the enormous mess bills which were so much a part of his two contemporaries' lives, and his men gave him that highest of all soldiers' accolades, 'You ken where you stand wi' Captain Murray.' Dour, in true Scots fashion, perfectly disciplined, as he expected every one of his men to be, he would, though possessed of plenty of physical courage, never take an unnecessary risk. Yes, Murray was really the obvious choice.

Willie looked back at his orders, trying to picture the situation. Egypt did not seem to be so bad. The trouble now lay in the Sudan, and as their port of disembarkation was 'somewhere south of Suez', it seemed obvious that the Sudan was where the Maclarens were headed.

General Charles Gordon, a fellow Scot for whom Willie had infinite respect, had been sent to Khartoum, and Major-General Sir Gerald Graham was raising a force at Trinkitat, a small harbour some hundred miles south of Port Sudan on the Red Sea. Graham was due to mount an expedition against Osman Digna, who had recently defeated a large force, mostly Egyptian, under Major-General Valentine Baker near El Teb.

The Maclarens were to join Graham, presumably at Trinkitat. There they would be placed under the command of Major-General Sir Redvers Buller, V.C.

Buller was another reason for giving the command to Murray. A gallant soldier who had won his Victoria Cross in the Zulu wars in '78 and '79, he was none the less a cautious man who would be liable to clash with the ebullient Farquhar or Grant, and would be much more likely to get on with the sober Murray.

Of course, if Murray was to get his majority, then Donald should, in the normal course of things, get his captaincy and A Company, but his son was another worry.

It had really been a hell of a fortnight. Donald had gone about his duties in a mechanical and uninspired fashion. Willie found it hard to believe that the Grigor business was entirely responsible for his son's lethargy, yet what else could it be? He had had half a mind to transfer the boy to H.Q. Company and keep him in Scotland. If it had been anyone other than his own son, he would have probably done that. But as it was Donald, there would always be the faint suspicion of nepotism, and Willie Bruce would have no part of that.

And now there was this damned business of Ian Maclaren. He had been absent from his quarters the night following the issue of the Martini-Henry rifles. Unfortunately, Willie had heard about this in casual conversation in the mess. He had had to obey the unwritten law which allows freedom of speech in the mess, and had therefore taken no action. But he had kept an eye on Ian and what he had seen had not been very encouraging. The boy had been turning up for parades half asleep. It was quite clear that for some reason or other Ian was utterly exhausted. And now, as if Donald were not enough, Ian had put in a request for transfer to H.Q. Company.

Willie could not believe that Ian Maclaren was afraid of going on active service. Granted the boy had never been tested under fire, but there had to be another reason. Willie could read a man and he knew that there was no lack of courage there. He had sent for Ian, determined to find out what this was all about, and he was now rereading the request for a transfer.

He glanced out of his window and saw Ian Maclaren walking across the square in the direction of H.Q. Block. Willie scratched his chin. It must be something pretty important, he thought. He had better try and put the young man at his ease and not approach the subject directly. He dropped Ian's letter into one of the three plywood trays on his desk. Then he opened the bottom drawer and pulled out a Morse key. This he placed in the centre of his desk where Ian would be sure to see it.

Ian came into the office and saluted and then glanced down to where Willie was tapping away at the key.

'Wonderfu' things these modern inventions,' said Willie. 'Interesting eh?'

'What is it, sir?' replied Ian.

'Tak' your hat off and sit ye doon. That's a Morse key.' He continued stabbing it with his finger.

'Something to do with sending messages, isn't it, sir?'

'Aye that's right,' said Willie conversationally, 'Ye ken well that I was never a one for newfangled ideas, but this might be useful tae us. Do you no think so?'

'I don't know, sir,' said Ian.

'Well let me put it this way. If I was to ask you for a good N.C.O. to learn how tae work this, send him awa' on a course wi' the Sappers, would ye hae anybody in mind?'

'He'd have to be somebody who could read, sir, wouldn't he?' Ian was beginning to wonder if Willie had read the letter.

'Aye, that's for sure. Ye understand the idea of the thing?'

'Well, only vaguely, sir. They've been using it since the Crimea, haven't they?'

'Aye. But they is the army and the army is us. Now it's getting important. Ye see, all ye need is twa o' these and a bittie o' wire and a battery and ye can send messages as far as ye need tae. But o' course ye've got tae ha' people who can operate it. The engineers dae it mostly, but I ha' an idea tae ha' a telegraphic unit in the battalion. Then we could dae oor own.'

'Yes, sir, it's a very good idea,' said Ian without enthusiasm; then, 'What about Lance-Sergeant Smith?'

'Smith. That's a verra good suggestion, he's a guid man.'

'Is that all you wanted to see me about, sir?'

Willie looked hard at Ian, 'Now, laddie,' he said, 'just you relax. I can see weel that there is something else on your mind.' He picked the note up from the tray, 'I ha' to say that this gave me quite a surprise.'

'Yes, sir,' said Ian.

'You applied for a transfer to Headquarters Company.'

'Yes, sir, that's right.'

Willie picked up a tiny piece of fluff which had dared to land on his desk and dropped it in the wastepaper basket. 'The damned place is like a pigsty,' he said.

'Yes, sir, I mean . . . no, sir.' said Ian.

'You do not give me any explanation as to why I should grant this request.'

'That is correct, sir.'

'Well, laddie, I have a few questions tae ask you before I can gi' a decision on this.'

'Of course, sir.'

'First of all, does your father ken anything aboot this?'

'No, sir, nothing.'

'I see,' said Willie who did not see at all. 'Are you prepared to tell me more?'

'I don't understand, sir.'

'Ian, I canna believe that you, a Maclaren, are afraid of active service, or that you dinna want tae go overseas. So there's got tae be another reason. I'm right, am I no?'

Ian did not reply.

'Answer me, boy.'

'Yes, sir, you're right.'

'Then I want tae know that reason and you had better mak' it a guid yin.'

'I don't want to leave Scotland, sir. Not just now.'

'You're a soldier, Ian. Soldiers go where they're sent, it's part o' the trade.'

'Yes, sir. I know that this is true, but there is no reason why I shouldn't try to stay at home.'

'Why dae ye want to try, Ian? Is it a woman? It usually is.'

The colour rising in Ian's cheeks gave Willie Bruce his answer. 'So that is what it is. You've fallen in love and ye dinna want tae go awa' and leave the lassie.' And as Ian opened his mouth to protest, 'I'm no mocking ye, Ian. I can understand.'

'I did not say it was a woman, sir.'

'Ye didna have tae. Might I ask who the lady is?' He waited for a reply but Ian did not answer. 'Ian, it is not trouble that you are in?'

'Really, sir!'

'Och, it happens in the best o' families, yours and mine included. Ian, I want to know the truth. Maybe I can help ye, but I canna help you if I dinna ken.'

'I don't think that anyone can help, sir. Please, sir, I've got to get out of the army,' Ian blurted out.

'For why?' said Willie. This was getting to be too much. He had been through all this with Donald only two weeks ago. 'Because you are under the regulation age to marry? These things can be dealt wi' you ken that. Well?'

'This one cannot, sir.'

Willie was really puzzled now. 'Look, laddie,' he said, 'I've known you since you were a wee bairn. I've watched you grow up and I've been as proud o' ye as if you were ma ain son. It's no difficult tae see that you're a badly troubled boy. And ye say that ye canna talk it over wi' your father.'

'That's right, sir, I can't,' said Ian gazing down at his boots.

'Then mebbie you can talk it over wi' me. Not wi' your commanding officer, but wi' your Uncle Willie, your friend.'

'I can't, sir, honestly I can't.'

'Do I know the lady?'

Ian nodded.

'Then perhaps I can help a bittie.'

'No one can help me, sir.'

The boy was almost in tears and Willie was embarrassed in his presence. 'Come on, now, laddie. Oot wi' it. Who is this lassie?'

'Naomi.'

There was a long silence. Willie picked up a battered meerschaum which was lying on his desk and twisted the stem round and round. Several times during the pause, he glanced up at the embarrassed Ian.

For his part, Ian could not understand his uncle's reaction. It was not pleasure, nor was it anger, either of which he could have understood. He looked as the bushy eyebrows opposite him drew together and the two deep lines above the nose deepened and darkened. There was more of sadness in Willie's face than there was of any other emotion. Ian gnawed at his bottom lip.

'Sir?' he said. 'Are you annoyed with me?'

'Sir?' he said again, after another pause.

'Bide a wee, laddie,' replied Willie. 'I'm thinking.' He looked up at the boy sitting in front of him. 'So you're in love wi' my Naomi?'

'Yes, sir. I'm sorry, sir, but it just happened.'

'And Naomi?'

'Sir, she says that it is hopeless.'

'Aye, she's no far wrong there. I've always been afraid of something like this. Do you ken how she feels about you?'

'The same, sir. At least, I think she feels the same.'

'Are ye sure o' that?'

'Oh, yes, sir. I'm absolutely sure. It's just that she says the whole thing is impossible.'

'Aye,' said Willie, 'I ken it is. Ian, you'll have tae give me time to work this out. I canna see that letting you stay behind is going to help you at all. I'm involved in this, and not just as your C.O. I am the lassie's father.'

'Begging your pardon, sir, but she did tell me that you are not her father.'

'Ian, if I'm no her father, then no one is.' Then, when Ian did not reply: 'She told you all about it, did she?'

'Yes, sir, everything.'

'Then there's nae mair that I can say. Not just now. Away you go, Ian.'

'Sir,'s aid Ian, rising, 'when do you think that you will be able to let me know?'

'Tomorrow, maybe.'

'Thank you, sir.'

Ian left, and after sitting in silence for several minutes, Willie got up and threw the door open.

'Orderly!' he bellowed.

A clerk appeared from the adjoining office. 'Sir?'

'Get ma horse. If anybody wants me, I've gone hame.'

That night Naomi told Ian that under no circumstances could she ever see him again. Nor could he move her to reconsider. All of his protestations could in no way persuade her to change her decision.

It was three days before Ian returned to barracks. But in spite of the fact that he had gone absent without leave, no one said a word to him. He was left very much alone to wallow in the miserable self-pity of frustrated young love.

Willie knew that he should have done something about it. It was very unlike him to allow one of his officers to take himself off and go absent without leave and yet say nothing. But he held an enormous sympathy for his nephew. He remembered his own beginnings with Maud, when he too had wished for the unattainable, though unattainable in an entirely different way. For him there had been a happy outcome, but he could see no happiness for Ian. So he overlooked the three days and prayed without much confidence, that Ian Maclaren could get it out of his mind.

5

On December 20, 1883, in accordance with their orders, A, B, and C Companies of the First Battalion, the Maclaren Highlanders, under the command of their newly promoted Major Murray, sailed from Liverpool in Her Majesty's Troopship *Avonside*. She was a big ship and fairly modern. She carried a staysail, but apart from that, no other canvas. Her tonnage was near six thousand and she would have provided reasonable if not luxurious accommodation for about four hundred. She had two thin funnels which were already belching forth black coal-smoke as the men marched aboard with their packs. The soot was dropping down onto the decks in the still air. Those who had done it all before watched this with extreme distaste. The more she dirtied herself the more work there would be for them. Not for the seamen, of course. They never dirtied their hands on a trooper. After all, their cargo was the scum of the earth, let them do the dirty work. *Avonside* was about four hundred feet long, but narrow in the beam, and as they were marching aboard an old man with a grizzled weatherbeaten face and a straggling wnite beard, and wearing a greasy peaked cap, shouted at them.

'I hope you're good sailors, Jock. Yon's going to roll like a pig.'

Before the men lay the prospect of over a week at sea in cramped and crowded conditions in the all-pervading stench of their own sweat which would get worse as the journey continued southwards until it permeated every nook and cranny of the iron hull. There were nearly a thousand of them on board. The Maclarens were not alone; they were accompanied by half a battalion of the West Yorkshire Regiment, condemned to share their boredom.

For the men aboard, there was no drink. No beer or spirits were obtainable. There was, for those of them who had money, a dry canteen, which opened three times a day for about an hour and made vast profits for the shipowners who ran it. Queues of fifty to a hundred tommies and jocks formed fifteen or twenty minutes before opening time and naturally the inevitable fights broke out. The jocks held the tommies in complete contempt and the tommies regarded the jocks as savages from another world. Within forty-eight hours this had become so serious that the canteen openings had to be taken on a strict rota basis in order to keep them apart.

The officers and the N.C.O.s tried hard to keep the men occupied. The smoke and the coal dust helped; there was a lot of deck swabbing and holystoning and scrubbing. Then there were guards, pickets, and fatigues, and work on the mess deck. But there were too many men. Only a few of them could be set to work at any one time, there just was no room to do otherwise. Most of their time was spent either lying in their hammocks or sitting around in little groups and talking.

Whenever they were not grumbling about the conditions on board they talked and fantasized about women. After the incident in the barrack room when Private MacTavish had come to his aid, young Peter Leinie had attached himself to him, even when it meant also being in the company of Private Anderson. Anderson's coarseness and his lurid recounting of sexual experiences shocked and awed the youngster. They would gather in the well deck in a corner between the after-funnel and the quarterdeck and sit down in the shade, if they could find any, and listen while Anderson reminisced or gave forth on women.

'I'll tell ye,' he would say, 'pushers are guid fer a screw and naethin' else.'

'What happens if ye get them in the puddin' club?' inquired Leinie cautiously.

Anderson laughed uproariously, 'Ye daft bugger, ye dinna tell them yer name and ye never tell them yer regiment. If ye dae, they'll be up there in the orderly room and tell the C.O. that their next bairn's yours.'

'Do you really dae that sort o' thing?'

'He'd like tae think that he did,' said MacTavish.

'Watch it,' said Anderson.

'We all dae 'em,' said MacTavish ignoring Anderson, 'but no the way he says. Ye'll dae it yerself. Jest wait till ye get tae the whore hooses in Egypt.'

'I wouldna gan in yin of them,' said Leinie.

'Then ye'll hae tae wank and ye'll get hair all over the palms o' yer hands,' hissed Anderson.

Leinie looked guiltily at his hands and Anderson laughed.

There were a couple of parades every day, usually physical training in the morning and a kit inspection in the afternoon. But apart from this they were at liberty to spend their time as they wished. The great enemy was boredom; those who could read did so, and those who could not spent most of their time up on deck, leaning over the rail and looking at the water. Gambling schools cropped up all over the ship and many an innocent was relieved of what little he had by spirits more hardened than himself. Gambling was, of course, not permitted, so a lookout was always posted to warn of the approach of any officer or senior N.C.O. with the result that very few were caught.

The food was miserable – for breakfast, half a pint of coffee and half a loaf of dry bread, alternating occasionally with a bowl of coarse porridge. Dinner was at noon and this invariably consisted of a mug of watery soup which many maintained was last night's washing-up water. This was accompanied by a few greasy lumps of beef or mutton, which gave the impression that the animal had died of old age, and a few soggy potatoes. The last meal of the day was tea, a pint of brown liquid that defied description, and another half loaf of dry bread.

They spent Christmas Day in the middle of the Mediterranean. As a special treat they all received an extra few lumps of greasy meat and their dinner was served to them by the officers. In the evening, they gathered together on deck for a concert. The Maclarens' piper played, there was community singing and a great deal of dirty-story telling, and everybody was glad when it was all over.

After that they went to bed. Starboard watch below decks and port watch on deck. Those below decks who could not stand the stench of human sweat found little relief even on the deck itself. The hammocks of the port watch were slung so low that it was impossible to move around except on hands and knees.

So it was to a great feeling of relief that the ship docked at the little harbour of Trinkitat and the sea-weary men were able to go ashore. Even the ninety degrees of heat and humidity which greeted them was preferable to what they had been through.

Young Peter Leinie walked down the gangway and onto the harbourside. It was all brown and yellow, relieved only by small single-storied buildings of dirty white rising out of what passed for streets. Their dark-skinned, loin-clothed occupants were sitting on the shady side totally unimpressed with the arrival of the kilted Highlanders. Sweating under the weight of his fifty-pound pack and his rifle, Leinie found himself swept along by the tide of his comrades as they cursed and grumbled their way ashore.

It was three o'clock in the afternoon when they docked, and the dry, baked mud of the earth burned its way through the soles of their boots until they felt that they were walking on hot bricks. Some of them, those who had been out east before, either aired their superior knowledge with blood curdling warnings of snakes and scorpions, or simply viewed the whole scene with listless resignation.

At last they were all ashore, standing in two ragged lines, still sweating under their packs and leaning on their rifles.

'I say, are these the Maclarens? Pretty scruffy lot, what?'

Frankie Gibson eyed the speaker balefully. He was a young cavalry lieutenant wearing an immaculate uniform and an enormous blond moustache. Frankie knew the type, though it always astonished him how they could look so beautiful irrespective of the conditions. He would be the younger son of some great family, sent out here so that he could return home and thrill the debutantes with tales of cavalry charges and other heroic doings, while all the time his commanding officer was under strict instructions not to expose him to anything that could be construed as danger. Frankie made a grimace of contempt, which was unfair because the young man, popinjay though he might appear, had already been wounded twice.

The lieutenant was addressing Major Murray, looking down his nose at him, when he noticed the crown on Murray's collar. He added, 'Sir'. But he managed to make it sound like an insult.

'Yes,' replied Murray, eyeing him without enthusiasm. 'Where do we billet?'

'What have you got here? The general would like to know.'

'Three companies of Highlanders,' replied Murray. 'We are supposed to be joining another company from India and the C.O.'

' 'Fraid they aren't here. You'll just have to soldier on without them.'

Murray was not surprised. Things never worked out as the planners intended.

'You're joining Major-General Buller, aren't you?'

'I'm glad to hear that we are expected,' said Murray.

'Yes, well, he's bivouacked just north of the town. I suggest that you make your way there. Can't really miss them. Find the lines and report to his A.D.C. Have you got your own bivvies?'

'Aye,' said Murray. 'They're unloading now.'

'Any transport?'

'No.'

'That's a damned nuisance. I'll have to see if I can rustle up some mules and wagons for you. If you could detail a platoon off to bring the gear, you can be on your way.'

'I'll do that,' said Murray.

Murray went in search of a subaltern. He spotted Ian Maclaren deep in conversation with Captain Farquhar and he went over to them.

To say that Ian was an unhappy man would be an understatement. He was utterly and completely miserable. After his interview with Willie Bruce he had seen Naomi only once. The following day he had gone down to the Priory Inn to meet her as they had arranged days ago, but she had not come. In the next few days he spent most of his time going to places where he felt she might pass, but he did not see her. Feeling unable to call, after what the colonel had said, he sent notes over to Cluny Cottage, but he received no reply. Wallowing in self-pity, he did not notice that the colonel never once mentioned his request for transfer. It was only a few days before they were to leave that he went to see Willie and tell him that he wanted to withdraw his application. Willie showed no surprise at this and simply tore the document up in front of him and flung it into the wastepaper basket.

Ian had found it impossible to believe that all was over between himself and Naomi, and yet he was beset by doubts and dark thoughts. The moment things got awkward, she had dropped him. Did she not know that he would have done anything for her? Did she not know that he would happily have sacrificed his career, or even his life, just to be with her? He would have done, too, if only she had given him the slightest encouragement; though how they would have lived was a question that had never occurred to him. A slave to his fantasies, he wondered if there could be another man; but he could not believe that, for they had given themselves to each other so completely.

If only there had been someone, anyone in whom he could trust and confide; he felt so alone. Finally he decided that the only course left open to him was to go overseas with the regiment, and there, he hoped, he would find the sweet oblivion of death. In his innocence, he never believed, not for a single moment, that Naomi might be doing this for him, and that she might be as unhappy as he was.

'Mr Maclaren,' called Murray, 'I've got a job for you. Fall out your platoon and wait here. Alex,' he said, turning to Farquhar, 'we've got to be on the move.'

'Sir,' replied Ian, 'what am I to wait for?'

'That clothes-horse over there,' said Murray, indicating the young cavalry lieutenant, 'says that he will get you some mules and carts. When he does, you can load the baggage and bring it up.'

'To where, sir?'

'I'm not quite sure myself yet. We'll find the lines and I'll send an N.C.O. back to direct you.'

'Yes, sir.'

Amid a great deal of shouted commands and noise and bustle, the Maclaren Highlanders moved out of the little town. It was hot and they were sweating and every time they put a foot to the ground the dust rose with it and found its way into their nostrils in a choking cloud. The streets were littered with animal dung, carpeted with flies of every variety and hue that could be imagined. The little town stank like a byre that had not been cleaned for a year or more. But they were still smarting under the obvious contempt of the cavalry officer and as Ron Murray placed himself at the head of his men, he called out.

'Piper!'

The sweet sad notes of the pipes sounded alien on the tropical air, but they reminded the men of what they were. They squared their shoulders and, proud and tall, marched out of the town. Not that it impressed the natives – hardly a one looked up. The British were a fact of life to them, they always did stupid things in the heat of the day when a man should be lying in the shade and waiting for the sun to go down.

Within minutes of leaving the town, they were on a vast empty, yellow plain; at least the stench had been left behind.

'Look at it,' said Peter Leinie. 'Just look at it.'

'Look at what?' said MacTavish who was marching on his right.

'There's nothin'.'

'Aye,' replied MacTavish. 'Ye'll see plenty o' nothin' oot here.'

Half an hour out of the town they found the neat lines of tents of the encamped force that they had been detailed to join. It was all very clean and military and extremely boring.

They sweated it out there for over a month until on the twenty-ninth of February, 1884, just before dawn, General Graham gave the order to march.

They formed square. It was the most massive square that any one of them had ever seen. Graham's force numbered four thousand men; so, with a thousand men a side, two seven-pounder guns and a Gatling at each corner, and the transport animals with ammunition and medical supplies in the centre, it made a huge mobile fortress walled with the flesh of the soldiers who formed it.

For a month now they had been practising manoeuvres, wheeling and turning in large square formations. It could have been the same today except that their centre, which in practices had been left empty, was now full of baggage and supplies. This looked like the real thing.

The three companies of the Maclarens were to the right of the forward side of the square. At their corner, beyond which marched the Black Watch, was their Gatling gun with Captain Farquhar in command and at his side Lance-Sergeant Smith.

'Pity the poor bastards at the rear, sir,' said Smith.

'Yes, a bit rough on them, eh?' said Farquhar, glancing back at the rear ranks, who were enveloped in the clouds of yellow dust which the front ranks were raising. 'Charming country though, doncher think?'

'It's fucking awfu'. Sir, I never believed that there could be sae much o' nothingness.'

'Plenty of flies.'

'Aye, bugger them.'

This mass of men was marching out over this barren uphill wasteland in the direction of a little village called El Teb. It was there, under General Baker, five months previously, that a force of some four thousand, mostly Egyptian, had been wiped out by the Sudanese. These Sudanese had fought with incredible bravery because, for them, this was a holy war. The Mahdi, they believed, was divinely appointed to purify Islam and rid the lands of all infidel governments. In only four years he had become a real threat to the entire presence of Britain. His followers did not care what risks they took for if they died in the Mahdi's cause, their eternal salvation was assured.

Graham had also under his command a squadron of the 10th Hussars. These rode forward in a scouting expedition to ascertain the dispositions of the enemy, whom they expected would be entrenched around El Teb, only a dozen or so miles distant.

Captain Donald Bruce, marching to the rear of A Company, which he now commanded, was gazing at the barrier of human flesh which would stand between him and the enemy spears when the fighting started. He was trying hard to persuade himself that he was not a coward, and hating every step he took. It was to Donald, as it was to so many of them, the first time. He could not see the sense of it. What difference would it make if those who died today were still alive tomorrow? What benefit would be bestowed upon the British Empire by their sacrifice?

He had been at the officers' briefing the night before, and he realized that this was just like one of the punitive expeditions on the Northwest Frontier, only it was much bigger and many more would die. The enemy had cannon. They had to have, because Baker had had two Krupp guns which were now undoubtedly in the possession of the Sudanese at El Teb. It all seemed so bloody pointless to Donald, and yet here he was marching along, obeying orders, and expected to reduce living, breathing, thinking human beings to the state in which he had left Jimmy Grigor.

In the second rank Peter Leinie had contrived to get himself next to Frankie Gibson. Frankie seemed to have taken a liking to the boy and Leinie believed that if only he could stay close to Frankie, he would be safe.

'Where are we gannin', sarge?' he asked. They were marching at ease and a limited amount of conversation was permissible. 'How the hell dae I know?' replied Frankie.

'Will there be fechtin' today?'

'Aye, it looks verra much like that there will.'

'What's it like?' asked the boy.

'What's what like?'

'Weel, when the fechtin' starts. What's it like just standing here and getting shot at?'

'Och, dinna worry yersel' aboot that,' said Frankie. 'They'll nae get close enough tae dae us any real harm, and if they miss ye, ye's got naething tae worry aboot.'

'Aye, but what if they dinna miss me?'

'Then,' said Frankie, 'ye'll hae even less tae worry aboot. But you'll get through, laddie. It's always like this the first time. It's always a bittie like this every time.'

'I'm scared, sarge.'

'That's nothing tae worry aboot. Everybody's a bittie scared. I ken I am. Why, the colonel told me himself that he's frightened every time he goes into action.'

'Colonel Bruce?'

'Himself. But once it starts you'll be too bloody busy tae think aboot being scared.'

'I hope you're right, sarge.'

'Just stay close tae me and you'll be all right.'

Ian Maclaren, temporarily in command of C Company,

marched silently, his head erect, his eyes fixed firmly on the horizon, and an expression of fixed grim determination on his face. He had resolved that he would die today. Perhaps this news would prove to Naomi that his was a great and true love, without which life was meaningless. Several times he fingered the letter which he had written her. He had left it in his sporran for them to find when the deed was done. They would find it and send it to her and she would weep for what might have been.

In front of him the two big men, Anderson and MacTavish, lumbered along together.

'Hey, Jamie,' said Anderson, 'hoo many wogs are you ganna get yoursel' today?' He grinned, showing a line of yellow stained teeth with a gap in the middle, the legacy of a barrack room brawl.

'I shall dae what I have tae dae,' said MacTavish, not wanting to be drawn into a conversation.

'Aye, and mind ye dae it right,' replied Anderson. 'Remember that you're next tae me and I like tae feel that I can trust the mannie on my right.'

'Well, I only hae ma left tae worry aboot,' said MacTavish.

'I'll sort you oot when this lot's over. Dinna turn your back on me, that's all,' rumbled Anderson.

'Stop chattering in front there and look where you're going.' Ian's thin voice put a stop to their conversation.

It was approaching noon and the sun was baking them with a relentless, steamy heat. They must have been less than a mile from El Teb and here and there, dotted around them, were the rotting remains of Baker's force, stinking to high heaven and making the more susceptible retch. They had got to within about half a mile of the village and the wells which they had to take that night – for if they did not take them, they would be out of water – when there was a puff of black smoke on the horizon. This was quickly followed by a crack and a series of high-pitched whistles, and two men to the rear of the square fell.

'Fuckin' shrapnel,' said Frankie Gibson.

'What's that, sarge?' asked Peter Leinie, who had nearly jumped out of his skin at the sound of the first shot.

'Shrapnel, laddie. Ignore it,' replied Frankie. 'The general will ken what to do.'

Indeed Graham was already wheeling the square to the right, bringing the Black Watch into his van.

'See that,' said Frankie. 'We're no in the front line, noo. We'll be going aroond their flank. I could nae ha done it better myself.'

The square was halted and they opened fire with their seven-pounders. While the barrage was on, those of them who had seen it all before lay down and relaxed, while the men who were seeing action for the first time waited tense and expectant for the shrapnel bullet with their name on it. The few wounded were being treated in the centre of the square. Usually there was nothing done for them beyond a rough bandage or if the wound was bad a rapid amputation and a dollop of tar to stem the flow of blood. A body wound meant a fifty-fifty chance of death as it was more than likely that gangrene would set in before the wound had been cleaned up enough to prevent it.

Within fifteen minutes the enemy's guns had been silenced and the men were on their feet again. The Maclarens were again in the front ranks. They moved forward shoulder to shoulder towards the enemy's flank.

Less than a quarter of a mile from the first line of entrenchments – now clearly visible as dark lines upon the yellow earth – Graham halted his square. As he did this, the air was suddenly filled with an incredible high-pitched yelling and wailing. The front rank knelt in firing position, their rifles loaded and ready, with the second rank standing behind them awaiting the order to fire.

'Christ, sarge, what's a' that noise?' There was a tremor in Peter Leinie's voice.

'That's them, laddie,' replied Sergeant Frankie Gibson. 'Dinna worry yersel', they'll be coming oot soon.'

As if in response to Frankie Gibson's words, a mass of figures appeared over the top of the entrenchments. They were all black-faced, stark against the dirty white cotton of their clothing.

At the corner of the square Captain Farquhar busied himself with his gun crew, checking the range, ripping open another box of ammunition, and awaiting the order to open fire. Private Anderson drew his dirk and started slicing the heads from his bullets.

'What are ye doin' there?' demanded Private MacTavish.

'These'll stop the bastards,' said Anderson.

'Ye dirty pig.'

'I told ye, sodger, I'll sort ye oot after this is aye ower.'

Anderson was not alone in what he was doing. Many of the men, those of greater experience, knew that within minutes those thousands would be upon them. A rifle bullet making a clean wound, though it might kill, would not stop a man in his tracks. The dumdum, which splayed out and made a hole that you could put your fist into, would stop a man dead when it hit him.

Closer and closer came the horde of black faces, howling and yelling as they came, brandishing spears and long-bladed swords. At last the order came.

'Fire at will. Pass the word.'

Frankie Gibson calmly licked his thumb and damped the foresight of his rifle. He took a quick glance at young Peter Leinie.

'Dinna hurry yersel', laddie. Yees'll be a sight quicker that way. Allus aim at the yin that's nearest tae ye.' Then he fired. 'That's yin that'll no be worryin' us.'

On their right the staccato chatter of Farquhar's Gatling started up. And soon in the still air the smoke from the black powder was obscuring friend and foe alike. But not before Donald Bruce had watched, horrified, as the machine guns swathed down line upon line of his fellow creatures. He tried to close his eyes and choke back the nausea that was rising within him, but when he did this, all he could see was Jimmy Grigor's torn body sagging at the post, streaming blood.

Now the men were firing as fast as they could reload their Martini-Henrys, and it seemed to Ian Maclaren that it was impossible for anyone to survive that massive barrage of fire. He fired off all six shots from his Webley and calmly set about reloading, waiting for the Sudanese to break into the square, waiting for the thrust that would end it all.

A few of the Sudanese, perhaps twenty or thirty, charged through the pall of smoke and broke through into the square itself. They had forced the line on the left of C Company. Donald Bruce suddenly found himself confronted by a giant of a man wearing nothing but a dirty white loincloth. The Sudanese's lips parted, revealing to Donald two rows of blackened teeth as he swung back his heavy cross-hilted sword. Donald raised his revolver. His hand was shaking as he tried to force himself to find the will to pull the trigger. But it was no good, he could not do it. He stood there waiting for the blow to fall when suddenly a great glob of blood welled out of the man's mouth as he coughed, spattering the liquid onto Donald's hand. The tip of a bayonet appeared through the front of the man's chest and he sank to his knees in front of Donald, as if in supplication.

'Ye'd better nae leave it sae lang the next time, sorr,' shouted R.S.M. Macmillan as he put his foot on the body of his victim and heaved his bayonet out. He pressed another cartridge into the breech of his rifle and turned away.

Within minutes all of those who, with desperate bravery or foolhardiness, had broken through into the square, were dead, and Donald, who had not moved, tried to hold back his tears of shame.

Suddenly as the attack had started, it ended, and the enemy was streaming away towards a second line of entrenchments.

'Come on, let's get after the buggers!' shouted Peter Leinie, filled with the lust for more blood.

'Just ye wait,' said Frankie Gibson as he reloaded his rifle. 'Ye'll be told when tae move by your betters.'

The square had not been given orders to advance. Instead the front lines stayed where they were while the flanks formed up on either side of them, making a double line of men nearly half a mile long. Leaving their dead and wounded to be dealt with by the medical teams, they advanced on the town itself.

Not all of them moved forward. There had been casualties. One man – it was a tommy – grabbed fitfully at Lance-Sergeant Smith's kilt as he was stepping over him.

'Don't leave me, mate. Don't leave me 'ere,' the man said, and coughed.

Smith glanced down and saw the trickle of blood coming from the side of the man's mouth and the great spreading wound where a sword had been thrust into his chest. 'You'll be all right,' he said. 'Dinna worry yerself, the doctors are comin'.' But he knew that the man would not be all right. He knew that he would be dead within the hour and the fat flies would feed on his corpse.

Over to their left they saw a detachment of naval ratings storming a fortified building. In front of them it seemed that every few yards the earth spewed up a Sudanese who opened fire, then dropped his weapon and ran until he was either out of range or cut down by the fire of the British.

By two o'clock in the afternoon the cavalry were recalled and the position had been taken. Behind and around them lay over two thousand Sudanese – grotesque, shapeless things, a mass of torn flesh and suffering. Some of them still moved. One man in his death agony tried with every ounce of life that remained in him to thrust his spear at Private Anderson. Anderson grinned and thrust his bayonet into the man's gut, twisting it as he did so and spitting into the brown face. What remained of the Sudanese force was rapidly vanishing over the horizon in the direction of Tokar.

As for the British, Graham's force, there were thirty-four killed and one hundred and fifty-five wounded. The Maclarens had not had a single casualty. Ian Maclaren was, much to his surprise, delighted to find himself still alive.

6

The winter frosts were upon them in the Highlands. The ground was hard and unyielding beneath the foot. Willie Bruce had spent the day following his interview with Ian Maclaren at his home at Cluny Cottage. Cluny Cottage lay about four and a half miles from Culbrech House, a little oasis cut out from the Maclaren estates and a small establishment by comparison. It was Maud's house really. She had bought it before she married Willie while he was still an N.C.O. The bare trees and the recently pruned rose-bushes, left to lie dormant in their neat patches of black earth until the coming of spring brought them back to life; the little patch of lawn which led down to the green wicket gate: this was home for Willie Bruce, and he wanted no other. He had no yearning for grand establishments. Home to Willie was a place where he and his wife could be alone and lock themselves away from the world, and if it was comfortable, which indeed it was, it was all that Willie asked. It was here in Cluny Cottage that he had spent the first tempestuous years of his marriage.

Willie Bruce was one of those rare officers who were more than willing to live on their pay alone. When he had first been commissioned, Sir Henry, Andrew's late father, had made him an allowance of three hundred pounds a year. This had been perpetuated in Sir Henry's will, for Willie was Sir Henry's son.

Sir Henry had always been proud of Willie, who, by an unkind mischance, had been born on the wrong side of the blanket. On the death of Sir Henry, Willie had objected strenuously to the allowance being continued. This matter, as Andrew pointed out, was not really in his hands, so finally Willie reluctantly accepted. At the time he was a lieutenant-colonel and he maintained that, as he was a man of modest needs, he was quite capable of living on his pay. Willie was a proud man. Maud, his wife, was blessed with a fairly considerable private income but she found no small difficulty in trying to supplement the family budget. Willie would accept nothing from her, his Highland pride demanding of him that he be the breadwinner in his home; nor, for that matter, would he take advantage of a law that said that a husband had complete right of disposal of his wife's property. He relaxed in only one thing. Maud insisted that as Naomi was not his daughter, she should at least be allowed to cover the expenses which that young lady added to their budget. When Willie had protested at this, they had had a flaming row, and he had given way for the sake of peace and quiet.

He had taken the day off for the quite specific reason that he wanted to have this thing out with Naomi. As soon as he was able to get her alone, he had tackled her on the subject of Ian Maclaren, and her association with him. He had reiterated to her the circumstances of her birth, and though it had hurt him to do it, for he regarded it as a near insufferable injustice, he had had to point out to her that marriage with Ian was just not possible if he was to continue his career in the regiment.

'Your mother,' he said, 'had to suffer just as you are suffering now, and for the same reasons. Mind you, I am glad that she lost that battle, for if she hadna, I'd no be sitting talking to you now. You don't hae to tell me that it's bloody unfair. I ken it is. Now, I'm as fond of your Uncle Andrew as any man could be. For that matter, I'm fond o' the whole brood o' them. But they are Maclarens, and they're no like us. They're a different breed.'

'But, Father,' she replied, 'I was totally aware of all this. If it is marriage you are worried about, you can set your mind at rest. I never had the slightest intention of marrying Ian. I know that it is impossible, and yet I was not strong enough to deny him to myself if only for a little while.'

'And just what dae you mean by that?' asked Willie.

'Father,' she said, 'I don't know whether I ought to tell you this, but I shall, if you will promise me something. You must regard what I say as a very strict confidence. You will never, no matter what the circumstances, either by thought, word, or action, indicate to Ian that you know.'

Willie was impressed by the gravity of Naomi's tone. 'All right, my dear. I promise.'

'For the past weeks,' she said, 'we have been lovers. Does that shock you?'

To her surprise, Willie's expression did not change.

'No, Naomi,' he said. 'It doesna shock me, nor does it astonish me. When I was a laddie, there was many a lassie I, well, you ken what I mean. And I know that society condemns the woman and applauds the man in these cases. But that's bloody unfair, too, for how could a mannie gain that applause if there were no a lassie tae help him wi' it? The real point is, Naomi, what are you going to dae? Dae you really feel serious towards Ian?'

'Yes, I do, and I don't want to hurt him.'

'You'll dae that whatever you dae.'

'I know. As I see it, the only thing I can do is to go away from here, because if I stay, I shall continue to see him.'

'And where would you go to? I'm not stopping you, mind. You're twenty-five years old and you should be able tae tak' care o' yourself.'

Naomi looked at him. No, he would not attempt to stop her. She knew him well enough to realize that here was, in another form, a reflection of her own independent spirit, and that he would have no brief with the convention which demanded that a lady should not travel alone and unaccompanied, much less have an establishment of her own. She smiled at Willie. They understood one another, these two.

'I think that I should go to London,' she said.

'That's an awfu' lang way.'

'Not really. London is easier to get to than most places. Once there I could get some sort of a job. Women do work, you know. They can be other things beside being a housewife.'

'But you don't need a job,' said Willie.

'I know.'

'And if you went to London, where would you live? It's a big place and some parts of it are no the sort of places I'd like you tae be living in.'

'Perhaps Uncle Andrew would let me stay in his house until I found a place of my own.'

Andrew had a tiny town house just off Sloane Square. It was unoccupied for almost fifty weeks of the year and he would probably be glad to have someone he knew living in it.

Willie was well aware of this. 'Well,' he said, 'dinna be too hasty. Think it over for a couple of days and if that's what you decide tae do, I'll no be the one tae stand in your way. I'll talk to Andrew about it and tae your mother, and then we'll see if something canna be arranged. That is, if you're still of the same mind.'

And that was the reason why, a few days later, Naomi was aboard the night train from Inverness on her way to London. She moved into the little pink house in Charlotte Street, finding it comfortably, if not extravagantly, furnished. She occupied only two rooms, her bedroom and the large kitchen where she cooked her own meals and generally attended to her needs. There were no servants. Sir Andrew, on the rare occasions when he occupied the house, always engaged temporary staff. It was totally sufficient for what she wanted and it was in a pleasant and comfortably well-to-do neighbourhood. It was one room wide, two rooms deep, and three rooms tall, built into a terrace of a couple of dozen houses, all of which were identical apart from the fact that they were painted in different pastel colours. All of this gave an airy, light, pleasant atmosphere to the area.

Every morning she studied the 'Situations Vacant' column in *The Times*. She was reasonably well educated and considered that she was a suitable candidate for any of those advertisements which began: 'Lady of gentle background required for . . .' Usually it was for the position of governess in a smart London household. However, on the two or three occasions that she went for interviews, her prospective mistress, seeing her beauty, 'regretfully' decided that she was not quite suitable. Not many women wanted to take the risk of anything as lovely as Naomi living in their house and in close proximity to their husbands.

Naomi did not worry about her failures. She was adequately, if not lavishly, provided for. Her mother made her an allowance of two hundred and fifty pounds a year, which was quite sufficient for her modest needs. It was primarily the boredom of having nothing to do which gave her the impetus to keep trying. She had come to the conclusion that she must not be cut out for a position as a governess, and had decided to try for a job in a shop in one of the more fashionable areas.

Not that her life was dull, not by any means. She had suddenly been transplanted from the slow-moving peace and quiet of her Highland glen into the largest city in the world. Most of her contemporaries would have taken fright, but Naomi found it fascinating.

At that period there were five million people packed into a tiny area. More than there were in the whole of Scotland. It was big and it was busy and it was the heart of the Empire and Imperial Britain.

Sometimes she would go down to the river. The Thames was turgid and swimming in filth from the thousands of sewers which cascaded their effluents into its slow-moving waters. She enjoyed watching the great Thames barges with their reddy-brown sails, their hulls only inches above the water as they plied up and down the river.

But she missed the blue skies and the clear unpolluted air of home. A million chimney pots, daily belching their coal smoke into the skies above the capital, left a permanent murky haze over the city and a permanent coating of grime over most of the buildings in the fashionable areas and all of the houses in the poorer parts. It was all bustle and Naomi treated herself as a spectator. She walked mostly, but sometimes she rode in a hansom and always she watched the seething life of London as it passed her by.

On leaving for London, she had been provided with a number of introductions, and gradually her circle of acquaintances grew. One of the people she met was a Mrs Bunty Worthing, who was related by marriage to Sir Andrew's late wife Emma. Bunty was a great socialite and moved in the circles of London's café society and it was at a party in her house that Naomi met Lord Charles de Vere-Smith.

Charles de Vere-Smith was the second son of the Duke of Beverley. When he was introduced to Naomi, he took her hand and held it too intently. He was obviously pleased with what he saw. Naomi herself was flattered by his attention. He was a very personable man, about thirty, she thought. Tall and slim, he had brown eyes rather like a spaniel's, sad and gentle. The eyes were, however, given the lie by his mouth, which always seemed to be twisted up at the left corner, giving him a permanent air of cynical amusement. He was dark-haired and immaculately dressed in white tie and tails with two large diamond studs sparkling from the front of his stiff shirt.

He had obviously taken more than a passing fancy to Naomi for he dominated her company throughout the evening. When the party was about to break up, he asked her if there was anyone escorting her home.

'No,' she replied. 'Bunty will send one of the servants for a hansom.'

'Totally unnecessary,' he said, 'I have my brougham here and I shall be only too pleased to see you to your home. It may take some time to get a cab just now, and I should not like to think of your parents worrying about your safety.' He had noted with satisfaction that the third finger of her left hand was bare of any rings.

'I'm afraid that my parents are in Scotland. I live alone.'

'How very brave of you.'

'I don't think so,' she smiled. 'But you may take me home.'

As she went to get her wrap, Bunty pulled her to one side. 'Are you going home with Charles?' she asked.

'Yes, why do you ask?'

'Well, my dear, I feel that I ought to warn you that he has a most terrible reputation. Of course, he is a delightful man and such fun. But I thought I ought to tell you. After all, he is married, you know.'

'I didn't know, but it doesn't matter. I'm glad he's fun, though.'

Cocooned in the blackness of the interior of the brougham, she snuggled comfortably and catlike into a corner. She was enjoying herself. She felt happy, a little excited, and just the smallest bit tipsy. She had had rather a lot of champagne.

'Did you tell the coachman where to go?' she asked into the blackness.

'He knows.'

She was silent for a moment, listening to the slow clip-clop of the horse's hoofs. 'He's not going very fast,' she murmured.

'I told him to go very slowly.'

'That's nice,' and she hiccupped slightly.

She felt rather than heard him move across the padded leather seat, and then his hand was holding her chin and he kissed her. For a moment she responded, and then turned her head away.

'You should not do that, you know.'

'Yes, I know.'

Now she could feel his body touching hers. His hand searched for hers, and, finding it, he held it palm upwards on his lap. She started to withdraw it and felt his grip tighten. She relaxed and let her arm go limp. He began to draw the tip of his finger across her open palm.

'I like that,' she murmured, very aware that he must be able to hear her heavy breathing. 'But I'm sure that you should not be doing it.'

He took his hand away and, for a moment, she thought that he had taken her seriously. But then she felt him move, and his lips were touching her palm with his tongue drawing quick circles on it. It was then that the brougham stopped.

'You're a damned attractive girl,' he said.

'Yes,' she said.

'Sink me if I can understand why the devil you're not married.'

'Because I'm too nice,' she said, 'much too nice for only one man,' and she giggled. 'It's the champagne.'

'Of course,' he said. 'Must say, you're forthright, aren't you?'

'Do you know, Lord Charles, we have been stopped for five minutes.' Her tone was rather cool and formal.

'Not as long as that, but I am aware of it.'

She looked out of the window. 'And your driver is lost. This is not Charlotte Street.'

'I know that, too, and my driver does know the way. This is my house.'

'Oh,' she said, 'are you going to take me in to meet your wife?'

'No,' he replied. 'My wife is in Yorkshire. My wife is always in Yorkshire. But I thought that you might like a cup of cocoa or something before I get Barker to run you home.'

Naomi was rapidly sobering up and was now completely aware of the situation into which she had allowed herself to be persuaded. However, she was interested in this man and curious as to what would be his next move.

'All right,' she said, 'I'll come in. But I think you should know that I am perfectly aware of what you mean when you say "or something". '

'Miss Bruce,' he replied, 'I will give you my word that nothing will happen this evening to which you are not a willing party. I shall not touch you or come near you without your full consent.'

'How do I know that I can accept your word?'

'You don't,' he replied. 'But there are servants in the house and I am not the kind of person who would drag you screaming into the bedroom. At least not in front of witnesses. Shall we go?'

He got out of the brougham and opened the door, taking for granted her acceptance.

She was not quite sure where she was except that she must be somewhere in Mayfair, that island of wealth and the establishment. Where the town houses of the ancient and titled families rubbed shoulders with the homes of ambassadors, foreign diplomats and the self-made tycoons of the industrial revolution. Here, behind closed doors, many decisions which affected the lives of hundreds of millions of people throughout the world were taken. Here many of the parties which were given were not given for entertainment but for information, that most valuable commodity in the mysterious world of secret international diplomacy. Here the Germans, now emerging with their illusions of Empire, would ferret out details of the British naval programme. Here the French and the British eyed each other with outward courtesy and inward suspicion born of centuries of conflict. Mayfair was the seat of real power.

They went up the stone steps to the front door. Then into an entrance hall and Naomi was immediately struck by the obvious opulence of the house. It had a high ornate ceiling, from which hung a polished brass gas chandelier. Two particular items caught her eye, a medieval painting and a huge Chinese vase sitting on a Grecian column of black marble. The whole place breathed of wealth, and the staircase flowed upward to an ornate gallery which led off to the upper reaches of the house.

They were approached by a man in tail coat and black tie, superior and formal, who glanced at Naomi with pallid eyes and downturned lips.

'Good evening, Watkins,' said Charles.

'Good evening, my lord,' replied Watkins.

'This is Miss Bruce. We'll go into the drawing room. Is there a fire there?'

'Yes, my lord. I think you'll find it most comfortable,' replied Watkins, opening a door on their right. 'Good evening, miss,' he said as Naomi passed him.

The floor of the hall was all highly polished parquet. When she entered the drawing room, she was conscious of the deep pile of the carpet which was now beneath her feet. The elegance of the soft inviting furnishings, the glitter of the cut-crystal glasses and decanters on the sideboard, and the huge fire burning in a beautiful Adam-green fireplace, gave an almost sensual aspect to the room.

'I have an excellent Napoleon brandy here if you would care for some,' said Lord Charles.

'I think I've had enough for tonight,' she said. 'Why don't you have one and I'll just sit here and watch you while you drink it.'

She seated herself in a silk-brocade-upholstered armchair near the fire. Opposite her was a long, low-backed matching settee, at right angles to the fire. Lord Charles poured out his brandy, came over, and sat in that.

'I feel that I owe you an apology,' he said.

'Whatever for?'

'My behaviour in the carriage. It was most ungentlemanly. Please forgive me.'

'I did not object at the time,' said Naomi. 'So I was a willing party. I think it was the wine. Your apology is quite unnecessary. I do, however, feel that you owe me an explanation.'

'I suppose you mean regarding my intentions.'

'You are a married man. You have invited a single woman into your house alone. Forgive me if I suspect that your intentions are not what gentlefolk would regard as honourable.'

'I can assure you, my dear young lady, that intentions I have not. Hopes? Yes, but I do not intend anything. As you have obviously found out, I am a married man. I am twenty-five years old and two years ago my parents arranged for me what they considered a good match. I am not the misunderstood husband. There has never been any love in our marriage, though we are good friends and do what we consider to be our duty. To that end, my wife has already produced me one child and another will be coming along within the next few months. She is quite aware that I look for my pleasures outside the marriage bed.

'Now forgive me for saying this so early in our acquaintance, but I think that you are the most beautiful woman I have ever seen, and I want you very much. There is nothing I desire more than to form a relationship with you. Perhaps you think that what I am saying is outrageous, but I mean it, every word. I want you to have no doubts about how I would regard our association. I can promise you that the door will always be open. You need never feel trapped. I also give you my word that I shall be most discreet, and in return I should require your promise that you would be likewise.'

Naomi studied him for a moment. 'Isn't this all very sudden?' she giggled. 'Are you not supposed to take time to work up to this sort of a proposition?'

'Yes,' he replied. 'That is quite true. But we would both know exactly what I desired whether I had spoken as I have or not. So, what is the point? Either you will become my —'

'Mistress?'

'Quite. Or you will not become my mistress. A few weeks of verbal sparring and playacting' – and here he laughed – 'and hand-clutching in dark corners, are not going to make any difference to the final outcome. I would much rather you were completely aware of what you are letting yourself in for, if you decide to go ahead. Now, shall I ring for Watkins and ask him to have you taken home?'

'Perhaps,' replied Naomi, 'but not for a moment. I want you to be quite silent while I think over what you have said.'

She gazed at him intently, and he, aware of her scrutiny, toyed with his brandy snifter and looked back at her with that faintly sardonic smile never leaving his face.

Now, Naomi Bruce was all woman. As such, she had no intention of going through life being denied all of those things woman's flesh desires. These were her right as a human being. By an accident of birth, she found herself in the position of the child who was invited to the birthday party, only to be told that the cake was for everyone except her.

This young man who had offered to make her his mistress, she found attractive. But she was totally aware that it was simply healthy womanhood within her which desired him. Whereas she could certainly give him her body, she could never give him herself. It would not be the way it had been with Ian Maclaren. Dear Ian, he was not for her; she had known that from the beginning. She did not have to be told by her stepfather. If she married Ian, all she could offer him would be social ostracism, and she loved him far too much to do that. She feared too that the burden of being married to her would have proved too much too soon. At least, that was what she believed.

Charles was different. As far as she was able to see, this would be an uncomplicated relationship. There was no question of marriage with anyone she had ever met in the circles in which she moved and lived.

She only had to look around the room she was sitting in to see that Charles was immensely wealthy. He could and probably would give her anything she ever wanted in return for her body. Of course, it would not last. In two, four, five, or even ten years, they would tire of each other and he would find someone else, and that would be the end of it.

If she accepted his offer, she realized that she was becoming, in effect, a prostitute. But half the duchesses in London were prostitutes, though they would never see themselves as such. A real prostitute was a damned sight more honest than this society which pretended that sex did not exist and jumped in and out of each other's beds, behind their opulent locked doors. There was always the possibility of children in such an alliance, but in this Naomi felt fairly safe. As far as she was able to tell, she was not capable of having a child; after all, she would probably have had one by now if she had been. So it was accept this offer or one like it or live a life of celibacy, punctuated by a series of hole-in-the-corner affairs.

Well then, she thought, if I say yes, what do I get out of it, apart from satisfaction in bed? She wondered what he would be willing to pay. She felt very coldblooded in this, but no more so than those who made the rules that made women like her unacceptable in any other way. She smiled as she realized that what they both wanted was simply sex. She, probably, as much as he. But the rules also said that she could call the tune and he must pay the piper.

She smiled again and Charles, sitting opposite her in silence, raised his eyebrows.

'May I speak now?' he asked.

'You may.'

'Are you ready to talk?'

'Yes,' she said. 'Yes, I think I am.'

'All right, my dear. I await my fate.' And the mocking smile was there again. 'Are you going to give me an answer? Now?'

'I will give you a conditional yes,' she replied.

'Conditional? I expected no less.'

'Yes,' said Naomi. 'I am as old as you. I am not a young blushing virgin. If I become your mistress, then I shall have sacrificed whatever chance there remains to me of having a husband and a family.' She felt that she was being slightly dishonest, knowing how minute the chances of her marrying actually were. 'But,' she continued, 'I am willing to do that if you, for your part, are willing to promise some insurance.'

'Insurance?' he said.

'Yes, Charles, insurance.'

'I think you had better explain.'

'Of course,' she replied. 'First, I am at the moment living in a house which is not mine; it belongs to my uncle. It is just off Sloane Square. A very middle-class neighbourhood where the sort of arrangement that you propose would undoubtedly lead to a deal of gossip. I would require you to give me an establishment of my own; not somewhere to live, but my own property. I would like it to be in Mayfair, preferably overlooking the park.'

'Do you know what they cost?'

'A great deal, I have no doubt. Now talking of money, I receive a small allowance from my mother. I would expect that you would supplement this in order to allow me to live in a style that you would expect of your mistress.' She paused. 'Do I make myself clear?'

'As crystal,' he said. 'Go on. I am sure that there must be something else.'

'There is. It is always possible that, in this sort of a union, a child would result. You will, of course, bear full financial responsibility should such a thing occur. Now, for my part, I will be completely faithful to you except for those periods when you are living in Yorkshire with your wife. Do you consider that fair?'

'Perfectly.'

'Very well then. On these terms, I will agree to become your mistress. Those are my conditions, the details I will leave to you. Well?'

'Dammit, I think you're wonderful. If anyone else had said to me what you have, I'd have booted them out of my house. But you are different. I suspect that there is a very deep reason for what you have said. I shall not pry. Perhaps one day you will be willing to tell me. If you ever do, I shall regard your confidence as a great privilege.'

'Thank you,' she said. 'I will make you as happy as I possibly can.'

'And I you, my dear. I agree to all of your conditions without reservation and in return —'

'In return,' said Naomi, 'you will have me. You will have my body. I find you most attractive, but I do not love you. I doubt I ever shall. But I shall give you everything that a woman can give a man whenever it may please you.'

'You're quite sure? You won't change your mind?' said Charles.

'Yes, quite sure,' she said. 'Now if you would ring for Watkins, I would like to be taken home.'

'But I thought —'

'But nothing, dear Charles,' she answered. 'You may visit me in my new house in Park Lane the day after I move in. Until then, goodbye.'

7

It was the first of March, 1884, the day after the battle. They had, the previous night, moved into the undamaged village of El Teb and found that the wells had not been tampered with. Then, almost as quickly, Graham's force moved out of the little village and bivouacked about half a mile away. They set up their neat lines of tents, thankful to be away from the few rude, square mud-and-straw buildings which comprised El Teb, together with years of animal droppings and a permanent stench.

Early in the morning, parties consisting of an N.C.O. and about ten men set out to scour the battlefield for any wounded who had been left behind. It was during this that Lance-Sergeant Smith almost ended his promising military career. From the mass of bodies that already stank with the cloying smell of death, a huge Sudanese with a heavy black beard, suddenly arose, a large double-handed sword in his hands.

'Look oot, sarge!' shouted a voice.

Smith whipped round and ducked just in time to avoid a blow which would certainly have decapitated him. The Sudanese did not have time for a second attempt, as he was immediately transfixed by four bayonets. After that every Sudanese they came upon was kicked, and, if he showed any sign of life, bayoneted. Private Anderson, who was in Smith's party, took particular delight in this exercise.

The back-up of the medical teams had obviously done a good job and they found no more of their own wounded, and so the parties made their way back to camp, where they settled down to wait. For what? They did not know.

'It's a bugger,' growled Frankie Gibson, swatting his face and addressing no one in particular, 'I think the bloody flies must send scouts oot wi' us and when we bivvy they send home for a' their relations.'

The men were looking forward with some distaste to the immediate future. There was nothing to do. You can only clean a rifle so much. And there was nothing else in that dreary, yellow, barren country that was the Sudan.

For the Maclarens there was much speculation about what the hell had happened to the second battalion. It was weeks ago now that they should have been reinforced by the second battalion's commanding officer and the two companies he was supposed to be bringing from India. They never did come; instead of sailing west they had moved up to the Northwest Frontier, much to their disgust. Instead of half of their number, those with the longest overseas service, going home, and the rest of them to the Sudan, it seemed like at least another year of India for them.

The Maclarens were therefore left with just three companies and Major Murray in command. In view of this situation, Murray had been gazetted acting lieutenant-colonel and second-in-command of the first battalion.

Bivouacking in the arid plains of the Sudan was no one's idea of enjoyment. Officers and men alike suffered the triple purgatory of heat, flies, and boredom. But for one man in their battalion, these things did not matter. For him there was only worry and shame.

Gordon Bruce had seen the incident during the battle for El Teb when his brother had failed to fire on the Sudanese who had broken through and into the square. This was something beyond his comprehension. Gordon, though he would not have put such a name to his actions, had conducted himself in a gallant and soldierly manner throughout the action, though he had not been within the area where the hand-to-hand fighting had occurred. But he had been not far away and had seen Donald trembling in the face of the threatening Sudanese before the R.S.M. had bayoneted him.

Gordon did not know what to do. Should he tackle his brother? Should he go and ask him why? There had to be some explanation for his conduct. But it was difficult, for Donald was not only his brother, he was also his superior officer, and the tradition that one did not question one's superiors in matters military had been bred into Gordon from birth.

As for Donald, he kept himself very much to himself. He was faced with the constant nightmare of what would happen next time, for there would surely be a next time. After El Teb, he knew that he could not kill. He had stood there awaiting the sword, his flesh cringing at the thought of his own death, knowing that he only had to pull the trigger and he would be safe. But he could not do it. He could not do it because even his own death would be preferable to taking the life of a fellow human.

Gordon, as soon as he joined the battalion, had realized that something had happened to his brother. The extroverted young man who, after three years of playing at soldiers at Sandhurst, had won the Sword of Honour, no longer existed. He was now a man who shunned all company, even of his brother officers, and was regarded as a nonentity by the men. If only Donald would speak to him about whatever it was. But Donald was silent, keeping his own company with his own thoughts, remembering Jimmy Grigor, staying alone in his quarters and coming out only for meals or when parades were ordered.

The differences between Gordon and his elder brother were mostly a question of degree. Gordon was one and a half inches shorter than Donald. Gordon could run a hundred yards in twelve seconds, Donald could run it in just over eleven. At musketry if Gordon got a one-and-a-half-inch group, then Donald would get a one-and-a-quarter-inch group. For most of his time at Sandhurst, Gordon had been reminded constantly by his instructors of how well his brother had done. This could have caused resentment but it did not, for ever since they had been children together Gordon had tried to copy Donald in everything he did. The longest separation they had ever had had been that between the time Donald left Sandhurst and the day Gordon joined the battalion. It was after this that the change in their relationship had become so noticeable. Donald had always helped him along. Gordon had always been able to go to Donald with any problem, however small, assured of a sympathetic hearing. But now all that had changed; Donald just did not seem to want to know him. The difference between them at Sandhurst had been the same as that which had existed throughout their lives, the difference between the good and the excellent. Now excellence had nothing to do with it and Gordon, who was basically a good, reliable regimental officer, keen and willing to learn, could, for the first time in his life, find no communication with his brother.

They had been at El Teb for almost two weeks when Major-General Sir Gerald Graham, V.C., called his officers to conference. The general was a small man, about five foot eight with a slightly greying moustache at which he constantly tugged while addressing his audience. He had a fine record of bravery and aggression in action, having won his V.C. in the Zulu Wars. He also had what was then an unusual attribute: he firmly believed in taking his officers into his confidence before any action. No great strategist, he was nevertheless regarded as a safe, reliable commander.

It was ten o'clock in the morning on the twelfth of March when they assembled in front of the commander's tent.

'Gentlemen,' he announced, 'Osman Digna, whom we thought we had defeated here thus avenging the annihilation of Baker's force, was not with the Sudanese that we engaged. As a matter of fact, the enemy we engaged represented only a small portion of his force. I have, as you well know, had reconnaissance parties out for over a week. I am happy to be able to tell you that we have discovered Mister Digna's whereabouts. He is at present lying in the area around the village of Tamai.

'This is important, for Tamai controls the route from Suakim to Berber on the Nile. Berber is held by an Egyptian garrison, but its rear is exposed as long as Osman Digna lies between us and the garrison. So you see, it is of great importance that the road is opened and the Egyptians' rear is safeguarded.

'Our job then is to remove Digna from Tamai. The men should be rested now. In fact, from my own observations, they are probably more than rested and could do with a spot of action. Tamai lies to the west of us, about three or four hours' march. If we march out at dawn tomorrow we should be able to engage the enemy before midday.

'The enemy is in considerable strength. Our intelligence reports that they number more than nine thousand. That is odds of over two to one. He has, however, few modern weapons. Though whether or not he has any of Baker's ordnance left, or machine guns, we just do not know.

'I propose to split my force into two brigades. One will be under the command of General Buller, and the second brigade will be under General Davis. The cavalry will be under my personal command. Both brigades will advance in squares. General Davis will be in the van and engage the enemy, with General Buller lying in reserve in echelon to his right and close enough to give supporting fire should that prove necessary. About five hundred yards would seem to me about right. Agreed, General?' he said, turning to Buller, who was seated on his right.

Buller, a tall, square-faced man who sported a large moustache and heavy eyebrows under his pillbox cap, tugged at his sideburns and nodded his agreement.

'Good,' continued Graham. 'To General Davis's left, I shall deploy the cavalry to deal with any attempt to get around that flank.

'The task would not be too difficult but for one unfortunate piece of topography which lies between us and the enemy. That is a deep, sandy-bottomed ravine which is situated five hundred yards north of the village of Tamai. However, I trust that we shall be able to clear this obstacle, take the village, and most important of all, destroy Osman Digna's force. If we succeed in this, then the road between Suakim and Berber will be clear and offer an alternative supply route. Berber is important because with General Gordon in Khartoum, and the Nile constantly under attack, it is most important to secure this route to ensure his supplies.

'I fear that I have kept you for quite a long time, but I wanted all officers to be aware of what we are doing and why we are doing it. Now I would appreciate it if all senior officers ensure that their commands are all ready to move off at dawn tomorrow. Are there any questions?'

'Sir,' called a voice from the rear of the group. 'Who exactly is Osman Digna?'

'I can tell you a little about him,' replied Graham, 'but there's not a great deal known. He is a most unsavoury character. The Mahdi is a religious fanatic but this fellah Digna is a slaver, or at least he was until he thought he could do better by open rebellion. He's killed an awful lot of Egyptians – and never forget the Egyptians are our allies! – Baker Pasha's force was wiped out by him; and the entire garrison at Sinkat was massacred. That's about all I can tell you. The only other thing I want to know about him is that he's dead.

'Anything else? No? Very well then, gentlemen, thank you for your attention and good hunting tomorrow.'

'When's there goin' tae be mair fechtin'?' asked Private Leinie.

He and Private MacTavish were seated outside their bivouac, cleaning their rifles. They seemed to do little else; the sand got into everything and it was a constant battle for the men both to keep it out of their equipment and avoid swallowing it. They were sitting beside their bivvy, one of the many little white ridge-tents arranged in neat straight lines. The army seemed to have a passion for geometric forms. Everything was in straight lines and squares, except around the flagpole which they erected whenever they bivouacked for more than a day. There the senior officers' tents were deployed, and they were in a perfect circle.

'It will nae be lang noo,' was the reply. 'Ye can bet your boots that when the officers hae a conference and Frankie Gibson comes aroond and tells us that there's a rifle inspection at six o'clock the night, the fechtin' is nae far off.'

'Och, I'm nae sae sure,' replied the other. 'But I hope that it's true. Fechtin's great, is it no?'

'Youse have changed,' said MacTavish. 'I mind the wee laddie whae was scairt o' a fight.'

'Aye, I suppose that I was at first,' said Leinie, gazing wistfully out into the yellow desert. 'But it's – different after yees have done it once. I kilt quite a few o' them buggers, ye ken.'

'I suppose that it is a medal that you'll be wanting next?' said MacTavish.

'And why not?' said Leinie, looking down at the bare left

breast of his tunic. 'It would look fine there.' And he patted his chest.

'Medals dinna come that easy, laddie.'

'I might even get a Victoria Cross. Ye get ten pound a year if ye get yin o' them.'

'If ye go on talking like that, it'll be a posthumous yin, that's what ye'll get.'

'What's a poth – poth – what ye said?'

'It means,' said MacTavish, 'that yer deed and buried afore ye get it.'

'Oh.' Leinie was silent for a while.

'Look ye here,' said MacTavish, 'you'll dae weel tae tak' a wee bittie advice from a auld sodger.'

'What advice?'

'Well, I'll tell ye. A soldier is best if he daes what he's telt tae dae and he doesna' try to dae anything other than stand in the line and keep himsel' alive.'

'Och, that's daft talk, you dinna get medals for that.'

'You'll see,' said MacTavish, 'you've only been under fire the once. We were lucky, we didn't lose a single man. You'd nae be talking like that if half your marras were deed or mebbe worse. I've watched men dying aroon me and it's no funny. You watch Sergeant Gibson. When he's in action, you'd think that he was on the parade groond; or the R.S.M. They dae it all according tae the book. They's the sort that lives. If ye gan trying tae get yersel' a medal and all o' that nonsense, we'll aye be awa' home tae Scotland wi'oot ye. Though I have nae doot that yer mither would be proud o' ye and hae a guid cry when they sent her your medal.'

With the prospect of action the following day, Gordon Bruce finally screwed up sufficient courage to go and talk to his brother. He waited until after the evening meal, then walked down the lines under the black velvet sky of the tropical night. He went into his brother's bivvy and found Donald sitting on his cot, just looking blankly at the white canvas wall in front of him. His face was lit by the guttering candle in a beautiful silver candlestick which looked incongruous against the background of a discarded tunic, spattered with sand, which lay on the groundsheet at his feet.

'Mind if I come in, Donald?'

'No.' But there was no welcome in Donald's voice.

'Thanks a lot. I've scrounged a bottle of whisky from Farquhar. You know, he's a remarkable chap. He always seems to be able to get supplies brought up when nobody else can get them.'

'He's very rich,' said Donald, as if that explained everything.

'Yes, I suppose that's why,' replied Gordon, and he poured out two whiskys. 'Donald, I wanted to ask you something.'

'What?'

'It's not about me, it's about you. Donald, what's wrong?'

'Wrong? Nothing.'

'No, Donald, something's very wrong. I know that I'm speaking out of turn. After all, you're a captain and I'm only a second lieutenant. But you are my brother and you did so much better than I did at Sandhurst. Well, I'm sorry, but I just felt that there was something wrong.'

'Thanks, Gordon.' Donald gave a wry smile. 'It's nice to know that you care. But I'm afraid that it's nothing that you can do anything about.'

'Are you quite sure? You know I'm a bit stupid and all that sort of thing, but it's not hard to tell that you've got a problem. Perhaps if you could talk about it, even to me, it might help.'

'I don't want to talk about it,' said Donald. 'Not to anybody.'

'Please, Donald. You know that we're going to be in action tomorrow, and I don't want to go in worrying about you.'

'Why should you worry about me?'

'Donald, I saw what happened here a couple of weeks ago.'

'Oh.'

'I could have understood it if you'd run away. But you didn't. You just stood there, just as if you wanted that man to kill you. Please tell me. I may not be able to do anything, but if you could just tell me, it might help.'

'I wonder. You see, Gordon, I should never have been a soldier.'

'But that's nonsense. You won the Sword of Honour.'

'Games, Gordon. Just games.'

'Donald, it's frightfully cheeky of me to say this, but are you afraid?'

'No, not really. That is, I'm not afraid of anything that might happen to me. It's just that I cannot do it.'

'What is this thing that you cannot do?'

'I can't shoot a man. It is impossible for me to point my gun at a man and kill him. I found that out four months ago. You heard about Jimmy Grigor?'

'Yes.'

'You know that I was in charge of the execution detail.'

'Yes.'

'Did anybody tell you that I funked giving the order to fire?'

'Oh, God.'

'Yes, I did. Grigor gave the order himself. I was a coward; not in that, but in not resigning my commission there and then. I wrote it out, you know. Then I took it to father and let him persuade me to tear it up. Now we're out here and, of course, I cannot do it.'

'Well, you could,' said Gordon. 'If that's the way you really feel. I'm sure that Ron Murray would understand if you put it to him.'

'Gordon, I can't run to Ron tonight and say, "I'm sorry, there's going to be a battle tomorrow so I'm going to resign my commission"!'

'No, I suppose you can't.'

'Besides, do you think that he would understand if I were to say, "I'm not afraid of being killed, but I'm terrified of killing anyone. I'm only afraid of having a man's death on my conscience." '

Gordon's expression became very solemn. 'It's worse than I thought.'

'How is it worse?'

'Well, if what you say is true, there's nothing that you can do about it.'

'I know. If I get home, I shall leave the army. So far as that is concerned, my mind is quite made up. If I get home.'

It was a quarter to seven in the evening and Frankie Gibson, with R.S.M. Macmillan and a couple of other senior N.C.O.s, were sitting on the dusty earth. They regarded their rations of hardtack – biscuits which, it was rumoured, had been used for the building of a fort – with disgust. The drill was that you broke a bit off, if you had the strength, and dipped it into water until it was softened enough so that you could eat it without breaking your teeth.

It was very quiet now. Along the lines small groups of men were gathered outside the neat rows of white tents. Some of them, those who had been fortunate enough to find some sort of fuel, had lit fires to guard against the cold desert night, and the flicker of these could be easily distinguished against the now gathering gloom. The men seemed, with the near certainty of action the following day, to have lost their bravado along with the daylight, and they talked, if they talked at all, in little groups, in subdued voices, and mostly they talked of home, their faces being brought into sharp relief whenever the fire flared as one of their number tossed on another piece of carefully husbanded fuel. The bits of wood they burned, and the dried grass, were hard to come by in that desert, and much of each man's spare time was spent in hunting for it, because, though the days were hot, when the sun went down the chill air was enough to make you shiver and huddle over whatever warmth you could find.

The night also gave rise to another pest, or series of pests. The flying beetles, huge heavy things that seemed to lack any sense of direction and would hit you in the face or land on your piece of hardtack just as you were about to put it into your mouth. Then there were crawling things, 'Bugs wi' footba' boots on,' Private MacTavish called them, that walked all over the exposed portions of your flesh, waking or sleeping, and most of them seemed to regard the British soldier as a sort of mobile lunch counter. For an area that appeared devoid of life, there seemed to be one hell of a lot of inhabitants.

The little group outside the R.S.M.'s bivouac were grumbling quietly about their dinner when Frankie Gibson cocked his head on one side.

'Hald your whist,' he whispered.

'What is it, Frankie?' asked Macmillan.

'Shut up, I canna hear a thing if youse keep talkin'.' He paused, 'Aye there it is again.'

They were silent for a moment as Frankie listened intently.

'What are ye on tae, Frankie?' asked one of the others.

Frankie turned to them, a broad grin on his leathery face. 'Hoo would yees like some real meat for your supper?'

'Eh???'

'Hae ye got your dirk there, Mac?'

'Aye,' replied Macmillan.

'Gie it here. Get the fire gannin' guid. I'll be back in a wee whilie.'

Frankie slipped the dirk into his stocking top and left the group, heading out through the lines in the direction of the village.

'Halt, who goes there?' It was the sentry whom Frankie had posted himself about twenty minutes ago.

'Shut yer gob or ye'll wake the whole fuckin' camp.'

'Sorry, sarge. Didn't recognize you.'

After he had passed the sentry, Frankie walked a few paces, then lay down close to the ground, listening. Yes, there it was again, the faint bleat of a sheep or a goat. Frankie Gibson, stalker supreme, and poacher without parallel, grinned as he started to creep towards the sound.

About twenty minutes after he had left, Frankie returned to his comrades with the corpse of a small goat slung across his shoulders. He was greeted with much joy.

'Well done, Frankie,' said the R.S.M. 'Twa o' ye get it skinned and intae the pot.'

'The puir bloody beast didna hae a chance. Some rotten black bastard had tied it up.' He watched the men struggling with the carcass. 'It's a shame we havena any onions.'

Hugh Grant was duty officer and at nine o'clock started on his rounds. He did not expect to find anything, and if he did and could ignore it, he most certainly would. However, he could not ignore the appetizing smell which seemed to be emanating from the direction of the R.S.M.'s bivouac.

He approached the group sitting around the fire. They seemed to be arguing among themselves as to whether 'it' was ready.

'What are you doing?' asked Grant.

'Jest cooking up the hardtack, sorr,' said Frankie, his face expressionless.

'Smells better than ours.' He was sniffing rather pointedly.

'I suppose it does, sir,' said R.S.M. Macmillan, rising to his feet.

'All right, Sergeant-Major, at ease. What have you got there?'

'Weel, sorr,' said Frankie, 'it's like this. I was just taking a wee walkie into the desert for – weel, you ken what I mean. And this beastie just walked right onto ma dirk. Well, we couldna throw guid meat awa', so we're cooking it.'

'Mmmm,' replied Grant. 'That sounds a jolly good idea. I hope you have enough.'

'Och, aye, sorr,' said Macmillan. 'We could even manage a bittie for yourself if you had a mind tae it. But dinna go telling everybody.'

'That is very kind of you, Sergeant-Major, thank you.'

'A wee dram would go doon afu' well wi' it,' said Frankie.

'Sorry, haven't got a drop.'

'Oh, that's verra sad.'

'But I do happen to know where there is some if you think you could manage two extra portions.'

'I think that would be all right,' said Macmillan. 'Eh, Frankie?'

'Oh, aye, we could dae that, all right.'

'I'll be back in a few minutes,' said Grant, all thought of his duty round now forgotten at the prospect of fresh meat.

Captain Grant hurried along to Alex Farquhar's bivouac where he found that worthy deep in conversation with Ian Maclaren.

Ian, no longer intent on a hero's death after his discovery at the battle of El Teb that life was sweet even without Naomi, had come along to Farquhar's tent to discuss tactics for the morrow.

'You know,' Farquhar was saying, 'that Gatling is a damned good weapon, but if there's no wind tomorrow, we're going to have the same problem all over again.'

'You mean the smoke?' said Ian.

'Of course I mean the bloody smoke,' replied Farquhar. 'Why the hell they cannot invent some sort of smokeless powder beats me.'

'You know, I've been thinking about that,' said Ian. 'And I might have got an answer.'

'Then for God's sake, let's have it.'

'It sounds a bit daft. It's really so simple.'

'Most good ideas are.'

'Well, if you had a man standing alongside the breech with a big board, and he fanned like hell whenever you were firing, it might disperse the smoke enough for you to be able to see.'

'You know, I think you could be right. I'll take one of your jocks and we'll try it. Good thinking, Ian. Oh, hello, Hugh,' he said as Grant came into the tent. 'Ian here's got a great idea. We're going to have a punkah wallah for the Gatling.'

'Can I have a word with you, Alex?' asked Grant, ignoring that important piece of military information.

'Sure,' said Farquhar. 'I'll get a bottle out.'

'Er, Alex,' said Grant, looking rather pointedly at Ian.

'That's all right, Hugh. Ian's going to have a dram, too. Aren't you, Ian?'

'Oh, yes, rather. Thanks a lot.'

'Oh, all right,' said Grant, 'I'll have to tell you, because there isn't much time. Just you keep your trap shut about this, young Maclaren. Some of the sergeants have got a fresh meat stew and they're willing to share it with us if we can supply a dram.'

'How did they manage that?' asked Farquhar.

'Need you ask? It was Frankie Gibson. Apparently the beast impaled itself on his dirk voluntarily.'

All three men laughed. 'Where do we come in?' said Ian.

'I'm sorry, but you don't. They're only willing to share it with two of us, if there's a dram in it for them.'

'Ah,' said Farquhar, 'we can't very well leave poor old Maclaren out of it. Why don't we get our two shares and each of us give him a bit. How about that?'

'They mightn't like it,' said Grant.

'They'll like it, all right. I tell you what, Ian, you carry the bottle. They won't say no then.'

'Righto!' said Ian, grabbing the bottle of whisky. 'Where are they?'

'They're just outside the R.S.M.'s bivvy.'

Off the three of them went, heading for the flickering light of the fire outside Regimental-Sergeant-Major Macmillan's bivouac, their gastric juices flowing in anticipation.

Further along the lines Peter Leinie cocked his head on one side. 'What's that?' he said.

'What's what?' asked MacTavish. 'Awa' tae yer beed.'

'Whist. Dinna ye hear it? Dinna ye hear it?'

MacTavish was impressed and the two men were silent a while, listening.

'There it is again,' said Leinie.

In the distance they could just make out the unmistakable sound of firing.

'Aye, I hear it noo,' said MacTavish. 'There's shooting gannin' on. Awa' and tell the sergeant-major.'

'What, me?' said Leinie. 'Why dinna ye go?' He was appalled at the thought of approaching the august personage of R.S.M. Macmillan.

'Aye, you. Ye heered it first. Awa' and tell him.'

Grudgingly Leinie got to his feet and reluctantly walked down the lines towards Macmillan's bivouac. There around their fire they were just finishing their meal, and poor Leinie was assailed with the mouth-watering odour of the fresh stew. He stopped outside the group and, seeing officers present, he saluted. Frankie Gibson looked up.

'Weel, here's a smartie. De ye no ken that ye dinna salute wi'oot your bonnet on? What dae ye want, sodger?'

'Sorry, sarge. Please, sir, I ha' something tae tell the sergeant-major,' he replied.

'All right, lad, what is it?' demanded Macmillan, not very pleased at being discovered at their feast.

'Please, sir, there's shootin'.'

'Shooting? Where, in camp?'

'No, sir. If ye'll listen, yees'll hear it.'

'Quiet a minute!' said Captain Grant.

They were all silent. For a moment or two they heard nothing, and then, in the far distance, but quite unmistakable, there came a sporadic burst of firing.

'He's right, you know,' said Grant. 'Somebody's shooting. Have any of our chaps gone out tonight?'

'I saw a detachment of Black Watch move out about two hours ago. I thought that they were just drilling or something,' said Ian Maclaren.

'All right, Private – er – what's your name?'

'Leinie, sir.'

'All right, Leinie,' said Grant. 'You can go back to your bivvy now. Good work, lad.'

Relieved of his responsibility and the awesome presence of

superiors, Peter Leinie scuttled back to tell MacTavish how he had told the officers a thing or two.

'I don't suppose that it's any of our business,' said Farquhar.

'I certainly hope not,' said Grant. 'And if the top brass don't know, I don't see why we should disturb them and maybe lose a night's sleep. And talking of sleep, we had better get our heads down in case the balloon does go up.'

'Aren't you going to tell anyone?' said Ian.

'No, sonny,' said Farquhar. 'Thou shalt not have converse with those set above thee. You'll only end up with a bloody sight more work to do. That's the eleventh commandment. Anyhow, they'll know what's going on. The sentries are sure to have reported it.'

'I still think we should tell somebody,' said Ian.

'Look, laddie,' said Farquhar, 'you go along to the general and tell him what we've heard. Just at that moment, he's pretty sure to be looking for someone to go out on a recce to find out what's happened, and you are standing right in front of him; who do you think gets the job?'

'Me?' said Ian.

'You,' replied Farquhar. 'Right, Hugh?'

'Right, Alex.'

'Right, Sergeant-Major?'

'Right, sir.'

'So now, if you want to go and tell the general, you can go. But don't say we didn't warn you.'

'All right, I'll go,' said Ian almost petulantly.

And he did, and everything that Farquhar had predicted happened just as he had said it would. It was over two hours later that a tired and dusty Ian rode back into camp on a borrowed cavalry charger to tell General Graham that the detachment of Black Watch had achieved their objective. They had taken a *zariba*, an enclosed square fortified by palisades and thick thorns. This lay about a mile north of the ravine beyond which lay Osman Digna's main force. It was all very satisfactory to the general. The detachment he had sent out would hold the *zariba* until he arrived with his main force tomorrow. And moreover, it would provide a fortified base, should that prove necessary in order to secure his rear.

'Well done, Mr Maclaren,' said the general. 'You've done a

good job. And now, you had better get to sleep. It's almost two o'clock.'

At five thirty the following morning the bugles sounded reveille. After a hurried breakfast of hardtack and water from their canteens, the brigade formed in two squares, as General Graham had decreed, and began their march on Tamai village.

By about ten o'clock, they were in sight of the *zariba* and received a resounding cheer from their comrades who were now occupying it. They were marching at ease, each man carrying his rifle in whatever manner was most comfortable for him. They marched in light field order. They had no packs, only their rifles, fifty rounds of ammunition, their canteens, and a couple of biscuits stuffed into their sporrans.

But an army on the move is not a machine. It is men, individuals, each one with his private fears and thoughts. Private Brady, a Glasgow Irish Catholic, nineteen years old, had seen action for the first time at El Teb; he was a member of A Company and A Company had been in the front ranks. He had seen the hordes of Sudanese rise to attack and he was now scared. A man of uncommon imagination, he could, in his mind's eye, see, over and over again, a spear thrusting towards him and tearing at his guts. He complained bitterly that there was no priest to hear his confession, though he had not been inside a church since he was ten when he used to steal pennies out of the collection plate until he was caught and given a most memorable thrashing. Private Doig of B Company was sick but afraid of reporting himself so in case they found out about the bottle of evil-smelling liquid which he had found in the village of El Teb and drunk the night previous. Doig's marras managed to get him to his feet and into the square where, after vomiting up his breakfast, he was able to move, albeit somewhat unsteadily, of his own volition. But Doig and Brady and the rest were really quite ordinary men; it was the task which confronted them, the killing and being killed, which was extraordinary.

And now they were on the march again, out into that barren thankless country only describable by the complete sameness of the vista whatever direction you went, whichever way you looked.

Davis's square moved out first and Buller, with the Maclaren Highlanders in his formation, followed some five hundred yards to the rear and in to the right. They talked and smoked as they marched over the barren, empty yellow earth.

'Where the hell have they gone, Sergeant?' Ian inquired of Frankie Gibson.

'They're no sae far off, sir,' was the reply. 'We're no disturbin' any birds or wee animals. That means that there's men around. Men whae got here afore us.'

From their position in the front of Buller's square, the Maclarens could see Davis's square approaching the ravine, when suddenly, out of the seemingly deserted earth, where a moment previously no living thing could be seen, thousand upon thousand of Sudanese appeared. They rose, it seemed, from nowhere, and fell upon Davis's square.

The Maclarens in Buller's square watched helplessly as Davis's men, without awaiting orders, opened a frantic fire on the hordes which now surrounded them. Soon they were almost obscured from view by the black pall of smoke which hung over them in the still air – almost, but not quite.

'Jes' look at yon daft buggers,' shouted Private Anderson.

The Black Watch, who formed the front ranks of Davis's square, had rushed forward with bayonets fixed, leaving a gap between themselves and the two flanks of the square. In a trice the Sudanese, with that intense ferocity and courage which was the hallmark of their fighting men, had seen their opportunity and charged into the gap. Hundreds of them were now inside the square engaged in bloody hand-to-hand fighting.

Buller halted his square and gave the order for covering fire. The Maclarens and the rest poured volley after volley into the masses who were still far enough from Graham to offer a safe target. There was, however, nothing they could do to assist their comrades who were engaged within Davis's square.

Even above the noise of the battle they could hear the bugles as they called the square to re-form, and the shouts of the officers and N.C.O.s as they rallied their men into some sort of formation. They seemed to be broken up into small groups standing back to back as they fought and died. Isolated, the Gatling guns wrought a terrible carnage until their naval crews were all killed or wounded. A little to the rear the gunners, with a battery of four eight-pounders, stood firm and fired off round after round of shrapnel at the advancing foe.

The battle had been raging for a few minutes only when another horde charged towards Buller's square. But this time they were ready. Calmly they opened fire at this new threat, mowing them down like the corn on the hill before the scythe. Captain Farquhar opened up his Gatling, complete with the ministrations of his punkah wallah, and to his utter delight, it worked. They managed to keep the smoke away from the gun as it poured hundreds of rounds into the advancing enemy.

While Buller's square was blowing the enemy off the face of the earth, many anxious glances were cast towards the other square. But the hand-to-hand fighting seemed to be diminishing, and at last they started to re-form. As Davis's square became once again coherent, Buller was able to resume giving covering fire across the open ground which separated them. Ian Maclaren was standing just to the rear of his platoon holding his Webley and wishing he could get hold of a rifle, for not a single one of the enemy had yet come within range of his pistol. Donald Bruce had not even unholstered his revolver; he simply stood there, watching, sickened at the carnage.

Private Leinie had killed four, perhaps it was five, or even six, of the enemy, and the strange, almost sexual excitement of watching men die at his hands made him mad. Suddenly and without warning, he broke ranks and charged a small group of Sudanese. He shot one and bayoneted another, and then he was among them being hacked at by their swords.

'Come back, you bloody fool!' roared Frankie Gibson.

'He's a goner,' said R.S.M. Macmillan, who was standing next to Donald Bruce.

Those of them who had seen Leinie shifted their fire to try and cover him, and give him a chance to get back to the square. Leinie went down, still fighting, blood streaming from him, and only about twenty yards to their front.

Donald had seen it all as well, and as Leinie charged into the group of Sudanese, he had turned and shouted at the R.S.M.

'Cover me, Sergeant-Major, I'm going to bring him in.'

'You'll be killed, sir.'

'That's an order, Sergeant-Major.'

'Aye, sir.'

Then, calmly unholstering his revolver, he stepped out of the square and walked, the shots of his own men whining around him, towards Leinie. There were three Sudanese left. All of them were wounded, but just about to give Peter Leinie the *coup de grâce*. Donald, his face grim, shot each one of them. He then went to where the wounded man was lying, threw his revolver to the ground, heaved Leinie over his shoulder, and carried him back into the square.

As he returned, an enormous cheer rang through the ranks, and Gordon Bruce, who had seen it all, uttered a silent prayer of thanks for the manner in which his brother had acquitted himself.

By now the battle was virtually over and the Sudanese were in full retreat. Davis took his square back to the *zariba*, and Buller formed line and marched into the village of Tamai. There they set fire to all of the buildings and then returned to join up with Davis once again. The ground was covered with Sudanese dead, and as the men returned across the Khor Gwob, the ravine by which they fought their battle, they were silent in the presence of so much havoc. Frankie Gibson looked down on one of the corpses, soon to become bloated and flyblown, and wondered who and what the man had been. Frankie, true professional that he was, held no hatred for the enemy and he could see, in the body of the man he was looking at, someone who had probably got a home somewhere. Maybe he had lived in one of those little square mud huts at El Teb, perhaps he had a wife and children who even now were waiting for their father to return. Frankie shrugged, it was all luck. It could just as easily have been himself lying there and the Sudanese standing where he was and looking at him. They had fought their battle and won it and the price was over two thousand Sudanese dead. As for Graham's force, their casualties were 109 killed and 102 wounded. The proportion of dead to wounded bore tribute to the tenacity of their opponents. But of the man they were after, Osman Digna, there was no sign.

Most of the British casualties had occurred in Davis's square, which had borne the brunt of the fighting. As for the Maclarens they had got off very lightly with only six of them wounded and of them, only one seriously, Peter Leinie.

Osman Digna excepted, Graham had achieved his objective.

The road from Suakim to Berber was open, and perhaps now Khartoum could be relieved and Gordon saved. But that was not to be their decision.

They headed back towards Suakim where their lines were ready to receive them. Two companies of the Yorks and Lancs had been left out of the fight to do this. When the men got there, footsore and battle weary, the neat rows of bivouacs, the smoke from the cooking fires, and even the hard ground on which they would lie looked like paradise. There was even a stew, real meat heaped onto their tin plates, and they were able to gorge themselves before bivouacking for the night. At first most of them could not sleep and they sat around bragging about one another's deeds and many a story was told of the action of Captain Donald Bruce on that day. But suddenly fatigue overcame them and one by one they drifted into sleep, many of them without moving from where they had been sitting, tin plates still on their knees and fingers still through the handles of their mugs.

But it was the Maclarens who talked most and longest and many a bet was laid that Captain Donald would be getting a Victoria Cross for his deeds.

The medical staff worked throughout the night, treating the wounded. 'When in doubt amputate,' said one young R.A.M.C. captain. 'God, it makes you sick. We've got nothing and half of these men are going to die because they won't give us an extra couple of hundredweight of supplies.'

'Get on with your job, Captain Walker,' said the major in charge. But there was no reprimand in his voice because he knew that what the young man was saying was true.

Those of the casualties who were bad, but not too bad to be moved, and this included Peter Leinie, they were transporting to Port Sudan. At least there was a reasonably well-equipped hospital there.

After the battle and after they had bivouacked their men, the three major-generals gathered together in Graham's quarters. General Graham had a large tent and he lived in comparative comfort though nothing like the luxury in which generals had managed to live as little as thirty years ago or less. They had a meal of soup followed by the same stew which had been served to the men, and here was the luxury, Stilton cheese washed down by a bottle of the general's excellent claret, the second last of the dozen he had carefully hoarded through the Sudan campaign.

There were no tablecloths and no expensive silver to polish and only the general's batman to serve the meal. So with the meal over and the servant having cleared the table they sat on at table to review the day's happenings.

'Well, sir,' said Buller. 'It worked.'

'Yes,' said Graham. 'It worked. Now they've got to get to Gordon.'

As Graham ordered the last bottle of claret, Buller said, 'I think we got a V.C. today, sir.'

'Who, you?' said Graham.

'No, thank you, sir. I already have one,' replied Buller, a smile crossing his usually grave countenance. 'I'm referring to a young captain in the Maclaren Highlanders.'

'What did he do?' asked Davis.

'Just about the bravest thing I ever saw,' replied Buller. 'One of his men had broken ranks and was surrounded by half a dozen Sudanese. Well, this chap calmly walks out of the square with nothing but his revolver. It was the coolest damned thing I have ever seen.'

'Well, go on, man,' said Graham, 'let's hear the rest.'

'The soldier, damned fool, dealt with some of them, but there must have been three or four of them left, and this young fellah picked them off as if he had been at target practice on the range. Then he picked up the soldier – he was in a sorry state by then – and carted him back into the square.'

'I suppose we ought to court-martial the soldier,' said Davis.

'No,' said Buller, who was always one to excuse the indiscretions of the ranks. 'He's suffered enough. I hear that he's in a pretty bad way.'

'Well, it's your decision,' said Graham.

'I don't want to punish him. After all, he showed a wonderfully aggressive spirit. He'll need taming, of course, and I'll get his C.O. to give him a good dressing down. But not until he's better,' he added. 'He got cut up rather badly.'

'All right, have it your way,' said Graham. 'Now, what are we going to do about this young officer? I think you are right, we ought to recommend him. Why don't we get him in and have a word with him? Not wounded, was he?'

'No, sir,' said Buller.

'Who's the C.O.?' asked Davis.

'Lieutenant-Colonel Murray is acting C.O. Actually the regiment is commanded by the boy's father, a ranker,' said Buller.

'Well, I'm damned,' said Graham. 'Anyhow, let's have him in and give him a glass of wine. Orderly!' He turned to Buller. 'What's the lad's name?'

'Bruce, sir. Captain Donald Bruce.'

'Go along to the Maclarens' lines, orderly,' said Graham, 'and tell Captain Donald Bruce to report here at once.'

About fifteen minutes later the orderly returned accompanied, not by Donald Bruce, but by Colonel Murray.

'You're not Captain Bruce,' said Graham.

'No, sir. Lieutenant-Colonel Murray.'

'But I sent for Captain Bruce.'

'I know, sir. We can't find him.'

'Can't find him? What the blazes do you mean, Colonel?' demanded Graham.

'He's vanished, sir. All of his kit has been left in his bivouac and he left this.' Murray held out an envelope.

Graham took it. 'It's addressed to you.'

'Yes, sir, but I think you ought to read it.'

Graham took out the letter and unfolded it. He read it through slowly, then looked up at the others.

'Good God!' he said.

'What's in it, sir?' asked Buller.

Graham began to read aloud without further comment.

'Sir,

I have the honour to request that you will accept the resignation of my commission. I wish this resignation to take effect from today, March 13th, 1884.

After careful thought, I have come to the conclusion that I am not a soldier, and that I never will be one. War and killing are abhorrent to me.

Today, I killed three of my fellow human beings and this will be on my conscience for the rest of my life. It does not make any difference to me that they were black and the enemy.

They were people. I know that I could never do it again. I would have submitted my resignation earlier. I had intended to write it yesterday, but the coming action would have left me open to a charge of cowardice. That would have mattered little to me, but it would have caused my family a great deal of grief. So I went through today's action determined that it would be my last. I have never killed before and I shall never kill again. I almost died at El Teb, and but for the action of Sergeant-Major Macmillan, I would have done.

In spite of all I have said, I know that this decision will cause my father and my family much distress, but there is no other way open to me.

I have the honour to remain, sir,
Your obedient servant.

It is signed, Donald Bruce.' Silently Graham handed the letter back to Murray.

'Dammit,' said Davis, 'the man's a deserter. He's gone, you say, Murray?'

'Yes, sir.'

Buller raised his eyebrows. 'A moment ago we were recommending him for a Victoria Cross.'

'But,' said Davis, 'you can't resign your commission on active service in the middle of a campaign.'

Buller looked at Graham. 'What are you going to do about it, sir?'

Graham thought for a moment. 'I'll do the only thing I can do,' he said. 'I shall take no action myself. I shall report the whole facts, including his gallant behaviour in the field, to the C-in-C Great Britain. Let him deal with it.'

Four days after the conversation in General Graham's tent, a dishevelled Donald Bruce, dressed in an old pair of trousers and a dirty shirt, signed as a junior stoker on board the SS *Wayfarer*, homeward bound from Port Sudan to London.

It was easy. Three of the crew had jumped ship in the port and the master would have taken anybody who was willing to work. It happened all the time at every port in the world. The master did not care who or what his new crew member was as long as he shovelled coal; and that he did, losing a stone in weight in the process.

8

It was ten o'clock in the morning. It was June, and the temperature in London was approaching the seventies when Mr Wilson left his rooms in Jermyn Street and started walking, as he did every morning, in the direction of his shop. Mr Wilson's shop was in Bond Street, and he sold high-class jewellery to a very high-class clientele.

It was late. The shop would already have been open for over an hour. But Mr Wilson had no worries, for he had an excellent manager. Mr Wilson thought everything was just as it should be. The Marquess of Salisbury was Prime Minister, much better than that dreadful radical Gladstone. Mr Wilson's politics were, like those of the Queen herself, firmly with the establishment. He had no business worries; his establishment – he never thought of it as a shop – was in the very capable hands of Mr Kevin MacDonald.

A spry sixty-five-year-old, Mr Wilson was already contemplating retirement while he was still possessed of sufficient energy to enjoy his declining years. Not that he would lose touch with his business, but he felt that he could now, with safety, offer to Mr MacDonald a junior partnership.

He was a grateful man, and the thought occurred to him as he walked along, how good life had been to him, and that not the least of his good fortune had been taking Mr MacDonald onto his staff. He had had grave doubts when he had first employed him. He had placed an advertisement in *The Times* offering a position to a person of refined habits and gentle bearing. Mr MacDonald had replied to the advertisement in person, with little or nothing to recommend him except the obvious fact that he was a gentleman who had fallen upon hard times. What had impelled him to accept the young man would forever remain a mystery to Mr Wilson. He supposed it was some sort of instinct that had made him decide to give Mr MacDonald a try. He had never regretted it. His assistant had proved himself honest and trustworthy, quite apart from being most popular with his customers. Mr Wilson was now in the happy position of being able to take time off from his business without the slightest worry, knowing that it would be handled as efficiently as if he were doing it himself.

Mr MacDonald spoke with an educated, well modulated accent, with just that trace of Highland lilt which indicated that he was Scottish born, as his name implied. On more than one occasion Mr Wilson had attempted to persuade Mr MacDonald to tell him something about his past, but Mr MacDonald had always changed the subject. Anyhow, that was Mr MacDonald's business, and Mr MacDonald was an efficient and honest servant, and what more could any master ask? Mr MacDonald lived in a small lodging near Golden Square; not fashionable, and on the wrong side of Regent Street. But Mr MacDonald would not be able to afford anything very much better on a wage of two pounds a week and an occasional bonus when he had made a particularly good sale. He did seem to come from a good background. The referees he had given were two titled gentlemen in Edinburgh. Mr Wilson had not written, so impressed had he been by the man's initial demeanour, and this impression had been borne out by time. He was never late for work, never even seemed to want time off. He was always in the shop by nine in the morning, and seldom left before seven-thirty in the evening. What, if anything, he did outside of his work was a complete mystery to Mr Wilson, and he did not feel that he had the right to inquire.

He paused for a moment, as he always did, to admire the front of his premises: a heavy-black, gilt-lined door with a little barred viewing hole at about eye height, a small window on either side set back in the heavy stone of the façade and each containing a single article of jewellery. It was flanked by shops of equal quality and like most of the shops at that end of Bond Street it would still be there many, many years hence.

Mr Wilson went in through the door without touching it. His doorman had seen him approach through the little grille. Moffat, the doorman, was an ex-policeman, one of the original Peelers who had retired from the force while still a very fit and healthy man. He was responsible for the security of the shop and his impassive blue eyes never left anyone, no matter who they were, as long as they were on the premises.

Mr Wilson handed Moffat his top hat and silver-topped cane, flicked an invisible speck of dust from the silk lapel of his frock coat, and smiled a greeting.

'Good morning, Mr Wilson,' said Moffat.

'Good morning, Moffat,' replied Mr Wilson, glancing down at the heavy wool carpet which deadened all sound, and running a speculative finger over the glass-covered counter on his right, beneath which lay a selection of cameos, gold bracelets, enamel brooches, and the like. Not the best, of course; like all jewellers, he kept the very valuable pieces locked away in the safe in the office at the other end of the showroom. It was in the office that he found Mr MacDonald; he was busy, as usual. On this occasion he was polishing a silver teapot.

'Good morning, Mr MacDonald,' said Mr Wilson.

MacDonald looked up. 'Good morning, sir,' he said. 'There has been no business yet, sir.'

'It is early yet. The customers will come, you mark my words.'

For five years they had exchanged the same remarks every weekday morning. It was true, however, that the business was lucrative. So lucrative in fact that Mr Wilson had thought of moving into The Albany; but he had decided against that. Several of his clients lived in The Albany and it would not do to let them see that he was as wealthy as they.

'Mr MacDonald,' he said in a tone that indicated that the day's work was about to begin, 'I would like to have a word with you when you can spare the time.'

'Certainly, sir.'

'No. I have a better idea. Why don't you come and take luncheon with me tomorrow? Would Rules suit you? I have something to tell you which I think that you will find to your advantage, and it would be pleasant to discuss it over a good lunch and a half-bottle of claret.'

'You are very kind, sir,' said Mr MacDonald.

Mr Wilson had always closed the shop between one and two P.M. It saved employing extra staff, and the type of people with whom he dealt would in any case be at lunch themselves between those hours.

'Mr MacDonald, I have a mind to check the inventory of what valuables we have in the safe. Would you be kind enough to do that? I will attend to any customers while you do.'

'Certainly, sir,' replied Mr MacDonald, and he went into the office.

Mr Wilson reflected that it was good to have someone working with him in whom he had absolute trust; who could hold the keys to the shop and the keys to the safe and never give one a moment's worry.

The door opened and a lady and gentleman came in. He recognized the gentleman at once. It was Lord de Vere-Smith, a very valued client, though this was the first time he had ever seen him in the company of a lady.

'Good morning, my lord. How nice to see you again,' he said in his most unctuous manner.

The lady who was with him was wearing a heavy veil which completely hid her features.

'What service may we be of to your lordship today?'

'I had in mind to buy my cousin here a small present for her birthday. See what you can do for her.'

'Ah, quite so, sir,' said Mr Wilson. It was surprising how much money gentlemen like his lordship here were prepared to spend on their 'cousins'. 'Had madam anything particular in mind?'

'I love pearls, Charles,' she said, and Mr Wilson noted that her voice was low and soft, not a voice that one was likely to forget. 'Would pearls be all right?'

'Anything you want, my dear. It has been difficult enough to persuade you to come here anyhow. Pearls, diamonds, emeralds, the choice is yours.'

'Then I should like pearls.'

Mr Wilson stood a little aside from the conversation. He knew well that this was not the moment to make any suggestion.

'Pearls are for tears,' said his lordship.

'For me, they will be for five happy years. But if you would rather I had something else —'

'Don't give it another thought. Pearls it shall be. Mr Wilson.'

'Sir?'

'Pearls, Mr Wilson.'

'Of course, my lord. We have quite a nice selection here if madam would care to glance at them?' He reached down beneath the glass-topped counter to draw out a tray of pearl necklets.

'No, no, Wilson, not those,' said his lordship. 'The ones you keep locked away in the safe.'

'With the *greatest* of pleasure, my lord,' said Mr Wilson, backing into the office.

'Something very special,' called his lordship to the retreating Mr Wilson.

'Mr MacDonald,' he said, as soon as he had closed the office door, 'do you know Lord de Vere-Smith?'

'Not by name, certainly, though I may know him by sight.'

'Well, he's one of the richest young men in town, and he's got his lady with him. He wants to give her pearls. Where is that string of pearls that may have belonged to Marie Antoinette?'

'Right here, sir. Good heavens, that's fifteen hundred guineas' worth.'

'I know, Mr MacDonald, and his lordship will buy them.'

He took the black leather case and went back into the shop. 'Here we are, madam. These pearls may once have belonged to Marie Antoinette, though I doubt if anyone would ever be able to prove it.'

As he spoke, he reverently laid the long rope of iridescent, perfectly matched pearls onto the black velvet cloth on the counter where they seemed to be infused with a soft glow.

'They are so beautiful,' said the lady.

His lordship watched her, his slightly crooked smile playing around his lips. 'They're yours if you want them,' he said.

'I have others,' said Mr Wilson as he saw the lady hesitate.

'Well?' said his lordship.

'But you have not even asked how much they cost,' said the lady.

'And I shall not do so, in your presence. They are yours if you want them.'

'There is just one thing.'

'Yes, my dear?'

'I should like the clasp altered.'

'You would alter Marie Antoinette's pearls?'

'She means nothing to me. You see that the clasp is in the form of an "L"? Well, I should like it to be changed to a "C", for Charles.'

'Can that be done right away?' inquired his lordship.

'We could have it ready by this evening, sir.'

'In that case, you will have to send it round to madam. I leave for York on the afternoon train.'

'With the greatest of pleasure, my lord.'

She took off her glove to touch the pearls and Mr Wilson admired the delicate creamy skin of her hand as she fingered the gems. Her fingers were long and elegant and Mr Wilson was quite embarrassed by the manner in which they fascinated him.

'They can wait till you get back, Charles.'

'Not a bit of it. What time can you deliver them, Mr Wilson?'

'Would seven thirty be too late, sir?'

'That would be all right,' said the lady.

'Unfortunately, I shall not be able to deliver them myself, but my – er, partner, Mr MacDonald, will be able to, I am sure,' said Mr Wilson.

'Thank you very much. The address is 182 Park Lane.'

They left, and it was only after they had gone that Mr Wilson realized that he had not got the lady's name. Still, it did not really matter; 182 would be one of the small houses near Hyde Park Corner. Mr MacDonald would certainly find the right recipient.

They got into a hansom outside the shop and Lord Charles gave the cabby instructions to drive to the Park Lane address.

She reached out and put her hand into his, and after a while he turned to her.

'Well, Naomi, this is really goodbye.'

'Yes,' she replied, and the word was soft and long drawn out. 'But we will meet again.'

'Whether we shall meet again, I know not.'

'Therefore our everlasting farewell take,' she murmured. '*Julius Caesar.*'

'At Philippi,' he answered.

'If we should meet again, why then we'll smile.' He looked at her. 'I know only that I shall pray for the day. It can never be the same again, but perhaps one day —'

Gently she placed her fingers over his lips. 'Do not say it, my dear. Now that you know all about me, you know how impossible it is. Even if you were free, you know that it could not be. Perhaps in a way your father's death has been a blessing to us. We could not have gone on forever.'

'I suppose you are right. Our parting is of our own choosing. But if your brother were not returning to England tomorrow —'

She thought for a moment of Gordon. She would see him tomorrow when the regiment docked at Tilbury. If only Donald were to have been there, too.

'There are so many buts,' she said.

'I know that, and if Phillip had not insisted upon remaining in the United States, we could have gone on a little longer. He should have come home, you know. After all, he is the eldest son and he has inherited the title, though it is highly improbable that he will ever marry, so it will eventually come to either me or my son. I know that it is only a chunk of land, but the estate means more to me than my own happiness. I cannot tell you why, I can only tell you that it is so. I don't suppose that you are able to understand that?'

'I understand it only too well,' she replied. 'We have no estate, but we have a regiment.'

'You've told me often,' he said with a little smile.

'It's true, though, that one's happiness, everything, must be sacrificed on its altar. I suppose that your estate, and your ancestral home – no, no, I'm not laughing – and my regiment are in a way a little bit of eternity, and we've all been bred to cling to them.' Her tone changed. 'Please, Charles, don't write to me when you get home to Yorkshire. And if you come to London, don't let me know, just come. Have no fear, I'll be waiting.'

They were turning into Park Lane now.

'We're nearly there,' he said.

'Yes, are you coming in?'

'No, Naomi. You know how dearly I should love to. But I think it is better this way. I shall go straight to the station, get a bite of lunch there, and then catch the train. I do want you t know that I shall be forever in your debt.'

'And I in yours, my dear,' she replied.

'Just one other thing: the house is yours and your allowance will continue for as long as I live, and when you wear your pearls, give a thought to the one who gave them to you.'

'You know I shall,' she replied. 'And you are quite right. Pearls are for tears.'

The hansom had stopped.

'Goodbye, Charles.' There was a little catch in her voice.

He took her hand and gently raised it to his lips. 'I think I love you more than anything else in this world. If love were all . . .'

'I know, but it's hopeless,' she said, and then in a whisper, 'Goodbye.'

Suddenly she was gone and he was alone. 'King's Cross, cabby,' he called.

She went up the stone steps and paused with her hand on the polished brass doorknob. She turned and looked up Park Lane trying to distinguish Charles's cab ploughing its way, in the maelstrom of London traffic, up towards Marble Arch. It could have been one of a hundred. She turned and went into the house.

In the hall Barker was waiting for her as indeed she always was, in her long, severe, black housekeeper's gown, her greying hair tied back in an equally severe bun; Barker whose forbidding appearance concealed a great deal of affection for her mistress.

Barker had engaged the staff with care; none were too young, none were obtrusive when they went about their duties, and all of them – there were six – contented with their station in life. They were all women, even down to the cat who proved her femininity time and again by the number of litters of kittens she produced. On each of these occasions the entire household, Naomi included, spent many long hours searching for homes for the offspring.

Things would be different now, for Charles, who had made all of this a reality, had gone out of her life. But he had been with her long enough for her to be able to create a life satisfying and completely her own. It was quite true to say that Naomi was one of the most sought-after hostesses in London. Anyone who was anyone in the world of art and letters, or the theatre, could at some time or other be found at her house. An invitation to one of her 'Salons' was eagerly sought.

She took the pins out of her hat and handed it to Barker together with her velvet cloak.

'Will you be taking luncheon, madam?' asked Barker.

'No, thank you, Barker. Perhaps a sandwich and a pot of tea in my sitting room in about half an hour.'

'Very good, madam.' And Barker left her.

She went into her sitting room, which, like everything else in the house, was furnished in the most exquisite taste. This in a way was Charles's legacy to her. Though not in any definable way a patron of the arts, he loved beautiful things and he had gently guided Naomi along the path of appreciation of the delicate and the tasteful. In her house she was able to blossom and express her secret self and wherever one turned there would be a delicate piece of porcelain, or a gilt-framed picture – not like the heavy portraits of the Maclarens, but landscapes and seascapes all bright and cheerful, reflecting the whole demeanour of the house. Silk brocades, always gentle in tone, patterned much of her furniture, most of which belonged to an earlier and more delicate era than the heavy plush and horsehair of the present.

In the sitting room the ceiling was Adam green, with the intricate plaster ornamentation picked out in white. A huge mirror which, in its heavy gilded frame, dominated one wall, made the room appear twice as large as it really was. The tall rectangular windows which looked out over Park Lane and Hyde Park beyond were hung with heavy curtains of deep green velvet. It was a warm house. Even in June the fires were always lit early and kept going throughout the day if need be and then banked up at night so that the house was never allowed to suffer from an early morning chill.

Naomi had come to love this place. It was hers and it had become her home. In the beginning it had been a little difficult explaining it to her father and mother. Willie had come to visit her and she had explained to him how Charles had been looking for a London hostess, which was part of the truth, to assist him in entertaining his many business interests, and she had been given the job. Willie gave no hint as to whether or not he believed what she told him, but knowing his stepdaughter and knowing her position, he had held his counsel and gone along with the story. She saw Willie more often now, of course. Willie, as a staff officer of Scottish Command, had to make not infrequent trips to London. He hated every moment of these. Willie Bruce would far rather have given battle to Osman Digna than fought the constant skirmishes with uninterested brass hats in the high-vaulted corridors and oak-panelled offices of Whitehall. His only relief in London was the fact that Naomi insisted that he stay with her. Mind, he never stayed long. Naomi's establishment was too delicate for him, Willie did not fit into the sophistication of Naomi's world. When he had been promoted brigadier and Murray had been confirmed as commander of the first battalion, he had for a while imagined that he could get a few things sorted out and improve the lot of the Maclarens. But too soon he discovered that all the unpleasantries he was in the habit of directing against the controllers of the army's destiny were sadly true. So he went to London as infrequently as possible and told himself that he would not damned well go there at all except for the chance of a day or two with Naomi.

In all of this Charles had behaved wonderfully. Ever maintained the fiction of a business relationship, excepting for those golden moments when they were alone. Funny, Naomi thought, it really had started as a business deal, but that had not lasted very long.

Of course, Willie would be arriving in London tomorrow. The regiment was due at Tilbury after five and a half years overseas. She would see Gordon again. As for Donald, she had no idea what had happened to him. No one ever talked of Donald. Willie had told her once that he had been reported missing, and he had left it at that. She sensed more than that. She was certain that there was a lot more to it. But Willie had shown very obviously that he had no intention of explaining further, and knowing Willie, she did not try to find out.

Gordon could tell her nothing. He kept writing to her, asking if she had had any news. It was as if her dear brother had become a dark skeleton in the family closet.

As for Charles, even after five years she still questioned herself as to whether or not she loved him. That apart, she knew that he was her best friend, and she his; nothing could ever take that away from them. But love? What was it, anyway? Was it what she had felt for Ian Maclaren? How strange and long ago all of that seemed now, an episode which seemed to spring from her childhood. She would most certainly see Ian again; in fact, Gordon would most probably bring him with him when he called before they moved back up to Scotland.

Naomi counted herself fortunate in that she had no material worries. She had desires, of course, but she could not name them so they did not really count. She was quite content for life to continue just as it was. There was really only one sadness, how much she would miss Charles. There was a new emptiness in her house.

Mr Wilson looked at his watch. 'It is seven o'clock, Mr MacDonald,' he said. 'I think you had better be on your way to Park Lane.'

'Yes, sir.'

'Don't worry about locking up, I shall attend to that.'

'Thank you very much, sir.'

Mr Wilson opened the till and took out a florin. 'I think you had better take a hansom. After all, you are carrying something rather valuable.' And he handed the florin to Mr MacDonald.

'Shall I take the account with me, sir?'

'Er – no, Mr MacDonald, that will not be necessary. Lord de Vere-Smith is a very old and valued customer. I shall send the account to him in Yorkshire.'

'Very good, sir.'

Mr MacDonald carefully wrapped the jewel case in brown paper and put it in the inside pocket of the jacket of his dark-grey lounge suit. He then asked Moffat to call him a hansom. It had been a very pleasant day, and from the first of next month the firm would become Wilson and MacDonald. He would be a very junior partner, but nevertheless it was all very satisfactory and Mr MacDonald was able to contemplate the fact that he was, at last, carving out for himself a completely new existence.

The hansom stopped outside the door of 182 Park Lane and Mr MacDonald got out, paid the cabby, and gave him a two-penny tip. He walked up the steps to the front door and rang the bell.

After a moment or two the door opened. 'Good evening,' he said, 'I should like to see the lady of the house. I am sorry, but I omitted to get her name. I have an important package for her from Wilson's the jeweller's.'

'I'll take it,' replied Barker.

'I'm sorry,' said Mr MacDonald, 'but I must deliver it personally. It is rather valuable and I shall have to establish her identity before I hand it over.'

'I understand,' said Barker. 'Mrs Bruce told me about it.'

At the mention of the name, MacDonald raised an eyebrow.

'If you will wait in the hall, I will tell madam that you are here,' said Barker.

Barker went into the sitting room. 'There is a man here from Wilson's,' she announced.

'Oh, good,' replied Naomi. 'Ask him to come in, will you?'

'In here, madam?'

'Please.'

Barker went out and returned in a few moments with Mr MacDonald. What happened then made Barker for the first time in her life forget her place and simply stand and stare at Mr MacDonald and her mistress.

'Good evening,' Naomi said as the door opened. 'I think you have—' She stopped. An expression of utter astonishment crossed her face. 'It cannot be,' she said very slowly.

But she knew that it was. He was thinner. He was dressed in dark serge, the sort of clothes that clerks and shop assistants wore. There were more lines on his face and a gravity born of suffering. But the back was straight, there was the echo of a soldier in his bearing. The only thought that she was capable of in that instant was, Thank God he is alive.

Naomi sped across the room and put her arms around her brother. 'Oh, Donald, Donald,' she said. 'After all these years, where have you—What have you—?' And then, realizing that

Barker was still standing there, 'Barker, go and get us a pot of tea'; and, as Barker hesitated, 'This is my brother, Barker. It's Donald whom we thought was dead.'

A beaming smile crossed Barker's normally rather grim face. 'Well,' she said, 'isn't that wonderful!'

'Yes,' said Naomi, 'this is my brother Donald. Please leave us and – and – and bring us some tea.'

Donald almost smiled as she said it. In any moment of stress his sister would always fly to the teapot.

'Sit down here beside me,' she said, her voice coming in little gasps. 'Sit down, Donald, and let me look at you.'

Silently, for his emotions were such that speech was impossible, Donald did as he was asked.

'Oh, Donald,' she said, 'why have you hidden yourself away from us for so long? We all thought that something terrible had happened to you.'

He looked at her and smiled, and it was a sad smile. 'Naomi,' he said, 'I knew it could not last. I knew that one day you would find me.'

'But why shouldn't we, my dear? Why shouldn't we find you? Do you know how we have worried? Every letter I have had from Gordon has talked about you, asking me if I had any news. Why should he ask me? I could never understand it. How could I have had news?' And suddenly her voice took on a graver tone. 'You have been hiding, haven't you, Donald?'

'Yes,' he replied. 'I've been hiding.'

'Is that all you have to say?'

'I'm afraid so. How are the family?'

'Do you care, Donald?'

'Yes, I do. I care very much.'

'Donald,' she said, 'what have you done? Why won't Father talk about you?'

'That doesn't surprise me. You see, I ran away and the Maclarens don't run away.'

'But you couldn't have run away,' she said. 'Gordon wrote and told me that you did the bravest thing he had ever seen.'

'No,' replied Donald, 'that wasn't bravery. I was trying to say something, something that they would understand. I was trying to tell them that I wasn't running away because I was a coward. Doing what I did was not brave; running away was.

I was trying to tell them that I didn't believe in their bloody army, that I was done with killing.'

Naomi was silent.

'None of them will ever understand; they don't think like I do. I don't suppose that even you will understand.'

'Gordon will be here tomorrow,' she said quietly. 'I am sure that he will understand. He'll be thrilled when I tell him that you are safe.'

'No, Naomi,' said Donald, 'that you must not do. No one must know. Not even Gordon.'

'But that's unfair, Donald,' she said. 'What earthly reason can there be? Gordon has been miserable ever since you disappeared. I've got to tell him.'

'No.'

'He worships you, you know that.'

'Not any more,' said Donald. 'Will you keep my secret?'

'How can I? Why should I?'

'Please.'

'Not even Gordon?'

'Not even Gordon. I don't want the regiment to know. I have a completely new life. The Donald you knew no longer exists. I have worked very hard and I have tried to forget. I don't want all that wiped out.'

'Is it Father?'

'Yes.'

'You know that he is not with the regiment any more. He was promoted to brigadier. He's at Scottish Command now. Ron Murray's got the command now.'

'It makes no difference, Naomi. Please promise me that you will help me to keep my secret.'

'Did you know that the regiment is coming home?'

'From Africa?'

'Yes. They dock at some ridiculous hour tomorrow morning. Wouldn't you like to see Gordon again?'

'Of course I would but it's just not possible.'

Somewhere in the distance a bell rang, but they were both too engrossed in each other to notice.

'Where are you staying, Donald?'

'I have rooms in Soho. I may be able to move soon, though. I'm doing quite well, really. I've been offered a partnership in the shop. Very junior, of course, but it starts next month. I like the work. It's nice being among beautiful things all day, and it's interesting. You meet so many people.'

'Well, you certainly did today,' said Naomi, and for the first time he really smiled. 'Is it really better than the army?'

'Oh, Lord, yes. It's much better than the army.'

'And are you happy?'

'I think,' replied Donald, 'I am as happy as I ever can be. You see, I started wrong. I should never have been a soldier.'

Barker came in.

'It's the brigadier, madam,' she announced, smiling all over her face as Willie Bruce strode into the room.

At ten o'clock the following morning Mr Wilson arrived at his shop and was surprised to find Moffat standing outside the door.

'Mr MacDonald is not here, sir,' said Moffat by way of explanation.

Mr Wilson could not recall any similar incident in the whole time he had known Mr MacDonald. His first reaction was to assume that Mr MacDonald was ill. He told Moffat to hurry round to Mr MacDonald's lodgings and see if there was anything that he could do to help. He became quite agitated, however, when Moffat returned half an hour later and told him that Mr MacDonald was not in his lodgings, and that he had managed to ascertain that Mr MacDonald had not been there since he left to come to his work yesterday morning.

Mr Wilson felt quite guilty at the terrible suspicions which raced through his mind. He could hardly credit that Mr MacDonald had done anything criminal. But Mr MacDonald had been entrusted with a very valuable piece of jewellery last night, and Mr Wilson could not afford to take risks.

Leaving Moffat in charge, he called a hansom and went to the Park Lane address. When he arrived at the house, the housekeeper assured him that Mr Donald, as she called him, had been there last evening. At Mr Wilson's insistence, the housekeeper went and asked her mistress if indeed the pearl necklace had been delivered. She returned to inform Mr Wilson that the necklace had been delivered, but that her mistress was not very well and regretted that she could not receive him.

Mr Wilson returned to his shop utterly mystified. By twelve noon, he had taken an inventory and found that nothing was missing. It just did not make sense. Why should a promising young man like Mr MacDonald disappear the day after he had been offered a partnership in the firm? Mr Wilson could not understand it, and he doubted that he ever would.

It was around six o'clock that same afternoon that the London train pulled into the twenty-five glass-covered acres of Edinburgh's Waverly station. The carriage doors swung open onto the steamy, smoky platform and Donald Bruce, under close arrest and accompanied by two captains of the Lancashire Fusiliers, stepped out. It had been a tense, uncommunicative journey. The escort, only too aware of their task, had been too embarrassed to indulge in anything approaching normal conversation and hardly a word had passed between them in eight hours.

Donald had not been left alone for a moment. Even when he had had to go to the toilet one or other of them had taken him along the corridor and stood outside waiting for him. For himself, Donald was glad that there had been no attempt to force conversation upon him; he wanted to be alone with his thoughts. In a way he was glad that it had happened this way and that he was no longer required to live as another. He was himself again, whatever that might be. The young captains, smart, clean shaven, had taken refuge in behaving absolutely correctly in what to them was an unusual and unpleasant task.

Outside the station, just for a moment, Donald got a glimpse of the castle which was to be his destination, standing grim and timeless on its rock, and then he was thrust into a closed wagon and driven off up the Mound and along the eastern approach and into the castle yard.

There he was escorted into the building, through the thick grey walls, and taken to a bare room containing the minimum of furnishing: a cot, two chairs, a small wooden table, and a Bible. This room, which he would share with an escort, was to be his home for the next three weeks. He would eat, sleep, and exist here while the General Officer Scottish Command had the summary of evidence prepared which would be offered at his General Court Martial.

9

The president of the court was a Colonel Gordon, late of the King's Own Scottish Borderers, that lowland regiment recruited mostly in Glasgow, who wore trews and held the Highlanders in their 'skirts' in the deepest contempt. The colonel however did not feel that way; he had fought with the Highlanders and knew of their qualities. Approaching fifty, with his dark hair greying, he maintained a soldierly manner and an iron control of the court which served under him. He was a veteran of many campaigns in the field. A man who had spent most of his service as a line officer. A man who had stayed on in the army when active service was no longer open to him, because he neither knew nor wanted any other way of life. There was in his cheek a deep indentation where it had been pierced by a ball during the Crimean campaign. It was not his only scar, but it was the only one which was visible. He well understood soldiers and the way they reacted. While his love of the army and all that it stood for gave him the outward appearance of a strict disciplinarian, he was at heart a kindly man who understood soldiers as people. It was he above all others who held the fate of Donald Bruce in his hands and he already felt a certain sympathy for the young man who was now before him on trial for his life. But he was too much of a soldier to allow his personal feelings to cloud the due process of military law.

Colonel Gordon glanced slowly around at the other twelve members of the tribunal, and after a short, whispered conversation with the Judge Advocate, whose job it was to rule on all matters of law, turned to the 'Prisoner's Friend'.

'You may call your first witness, Captain Maclaren.'

Donald Bruce had been surprised and not a little grateful when, less than twenty-four hours after his arrival in Edinburgh Castle, Ian Maclaren had walked into his room.

'Hello, Donald,' he said. 'I'm sorry about all this.'

'Thanks for coming to say so. But it's no use being sorry,' replied Donald. 'It had to happen one day, sooner or later. I'm sorry that it wasn't later, but now it has happened, I'm quite prepared to take what is coming to me.'

Ian got straight down to business. 'Well,' he said, 'what are we going to do about it?'

'We?' Donald was surprised at the determination in Ian's tone.

This was not the boy that he had known five years before. Though they were much of an age, Donald had always regarded himself as the man and Ian as the boy. But this man who had come to see him was not the same boy who had gone away with him. The Ian who had gone away had been a moonstruck, quiet-spoken, gentle adolescent. After his five years on campaign, his face, bronzed and leathered by the African sun, his eyes looked paler, harder, and more determined than Donald could remember. The boy he had known had grown up. For the first time Donald felt less of a man than Ian. There was a preciseness and determination about him, reflected in every movement that he made. And though when Ian spoke his phraseology had not changed, it was the way that he said it.

'I know that the decision is yours and you may consider it damned cheek on my part, but you have to have someone to defend you. I thought that I might be qualified to take the job on.'

'You? Nobody's going to be able to help me, Ian. The facts will speak for themselves.' Donald spoke quite calmly. 'I know as much military law as you do. I did rather well at Sandhurst, remember?'

'Don't you care, Donald?'

'No, I don't. You can have the job if you want it. It won't make any difference.'

'I think it will. Remember, I know you. I'm a brother officer who has served with you. I don't believe that the facts, as you call them, are in any way the deciding factor in this case.' He paused. 'They will charge you with desertion, you know that.'

'Of course. But I did resign my commission.'

'You know as well as I do that you cannot resign your commission while you are on active duty in the middle of a campaign.'

'In which case I have no defence. They'll take me out and they'll shoot me, just as I took Jimmy Grigor out. And, Ian, I don't care.'

'Whatever you say, I think that we can beat this,' said Ian. 'I know that I am no lawyer and your father is willing to employ the best that money can buy.'

'It was my father who had me arrested.'

'Of course he did. Do you imagine for one moment that Willie Bruce would treat his son in any way different from how he would treat the most humble private in the regiment? Well, would he?'

'You're right, of course. Father would not be capable of anything else.'

'The point I am trying to make,' said Ian, 'is that no lawyer knows what it is like on active service and they certainly have no conception of what it is like in battle.'

'Well?'

'The court will be comprised of officers, many of whom will have spent years on campaign. There are things that only a soldier can understand.'

Donald was surprised to find how much Ian Maclaren had matured in the five years since he had last seen him. They said that the army either made you or broke you. Well, it had made Ian, all right. As for himself, it had broken him.

Donald looked up at Ian and smiled. 'I'm very grateful, Ian. We won't bother with lawyers. You can tell whoever it is that you have to tell, that I have asked you to be Prisoner's Friend.'

Between that moment and the commencement of the trial, Ian used every moment he had studying case histories and preparing Donald's defence. He knew the facts from the summary which was presented to him as soon as it was completed, and he knew that he would not be able to dispute those facts. But dammit, Donald would not help. Ian tried every method that he could think of to persuade Donald to take an interest in his own case. In his own survival. He talked of the glen, of Donald's father and mother, of Sir Andrew his own father, all to no avail. The awful thing was that he understood, or felt that he did. He believed that Donald had just given up on life. That the Donald Bruce who had come to them from Sandhurst with such a glowing reputation, had never really existed. That was not the real man, it was a sham, a façade, created by family and fear. Not a physical fear, but that moral fear which expresses itself in an inability to say no. And all the time that Donald had been in the army he had not been able to say, 'No, this is not the life for me.'

Ian Maclaren knew that he was dealing with a very complex human being. At first he thought that Donald had changed, until he began to believe that this was not true and Donald had not changed and that the man he was now dealing with was the real Donald and that he had always been there.

It was out of these thoughts that the idea came which, though it did not conflict with those indisputable facts, gave him, Ian believed, a chance to win his case. It was not a very good chance, but it was just a chance – if the prosecution would let him get away with it.

'Captain Maclaren,' the President said, glancing sternly in Ian's direction, 'I asked you to call your first witness.'

Ian looked around the improvised courtroom. The high stone walls of the castle interior, the cold light creeping in through the arched windows, the trestle tables for prosecution, defence, and the court, all covered with grey army blankets. It was a dismal setting, relieved only by the red tunics and shining brasses of the assembled military personnel. What a lousy hole in which to try a man for his life, he thought.

'Yes, sir, I'm sorry, sir,' said Ian, rising from the defence table at which he had been seated next to Donald; Donald was feeling strange and uncomfortable wearing for the first time the fine worsted kilt, silver-mounted sporran, and gold-braided doublet of his full dress uniform. He was of course bare headed and carried no sword, that sword which had been presented to him by the Duke of Connaught at Sandhurst and which he had told Ian was to go to his younger brother Gordon when this was all over.

'Sir,' said Ian, 'for my first witness, I call Brigadier William Bruce.'

The President looked at Ian. 'That is the accused's father, is it not?'

'Yes, sir. But he was also, at the time of the alleged offence, the accused's commanding officer.'

'But not present in North Africa,' the prosecution murmured.

Willie Bruce came into the courtroom. He made a drab figure against the regimental finery of the junior officers. He wore the black, black braided frock coat and trousers and the little pillbox cap with the tiny peak, of a staff officer. He took the stand and read the oath from the card. He tried to look at Donald, but his son avoided his gaze. It was hell. At what point did love supersede duty? Willie wished that he knew. He regretted what he had done, but knew all the while that he would have done it again.

He sighed; they all avoided him now. Maud, Naomi, and even Gordon. But what the hell else could he have done?

After the preliminary questions establishing his identity and rank, Ian asked, 'Brigadier Bruce, I would like you to cast your mind back to the month of November in 1883. There was – I'm sorry, I'll rephrase that,' he said as he saw the prosecution start to rise. 'Was there an incident during that month which caused great distress to the accused?'

Again the prosecution started to rise, but the President waved him down. He knew that Ian was no lawyer, and he had no intention of allowing the boy's case to be damaged on technicalities. Willie looked at him inquiringly and he nodded.

'Aye, there was.'

'Would you please tell the court about that incident?'

'A private soldier by the name of Grigor, a member, I'm sorry tae say, of the Maclaren Highlanders, was convicted and found guilty of a most brutal murder. He was, of course, sentenced to death. My son – I'm sorry, Lieutenant, as he then was, Bruce, was unfortunate enough to be detailed as commander of the firing squad.'

The prosecuting officer rose to his feet. 'Sir, I cannot see what relevance an execution in 1883 can possibly have to the present case.'

The President looked towards Ian inquiringly.

'Sir,' said Ian, 'I think that this matter is of the utmost relevance. We are not disputing the facts as they have been presented. It may not have escaped your notice that I did not cross-examine any of the prosecution witnesses. I know all of them, and I know that the accounts which they gave of the occurrence were true, and as full as they were able to make them. But, with respect, sir, I think that I have a right to show both the motive and the reason for Captain Bruce behaving in the manner in which he did.'

'Harrumph,' said the President, turning to the Judge Advocate, a thin-faced, beaky-nosed individual wearing a legal gown over his civilian clothes.

The Judge Advocate looked towards Ian and pressed the tips of his bony fingers together. 'Captain Maclaren,' he said in his high-pitched, reedy voice, 'are you trying to establish mitigating circumstances?'

'Well, not exactly, sir.'

'Because if that is your purpose, you should have entered a plea of guilty, and this you have not done. What have you to say to that?'

Ian suddenly felt for the first time that perhaps he should have persuaded Donald to get a skilled lawyer.

'Go on, Captain Maclaren, we are waiting,' said the President.

'Sir, I honestly believe that the facts which I hope to present to the court have a great bearing on this case. I am, moreover, sure that, unless the court is fully in possession of these facts, it will be most difficult for justice to be done. Now what I am doing may not be strictly according to law, but I believe that justice is very much more important.'

'That is for the court to decide,' said the President, silencing the Judge Advocate with a glare just as he was about to speak. 'I shall permit you to continue with your present line, for the moment at least.'

'Thank you, sir,' said Ian, suddenly realizing that an experienced lawyer may have had much more difficulty in getting this evidence to the court, which, because of his lack of that experience, was going to deal with him leniently. He turned back to Willie.

'Brigadier Bruce, would you please tell the court what happened on the morning after that execution?'

'Nothing!'

'But you told me that —'

'Captain Maclaren,' said the President sternly.

'Nothing happened of any significance regarding Captain Bruce's part in that execution?'

'Och, aye,' said Willie, 'but it happened on the same afternoon.'

'Oh,' said Ian, 'I'm sorry, sir.' He felt rather foolish.

The President turned to Willie. 'Why don't you just tell us, Brigadier?'

'Aye. Well, it happened like this. I was in ma office and I sent for Lieutenant Bruce. He brought me a letter.'

'What were the contents of that letter?'

'That he wished to resign his commission.'

'I see,' said the President. 'Continue, Captain Maclaren. That is what you were trying to establish, is it not?'

'Yes, sir, thank you, sir,' said Ian. Then turning back to Willie, 'Brigadier, did you speak to the accused on that occasion?'

'I did,' replied Willie. 'I told him that he was being a damned fool.'

'And what did he tell you?'

'He told me that he was not cut oot tae be a soldier. He said that he hated killing. I canna remember his exact words, but he did tell me that he'd rather not be in the army.'

'What action did you take, sir?'

'I persuaded him to let me tear up his resignation. I could not believe that a son o' mine – but perhaps I was wrong.'

'Thank you, Brigadier,' said Ian, and he sat down.

Captain Roger Brown, the prosecuting officer, of the King's Royal Rifles, was not and never had been a line officer. He was a fully qualified lawyer who had spent almost his entire military service sitting behind a desk and appearing at military courts. He was a man of about thirty-five, with a receding chin, a high, domed forehead, and gold-rimmed spectacles. His uniform looked a little out of place on him. It wasn't that it did not quite fit, it just seemed out of character. He had presented his case in a quiet, precise manner, never raising his voice and never appearing in the least flustered. Ian had watched his obvious professionalism with something approaching envy, sparked off by his own feeling of inadequacy which had grown as the trial had progressed. Now he looked at Captain Brown as he rose and calmly tapped his notes with a long finger, and then looked up and smiled slightly at Willie Bruce.

'Brigadier,' said Captain Brown, 'was Captain Bruce a good soldier?'

'Then?'

'Yes, then.' He spoke gently. He was not there to get a conviction. He knew that justice was a rare thing and that the law, especially military law, had little to do with it. But he had to do his job. He felt the tension building, 'Please answer,' he said.

'I always say that ye canna tell a good soldier until he's been in action under fire. That's what separates the men from the boys.'

'I'll put it another way. Had you any reason to believe that Captain Bruce was not a good soldier?'

'As far as I could tell, he was the best.'

'He did, I believe, very well at Sandhurst?'

'Aye,' said Willie. 'He won the Sword of Honour.' He looked across at Donald, who again avoided his gaze.

'Now,' said Captain Brown, 'we are all aware of how distasteful it must be to be given the job of commanding an execution detail.'

'Aye,' said Willie, 'thank God I've never had tae dae it.'

'Of course. Now do you not consider that Captain Bruce's attitude on that particular occasion was an emotional and perfectly natural attitude for any man, certainly any thinking man, to have after performing such a distasteful task?'

'I did at the time,' said Willie. 'But it was more than that. You see, he couldna do the job.'

'A moment, Captain Brown,' said the President. 'Brigadier,

I would like you to explain just what was implied in your answer to Captain Brown's last question.'

'Lieutenant Bruce, as he was then, never gave the order to fire. He waited and waited. I never forgot that moment. It was Grigor himself who shouted out the word.'

There was a long silence. Ian looked down at his boots; he felt that he was making a mess of the whole thing. Captain Brown allowed the implication of Willie's last remark to register fully on the court.

When he broke the silence, Captain Brown said to Willie, 'Would you consider then that a man who failed to carry out what was, however unpleasant, a very simple duty, was lacking in courage?'

Willie glared at him. 'Nothing of the sort. Besides,' he muttered, 'it's nae for me to say.'

'Thank you, Brigadier,' said the prosecutor, and sat down.

The President glanced across at Ian. 'Have you any further questions?' he asked.

Ian wished that he had, but he could not think of any. 'No, sir,' he replied. 'No further questions.'

The President turned to Willie. 'Brigadier Bruce,' he said, 'I am still not quite sure what the defence's line is going to be. But I think there is one question which has not been asked which should have been. With the knowledge which you possess today, do you feel that you were wrong in not accepting Captain Bruce's resignation in 1883? Or do you feel that you acted correctly at the time?'

Willie looked hard at his son. Again he got no response. When he spoke, his voice was heavy with emotion. 'Aye,' he said, 'I should ha' taken it. I should ha' made the decision a lot earlier. Donald should never have been a soldier. I am every bit as responsible for him being where he is today as he is himsel'.'

'Thank you, Brigadier,' said the President. 'That will be all, sir.'

The President looked at the clock on the wall facing him. 'Captain Maclaren,' he said, 'have you any idea how much longer it will take you to present your case?'

'Not really, sir,' replied Ian. 'At least a couple of hours, possibly longer.'

'In that case,' said the President, 'I think we will adjourn and resume here tomorrow morning at ten o'clock.' There was a pause as they gathered their papers together and then, in muted conversation, the President and the members of the court left the room. As soon as they had gone, an orderly came up to Ian and handed him a slip of paper. It was from Willie Bruce, inviting him to dine with him that night at the George Hotel.

Donald's escort was hanging around, waiting to take him off to his room.

'I shall not be able to see you tonight, Donald,' said Ian. 'I'll come in at half past eight in the morning so we can have a chat before they start.'

Donald did not reply. He nodded briefly and then went to the officer who was waiting for him and left the court.

Ian looked after him as he left. He had not done very well, but what the blazes could he do? Here was a man who had already decided that the verdict would go against him. He moved like an automaton. The real trouble was that he did not care. Hell, tomorrow, perhaps, he might do better. Feeling that he had let Donald down by even offering to act for him, Ian started to gather up his notes.

While he was at this, Captain Brown came over to him.

'You'll have to do better than this, you know,' he said not unkindly.

'Well —' Ian stopped. Dare he ask the other man's advice? No, he could not.

'Look, Maclaren,' said Brown, 'I'm not the enemy. I'm not here to see your fellow convicted. My job is just to present the facts.' He smiled. 'I know you're new and this is a damnable case. I'll give you as much leeway as I dare. Good luck.'

Captain Brown went out and Ian stood looking after him feeling sick in the pit of his stomach.

10

After the arrest of his son, Willie Bruce had caught the next train north. He was determined to get to Strathglass as soon as possible. He did not even wait to greet Gordon from the boat and left behind a very angry Naomi to make the explanations. Throughout the journey he sat gazing sightlessly out of the window of his compartment. He was aware of nothing of the countryside through which he passed, the rolling broad acres of Yorkshire, the smut and grime of Newcastle and industrial Tyneside. The magnificence of the coastline around North Berwick, where the train runs in a great sweeping curve along the sea wall, meant nothing to him. Not even when he got into the Highlands and the train struggled through the passes in the Cairngorm mountains did his thoughts allow him to see the beauty of the land that was his. He had only one thought in his mind. He had to get to Maud. He had to tell her to her face, before she heard the news from any other source. He knew that the interview would be painful and that he would have to face her wrath; but he hoped and he prayed that she would understand that he could have done no other thing.

He would have had to wait for three hours at Inverness for the next train to Beauly, and he was too impatient for that. He hired a cab which took him as far as the Maclaren barracks where he borrowed a charger and galloped across country to Cluny Cottage.

His home looked so beautiful and peaceful in the late August sunshine. The rose garden was a mass of colour, the lawn inside the little wicket gate neat and well tended, and very, very green. Willie saw none of this. He could think only of the woman inside the house, and what he was about to tell her. They had reached middle age together after a turbulent and sometimes heartbreaking early marriage. For many years now, though, they had carried on an almost idyllic life together, and Willie was afraid, desperately afraid, that he was about to shatter all of that.

He arrived at Cluny Cottage just twenty-four hours after he had walked into Naomi's sitting room. He went in through the front door, bending his head as he had done ever since the low lintel had knocked his feather bonnet off many years ago. Maud Bruce was astonished at the sight of her husband whom she had not expected to see for at least another week.

'What has happened?' she asked, for it was easy to tell from the expression on his face that something was radically wrong. 'It's not Gordon. Don't tell me that something —'

'No, lassie, it's no Gordon. Maud, I want you to sit down. I have something verra serious to tell you. Please, lass, sit down.'

Slowly she did as she was bid. She knew from the turn down of his lips that whatever it was, it was not going to be pleasant listening.

Willie had not even paused to remove his greatcoat. He stood there with his back to the fire facing her as she waited.

'It's Donald,' he said.

'Donald?' There was hope in her voice and for a fleeting moment there was happiness in her eyes.

Willie could hardly bear it. Slowly he shook his head and watched her expression change again.

'You've found him?' she asked nervously. 'Is he – no, don't tell me, he's – he's dead. Willie, what is it about Donald?'

'Maud, me wee love, he's no dead. He's in the best o' health.'

Again the hope transformed her face. 'Then what can possibly be wrong?'

'He's under arrest.'

'Arrest? What for? What has he done? Who arrested him? Willie, if it's the army, you can fix it, can't you?' She looked up at him. 'Well, can't you?'

'I arrested him, Maud.'

'You?' She could not believe what she was hearing.

'Aye, me. I did it. I found him in Naomi's house. He'd been working in London for the last five years, in a jeweller's shop or something like that. Dinna look at me like that. What else could I do?'

'You arrested Donald? Your own son. What for? What had he done?'

'Maud, he'd been posted as a deserter.'

'And you didn't try to help him? Your own son? You just arrested him, just like that?'

'What the hell else could I do?'

'Your own son.'

'Maud, Donald is a soldier. Could I treat him any different to the way I'd treat any other soldier? Well, tell me, could I? Dae ye think it didna hurt me? Dae ye think I didna curse the fate that had made it me that should find him?'

'What will they do to him?' she asked, and her voice was flat and lifeless.

'They'll court-martial him. He's got to have a court martial. After that, I don't know.'

'Oh, but you do know, don't you, Willie Bruce? You know exactly what they'll do to him, only you won't tell me, and you won't tell me because you're afraid. I know what they do to deserters.'

'Don't, Maud. You're just torturing the both of us.'

'Shall I tell you what they do to deserters, Willie? Because they're going to do it to Donald. They're going to do it to our son.'

'Please, Maud.'

'You're afraid to hear, aren't you? But you're going to hear. They'll march him out in the half light and they'll tie him to a post and as the sun breaks over the horizon, they'll kill him! Your son. My Donald.' She was near to hysteria.

'Maud, please, I haven't got much time.'

'Why, have you more to do?'

'I'm going tae tell you, Maud, and you are going to listen.'

'Go on, I'm listening.'

'I'm going back to Edinburgh on the overnight train from Inverness. They're bringing Donald there. I've done ma duty as a soldier. Now I must dae everything in my power tae get the laddie off.'

She just sat there staring at him. If only she would say something, scream, break down. But she did nothing.

'Maud,' he pleaded, 'dae ye no ken how hard it is for me to ha' to tell you this? Dae ye no understand what this has done tae me inside? I feel that I hate the army and yet . . . Maud, I dinna ken who I am. Help me, Maud.'

He waited but she seemed to be turned to stone. Finally he could stand it no longer. 'Woman, have you nothing tae say?' he blurted out.

'Only this. I shall not see you until the outcome of this is known, and if the worst happens I shall never see you again. I love you, Willie Bruce. God help me, I cannot stop. But if you fail to save our son, that will be the end.' She turned away from him and then added quickly, 'You had better go now.'

He opened his mouth to speak but there were no words. Silently he turned and left her.

Ian found Willie in the company of two others in the hotel lounge. They were seated in comfortable leather armchairs at a low table with drinks in front of them. There was an elderly man who had a round, jovial face with pink cheeks and white hair, and a most incredibly clear skin. He was dressed in formal evening attire. But it was the lady sitting next to him who really caught his eye and promptly captured all of his attention.

She was small, almost tiny, and Ian thought that he had never seen anything quite so delicately beautiful. For a moment he forgot the grim purpose of his visit and only stared. She was like a piece of precious porcelain, beautifully moulded. Her fair, tending to golden, hair was drawn back from her clear forehead and from a centre parting, falling in soft ringlets which seemed to caress the sides of her face. Her deep blue eyes seemed to sparkle as they twinkled a greeting at his approach. She smiled and he couldn't take his eyes off her.

'Ah, Ian.' Willie's voice brought Ian back to reality. 'Glad you could manage to come. This is Sir Godfrey MacAdam, and his daughter Victoria.'

If he had not known Willie all his life, Ian would have thought that he was behaving as if on any normal social occasion. But knowing him as he did, he realized the tension behind the careful words and precisely enunciated syllables.

'Miss MacAdam,' said Ian, looking again at that vision. He bowed his head in acknowledgment of the introduction. 'Sir Godfrey.'

They accepted his greeting with a murmur. 'Hello, Uncle Willie,' he said. 'Thank you for asking me.'

'It would have been sooner, but I had to give evidence first.'

'Yes, of course, sir.'

'Well now, would you like a little something before we go in and eat?' And without waiting for a reply, Willie ordered a Glenlivet for Ian.

'Thank you, sir.' Ian sat down beside Miss MacAdam while the waiter brought his drink.

'This must be a very worrying time for you, Captain Maclaren,' said Miss MacAdam. 'Your uncle has been telling us all about it. He and Daddy have been spending days together.'

'Sir Godfrey,' said Willie, by way of explanation, 'is a Queen's Counsellor and a very distinguished member of the Scottish bar. I have told him everything that I can, and he thinks that you have a chance. Certainly he will be able to help you in the presentation of your case.'

'That is very kind of you, sir,' said Ian.

'Sir Godfrey,' continued Willie, 'is quite willing to take over the case but he feels, and I think that he is right, that a soldier will have more sympathy from the court than a high-powered advocate.'

'But wouldn't he be much better?'

'We don't know,' said Willie. 'After dinner, you two can put your heads together and make that decision between you.'

'Well, thanks a lot,' said Ian. 'But why do we have to wait till after dinner?'

'I want to get to know you a little first. Your uncle has given me a very strange brief, but it intrigues me; and more than that, Brigadier Bruce is a man I admire, and from what I have heard, I think I admire his son even more.' Sir Godfrey's clipped, precise speech belied his round friendly appearance. 'Just try and be yourself during dinner and then after we have eaten, you and I will have a long session. And tomorrow, one of us, probably yourself, will go in there and get that young man off.'

'I can only pray that you are right, sir.'

'Amen to that,' said Willie. 'Well, shall we go in? You two youngsters might as well go in together.'

'May I, Miss MacAdam?' said Ian, offering his arm and praying that she would not prove too much of a distraction from the task at hand.

'Thank you, Captain Maclaren.' And there was that smile again.

In spite of the undoubted effect which this charming young lady had had upon him, Ian was trying very hard to concentrate on the main purpose of this meeting. He was well aware that his overconfidence may have placed his friend's life in jeopardy. After all, this was not a game, and though anyone might lose it, Ian viewed with horror the thought that he might have to be that one.

Ian was very quiet during dinner. Most of the talking was done by Sir Godfrey, who was obviously trying to draw him out. What kept Ian even more quiet than he would otherwise have been was that Sir Godfrey discussed anything and everything except the case.

At the end of dinner Willie announced that he was going to escort Victoria home, leaving Ian and Sir Godfrey to get on with their discussion. Willie took his time, and it was approaching ten thirty, an hour and a half later, when he returned. He found them sitting together in the lounge. Sir Godfrey was smiling quietly and Ian was sipping a drink, his brow puckered, obviously deep in thought.

'Well,' said Willie anxiously as he approached them, 'how's it going?'

Sir Godfrey looked hard at Ian. 'It's going very well. What do you say, Ian?'

'I only hope that you are right, sir.'

'I think,' said Sir Godfrey, 'that this young man can win the case and I think that he ought to handle it himself.'

'You're quite sure about that, sir?' said Ian.

'Quite.'

'It's my boy's life you are playing with,' said Willie.

'I know,' said Sir Godfrey. 'But I am sure that Ian here would have a better chance than I. After all, I am a professional and a civilian and soldiers are notoriously suspicious of both. In a court martial you have to take greater cognizance of people and their emotions than you would ever dream of doing in a civilian court.'

'Well,' said Willie, and there was still a doubt in his voice, 'How do you feel about it, Ian? Can you do it?'

'I think that we have a very good chance, sir,' he replied. 'Besides, Sir Godfrey has promised me a reward if I win the case.' He smiled slightly.

'Reward?' said Willie, raising a questioning eyebrow. 'What reward?'

'I told the lad,' said Sir Godfrey, 'that if he wins the case, he has my permission to call on my daughter. But we have little time, and there is a job for you, Brigadier, one that has to be done at once.'

'Name it and it'll be done.'

'We want to call another witness, sir,' said Ian.

'I believe, at least your nephew told me, that the man we want is at this moment in the Maclaren barracks at Beauly. Have they got the telephone up there?'

'Och, aye,' said Willie, 'they have that.'

'Well, then, there's a train that leaves Inverness some time after midnight and gets into Edinburgh some time in the small hours. Do you think you could get him on that train?'

Willie looked at the clock. Whoever it was would have to ride posthaste from Beauly if he was going to make that train. 'It'll be pretty tight,' he said.

'Can it be done?' asked Ian.

'It will be done,' said Willie, 'and I'd better go and do it right awa'. What's his name?'

It was just before nine o'clock the following morning that Ian tapped on the door of Donald's room. The escort answered.

'I want to see the prisoner alone,' said Ian.

'I'll be just outside,' said the escort, and he stood aside to allow Ian to enter.

Buoyed up with renewed confidence after his long talk with Sir Godfrey, Ian went in. It was a depressing sight. Donald was sitting on his unmade bed in his shirtsleeves. The place was beginning to look more and more like a cell and Donald was looking more and more like a man who had lost all hope, and, for that matter, all interest in what was happening. Ian paused silently for a moment, feeling the confidence oozing out of him. Donald did not even bother to look up.

'Donald,' said Ian, 'I'm not sure at this point whether or not I shall ask you to give evidence. It depends entirely on what happens this morning. I have two more witnesses to call and one of them is new. Until we have had this evidence, I cannot be sure that your own evidence would be of any value to your case.'

'What are you up to, Ian?' asked Donald. 'We both know that I have very little chance. I don't suppose that it will make any difference if I give evidence or not.'

Ian ignored Donald's question. 'Your father has been working very hard and I think that he has come up with something.'

'Has he?' said Donald. 'You know that I haven't spoken to him since I was arrested?'

'I know. I think that he's a bit ashamed.'

'Ian, if you do see him, will you tell him that I know that he did what he had to do. I bear no grudge.'

'He'll be glad to hear that,' said Ian.

'Well,' said Donald as Ian paused. 'Is that all? Aren't you going to tell me what is going to happen?'

'No, I'm not,' said Ian. 'I have taken the best possible advice on this and we decided that it would probably be better if you did not know.'

'We? Who are we?'

'Sorry, Donald.'

'You've found something out, have you?'

'No, Donald, don't try and draw me. I've had some very high-powered advice and I'm going to follow it. I'll see you in court.' He smiled at his friend. 'Good luck.'

'Aye,' said Donald. 'We'll need that, all right.'

At ten o'clock exactly the court reconvened, and Ian rose to his feet.

'Sir,' he said, addressing the President, 'I shall be calling an additional witness.'

The Judge Advocate glanced sharply in the direction of the President.

'Oh?' replied the President. 'How nice of you to let us know. Captain Brown?'

The prosecutor rose to his feet. 'Captain Maclaren has already discussed the circumstances with me, sir. We have no objection.'

The President looked at the Judge Advocate, who shrugged his shoulders disapprovingly, and then back to Ian. 'Very well. Do you propose to call him now?'

'No, sir. First I wish to recall Colonel Murray.'

'Lieutenant-Colonel Murray,' said the Judge Advocate with pedantic formality and the President glared at him.

'Just a moment, Captain Maclaren,' said the President. 'Are you calling Colonel Murray as a defence witness? It appeared to us that his evidence, when he gave it for the prosecution, was very concise and very complete.'

'Sir, there are a couple of questions which I wish to ask him, and as they are on matters arising out of his evidence and do not involve anything new, I should imagine that they would be regarded by the court as cross-examination.'

'You seem well versed in the law, young man,' said the Judge Advocate, 'but you did waive cross-examination when this witness testified.'

Sir Godfrey had warned Ian about this. 'Yes, sir,' he replied, 'but it has a direct bearing on the new evidence which only came to my notice last night.'

'For heaven's sake, man,' the President snapped at the Judge Advocate, 'I don't give a damn how we get at it as long as what we end up with is the truth. Does the prosecution object?'

'No, sir,' said Captain Brown.

'Captain Brown appears to be very accommodating,' mused the President. 'Very well, you may recall Colonel Murray. There will be no need to readminister the oath.'

Colonel Murray was called and took the witness stand.

'Sir,' said Ian, 'there are a couple of points arising out of your evidence which at the time I did not think were very important. Certain facts have since come to light which render it necessary, however, that I ask you one or two further questions.'

'Get on with it, Captain Maclaren,' said the President.

'Colonel Murray, you will remember that, in your evidence, you said that the general's orderly came to you and asked if you knew the whereabouts of Captain Bruce?'

'That is correct.'

'Did you know why?'

'Not at the time.'

'But you do now?'

'Yes.'

'Please tell us.'

'I heard from various sources —'

'I'm sorry,' interrupted the Judge Advocate, 'I am afraid that this falls into the realm of hearsay.'

'Did you have reason to believe that Captain Bruce had committed some offence?'

'No, on the contrary, I gathered that he was about to be commended.'

'Thank you Colonel, that will be all.'

The President looked at Captain Brown.

'No redirect, sir,' he said.

'Call your next witness, Captain Maclaren,' said the President.

I call Private Peter Leinie of the Maclaren Highlanders.'

Peter Leinie was as changed as Ian. Straight backed and smart, he had filled out a lot in the last years. He marched into the courtroom buttons shining and kilt swaying, and stamped to attention at the witness stand, in no way showing that he had just spent a sleepless night. He took the oath.

'Your number, rank, name, and regiment,' said Ian.

'One oh four three six one, Private, Leinie, Peter, the Maclaren Highlanders, sir,' he roared.

'There is no need to shout, Private Leinie,' said the President.

'Yessirr,' said Leinie, with only slightly less volume.

'Private Leinie, I want you to cast your mind back five years to March the thirteenth, 1884. What were you doing that day?' asked Ian.

'I canna tell ye that, sirr.'

'Don't you remember?'

'I dinna ken a thing aboot dates.' Suddenly light dawned upon him. 'Was that the battle at, what the hell was it called?'

'All right, Private Leinie,' said the President, 'I think that we can take it for granted that the day in question was the day upon which Captain Bruce left his battalion.'

'Thank you, sir,' said Ian. 'Now, Private Leinie, I want you to tell the court what happened to you on that day.'

'Sirr. We had formed square. Oor company, that is, Captain Bruce's, were in the front o' the square. It was nae sae bad at first. The poor buggers in the other square was getting all the stick.'

'Watch your language, Leinie,' snapped the President.

'Yessirr, sorry, sirr. Well, some o' yon fuzzy wuzzies had a go at oor square. We soon sorted them oot and we got orders to open fire across the ground between us and the ither square. A wee group, mebbe six or seven o' them, were coming at us, and I saw them. I was young and daft at the time, and I dashed oot o' the square yeelin' ma heed off right in amaingst them. Weel, sirr, they cut me down. I mind thinking that this was it, when oot o' nowhere, there was Captain Bruce standin' ower me, and the next thing I remember, was him carting me back and dumping me in the middle o' the square where I could get tended.' He looked over at Donald. 'I never got a chance till noo, sir, but I want tae thank ye for ma life.'

Donald looked embarrassed, but there was no response to Peter Leinie's remark apart from an admonitory grunt from the President.

'So,' said Ian, 'to put it simply, you believe that you are alive today solely because of the heroism of Captain Bruce?'

'Och, aye, sirr. I ken weel that I'd ha' been as deed as mutton if it hadna been for him.'

'And this was the same day that Captain Bruce disappeared from the regiment.'

'Aye, sirr, I suppose so.'

'You are not allowed to suppose, Private Leinie,' interrupted the President. 'Just answer the question. Was it the same day?'

'Weel, sir, I dinna really ken aboot that. I was in nae condition tae ken what was happening.'

'You were badly wounded?'

'Aye, sirr, I was cut up something awfu'.'

'Thank you very much, Private Leinie,' said Ian.

Captain Brown got to his feet. 'Private Leinie,' he said, 'you say that when you were rescued from this situation into which your own foolhardiness had placed you, that Captain Bruce stood over you and dealt with the enemy around you until he was able to carry you back into the square?'

'Aye, sir, that's reeght.'

'How were you lying?'

'Eh?'

'Where were you while this was happening?'

'I was on the groond, sirr.'

'And were you face up or face down?'

'I canna remember.'

'You cannot remember whether you were lying on your back or whether you were lying on your stomach with your face pressed against the earth?'

'I suppose that's reeght, sirr.'

'So if you cannot remember that, I suggest that neither can you remember what it was you saw there. If indeed you saw anything. You could not even be sure that it was Captain Bruce that rescued you.'

'I ken fine it was Captain Bruce.' There was a note of belligerence in Leinie's voice. 'Everybody telt me that it was.'

'Thank you, that will be all.'

Captain Brown sat down and Ian got to his feet again. 'Just one more question, Private Leinie. Could it have been anyone other than Captain Bruce that rescued you?'

'No, sirr.'

Ian resumed his seat. Peter Leinie looked around uncomfortably as there was a whispered conversation between the members of the court.

'Private Leinie, do you believe that Captain Bruce is a brave officer? One with whom you would willingly go into action again?' asked the President.

'Aye, sirr, he's the best.'

'All right, Private Leinie, you may go.'

The President looked inquiringly at Ian.

'I would like to call my last witness, Regimental-Sergeant-Major Macmillan.'

Originally Ian had intended calling the R.S.M. in order to give general evidence to Donald's qualities as an officer, but Sir Godfrey had advised him that he should restrict his questioning to the events during the battle. Sir Godfrey feared that the prosecution might be able to make too much capital out of any shortcomings that Donald possessed if Ian were to be too general in his examination.

'Don't open any doors that you don't want the other side to barge through,' Sir Godfrey had said.

So Ian confined his questioning to the events in the square during the battle, and managed to get a first-hand eyewitness account of Donald's behaviour during the action. He was extremely careful to keep his questions within very strict limits and had the satisfaction of seeing that the court was obviously impressed with what they heard.

So well did Ian handle this final piece of evidence that Captain Brown did not even bother to cross-examine.

When Macmillan stood down, Ian, addressing the President, said, 'That sir, concludes the case for the defence.'

'Very well, Captain Maclaren,' replied the President. 'Do you wish to address the court now? Or would you like a few minutes to consider your closing remarks?'

'No, thank you, sir.'

'Then you may address the court now if you wish to make any statement.'

'Thank you, sir,' said Ian, MacAdam's precise instructions still in his ears. 'Gentlemen, you have before you an officer who is a highly intelligent and sensitive person upon whom you now have to pass judgment. I would beg you that in considering your verdict, you judge him, in so far as you are able, not by your standards but by his.

'Of his abilities, I think that there can be no question. His record at the Royal Military College and the obvious satisfaction which he gave to his superior officers during garrison duties in Scotland speak for themselves. I feel also that you must take into account the affection that was felt for him by those who served under him.

'However, we are, and we do not challenge this fact, dealing with an officer who, while on active service, though - and I must stress this point - not in battle, wrote a letter resigning his commission, and without waiting for its acceptance, left his unit.

'The bare facts of this case tell us that this man did in fact desert, albeit that he believed that at that point he was a civilian. The army does not permit officers to resign their commissions whilst on active service. Therefore, he was technically a deserter.

'Why, then, you will say, did we not plead guilty and simply submit our evidence in mitigation? I will answer that. This is not a simple matter and there are other considerations which, in the view of the defence, make it reasonable to return a verdict of not guilty.

'Let us first recall the evidence of Brigadier Bruce. In 1883, Brigadier Bruce was not merely Captain Bruce's commanding officer, he was also his father. I believe, and subsequent events give credence to my belief, that Captain Bruce is a man of high courage. But he did fear one thing; he feared his father.' Ian paused to allow the point to get home before continuing.

'We heard in the Brigadier's evidence that Captain Bruce did, in 1883, attempt to resign his commission. Before going overseas, he had taken a letter of resignation to his father. This, and I do not think that I am overstressing the facts, he was bullied into withdrawing. Under normal circumstances I would not try to present this as a valid defence, but these circumstances were far from normal. Had he persisted, as indeed you may consider he should have done, in resigning his commission, then I am sure that he would have found himself without, not only the regiment, but also his family and his home. One cannot divorce this case from its filial aspect. Donald Bruce was afraid of only one thing, his father.

'I maintain that Colonel Bruce, as he was then, was wrong in not realizing that the man who tendered his resignation was not a man who should be in the army. I suggest that Colonel Bruce was somewhat blinded by his very laudable love of his regiment and its traditions. He could not believe that his son did not feel the same as he did, and there was a certain selfishness in Colonel Bruce's action. Had the Colonel accepted that resignation, it would have been, in his mind, a slur upon himself and his family.

'Captain Bruce, then, went unwillingly to the Sudan with his regiment. There he behaved, as we have heard from Colonel Murray, in a most gallant and exemplary fashion. Exemplary to the point that the general officers of that campaign were at the very moment of his desertion contemplating submitting Captain Bruce's name for the highest gallantry award that this country of ours offers.

'I am aware that we have not offered any direct evidence to support this claim, but I see no reason why, should the court have any doubts about its validity, they should not take evidence from any of the three generals concerned. Gentlemen, those three eminent soldiers are far afield, performing very important tasks. Therefore, I would beg you to accept what I have said as fact. However, if you have doubts, then I would beg that your decision be delayed until their evidence can become available to this court.

'I believe that Captain Bruce is a man who loathes and detests killing. I would like you to remember that the only time he committed an act of aggression was in order to save the life of a comrade in the field. A soldier whom you have seen after five years of active service – enjoyed thanks only to the gallantry of Captain Bruce – has become a credit to the army and the regiment he serves.

'Whether or not Captain Bruce was fully aware of the law regarding his leaving his unit whilst on active service, I do not know. I do not think that Captain Bruce could answer that question and that is one of the reasons I did not call him to give evidence on his own behalf.

'I must say, gentlemen, that if Captain Bruce is guilty, then by implication his commanding officer is equally guilty. For without the action of his commanding officer, Captain Bruce would never have been in the situation in which he finds himself today, and Private Leinie would be a dead man.'

Ian stood silent for a moment looking hard at the President, and then abruptly he sat down.

In the ensuing silence, while Captain Brown was glancing through his notes, Donald turned to Ian and whispered, 'Listen, Maclaren, I did not like the things you said about my father.'

Ian glanced at him with a half smile. 'Don't worry, he did. Your likes and dislikes don't come into it, Donald. Your father will be delighted.'

Captain Brown got to his feet and made a very brief summing up, running rapidly through the facts. He pointed out, with great emphasis, that there was no dispute between the prosecution and the defence on this. He then formally asked for a verdict of guilty and sat down.

The President glanced around the court. 'Well, gentlemen,' he said, 'we will retire now and consider the case as it has been presented.'

Ian watched them as they filed out of the courtroom, intently scrutinizing the face of each officer as he passed, looking for some indication of what he thought. More than one of them glanced over towards Donald as they left. That at least was a good sign. Sir Godfrey had told him that a jury never look at a man they are about to condemn.

After the court had retired, Donald was taken away to the prisoner's room to await the verdict. Ian hurried along there and, much to his surprise, was refused admittance.

'I'm sorry,' said the officer who was guarding Donald, 'but Captain Bruce does not want to see you.'

Ian wandered off along the dim stone-walled corridors, where he was astonished to run into Gordon Bruce.

'Gordon, what the hell are you doing here?' he asked.

'It doesn't matter what I'm doing,' was the reply. 'How long before the verdict?'

'Could be minutes, could be hours. But —'

'Thanks, Ian. If you do happen to see father, don't tell him that I'm here.'

Ian was well aware that he had deeply wounded Donald by attacking his father and wondered if Gordon was aware of what he had said. However, there was nothing he could do about that now, and he headed in the direction of the mess, where he found Willie Bruce.

'I'm sorry, sir, that I said what I did, but I thought that it gave us our best chance.'

'Ye did well, laddie,' said Willie. 'Whatever happens now, I dinna think that any man could ha' done better.'

'Thank you, sir,' said Ian. 'I'm afraid I've upset Donald, though.'

'Och, that doesna matter,' said Willie. 'If we can get him off this, nothing else matters.'

'I agree, sir.'

'Besides, you were right.'

'Was I?'

'Aye, it was ma pride that did it.' He paused. 'I've got permission tae come into court to hear the verdict.'

'Have you seen Donald yet?' asked Ian. 'You know he asked me to tell you that he bore no grudge.'

'Nae, I haven't. I've been a wee bittie shamed of myself. But I'll see him after we know. For now, we can only pray. I've been daeing an awful lot o' that lately.'

'Is Mrs Bruce here?' asked Ian.

'I dinna ken, she hasna spoken tae me since I told her that Donald was arrested. I don't blame her.'

But Mrs Bruce was there. It was she who persuaded Gordon to bring her down. Unknown to any of them, she had taken a room at the White Hart Inn, not nearly so luxurious an establishment as the George, but a place where she knew that Willie would not be staying. The White Hart had also the added advantage that it lay right at the foot of a flight of steps which led directly up to the castle. She was within two minutes' walk of her son.

She had used Gordon to get her information as to how things were going, giving him strict instructions that he was on no account to approach his father. But he was to use every other means to find out what was happening and to bring her news.

After meeting Ian, Gordon had hurried down the steps to the White Hart and told Maud that the verdict might be in at any time. She had immediately put on her green velvet cloak and accompanied her younger son up the steps to the castle. There the magic mention of her husband's name gained her immediate admittance.

'Where's the court?' she asked.

'It's on the second floor,' said Gordon, 'but they won't let you up there.'

He took her into a small anteroom of the officers' mess and

left her there while he went upstairs to hear the verdict.

The court had been out for over an hour when at last the order was given to recall those taking part in the proceedings. They all took their places, with Donald at the prisoner's table, made conspicuous by the fact that he was the only person in the room whose head was bare and who carried no sword.

They all rose as the court filed back to their places. The atmosphere was tense and silent. The only sounds were made by the shoes of the court members as they walked in, echoing in the vaulted emptiness of the room. Ian scrutinized each face as they came through the door facing him but he could read nothing. They were all solemn and expressionless. He had a queasy feeling in the pit of his stomach. This was the moment of truth. God, he wished that they'd hurry and get it over with, tell him if all of his effort had been vain or not. But they did not hurry. One by one they entered, each as impassive as the next. Maddeningly slowly they stood behind their chairs and waited for the President to sit. At last he did so. This was it, thought Ian. But no. As they sat down the President started leafing through the bundle of papers he had carried in with him. It was only after what seemed an age that the President looked up in Donald Bruce's direction.

'The prisoner will approach the court,' he said.

Still Ian could read nothing in the man's expression, as, with Donald on his right and the escort on Donald's right, they approached the blanketed table. They stood to attention waiting for Donald to hear the judgment.

Infuriatingly, the President looked down at his notes once again and then, at long last, looked sternly up at Donald.

'Captain Donald Bruce,' he said, 'it is the verdict of this court that you are guilty of a most serious offence: that of leaving your unit without permission whilst that unit was on active service in defence of Her Majesty's territories overseas. Is there anything you wish to say in mitigation before sentence is pronounced.'

Ian was about to speak but was stopped by Donald who, in a firm and clear voice, replied, 'No, sir.'

'Very well,' said the President. 'You will no doubt have observed that in stating our verdict, we did not use the word "desertion" which would have carried with it a mandatory sentence of death. The charge upon which you have been convicted is a little less grave and carries the sentence of death or such lesser punishment as the court might determine.

'We have taken into consideration all that has been said by the Prisoner's Friend. And at this point we feel that you should be grateful at having had so able an advocate. Your conduct in leaving the regiment when you did was inexcusable, and must be punished.

'We have also taken into consideration the gallantry which you displayed on the very day of your offence on the field of battle. We have decided that the proposition advanced by the Prisoner's Friend, that there had been a strong possibility of you becoming the recipient of an award for gallantry, was true.

'We have also noted that for several months preceding the offence you had made it known that you had no desire to continue in the army; at one point even attempting to resign your commission. We believe that filial fear was a contributory factor in your withdrawing your resignation.

'Having then taken all of these matters into consideration, the sentence of this court, subject to confirmation by the General Officer Commanding Scotland, shall be as follows:

'Captain Bruce, you are hereby sentenced to be cashiered and to serve a term of five years' penal servitude.'

Donald was probably the only man in the room who showed no emotion at the verdict. Ian, who had hoped so much for an acquittal, felt his shoulders slump. Willie Bruce at the rear of the room took a deep breath, audible throughout the court, and bowed his head. But the President had not finished. He looked up again at Donald.

'This sentence,' he said, 'is to take effect from the date of the offence. That is all. The court is adjourned.'

The members of the court rose and filed out of the room. Willie rushed across to Donald and flung his arms around him. 'Thank God,' he said, 'Thank God, lad.'

Donald looked at his father, smiling wryly. 'I'll see you in five years,' he said.

'Did you no listen tae what the man said?' Willie almost shouted. 'If I havna got a soldier for a son, at least dinna let me have an idiot. You are free. Your sentence started in 1884. It's over. Mister Bruce, you're a civilian now. I've got a hansom waiting. Come on. We'll get over tae the George – I'm sorry, lad, but I canna take you into the mess – and we'll all have a drink tae celebrate.' He turned, a little embarrassed, to where Ian was standing, 'Ian Maclaren,' he said, 'I shall forever be in your debt.'

'Thanks, Ian,' said Donald, and he offered his hand a little shamefacedly. 'Sorry I lost my temper. I understand now that what you did, you had to do. Thank God you did it.'

'Come on, then, let's awa',' said Willie.

The three of them hurried out of the castle and into the waiting cab. As soon as they arrived at the George, Donald went up to his father's room to change into the civilian clothes which had been brought down from Strathglass. Willie meanwhile ordered the drinks.

They were just sipping their first whisky when Gordon, accompanied by Maud, came into the lounge. She ran over to her son with her arms outstretched.

'Where did ye come from?' demanded Willie. 'Nae, don't tell me, it doesna matter. You're here and the lad's safe. We got him off.'

'Yes, Willie,' she said. 'You got him off.' And she kissed him. Turning again to Donald, she said, 'Oh, Donald, I've spent more time on my knees in these last weeks than I did in all the rest of my life put together.'

'Is everything all right, Maud?'

'Yes, Willie, everything is all right.'

'Come on, now,' said Willie, 'we'll drink up, and then we'll all have the biggest, most expensive meal that this hotel has ever seen. You'll stay, of course, Ian. You're the hero of the hour.'

'Well, sir,' replied Ian, 'actually, no, I cannot. If you'll forgive me, I have a prior engagement.'

'Who with?' demanded Willie.

'Sir Godfrey promised me a reward. I'm going to claim it.'

'Oh,' said Willie, laughing. 'The beautiful Victoria.'

'Yes, sir,' said Ian. 'I hope you understand.'

'I do that. She's a bonny wee lass.'

'I say, Ian,' piped up Gordon. 'Who's Victoria? I always thought you were rather keen on Naomi.'

'I was,' said Ian. 'But that was a long time ago.'

11

The spring of 1891 was exceptionally mild. The tight green buds of the silver birch trees were already bursting into leaf, the broom was in flower giving great patches of brilliant yellow among the rocks and crags, and the winter snow had receded until only the very tops of the mountains retained their white winter coating.

The salmon had started to run up the River Glass and Sir Andrew Maclaren would spend many a day sitting on a wooden stool by the river bank, vainly trying to persuade one of the silvery creatures to take his fly. Frankie Gibson, when he could get away from the barracks, would creep stealthily down to a secluded spot in the gorge at Aigas with his otter board and take a fish with consummate ease. Of course, everyone knew that Frankie did just that; it was the habit of a lifetime. And when Lady Maclaren asked her son to get her a salmon for the Great Day, he had replied testily, 'Why don't you ask Frankie Gibson?'

'All right, I will,' she replied.

She did and Frankie obliged with a fine eighteen-pounder the day before the Event.

Culbrech House was bursting at its ancient seams as the clan gathered for the Great Event. It was many years since the old house had seen a wedding. Andrew had married his bride in

St Margaret's, Westminster. Shortly after that his sister Margaret had married old Sir Henry Maclaren's English factor, Richard Simpson. The regiment had been in India at the time, having left shortly after Andrew's wedding, and since then there had been nothing. Andrew's other sister Jean had remained a spinster.

Andrew had broken all the rules, but he had managed by dint of persuasion and just a suggestion of bribery to convince Sir Godfrey MacAdam that it would be a good idea for his daughter to marry in the Highlands where she would be fated to spend most of the rest of her life. That eminent advocate, whose quite considerable wealth had been accumulated in no small way by a consummate ability to always allow someone else to pay the bill, had, after an insincere show of reluctance, agreed.

As for Victoria herself, she had stated categorically that she did not care where she got married.

It had been a gentle courtship in spite of its brevity. It had flowed serenely along conventional lines until the MacAdams' first visit to Culbrech House. That was when Victoria had met Robert.

Ian had not seen his younger brother for well over six years. When they finally met again – it was just after Ian's return from Edinburgh – he barely recognized him. Robert had been a tall, gangling youth when he went off to Sandhurst. But now, at six feet four inches, he towered over them all. When he stood apart, he did not look his height, so beautifully proportioned was his body. A great gentleness was probably his most outstanding virtue, though if you asked him, he would bend a six-inch nail with his bare hands; not in any spirit of pride, but because you had asked, and Robert always wanted to please. Robert had never known his mother; she had died before he even had a name. And Andrew, probably more from a feeling of guilt than for any other reason, had always over-indulged his younger son.

In the nicest possible way, Robert oozed charm; he was unable ever to say no to anyone, and he found the three hundred pounds a year that his father allowed him totally inadequate for his needs. But everybody loved Robert; nobody minded his extravagances. Robert never saw beyond the moment in which he lived. If he took a girl out to dinner, it had to be the best and most expensive that money could buy. Not because he wished to impress, but because he wanted to please. He would never ignore a call for help, whether it was to pick up a lady's glove, or to chop a winter's supply of wood for an ageing pensioner on his father's estate. Robert was one of those people who tried to be all things to all men; the only trouble was that he could not afford it. But the men admired him and the women adored him.

Ian had seen the danger signs the moment Robert and Victoria were introduced. There was nothing unusual in Victoria's reaction to Robert. She reacted as practically every other woman did when they met him for the first time. But this had hurried Ian in his resolve, and within three days of her meeting Robert, Ian had proposed, been accepted, and the date arranged.

They would all be there at the wedding in St Andrew's Cathedral in Inverness. The Bishop himself was going to perform the ceremony. Staunch Church of Scotland though the Maclarens were, they could not deny this charming girl the right to be married in her own, Episcopal, church. Ian's father, grandmother, and two aunts – Aunt Jean who would pray for him because she disapproved of marriage, and Aunt Margaret now married and with a family of her own, who with her husband practically ran the Maclaren estate – all would be there to witness the marriage nonetheless. Margaret would give him a lecture on economics. Of course, the Bruces would be there. Willie and Maud and Gordon. Naomi was arriving from London, apparently bringing someone with her. As for Donald, he had been invited, but no one was quite sure whether or not he would arrive and face all of his ex-brother officers again, for of course the whole officers' mess and the senior of the senior N.C.O.s were coming.

Donald, after a fleeting visit to Strathglass, waiting for the sentence of the court martial to be confirmed, had returned to London. There he had met a very surprised Mr Wilson on the step of the shop in Bond Street. Mr Wilson had taken him out to lunch at Rules, where Donald had told him the whole story.

'Well,' said Mr Wilson after he had heard Donald out, 'one

can only take people as they find them, and I have found you a good and reliable employee. If you wish to come back, you will be more than welcome. Though I must confess, I shall find it very strange calling you Mr Bruce, Mr MacDonald.'

Donald was very moved by his old employer's belief in him and expressed his gratitude.

'No, Mr – er – Bruce, I am the one who should be grateful,' was the reply. 'Now, Donald, we will just pretend that none of this ever happened and start again just where we left off. I shall see about the new shop sign tomorrow.'

Gordon Bruce, who was to be Ian's best man, had collected him that morning and taken him to rooms in the Caledonian Hotel in Inverness. He had done this because he had to get Ian out of the house before the bride and her party arrived on the afternoon before the wedding. It was, of course, Robert who had arranged the stag party.

Ian had got out of the house just in time. Within half an hour of his departure, the MacAdams had arrived. Lady MacAdam was a small mouselike little person who hardly ever spoke and always agreed with everybody. She would inevitably reply, 'Quite' to any suggestion that was made, and then observe her questioner through a pair of lorgnettes which she always carried on a black cord around her neck. They had brought with them only one servant, Michelle, who was Victoria's French lady's maid. As soon as they arrived and had been greeted by Andrew and his mother, they were shown to their rooms in the east tower, and then brought down and introduced to the Bruces.

It was Andrew who had insisted that Willie and Maud should come and stay with them over the period of the festivities. His wish was engendered by panic at the thought of being shut up in his own house with a lot of women. He was determined that, if his home was going to be turned into a female enclave, at least he would have Willie to lend support to himself and Sir Godfrey.

Lady Maclaren, upon whom the bulk of the preparatory work had fallen, had enlisted the aid of Maud Bruce. As soon as the MacAdams had unpacked, Maud whisked Lady MacAdam into Inverness to the Station Hotel to spend an hour with the banqueting manager in order to obtain her ladyship's approval for the arrangements for the wedding breakfast. Lady MacAdam listened to all that the manager had to say, and then raised her lorgnettes and said, 'Quite,' in an approving tone, so everything, Maud presumed, was all right.

Closeted in his study with Willie, Andrew asked if he knew whether or not Donald was coming.

'I've nae idea,' said Willie, 'we've hardly heard from him since the trial.'

'He went back to his jewellery business?' asked Andrew.

'Aye, he did that,' said Willie. 'Naomi told us, but more I canna tell you for I don't know myself.'

'I wouldn't be surprised if he doesn't come,' said Andrew.

'Why?'

'After all, it would be quite a strain for him to have to face the regiment again.'

'He's no a coward,' said Willie.

'I wasn't suggesting that he was,' replied Andrew, 'at least, not in the way we normally judge cowards. But just because you can face an enemy does not mean that you have the courage to face the disapproval of your friends. I know that only too well.'

Willie looked up at him quickly. He was well aware of what it was to which Andrew referred. For Andrew would have married Maud had he not been faced with social ostracism in the event of marriage to a woman who was carrying a bastard Eurasian child.

'Aye,' said Willie, 'you're right, of course. I must say that I'm damned glad that you are.'

They smiled at each other and Andrew poured another whisky. 'We'll just have to wait and see if he is going to show up then?'

'Right,' said Willie. 'Slainte.'

That evening, after Maud and Lady MacAdam had returned from Inverness, they gathered in the small dining room for dinner. Lady Maclaren and Andrew sat at the foot and head of the table respectively. Sir Godfrey was on Lady Maclaren's right, and Willie Bruce on her left. Lady MacAdam and Maud were on either side of Andrew. Between Sir Godfrey and Maud were seated Jean Maclaren and Richard Simpson, with

Richard's wife Margaret opposite them between Willie and Lady MacAdam.

They had a new butler, Seamus McLeod. He had adopted the mantle of MacKay, who had retired two years previously to a small house on the estate. McLeod was a veteran of twenty-four years' service with the regiment. He had risen to the rank of sergeant and had had his eye on MacKay's job for some time. An intelligent man, he had taken the trouble to hang around Culbrech House and pick up various details of what the work entailed, long before he applied for the job. He was tall and thin, cadaverous in fact, and he lacked the lobe of his right ear; it had been sliced off by a bullet while he was serving in India. When he started he retained a disturbing habit of noisily stamping to attention whenever addressed by a member of the family. After a little chat with Lady Maclaren he stopped stamping, but he still stood at attention. He had had to learn also that one did not speak to the other servants in the same tone and volume as one shouted at recruits on the barrack square. But he learned quickly and soon settled down and gave the same efficient service which had been the hallmark of MacKay.

McLeod began serving the meal assisted by the footman. Conversation was scattered and spasmodic; the army and the law had little common ground. And they in their turn had even less with the agricultural Simpsons or the professional spinsterhood of Jean Maclaren. In spite of this, both Andrew and his mother did their best with Sir Godfrey and Lady MacAdam.

Jean Maclaren, dressed in sombre, shapeless, deep brown, with touches of grey creeping into her lacklustre red hair, sat silently through the first two courses, and Richard Simpson on her right, knowing his sister-in-law's feelings towards any sort of relationship involving men and women, did not risk trying to draw her into conversation.

Over the soup Margaret informed the assembled company that the spring lambing had gone well and that they already had fourteen new calves, nine heifers, and five bullocks. This piece of information was of interest to no one but herself and her husband. Of course, it should have been of interest. Andrew, who now owned the estate, should at least have made an effort to know what was going on. But Andrew was not interested. The estate was well husbanded by the Simpsons and showed a handsome profit each year, and Andrew felt, probably wisely, that for him to interfere would only complicate matters. Andrew spent most of his time either out on the hill with a ghillie, or reading military history and indulging himself as the father figure of the regiment. His mother showed even less interest than Andrew did. Lady Maclaren always maintained that her duties were to be devoted to the memory of her husband, to her children, and to her home, and that was sufficient.

They were halfway through the fish, that fine piece of salmon poached by Frankie Gibson and then poached by their cook, when McLeod came over and whispered something to Andrew.

'Oh, good,' said Andrew, 'bring them right in and tell James to lay an extra two places. We'll wait for the main course.'

They all looked inquiringly at Andrew.

'Who is it, dear?' asked Lady Maclaren.

'Donald has arrived.'

'Ah,' said Willie, rising. 'Shall I —'

'No,' said Andrew, 'they've gone up to their rooms for a moment. They'll be down presently and McLeod's bringing them straight in.'

'They?' said Maud. 'Is Naomi with him?'

'No,' said Andrew, 'but there is a lady with him.'

'What lady?' asked Maud.

'I'd better let Donald tell you that,' replied Andrew.

'Oh, dear,' said Lady Maclaren, 'where am I going to put her?'

'Surely we can sort that out after dinner, can't we, Mother?'

'I suppose so, but it's very confusing.'

Just then the door opened and revealed Donald accompanied by the lady, who was a stranger to everyone present.

She was neither small nor tall, plain nor pretty. Her hair was not dark, nor was it fair. But her eyes were beautiful, large, and brown, and gentle and sincere. She appeared to be possessed of a calm and a maturity far in advance of her obvious youth as she stood there in her grey travelling costume, slowly glancing round the assembled company as if she was deliberately implanting each face in her mind. She was lightly holding Donald's hand, not seeming, in any sense, to require his protection but rather giving him of her strength for the ordeal of facing his family. Slowly, she allowed the tiniest of smiles to cross her lips. It was a signal, the gentlemen rose.

She looked up at Donald and he, still holding her hand, took her straight over to Maud. 'Mother,' he said, 'I want you to meet Brenda, my wife.'

'Good God!' said Andrew.

'What?' said Willie.

'Thank goodness, I don't have to worry about a room,' said Lady Maclaren.

Maud slowly rose to her feet.

'How do you do, Mrs Bruce,' said Brenda.

'Welcome, my dear,' said Maud, and she kissed Brenda gently on the cheek. 'Donald, you should have told us.'

'I know, mother, but we didn't want any fuss.'

'Bring your lassie over here and let me have a look at her,' said Willie from the other end of the table.

He walked around behind Lady Maclaren to meet them.

'So,' he said, taking both of Brenda's hands in his, 'you're ma daughter-in-law.'

'Yes, I am,' replied Brenda, calmly returning his gaze. 'So you must be Donald's father.'

'Aye,' said Willie, 'I suppose it follows.' He was not a little surprised at the calmness of the young woman before him, and the directness of her tone impressed him. 'You had better come and sit beside me. I think that you and I should get to know each other and I'm sure we have a lot to talk about.'

'But —' interposed Lady Maclaren, sensing that her table placings were about to be upset.

'It's all right, Mother,' said Andrew. 'I'm sure that Willie is right.'

'Oh, very well,' she replied disapprovingly. 'In that case, Donald, you had better sit next to Sir Godfrey. I do not think that you two have met.'

'No, we haven't,' said Donald as he took his place. 'I believe that I am very much in your debt, sir.'

'I think not,' said Sir Godfrey, 'but it is nice of you to say so.'

There was a long silence interrupted by Lady Maclaren, ever sensitive of the charged atmosphere in the room. 'McLeod,' she said, 'I think you should serve the main course now.'

'Very good, my lady,' replied McLeod, and out came the inevitable venison.

They were halfway through the main course before Willie broke the silence again. 'Donald,' he said, 'have you heard from Naomi? She was supposed to be coming up.'

'Oh, yes,' replied Donald. 'She's here.'

'Here?' said Lady Maclaren. 'At Culbrech House?'

'Oh, no,' replied Donald. 'We travelled up together and went straight to Cluny Cottage. That's why we are so late. We didn't know that you were all here. Naomi decided that she was tired, so they are staying there for the night. They'll be in Inverness in plenty of time tomorrow morning.'

'They?' said Andrew.

'Good God,' said Willie, 'dinna tell me that she's brought a husband.'

'Oh, no,' said Donald, smiling. 'He's a friend.'

'Oh, dear,' said Lady Maclaren. 'Donald, did you say "he"?'

'Yes, I did.'

'Oh,' said Lady Maclaren, and there was the faintest note of disapproval in her voice.

'Donald,' said Maud, 'you had better tell us, what is his name?'

'John Wilks,' said Brenda. 'You may have heard of him.'

'You don't mean John Wilks the actor?' said Andrew.

'That's right,' said Brenda.

'Good heavens,' said Lady Maclaren, 'an actor, whatever next?'

'He is a very famous actor,' said Maud, defending her young. 'I believe that he has even appeared before the Queen at Windsor.'

'Oh,' declared Lady Maclaren, indicating that all was therefore well.

'I am sure that Sir Godfrey and Lady MacAdam have heard of him,' continued Maud.

'Yes, indeed,' said Sir Godfrey, 'wasn't he that fellow we saw at the Lyceum in Edinburgh playing Richard the Second? Quite brilliant, I recall.'

'Quite,' said Lady MacAdam.

'Is Maggie at Cluny?' asked Willie, referring to their housekeeper, Maggie Buchannan.

'Yes,' replied Donald. 'Maggie's looking after them.'

'Och, weel, I suppose that it will be all right,' said Willie, glancing at Maud, who was looking a trifle worried. 'We'll meet him at the reception tomorrow.'

Again the conversation flagged.

After the ladies had gone into the withdrawing room the atmosphere eased appreciably and the men almost visibly relaxed. The port had been around the table, and the loyal toast had been drunk and cigars lit, when Willie turned to Donald.

'You ken that you should have let your mother know,' he said.

'I suppose that I should have, really,' said Donald, 'but we were in rather a hurry.'

'Oh,' said Willie knowingly, but without censure in his tone.

'No, Father,' said Donald. 'You're wrong. As far as we know, you are not yet destined to be a grandfather.'

'Sorry,' said Willie as the rest of them laughed. 'Well, how long are you going to be with us?'

'Only a couple of days, Father. I'm sorry that it can't be longer.'

Willie grunted. 'And how long have you been married?'

'Only two weeks.'

'I still say that you should ha' let us know.'

'Your father's right,' said Andrew. 'I think you should tell us a little more.'

'All right, Uncle Andrew,' said Donald. 'It was all rather sudden. I found out quite recently that I shall be leaving the country the week after next. Brenda and I decided to do it rather quickly so that we could go out together as man and wife.'

'Well, come on, laddie,' said Willie. 'Tell us where you're off tae?'

'We're going to South Africa, sir.'

'And what will you be doing there, might I ask?'

'There's been a lot of trouble in South Africa,' said Richard Simpson, 'most of it stirred up by bloody politicians.'

'Yes, I know,' said Donald. 'But things are quiet now. I don't think that there's going to be any risk.'

'I would not be too sure of that,' said Andrew. 'Whereabouts are you going?'

'Kimberley, sir.'

'Kimberley?' said Willie. 'That's where the diamonds come from, is it no?'

'That's right,' replied Donald. 'As you know, I've been working the jewellery business for several years now. I spent a lot of time studying diamonds, sort of specializing in them. My father-in-law —'

'Aye, that's a point,' said Willie. 'Who is your father-in-law?'

'Mr Wilson? Well, he founded the business. I'm a junior partner now. He's a very fine person, I'm sure that you'll agree when you meet him. Well, he decided that since the diamond business is booming, we ought to open an office in Kimberley where we could buy our stones much cheaper, direct from the mines. That's what Brenda and I are going to do.'

'Well, lad, I wish you every success,' said Willie. 'She looks a bonny lassie, and I hope that you'll tak' guid care o' her.'

'Oh, I shall, Father, I can promise you that. We love each other very much.'

'That's capital,' said Andrew, 'Come and see me after we get rid of the bride and groom tomorrow. I'll have a little wedding present for you. Well, gentlemen,' he continued before Donald was able to protest, 'shall we join the ladies?'

12

Inverness Episcopalian Cathedral stands foursquare on the north bank of the river Ness which drains Loch Ness into the Moray Firth. It is built of the same pink Moray sandstone as are the castle standing atop the hill on the other bank, and the home and barracks of the Maclaren Highlanders at Beauly. Twin turrets flank the west door giving it an air of a miniature Notre Dame de Paris.

'I now pronounce you man and wife,' said the Bishop, and the deed was done.

Ian had only a hazy recollection of what had preceded those words. He had, he assumed, remembered his part and made the correct responses, and the plain gold band on Victoria's finger assured him that he was now a married man.

He had arrived at the cathedral nursing a massive headache brought on by the overdose of alcohol with which he had been plied the previous night. The entire officers' mess had forgathered at the Caledonian Hotel determined that his last night of bachelorhood should be memorable, though Ian doubted if he would ever remember anything beyond the fourth or fifth whisky. Together they had drunk and sung until the small hours, and Ian, after losing all sense of time and happening, had been surprised to find himself lying on his bed, still fully clothed, when Gordon came to collect him and help him dress at half past eight that morning.

He glanced down at his bride with her small, delicate face peering out from the clouds of silk and organza lace, her veil now thrown back to reveal her features, and he smiled. She returned his smile for just a fleeting moment and then glanced demurely down. Together they turned and started the long walk down the nave, Victoria on Ian's arm. They saw no one; they were conscious only of each other.

The weather had been kind to them. The sun was glinting through the tall elms as they came out through the west door and through the arch of the sparkling blades of the crossed broad-swords of Ian's brother officers, all of them a mass of scarlet and gold and tartan in their full dress uniforms, and all of them just a little worse for the jollifications of the previous night. Down through the arch of the twenty crossed swords they went to where their open landau, newly polished and sparkling and decked with white ribbon, was waiting.

Ian helped his bride into the carriage and seated himself on her right, and they were off on the short journey across the river Ness, and then up the little hill to the Station Hotel.

The guests hung back respectfully to allow the couple time to get there and be in position to greet them when they themselves arrived for the reception. The landau, drawn by a matched pair of magnificent white hackneys and under their coachman's expert control, took no more than three minutes to get them to their destination. There the hotel manager, a dapper individual of medium height and sporting a neat black moustache under thinning, well-groomed dark hair, was waiting to greet them.

They went in through the main doors and stood at the foot of the sweep of the staircase which flowed away behind them, arching around until it reached a balcony which led off on either side to the upper floors.

'We have prepared room 201 which is the first on the right upstairs as a changing room for Mrs Maclaren. Her things are already there and unpacked, and you will find Captain Maclaren's clothes in the dressing room attached.'

'Thank you very much,' said Victoria, colouring slightly at being called Mrs Maclaren for the first time.

'Victoria Maclaren,' murmured Ian. 'How do you like the sound of it?'

'I like it very well,' she replied softly. 'But this is going to be the difficult part. I still have not met nearly half the people who are here.'

Of necessity the greater proportion of the guests had filled the bridegroom's side of the cathedral. Only a couple of dozen of Victoria's friends and relations had made the long journey north. However there was little time for discussion, as they had barely taken their places when Andrew, accompanied by Gordon Bruce and Lady MacAdam, approached them through the open doors followed by a host of other guests.

Andrew took Victoria's hand and planted a paternal peck on his new daughter-in-law's cheek; he felt he ought to say something, so he paused for a moment before grunting and moving on, having said nothing.

Lady MacAdam looked at the pair, blinking prodigiously, and then, as the tears came, shook her head and followed Andrew. Lady Maclaren was made of sterner stuff. She kissed Victoria noisily, then turned to her grandson.

'You have done very well, Ian,' she said. 'You have a most beautiful bride. See that you look after her.'

'Thank you, Grandmama, I shall,' replied Ian.

'Thank you, Lady Maclaren, I know he will,' said Victoria.

'Oh, no, no, no, no,' said Her Ladyship. 'I am Grandmama now, or Granny, if you prefer it. Never forget that you are family, you are a Maclaren now.'

They smiled at each other as Lady Maclaren moved away. Gordon Bruce claimed the best man's privilege and kissed the bride full on the lips, and then shook Ian warmly by the hand. 'You're a lucky devil,' he said, and started to move away.

'Hang on,' called Ian. 'I think you are supposed to stay with us, aren't you?'

'Oh, am I?' replied Gordon. 'Very well, then,' and he took up a position just behind Ian on his right.

'I think,' continued Ian, 'that the best man has to hang about in case we need anything.'

Led by Sir Godfrey, in they came, in a flood by now, over a hundred of them, to pay their respects to the newlyweds. They crowded in through the doors and waited, a most colourful throng, with a good half of the men in uniform, until it was their turn to shake hands and mutter some trite little pleasantry before passing into the banqueting hall.

There was a lull and it seemed as if the last guest had arrived.

'Is that everybody, Gordon?' asked Ian.

'I don't know,' said Gordon, 'but it looks like it. We might as well go in.'

They were about to move when Gordon continued, 'Hang on here for a minute. I'll go ahead and tell them that you're coming.' And he left them.

No sooner had Gordon left them than the doors swung open again and a couple entered. Victoria looked up at Ian, surprised.

'Is she one of the party?' she asked. 'How beautiful she is. Like a princess.'

Ian glanced at the approaching couple and recognition flooded his mind. She did indeed look like a princess. She was on the arm of John Wilks, tall and distinguished and just a little flamboyant in an immaculate frock coat with a grey cravat held in place with an enormous diamond pin. But it was the woman that they were looking at.

She was dressed in a purple and brown sari trimmed with gold which flowed across her body revealing the delicate contours of her figure as she gracefully came towards them. Victoria was sure that she was an Indian princess, and yet she did not look quite Indian. Her creamy skin was a little too light, and her carriage more self-assured than you would expect to find in an Eastern lady, no matter how highly born. She was by any standards incredibly beautiful.

Gently and gracefully she seemed to float across the floor towards them. What was it that he had said that evening after the court martial? It was impossible? It was a long time ago?

This fabulous creature, now standing before him and smiling a greeting, was many things, and all of them were beautiful. Ian glanced quickly at the doll-like creature beside him to whom he was committed for the rest of his life, and then again at the woman who was now extending her hand in greeting.

'Congratulations, Ian,' she murmured in her low, soft voice – a voice that flooded him with memories of those nights of passion at the Priory Inn and made him forget for a split second that he was standing there with his wife of less than an hour. 'You have a beautiful bride,' she concluded.

'This is Victoria,' said Ian. 'A very dear friend, Naomi Bruce.'

'May I present Mr Wilks,' said Naomi.

'How do you do,' said Ian, forcing himself to take his eyes off Naomi.

'How kind of you to come, Mr Wilks. You will find many of your admirers, among whom I number myself, are here today,' said Victoria.

'Charmed, ma'am,' said Mr Wilks in a resonant tone. 'If I may be permitted, I must say that you make a handsome pair. I understand that you and Naomi are old friends.'

'Oh, yes,' said Naomi before Ian could reply; and, echoing his words, 'very dear friends.'

'Naomi and I,' said Ian to Victoria, 'are cousins by adoption. You must have heard me talk about her.'

'Come, my dear,' said Mr Wilks, 'I fear that we are keeping the bridal pair from their other guests.' And he led Naomi towards the banqueting hall.

Inside the banqueting hall, all cream and gilt with its windows screened from the view of the vulgar by heavy salmon-pink curtains, its walls supported by pillars whose ornate and intricate plaster capitals moulded into a magnificent ceiling, all was ready. Down each of its sides the room had long tables swathed in snow-white linen and weighted down with every imaginable kind of meat and game and sweets too numerous to mention. At the far end, and in the centre of the room, stood a smaller table on which rested the four-tiered wedding cake. The room was by now a mass of people circulating among each other, shrouded by an intense hum of conversation as they smiled and accepted glasses of champagne handed around by the hotel staff.

Gordon Bruce pushed his way into the room and managed to find himself a chair. He stood on this and called, 'Ladies and gentlemen.'

There was absolutely no response.

'Ladies and gentlemen!!' he shouted at the top of his voice, and this time they heard him, and he waited until the conversation had died down before continuing: 'It is my most pleasant duty as best man to ask you to welcome the bridal pair.'

There was a polite murmur of pleasure and the company drew to the side of the room to leave a clear aisle for Ian and Victoria.

Gordon got down from his chair and signalled to the two periwigged footmen at the double doors. They opened the doors and a gentle handclap started, only to die away and give place to a series of gasps as Naomi Bruce and John Wilks walked into the room.

In the ensuing silence they moved a few paces inside the door and then stopped, a slight smile playing around Naomi's lips. Suddenly John Wilks's voice boomed out in carefully enunciated tones.

'Great heavens, me dear,' he said, 'it looks as if we have trumped someone's ace. We had better make ourselves scarce.' And he steered Naomi over to the side of the room.

As they moved, Ian and Victoria came in to a somewhat subdued welcome as half the guests speculated on the identity of the pair who had preceded them.

It was some time later, after the speeches and the cutting of the cake, during that hiatus while the bride and groom changed into travelling clothes, that Willie managed to buttonhole Naomi.

'I don't think that you have met Mr Wilks,' said Naomi as Willie approached.

'How de ye do?' said Willie, glaring at Naomi. 'Naomi, what the de'il do ye mean, coming here dressed like this?'

'Like what, father?' said Naomi, wide eyed and innocent. 'Don't you think that it is attractive?'

'You know fine that it's bonny, and I'm damned sure that you ken well what it does tae your mother!'

'What?'

'It makes her remember. It makes her remember things that are best forgot.'

'You mean,' said Naomi, 'that it reminds her that I am her daughter?'

'You can put it any way you like,' growled Willie, 'but there are things in your mother's life that are best forgot and you know fine what those things are.'

'Would you rather we left?' she demanded, stung by Willie's disapproval.

'That would only make things worse.'

'In that case we shall stay.'

'Aye,' said Willie, 'you stay, but I want you to know that I am not verra pleased wi' the way that you have behaved today. Excuse me, Mr Wilks,' and Willie left them.

Ian had taken his bride away to the room which had been set aside for them. Victoria's travelling clothes had been carefully laid out on the bed and Ian's civilian suit in the adjoining dressing room. When they went in and shut the door, Ian felt all the awkwardness of adolescence returning to him as he looked at this girl with whom he was destined to share the rest of his life. He knew what was expected of him, but he was suddenly afraid. The only other woman in his life had been Naomi, and she had done all the leading. Now it was up to him, and he felt lost and unsure. Naomi had been an exciting adventure, with the added spice of illegality, but now of course everything was legal, and the marriage bed awaited him.

They were to catch the afternoon train to Perth. There they would spend the night at the Royal George before catching the morning train for London where they would have two weeks before Ian had to return to the regiment. Tonight was scary, but it was still a long way off and he told himself that he did not have to worry about his performance just yet. It was not that he did not want her; it was just that Naomi's arrival had given him a feeling of guilty nostalgia.

He had grown up in the past few years, but he had grown up in a society devoid of women. When he had left Scotland for Africa, he had left nursing what he believed to be the great love of his life. He had come back and found Victoria and believed that that love was all over, and that Victoria must be the one. But now he had seen Naomi again, and with the vision of her had flowed back all of those erotic memories of their brief relationship.

He had undressed when he heard a small voice from the adjoining room.

'Ian.' There was a pause, and then again, 'Ian, Ian, come here.'

'I can't, I'm not changed yet,' he said, viewing his nakedness.

'Don't worry about that,' said Victoria's voice. 'Come in just as you are. You're my husband, remember?'

Among the things which had been laid out for him was a heavy quilted blue dressing gown. He quickly slipped into this and went into the main bedroom. As he stepped inside the room, he gasped, for his bride was standing there completely naked. She had closed the curtains and the contours of her body were lit by the flickering light of the big fire burning in the grate.

He stood there transfixed, staring at her until she cast her eyes down and covered her full breasts with her hands crossed in front of her.

'I thought that you would like to see,' she murmured, without catching his gaze. She waited, but he could not speak.

'Ian,' she said. 'Do you like what you see?' Still he could not reply. 'It's a little chilly like this,' she said. 'Won't you come closer to me?'

Slowly he took the three or four paces which separated them until her body was brushing his dressing gown. Without looking up, she slipped her hands inside his robe and he felt her fingers fluttering over his back as she investigated his nakedness. Ian put his arms around her and drew her close so that his robe enveloped them both.

'Hello, husband,' she said, looking up at him with a little smile. 'Are you going to make your bride your wife?'

Still he could find no words. He led her over to the bed where they lay together, still for a minute or two, and then he took her.

He tried to be gentle, but was astonished at the ferocity with which she responded to him. Her strong young body moved beneath him and she moaned quietly as they panted in unison until, as they reached their climax, she gave forth a long 'Aaaaaah' and then was still.

Very gently he withdrew from her. 'Oh, Victoria,' he said. 'Oh, Victoria.'

The matter-of-fact tone of her voice brought him back to reality. 'Come on, Ian, we'd better get dressed, they'll be waiting for us.'

'Was it all right?' he asked.

'It was delicious, my darling,' she replied. 'Absolutely

beautiful. I'm not a virgin, you know. Mummy and Daddy think I am, but I'm not. Do you mind?'

'What right have I to mind?' he asked.

'Well, it's different for a man, isn't it?'

'Is it?'

'You are not a virgin,' she said. 'You don't have to tell me, I know.'

'How do you know that?' he asked, feeling guilty.

'Was the Indian lady as nice as me?' she asked.

Oh, my God, thought Ian, she knows. 'But that was years ago, how do you know about it?'

'A woman does.'

'She was the only one.'

'Then, my dear,' said Victoria, 'she will always be very special to you because she was the first. No,' she said as he was about to speak. 'Don't ask me to forgive where there is nothing to forgive. Just remember this, I am truly your wife now that we have consummated our marriage. All that has gone before is of no consequence, there is nothing to forgive or to be forgiven. I love you and I am yours.'

'My darling, what can I say except to thank you, and to tell you that there is nothing I would not do for you.'

'In that case,' she said, suddenly jocular, 'we had better get dressed and go down or they will surely know what we have been doing.'

They dressed hurriedly, he in a grey frock coat and she in a brown worsted travelling costume; it was dark brown and trimmed with little bits of even darker brown velvet. He looked at her, wondering. Could this poised, self-possessed lady — But then, she could be, because she was, the same as the voluptuous animal he had known only minutes ago.

'Ian,' she said, 'you must stop looking at me like that.'

'Why?'

'If you don't, when we go down it will show.'

'Is it so obvious?' he asked.

'You're a man, darling,' she said. 'Men are always obvious.'

He smiled at her. 'Shall we go? I'll try not to tell them, but I really don't care.'

'Come on,' she said, with a half laugh, and put her hand into his.

They walked out of their room and down that beautiful staircase, across the lobby, and into the banqueting hall.

Ian knew then that everything was all right. He could face Naomi now. He glanced at his wife and murmured something.

'What did you say, dear?' she asked.

'I said that everything is all right. I love you, Victoria. Thank you for marrying me.'

2
The Great Boer Wars

1

It was a glorious afternoon in the summer of 1899. Major General Willie Bruce was standing with Sir Andrew Maclaren looking out of the windows of the library at Culbrech House down on to the sunlit lawns. Outside, amidst the hum of the bumblebees and the scent of the newborn roses, Andrew's grandchildren were playing. Emma, the eldest, was seven. Henry, named after his great-grandfather, was six. Albert was four, Phillipa three and wee James in his high perambulator, not yet a year old.

Victoria had gone out to spend an hour with her children and they were enthusiastically throwing a large woolly ball from one to the other.

It was two years since the old Queen's Diamond Jubilee, during which Willie had been promoted major-general and had promptly retired. Upon his retirement, he had been given the singular honour of the appointment to colonel-in-chief to the Maclaren Highlanders. This event had stirred in Andrew a slight twinge of jealousy. After all, he was The Maclaren, even though Willie was a couple of years his senior and born of the same father. But the jealousy did not last long; these two were bound together too tightly by ties of blood and comradeship.

Ian and Victoria had moved permanently into Culbrech House where they had settled down as the Laird and his Lady.

There had been a lot of changes in the past nine years, changes that had affected both of their families. Apart from his brief visit of a month timed to coincide with the Jubilee, Willie had not seen Donald since the day that Ian and Victoria had married. Donald had gone off that night on the train which was the first leg of his journey to South Africa and the diamond mines of Kimberley.

Naomi contacted them occasionally by letter, but seldom came up to the Highlands now. She seemed to be more contented with her life in London, where she moved in the highest circles of literature and the arts. In the context of the society in which she moved Naomi was one of the most sought-after hostesses in London. It was in the world populated by actors, artists, and writers that she had made her niche. 'Polite society' was barred to her. She was not acceptable within the doors of the establishment. She had not been presented at court. Never would she receive an invitation to a garden party at Buckingham Palace and matrons of the establishment would never countenance any sort of liaison between her and their sons. And Naomi did not give a damn. She wanted no part of the establishment cattle market. Her friends and acquaintances were interesting people whose company was never dull and if she occasionally went to bed with one of them, well, that was her business.

Ron Murray, that hard-working and truly professional soldier, had been transferred to the General Staff in London and was now, according to Willie, a Something-or-other in General Wolseley's headquarters. The command had passed briefly to Alex Farquhar who had soon tired of the responsibilities and within a year had resigned his commission and gone back to his estates and his beloved thoroughbreds. He used to invite the serving officers over to his home and proudly show them around his stud with the remark, 'You see? Not a bloody mule in sight.'

Ian had been promoted over the head of Hugh Grant with the rank of lieutenant-colonel, and been given command of the first battalion. Not that Grant minded. He had been offered the second battalion but turned it down, maintaining that he wanted to see out his service among the officers and men he had known and loved for so long. So he had remained a very senior major and second-in-command. Gordon Bruce was now adjutant and a major, and Robert Maclaren commanded C Company. R.S.M. Macmillan had retired, and Frankie Gibson had taken his place, and, with the royal coat of arms on his sleeve, had become a staunch upholder of the law which he had so long ignored.

For three of the intervening years the regiment had been on the Northwest Frontier where, apart from the odd skirmish, they had lived their tour of duty in the comfort and ease provided by the loyal native subjects of the Queen Empress, while none the less remaining ever vigilant to the possible threat of the Russians from the north. Victoria had settled down instantly into the role of army wife and mother. She had gone out to India with the regiment, and had refused to return home for the birth of her first child in spite of the knowledge that her late mother-in-law had done the same at the cost of her life. She proved herself a woman of great strength and of absolute devotion to both her husband and her children.

Willie, too, was a grandfather. Brenda had given Donald two fine boys and a daughter during their years in South Africa. But Willie had never seen any of them, and duty now kept him where he was, much to his own private sorrow. Maud had, however, determined to see them, and was even at this moment on the high seas bound for the Cape, where she intended to spend the winter with her son and his family.

As for Gordon Bruce, he had been married recently to the daughter of a hill farmer. Grisel was a strong Highland lassie, and the last person on earth that anyone would have imagined Gordon marrying. He had courted her quietly for over a year, saying nothing to anybody until the day, about six months ago, when he had told his father that he intended to marry. Only the dashing Robert remained a bachelor, but his bachelorhood was always at risk, for his liaisons were many and his prudence limited, to say the least. In 1899, birth control was still a primitive science.

Willie turned to Andrew. 'Shall we go oot and join them?' he asked. 'They're going tae have tea now.'

Kirsty, their attractive parlourmaid, about whom Andrew had several times had to warn Robert, was crossing the lawn with a great silver tray covered with little pink cakes and cucumber sandwiches, her neat little bottom swaying in the sunlight beneath a skirt too tight for the ladies but a delight to the men.

'No, I don't think so,' said Andrew, turning away from the window. As a grandfather he was more than adequate, except when his grandchildren were, as they were now, en masse. Then their boisterous pleasures made him all too aware of his own infirmity as he tried to keep up with them, stomping about on his wooden leg.

'Shall I get us some tea in here, Willie?' he asked.

'Nay, Andrew,' said Willie, looking at the marble clock on the mantelpiece. 'I ken it's a bittie early, but I have a feeling that I could take a dram.'

Andrew grinned and started to stomp over towards the sideboard.

'Sit ye doon, Andrew,' said Willie. 'I know fine where you keep it. I'll get it.' He took out the bottle of Glenlivet and poured out two generous measures.

Andrew lowered himself gratefully into one of the heavy leather armchairs which they had moved so as to be able to watch what was going on outside. 'Well,' he said, sipping his drink, 'what's going to happen in South Africa? This must be pretty worrying to you with Maud on her way there.'

'Aye, it is, though I couldna persuade her not to go. As to what's going to happen, I can tell you that, all right. I doubt that you'll believe me, though.'

'Try me,' said Andrew. 'The invincible Boer?' he added with a little smile.

'Och, no, man, it's not as simple as that, and there's nae point in you mocking them. If yon bugger Joe Chamberlain gets his way, we'll be fighting them soon enough, though, and we'll lick them, but it'll cost us dear. Never forget that they've already beaten us once at Majuba. If they did it again, it would mean the beginning of the end of the British Empire; and the Germans and the French would all be there picking up the pieces.'

'Oh, come now,' said Andrew.

'Nae, Andrew, I mean it. These men that we are going to be fighting, and mark my words there will be fighting, only oursel's can understand. They're like the auld Highlander.'

'How do you mean?'

'They havna got an army as we understand it. Their whole nation is their army. Every man jack o' them is a soldier and a damned good one. Every one o' them can ride and shoot, he's been weaned on it. And, damn and blast oor lords and masters, they're better equipped than we are.'

'We have the Lee-Metford.'

'Aye, and they have the Mauser,' retorted Willie.

'There's not much between them.'

'Och, awa', man. One press of the thumb and they've got five rounds loaded while oor laddies are putting them in one at a time till their magazine's full. That alone makes everv one of them worth three of us, for I have no doubt that they can get off fifteen rounds to every five of ours.'

'Well,' said Andrew, 'the Lee-Enfield is coming along fairly soon; that should put us on even terms.'

'Aye,' said Willie, 'they've got them in store already. But you ken what those cheese-paring bastards at the War House are going to do?'

'What?'

'They'll keep them in store until the Metfords are worn out or their owners are deed. Then they might start to issue them.'

'You're not very encouraging,' said Andrew.

'I see bloody little to be encouraged aboot,' replied Willie. 'I think that it's worse. One of ours canna match one of them in firepower. Any o' them can outride the best of our cavalry, and just now there are more of them than there are of us. You havena seen what they call the High Veld, Andrew. I have. I mind I was there fighting the Zulus, when I was only a drummer boy. I saw it then and that's where the fighting's going tae be. It's mile after mile o' nothing, it's bigger than all of Scotland, and it is just aboot the worst place I have ever seen to mount an attack over. There's nae point in trying tae tak' what they call a toon. It's never mair than a dozen or so wood houses and a church and they're no going tae sit there and wait for us.'

'Well, they do say that Buller is raising a corps to go to the Cape.'

'Aye,' said Willie, 'but they'll no move. Not until the war starts, and by the time he gets there the Boer will have been having his own way for a lang, lang time.'

'May I come in?'

They both looked around at Ian, who had just entered the room.

'Hello, Uncle Willie,' he said, 'you are spending a lot of time here just now.'

'Och, well,' said Willie, 'there's nothing much over at Cluny just at the moment wi' Maud away and all.'

'I thought that you were at the barracks today,' said Andrew.

'I've only just got back,' replied Ian. 'We've got our marching orders.'

Both of the older men showed interest. 'What's that?' asked Willie.

'When?' asked Andrew.

'We move at the beginning of August.'

'Well, come on, lad, tell us where,' said Andrew. 'India again?'

'Lord, no, nothing so interesting. Aldershot, so I suppose that will mean South Africa.'

'We've just been talking about South Africa,' said Willie. 'How do you feel about it, Ian?'

'I don't really know,' said Ian. 'I think it will be big; probably bigger than we've ever seen. Did you know that the rumour is that they're not going to send any Indian troops there?'

'Why ever not?' asked Andrew. 'The Indian regiments are some of the best we have.'

'I know,' replied Ian. 'But my information is that if it comes to war, they want to keep it a white man's war. No native troops, no Indians, only us.'

'I dinna know why they don't just hand the whole damned place over to the Boers on a plate. The Zulu is right behind us and the Bantu, after the way they've been treated by the Boer. He'd get no native help. Are you sure of your facts, Ian?'

'Well, it's just a rumour at the moment.'

'And I hope to God it stays that way.'

'Is the battalion anyway near up to strength?' asked Andrew.

'We're within a hundred and fifty of establishment, and we have a fair chance of making that up before we go. I have Sergeant Leinie out at the moment on a recruiting drive.

Amazing the way that man's come on. I'd rate him as just about the best N.C.O. we have.'

'Any hope of the Enfields?' asked Willie.

' 'Fraid not. I've been on to the War House; they don't seem to want to know. They say that they haven't got any.'

'Och, they've got them all right,' said Willie. 'They're sitting on them and hoping they'll grow.'

'We're getting another Maxim, though.'

'Aye, well, that'll help, if you ken how to use it,' said Willie.

'Come on, Uncle Willie,' said Ian, laughing. 'The army's changing, you know. We study these things now.'

'Aye, and you'd be as well tae study yon johnny you're going to be fighting. It's no going tae be easy.'

'I'm afraid,' said Andrew, 'your Uncle Willie feels rather depressed over the whole business.'

'Of course, nobody wants a war,' said Ian. 'But we can't let the Boers go on the way they are behaving. They don't allow the blacks any rights before the law, and the *uitlanders*, that's us, have no voice whatsoever in the Transvaal or the Orange Free State.'

'You're sounding a wee bittie like Chamberlain,' said Willie.

'Oh, no,' replied Ian laughing. 'Not I. I just came in because I thought you'd like to hear the news.'

'Will you be taking Victoria with you?' asked Andrew.

'Not this time, though it will be difficult to persuade her not to come. As I see it, Aldershot is just a staging post, and there's no chance of wives being allowed on a trooper. Not if we're going straight on to active service.'

'You're the C.O.,' said Andrew.

'And I'm not going to take advantage of that,' replied Ian. 'I wondered if you could have a word with her, father, and try to persuade her to stay here.'

Andrew looked out of the window to where the family were just finishing tea. 'I'll try,' he said. 'But you know what she is.'

'Aye,' said Willie, 'you did all right there, Ian. And she didn't do too badly, either.'

'Well,' said Ian, 'I suppose that I had better go and break the news to her. Wish me luck.'

It was not easy, as Ian had foreseen. Victoria dug her very small feet very firmly in and refused point blank to stay up in

Scotland when the regiment moved to Aldershot. Finally they reached a compromise, Victoria reluctantly agreeing to stay at the house in Charlotte Street while Ian was down there, at least for as long as it took them to find out what was happening.

At about the same time Ian had entered his father's study, Alasdair Maclaren, no relation to the Maclarens of Culbrech House, was setting out from camp. He was on his way to climb the little hill which ran up towards Glen Cannich just before you get into Beauly. Alasdair was seventeen years old and had served with the regiment for a full year. In that period he had completed his training and earned himself the right to be addressed by his juniors as 'trained soldier'.

He had joined the regiment just after his sixteenth birthday. It had all happened one evening in the 'bobbie's hoose' in Drumnadrochit. From these headquarters Alasdair's father pursued his duties of keeping the law as village constable. Sitting at the big wooden table in their kitchen along with his nine brothers and sisters, he had told them, over their tea of bread and jam, that his friend, Donnie Buchannan, had joined the Gordon Highlanders at Fort George.

Upon receipt of this information his sisters, all five of them, had taunted him and accused him of being afraid to become a soldier. This rankled and Alasdair said to himself, 'I'll show them whether or not I'm as good a man as Donnie Buchannan.' The following day he took the steamer into Inverness and sought out Sergeant Leinie of the Maclaren Highlanders who was recruiting in the city, and Alasdair had taken the Queen's shilling. From there he was taken to the barracks at Beauly and kitted out in Highland kilt, sporran, red tunic, and the rest. All of this, the glamour of the uniform, was, he now realized, the real attraction that the army held for boys of his age.

The initial glamour had palled within a very short time. His first months consisted of square-bashing, polishing and cleaning, and kit inspections and rifle drill and musketry and again square-bashing, and so on in endless repetition. But Alasdair had stuck it out and had already been noticed on more than one occasion for his soldierly bearing by Regimental-Sergeant-Major Gibson.

Alasdair was not a very big man. In looks he in no way

resembled the Maclarens of the big house, for he had the black hair and the blue eyes of the true Celt. He also had superstitions, inbred for centuries, and they were the main reason for his journey that day. Alasdair had decided that after the happenings of today, he would go and talk with Marhi Crow. Crow was not her real name, of course. She was called Marhi Crow because she was black. Her hair was black, her eyes were dark, and there was a touch of the Romany in her looks and in the colour of her skin. Marhi Crow had *the sight*.

Alasdair had never been to see her before, but he knew about people who had the sight and who could tell you what was to befall you, and sometimes warn of disasters to come. Many had the sight in the glens of the Highlands, but Marhi was something special. For Alasdair the exercise was a bit frightening, but he wanted to know what was happening.

The signs he had seen were nothing to do with foreknowledge, they were all of a very practical nature. That morning they had all been paraded and marched around to the quartermaster's stores. There they had been issued with two tunics, one khaki drill and one khaki serge, khaki webbing and ammunition pouches, even khaki spats to cover their white diced hose. And then the hat. It looked funny, more of a helmet. It was khaki, too, and so was the pugaree which he would have to practise binding round it. All in all it was an awful comedown from the bright red coat with its braided Inverness skirt and cuffs and the feather bonnet with its proud cockade. Rumour had been rife in the barrack room after dinner at noon, and the trouble with the Boers was high on everyone's mind. Only one thing seemed certain and that was that there was going to be fighting to be done, and that the fighting was not going to be anywhere near home.

He got to the door of Marhi's bothy with its straw thatch and its little wisp of blue peat smoke rising straight from the hole in the centre of the roof, for even though the day was warm and still, Marhi would never let her *lumb* go out.

He had never seen Marhi before and he hardly knew what to expect. Probably a haggard old crone with warts on her nose and a tall hat?

Summoning up his courage, he shoved his head in through the open door and into the blackness and called:

'Is onybody theere?'

Alasdair got the shock of his life when in reply a voice from behind him demanded, 'And what would you be wanting, Alasdair Maclaren?'

He whipped around and faced the speaker. She was dark, all right, just as he had been told, but she was young, and she was beautiful, made more so by the dark-haired child on her hip.

'I look for Marhi Crow.'

'Then you have seen her, so best be on your way,' she said in the carefully enunciated English of the native Gaelic speaker.

He found himself staring at the child. He had heard of it, of course. It was said to have been fathered by her familiar, in spite of its resemblance to John Doig, the butcher from Struy. He pulled himself together, fighting the temptation to run away down the hill, and with forced casualness he said, 'Och, I was just passin'.'

'And I would suppose,' she replied, 'that you always stick your nose into people's houses whenever you are just passing them?'

'No, I dinna.'

'You came to see me, did you not?'

'Aye.'

'Then you must have had something you wanted to see me about.'

'Aye.'

'Then do not stand there dreeching, and tell me why it is that you have come?'

'I heered ma faither talk aboot you, and he says that you hae the sight.'

Marhi's face suddenly became serious. 'That is not for any man to say, and the sight, if I have it, is not for the likes of you.'

'But I want tae know. I can pay if that's what you want. I hae money.' He took a florin out of his sporran and extended his hand towards her with the coin lying on his open palm.

She raised her head to look him in the eyes and suddenly her head darted forward as if it was a snake striking, and she spat on the coin. 'Away with you and your money. You must know that the sight cannot be bought.'

He pushed the florin back into his sporran and quite suddenly she put the child down and seized his hand, holding it tight between her palms. He watched her as she seemed to go far, far away from him, and he felt a shiver running all the way down his back.

'You did see something, and dinna tell me that you didna.'

Her expression came back to normal, and she looked at him kindly, but with a certain sadness. 'Go to the officer and tell him your real age,' she said.

'I canna dae that. I'll be oot o' the army if I dae that,' he protested. 'Besides, they wouldna believe me.'

'Then I cannot help you, though I would if I could. I will give you a promise, though.'

'A promise?'

'Yes. You will not die before you see me again.'

'Then I'll never come back and I'll live forever,' he said.

'But because of what I have seen, you can bed with me tonight, if you wish.'

'Och, woman, you're daft,' he said, but she only smiled sadly.

Something inside Alasdair snapped, and without another word he turned and ran off down the hill as if all the devils in hell were after him.

Regimental-Sergeant-Major Frankie Gibson knew. That is, he knew as much as his commanding officer did, and he was not looking forward to the prospect. At least, that was the impression he gave to Sergeant Leinie. Sergeant Leinie had just presented him with a batch of twenty-three new recruits. They had been kitted out, and they looked awful.

Frankie Gibson took a long pull at his pint of ale, and thumped the bar counter of the sergeants' mess.

'De ye think that we're going tae be able tae fight a war wi' that lot?'

The sergeants' mess consisted, to all intents and purposes, of three rooms. The dining room, where they ate the best food in the regiment; the anteroom, which was almost always empty; and the bar, which was hardly ever empty. The bar itself was a large spacious room with long picture windows heavily curtained. The curtains had been a gift from Sir Andrew Maclaren. Most of the senior N.C.O.s gathered here when they were off duty. A small group who were sitting playing dominoes at a table beside the stand which held the trophies won, in various sporting activities, by the members of the mess, looked up as Frankie hammered on the bar, and turned back to their game before allowing themselves to grin. It was highly dangerous to allow the R.S.M. to see himself as a subject for mirth.

Most of them would have denied that Frankie had changed at all over the years, though in fact his hair was now beginning to show touches of grey and the furrows on his bronzed weatherbeaten face were deeper. But his eyes were as bright and searching as ever and he held in deep contempt those under him who were unable to flout the law with the skill witn which he had done as a junior soldier.

'They're always like this,' said Leinie, replying to his question. 'Anyway I say the Boer'll back doon and then we'll nae ha' a war tae fecht wi' ony lot.' He took a pull at his beer. 'I tell you what, though, yon Donaldson, he's a funny yin, that.'

'Whae's Donaldson?'

'The yin that talks like an officer.'

'Och aye,' said Frankie. 'Ye get 'em like that sometimes. They mak' guid sodgers, though. I've seen them before.' He remembered Jamie Patterson, gentleman ranker, who had died in India. Most of them were like Jamie; they had nothing left to live for so there was nothing that they feared. 'It takes all kinds tae make an army,' he said. 'And if he's a guid sodger, shoots straight and keeps his boots clean, I'll ask nae mair of him.'

'De ye think that meybe I should nae ha' taken him?' asked Leinie.

'Och, mannie, ye've got tae take what ye can get. They're no men that ye bring in. They're babies and brutes and beggars and worse. Its oor job tae turn them into men. By God, we'll dae it, too. We move oot o' here in just over a month, and if by then there's one of these men that I wouldna want at me side in action, I'll hae somebody's guts for garters. Have anither pint.'

In the officers' mess Robert Maclaren was lounging in a leather armchair, his shoes propped on a small table while he admired the crease in the trousers of his mess kit. His was the unenviable task of looking after D Company, which was not really a company at all. It was the training company, or squad, or whatever you cared to call it, where all new recruits came for initial training. As soon as they were showing the slightest signs of becoming soldiers, they were taken away and shared out among the other, more illustrious companies. Then D Company waited for the next lot.

Robert did not spend many nights in mess, but tonight he had to be there. He was orderly officer. He too had been told that day of the impending move. It could not be a bad thing for Robert; at least, outside their catchment area, the likelihood of more green recruits was slender. After all, there would be English girls at Aldershot and English young ladies were remarkably easy prey for a man of six foot four, well built, and wearing a kilt. He reached inside the pocket of his mess jacket and took out a long slim black cigar and lit it. Well, he thought, if they were going to fight the Boers, the sooner the better, as far as he was concerned.

He lay back on his chair and watched the blue smoke of his cigar as it curled up towards the ceiling, just as the peat smoke did from Mahri's *lumb*.

On board ship in the south Atlantic a day and a half from Cape Town, Maud Bruce knew little of the impending war, and what she did know meant nothing to her. Within a couple of days she would be with her son again; with Donald in Kimberley. Nothing else really mattered.

In London, Lord Wolseley ordered General Sir Redvers Buller, V.C., to form an army corps of approximately fifty thousand men, and to be ready to sail for South Africa at a moment's notice.

Buller looked at his old chief. Wolseley was probably the most famous soldier that Britain had had since Wellington. Buller had served with him in 1870 and a year later he had entered the staff college. He had left there as soon as the chance came to join Wolseley again in the Ashanti war of 1873. In 1879, during the Zulu war, Buller had won the Victoria Cross. His entire career seemed to have been linked to Wolseley and always as number two and now he was being ordered on an independent command.

'Fifty thousand men,' he said. 'I don't want this job, you know that, sir.'

'I think,' replied the Commander-in-Chief, 'you must allow me to decide who is the best man for this operation. You'll have no trouble raising the men. If you opened the recruiting offices tomorrow you'd have three times the number you need by evening. The whole country seems to be after Kruger's blood.'

'It's trained men I shall need.'

'I know.'

'And what about equipment?'

'I'm sorry, Redvers, but that's another story. I fear that that is not so good. It's a damned sight easier to find the men than the supplies.'

'Ammunition?'

'For your artillery? Less than two hundred rounds per gun.'

'That's not so good, is it?' said Buller.

'No. And the Boer has a better rifle than we have.'

'Damn the politicians,' said Buller.

'Amen,' replied Wolseley. 'But you've got to do it. This talk we have had is off the record. You'll receive your orders in writing later. Then you can object if you want to. Training is what really matters now. I want you to get down to that right away.'

'I'll do my best, sir,' said Buller, 'but I don't like it.'

'Come and have lunch with me at Boodle's. We can talk some more over a bottle of claret.'

It was the first of October, 1899.

2

At an elevation of over a thousand feet, the town of Kimberley lay about six hundred miles north of Cape Town. It was only a matter of ten miles or so, within the border of Cape Colony, from the Orange Free State. Kimberley had been connected to the Cape by rail which passed through the town on its way to Mafeking and beyond. About thirty miles to the west, across the open veld, was the Vaal River. With only sixteen inches of rain a year, Kimberley was for most of the time hot and dry. There was little in the way of agriculture, and most of the provisions for the town had been transported there by the railway since it arrived there in 1885.

The town was built around a market square, the outstanding feature of which was a stone-pillared and porticoed town hall. The streets were wide, there was land in plenty, and most of the town centre consisted of shops and offices, some of which were stone-built though the majority were still of wood. Nearly all of the buildings had one thing in common, and that was the wooden awning which protected pedestrians from the heat of the almost ever-present sun.

Kimberley was the centre of the most productive diamond mines in the world, and thus a great financial prize for any predator. Kimberley also had within its bounds that high priest of empire, Cecil John Rhodes, who was at that time reputed to be the wealthiest man in the world.

All the diamonds which were mined in Kimberley and its environs were sold by the De Beers group which was effectively under the control of Rhodes himself. It was here that Donald Bruce purchased gem-quality stones in the rough and sent them by courier to Amsterdam for cutting. After that they went to their final destination, Mr Wilson's shop in Bond Street. It was here, too, that Maud Bruce arrived in the early August of 1899 to see her son, his wife, and the three grandchildren that she had never met.

The heat never bothered Maud; indeed she found it much more bearable than the Highland winters. She had been born in India and had returned there three times with the battalion. Kimberley, however, was not India. In India the army and army life dominated everything. But this was a commercial town, a business community with little time for the military. Of course, it was garrisoned and guarded by a series of forts, but one saw little of the army throughout the normal course of life.

It was Tuesday when she arrived and the day was pleasant enough with the temperature in the upper seventies. But this was early spring, and it heralded heat of well over a hundred degrees by the time summer arrived in November.

Maud got out of the train on to the dusty wooden platform. In some ways it was familiar and reminded her of India, both the natives who hurried about looking for someone whose baggage they could carry, and those who merely held out a plaintive hand in the hope of an offering. There were also one or two well-dressed Europeans going about their business and ignoring the cries of the throng. But in other ways, it was quite different. Here everybody seemed more purposeful, and there was no hint anywhere of social occasion. Maud watched for a moment with ill-concealed astonishment as a man with a straggling beard, obviously a Boer farmer, wearing a battered slouch hat and ill-fitting trousers with flapping shirt, tried to collect his wife, a tired, mousey-looking little woman, and eleven children.

Within a very few moments she had spotted Donald hurrying towards her, immaculate in white ducks and wearing a white pith helmet. Trotting along at his side was Brenda, dressed in the white linen costume and wide-brimmed hat that was almost regulation dress for ladies' daywear anywhere in the Empire.

'Welcome to Kimberley, Mother,' said Donald as he embraced her.

'It's good to see you, Donald,' smiling as she watched her son take his wife's hand. 'Hello, Brenda. But where are my grandchildren?'

'They're at home,' said Brenda. 'Donald wanted to bring them, but I thought it would be better to leave them there while we sorted out the luggage. Just in case any of them escaped, you know,' she added with a smile.

'Where is your luggage, Mother?' asked Donald.

'In the van.'

'Keep an eye on her, darling,' Donald said to Brenda, kissing her. 'I have a houseboy here. I'll get him to sort it out and bring it along. How many pieces?'

'Eight, I'm afraid,' said Maud. 'I plan to stay for some time.'

'It isn't very far,' said Brenda as Donald disappeared in search of his servant. 'But we've brought the gig in case you were tired. Did you have a good journey?'

'Oh, yes,' said Maud. 'It was most interesting. I find Africa very large and extremely empty. But after thirty hours in a train, even in my most comfortable compartment, one does tend to get a little weary. Especially at my age.'

'But you're not all that old, Mrs Bruce.'

'I'm nearly sixty, you know. And, Brenda, you must stop calling me Mrs Bruce. Mother sounds a bit foolish, so why don't you just call me Maud?' She was already warming to this rather plain, softly spoken woman, who was obviously so much loved by her son.

'All right, then,' said Brenda. 'Maud it shall be.'

They were rejoined by Donald, who escorted them to the gig, having assured Maud that her luggage had all been safely identified. They drove for a little way along the dusty streets towards the market square.

'I'm afraid,' said Donald as he helped his mother down from the gig, 'we live over the shop. But I am sure that you'll find that we have ample accommodation. We have a bungalow outside the town, but we do not use it just now. We have been advised to stay within the town limits.'

'Why?' asked Maud. They entered, through an unprepossessing front door, a corridor which was flanked by offices, the largest of which had a glass-topped door through which could be seen a heavy safe.

'It's all this talk of war, I suppose,' replied Donald.

'What are they saying about it in London?' asked Brenda.

'I haven't the faintest idea of what they're saying in London,' said Maud, 'but Donald's father seems quite convinced that there is going to be a war. He blames it all on Chamberlain.'

'It's all so bloody stupid,' said Donald. 'They'll never solve anything with a war. Men's attitudes don't change. Anyhow,' he said, deliberately changing the subject, 'come on upstairs, the children will be waiting.'

Towards the rear of the building a pleasant staircase led up to the first floor, where there was a bright landing lit by a large oblong window in the rear wall. They went across this and into what was obviously the sitting room.

It was furnished almost entirely by light cane and bamboo furniture, with a profusion of multicoloured scatter cushions. There was a series of large windows running the entire length of the opposite wall. These were open, but covered with screens of fine net, and the floor was tiled for coolness, with a couple of skin rugs placed with careful casualness.

But Maud saw little of this. She had eyes only for the three children who rose to greet her as she entered the room. They were all fair and had the reddish, freckled complexions which stamped them unmistakably as descendants of Willie Bruce. The two boys were dressed smartly in freshly laundered sailor suits, and the little girl wore a white dress with a blue ribbon around her waist, and little lace-trimmed pantalettes which peeped below the hem of her skirt.

'Children,' said Donald, 'this is Grandmama.'

'How do you do, Grandmama,' they said in well-rehearsed unison.

'Now, Mother, this is —'

'No, no, Donald, I must do this myself. Now let me see. You must be Harry,' she said, giving the tallest of the three a kiss. 'You are seven, is that right, Harry?'

'Yes, miss,' said Harry.

'You must always call me Grandma,' said Maud, smiling.

'And here we have Susan? Hello Susan, you are not quite six? Is that right?'

'I shall be six on December the second,' said Susan, anxious that her birthday should be firmly established.

'We won't forget,' said Maud. 'And this, of course, is Johnny.'

'Are you my gangma?' lisped Johnny. 'Did you bring me a present?'

'Johnny,' said Brenda, reproving, 'that's very rude.'

'Not a bit of it,' said Maud, laughing. 'Of course I have brought you a present, my darling. I have brought presents for all of you, and Grandpa has sent you presents, and Uncle Gordon has sent you presents, oh, dearie me, yes. There are so *many* presents.'

'Can we see them? Can we see them?' they chanted, their reserve completely broken down as they clustered around her.

'You will have to wait, my dears, until Grandma's luggage has arrived and we unpack. But there is one special bag which you must help me unpack because it has all of your presents in it.'

'Oh, I can't wait,' said Harry, and they all laughed.

There was another occupant of the room, a tall, statuesque young black woman. Her high, firm breasts and her rounded buttocks contoured the thin cotton print dress which Maud was quite sure was all that she was wearing.

'Nambi,' said Donald, addressing the native woman, 'this is my mother, Mrs Bruce.'

The girl nodded silently in Maud's direction.

'Would you go and tell cook that we will take tea now,' said Donald.

'Yes, Master Donald,' she replied in a low, husky voice. She walked out of the room with a sort of gliding grace.

'Nambi,' said Donald by way of explanation, 'is Zulu, as indeed all of our servants are. They come here from the tribal lands and work for a couple of years, and then go home and get married. Nambi is rather different, though. Her father was killed in a tribal raid and some friends of ours found her in the bush. She couldn't have been more than about ten at the time. Well, it was just after we arrived here, and when our friends brought her back to Kimberley, they gave her to us as a housegirl. In the years since, she's become more or less one of the family, hasn't she, dear?'

'Oh, yes,' said Brenda. 'I doubt if she will ever be able to go back to her tribe now. She'll probably end up marrying one of the town blacks. It'll be a pity, though. She's much too good for them.'

'Why?' asked Maud.

'Well, they tend to be the tribal dropouts. They live in the most appalling squalor around the outskirts of the town and spend most of their time stealing and begging. I should not like Nambi to end up with one of them,' said Brenda.

'I see,' said Maud. She had also seen the way that Donald had looked at Nambi as she left the room and hoped that she was wrong.

3

The Boer War began officially at, according to *The Times*, tea time on the eleventh October, 1899. The following day the man who had been chosen to command all the British forces in South Africa, General Sir Redvers Buller, V.C., broke off preparations for his imminent departure on the *Dunottar Castle*, which was sailing in three days' time, in order to grant an interview to a lady. He had done this in response to a request from an old comrade, Major General Willie Bruce.

Buller made no secret of the fact that he was not looking forward to his assignment. He had even again requested the commander-in-chief to find another and, in his, Buller's, opinion, more suitable candidate for the job. He had had a very gallant career since he had joined the army in 1859. But for fifteen years he had seen no active service. That time had been spent sitting behind a desk in Whitehall. Those fifteen years had added considerably to his waistline. He no longer had the trim, athletic figure with which he was portrayed in the illustrated magazines.

He had accepted the command in South Africa with a great deal of misgiving, having grave doubts about his own fitness for the job. But after much persuasion which culminated in an interview on the fifth of October with the Queen herself, he resigned himself to the fact that he would have to go through with it.

There was no more popular soldier in Britain. The rank and file of the army held him in the highest affection and knew him as a general who really cared for his men. The public in general, having been fed through the press with long and glowing accounts of his exploits, had made him their hero. For the last few days he had hardly been able to set foot outside his office or his home without running the risk of being mobbed by the crowds who, imbued with faith in the invincibility of Empire, were thronging the streets, waving Union Jacks and singing patriotic songs.

Buller was a gentle, kindly man who found it difficult to refuse any request. So even in the midst of all these preparations he had agreed to see his old friend's daughter. None the less he was most determined that the interview would be brief, and, if what she wanted to see him about was what he suspected, unfruitful.

'Miss Naomi Bruce, sir,' announced his aide, ushering Naomi into his office.

Buller heaved himself up from his desk, indicating a chair opposite him. 'Won't you sit down, Miss Bruce? Is there anything I can get you?'

He would have been less than a man if he had not paused to admire the lady as she walked across the room. She was dressed in a grey velvet town costume with dark-brown velvet trimmings. He put her age at about thirty-five, though in this he underestimated. Her huge brown eyes and the gentle smile on her full lips drew from him a smile in response, and the knowledge that before she had opened her mouth, he had lost the first round.

'Thank you, Sir Redvers,' the vision replied to his offer. 'I am here on a matter of urgent concern. I am aware that your time must be at a premium and I have no intention of wasting any of it in small talk or tea party conversation.'

'Thank you, ma'am,' replied the general. 'I assure you that I appreciate your concern.'

'I understand, Sir Redvers, that you are sailing for South Africa on the *Dunottar Castle* the day after tomorrow.' Naomi paused. 'Do correct me if my information is not accurate.'

The general raised his eyebrows. 'No, madam, you are quite right.'

'So am I.'

'Oh? You intend to visit the Cape? Perhaps I shall have the honour of meeting you during the voyage. You have relatives or friends out there, I presume.'

'No.'

'Then I should advise you to think again before leaving. You will no doubt be aware that there is a state of war between this country and the government of the Boer republics in South Africa.'

'I am quite aware of that, Sir Redvers. But mine is not a mission of peace. I am sailing to South Africa because of, and not in spite of, the fact that we are at war.'

'Madam, war is not for ladies. Ladies do not go to war.'

'Miss Nightingale did.'

'Perhaps you had better explain further,' said the general, taking out his watch and looking at it pointedly.

'Perhaps I had,' said Naomi with her sweetest smile. 'I, or rather I should say we, are a small company of six women. Four amateur and two professional nurses. All of our expenses are being met by the Duke of Beverley, so that we shall be a burden on no one.'

'I see,' said the general who did not see at all. 'Perhaps you will be good enough to continue.'

'We will travel at the Duke's expense to the Cape, and once there we propose to place ourselves at the disposal of the Royal Army Medical Corps.'

'Good God!'

'We believe,' continued Naomi, 'that there will be a great need for trained nurses, and though four of our number are untrained, including myself, we intend to spend the voyage learning the basic principles of nursing from the two real nurses who will be making up our party.'

'Indeed!'

'So the first thing that you can do for us is to put us in touch with the senior R.A.M.C. officer at whose disposal we can place ourselves.'

'My dear lady,' said Sir Redvers, 'I cannot in any way support you in such a venture. Have you any idea what war is like? Have you ever seen a man who has been maimed on the field of battle? I can assure you that it is not a sight that I would recommend to ladies of gentle breeding.'

'I don't suppose that you would.'

'I can assure you that it is no sight for a lady.'

'Have you ever seen a child born?' she asked.

'Certainly not.' The general was shocked.

'Well, I can assure you that that is no sight for a gentleman. I am quite sure that I and the ladies who are accompanying me will not be frightened by the sight of blood. Nor, if I may be so bold, will we be diverted from our purpose by the disapproval of persons in exalted positions.'

Buller looked at her for a long time until, under his steady gaze, even Naomi had to avert her eyes.

'Young lady,' he said at length, 'I admire your courage and I admire your motives. I am also very grateful that you came to me with this suggestion. I assure you that there is nothing more important to me than the welfare of the men whom I command. My first reaction was to have you thrown out of my office. But that was wrong, for I think that your offer is genuine, and you might in fact be able to be of service to those troops who are unfortunate enough to become casualties.' He held up his hand. 'Before you speak, I want you to know that I cannot promise anything at all. I shall discuss this whole matter with my principal medical officer and suggest that he accept your most generous offer. The final decision, however, will be his alone. If, as I suspect, this war upon which we are embarking results in heavy casualties, then we shall need the services of many ladies like yourself. We can always hope that you will not be necessary. But if you are, I have little doubt but that there are many who will follow you in the same spirit of compassion in which you offer yourselves. Thank you, Miss Bruce.'

'Thank you, sir,' said Naomi, surprised and moved by the general's ready acquiescence. She had come prepared for a fight and none had been offered.

'Remember, then,' said the general in a tone which indicated that the interview was over, 'no promises, but I shall do what I can. Perhaps I shall have the pleasure of dining with you ladies during our voyage to the Cape,' he added, steering Naomi towards the door.

*

It took them two and a half weeks from leaving Tilbury before they entered Table Bay and caught their first sight of Cape Town lying before Table Mountain, which was covered by its summer tablecloth of white cloud, and to its right, the two lesser mounds of Signal Hill and Lion's Head. The town itself ·-as thronged with people, many of them in uniform, for transports had been pouring men into the Cape for weeks past. On the pier where they docked, a full battalion of Highlanders was drawn up as a guard of honour, ready to greet their C-in-C. At last they would get some news. The ship carried not only the C-in-C and his staff, but also a large number of journalists, all of whom were news hungry after spending two and a half weeks cut off from the rest of the world.

There was a lot of coming and going before the general was ready to disembark, and during this time, while the battalion sweated on the quay, they discovered that on the day before, the thirtieth of October, General White had been defeated at Ladysmith and that Kimberley, with Rhodes, was under siege.

None of this seemed to dampen the spirits of the crowds who greeted them as they came down the gangway. Everyone got a cheer, but when Buller stepped on to South African soil, the noise was deafening. It was as if nothing that had so far passed mattered. And now that Buller was here, the whole of this irritating business would be dealt with speedily, and the Boers sent packing off back to their farms, having received a short, sharp lesson that it did not pay to tamper with the Queen's peace.

After Buller had inspected the guard and the battalion had moved off, he stood for a moment chatting with the colonel. Naomi watched this with an amused smile, and when Buller drove off in the carriage which had been provided for him, she excused herself from her ladies and went over to the Highland officer who was now hurrying to where his charger was being held by one of his men.

'Would you care to take dinner with us this evening, Colonel?' said Naomi.

'Really, madam, I have no time to — Good Lord, Naomi! Where the devil did you come from?'

'There, Ian,' she said, pointing at the ship. 'We are at the St

George Hotel and we may be leaving tomorrow. Try and be there by seven.' She turned to go.

'Naomi, wait!'

'Ian Maclaren, I must attend to my ladies. Till seven.' And she left him open-mouthed in the middle of the road.

Ian watched her walk away. Funny, he thought, after all those years. He could never think of Naomi without a sense of guilt. Victoria apart, she had been the only woman in his life, and though it had been such a long time since those days, and nights, at the Priory Inn at Beauly, every now and then he would find himself remembering. And when he remembered, he would feel remorseful, even while he dwelt on the memory and fantasized about every moment they had spent together, just as he was now doing. He tried to cast the thought out of his mind and told himself that, in any case, it would be impossible for him to go to the George that evening. The battalion was moving tomorrow and there was too much to do. He turned away, mounted his charger, and rode off in the direction of the Lion's Head.

Those three most prominent features of Cape Town, Table Mountain, Lion's Head, and Signal Hill, were well within Ian's view as he set out to return to camp. Signal Hill is over a thousand feet and lies within a mile of the coast. Beyond, Lion's Head overshadows it and still further inland the skyline is dominated by Table Mountain rising to well over three thousand feet.

It was at the base of Lion's Head, in open parkland, that the Maclarens had bivouacked. Ian could not help a slight thrill of pride as he saw the neat geometrical pattern of their lines of tents. Now that they were going to war, they had a double conceit: first, they were regular soldiers, trained professionals, and not like the many who had been hastily formed into Yeomanry battalions and the like, men who had rushed to volunteer for the army in the wave of war fever which had swept Britain, but amateurs nonetheless. Secondly they were Highlanders and there were no better fighting men in the world; at least that is how they saw it. As he looked upon those lines of tents, all so exactly alike and military, he thought to himself that they were a little bit straighter, a little bit more precise, and a little bit more army, than any of the other encampments which had sprung up as they prepared to move into battle.

In the centre of the lines their two flags hung lazily in the still sunlight. The Queen's Colour and the Regimental Colour, soon to be emblazoned with more battle honours. As he looked upon this he cast all thought of Naomi out of his mind. There was work to do. Tomorrow they were on their way to Durban and beyond Durban, the war. It would be good to get away from the Cape. The town was a seething mass of troops as almost every day brought another ship and with it another thousand men wondering what the hell was going to happen next.

Ian arrived at the lines and sought out Hugh Grant, his second-in-command.

'What's the situation?' he asked.

'We got back all right, and everything's well under control. All the gear's loaded. All that's left for morning are the tents and personal kit. There've been no problems. Your stuff's already on board.'

'Any problems with the men?'

'Not that I know of. I think the R.S.M. is a bit overprotective towards us. There's very little that he lets get past him. Look, Ian, why don't you take the night off? You've really had no time off since we sailed. Go and enjoy yourself. I'll hold the fort.'

Ian wished that Hugh Grant had not said that. He would have preferred a crisis which demanded his presence in camp. He was afraid of having the night off because he knew that if he did, he would go and dine with Naomi.

'Are you sure that you wouldn't rather take the night off and I'll stay here?'

'Quite happy where I am,' replied Hugh. 'I'm not one for the gay life. Can't stand crowds and there are far too many people in Cape Town.'

'It's going to be the same in Durban,' retorted Ian. 'Everybody seems to be moving up there. What do you suppose it's all about?'

'They've got Ladysmith bottled up, they've got Kimberley bottled up. Could be either of them. My own guess is Kimberley.'

'Why?'

'Rhodes.'

'And Mrs Bruce.'

'We've got to mount a relief column, but I think it's a toss-up as to which one Buller will go for,' said Hugh. 'Anyhow, we'll find out soon enough. You go off and enjoy yourself. We embark tomorrow at eight. Honestly, there's no need for you to be back before then.'

'Donald is in Kimberley as well,' said Ian, 'and his whole family. I hope it's Kimberley.'

'Well, you're not going to find out anything tonight. Far better spend it with a pretty girl.'

'What a hope,' lied Ian. 'But what if the C-in-C wants me?'

'If he does, I'll go. He can't expect you to hang about just on the off chance. The only thing we've got is a medical inspection after the men have had their tea, and I for one am not going to watch several jocks lift their kilts and cough. After that, they are not allowed out, but I think they've organized some sort of a concert. I'll go to that and that's all there is.'

Ian felt that he was being forced into a corner. 'Well,' he said reluctantly, 'I suppose it will be all right.' Damn it, he thought, why did they have to go and provide that bloody silly guard of honour to meet Buller. He knew the reason, of course. They had been in Cape Town a week, and it was a chance to give the men something to do. They were getting bored after two and a half weeks on a trooper and then sitting idly in camp; anything was better than having a thousand men sitting around with nothing to do. Still, he was surely making too much of this whole business. After all, Naomi was a great friend of the family, and it would be churlish of him to refuse her invitation. If he had seen her before she had seen him, he would certainly have invited her to dinner, especially as they would probably not meet again after tomorrow, at least until this lot was over. They were not dining tête-à-tête; there were six of them. No, he would have dinner, listen to a lot of female conversation, and come back to camp, and that would be all there was to it.

'Thanks, Hugh,' he said. 'I'll take the night off. Tell my servant that I'll probably be quite late.'

'Good man,' said Hugh. 'And don't worry. If anything crops up, I'll deal with it.'

Just as he was about to leave the lines, he ran into Gordon Bruce. The whole problem was solved. He would ask Gordon to go with him; after all, Naomi was his sister, so what could be more natural?

Gordon saluted. 'Hello, Gordon,' said Ian. 'Are you busy tonight?'

'No, sir, everything seems to be done.'

'Well, don't worry, we're off to the war tomorrow. There'll be plenty to do then.' He was about to say more, but he did not. He left the camp alone, almost furtively, committed at last to – what? He tried to tell himself that he did not know.

She was waiting for him in the lounge of the hotel. She had changed into an evening dress, low bodiced, tight waisted, which clung to the contours of her hips before flaring out into a bell-like skirt which swept the ground in a tiny train, emphasizing the curve of her back. It was trimmed with lace, and the bodice left her shoulders and the upper part of her bosom bare, revealing that near perfect creamy skin that Ian found himself remembering so well. Her long neck was completely without ornament, and her hair was piled up on top of her head and encircled by a single rope of pearls. She looked very beautiful, but it was the colour and the material of her gown which struck the most significant chord in Ian's memory. It was of orange silk, and though it lacked the polka dots, it took him back over the years to that first time in Beauly Priory Inn. But what was most obvious, more so than even the dress, was the fact that she was alone.

'Hello, Ian,' she said in her slow, husky voice. 'I thought that it would be nicer if we did not have anyone else here. I am sure that you don't want to listen to a lot of silly women's talk.'

And Ian felt guilty because he was glad that he had not brought Gordon.

'Gordon's here, you know,' he said.

'Yes, I do know. I was afraid that you might bring him.'

'Would you like a drink before dinner?' he asked.

'Why don't we go straight in; if you want anything, you can have it at the table.'

The meal passed quietly. There was a lot to talk about, family and friends, but there was really nothing new that they could tell each other, as they had both left England within the same week.

After dinner, as they sat in a quiet corner of the lounge and slowly drank their coffee, Naomi said, 'It's a long time, Ian, isn't it?'

'What?'

'Since we first sat together in a hotel lounge.'

It was a long time, all of those years which now seemed like only yesterday.

'You remember?' he said.

'How could I ever forget?'

'Do you regret any of that?' he asked.

She shook her head. 'How could I? Do you?'

'I don't know,' he said. 'I told Victoria, you know. She had already guessed that it was you.'

'Of course she did.'

They were silent for a while, gazing into their coffee cups.

'So tomorrow you go off to the war,' said Naomi.

'Well, we're off to Durban, anyhow. I suppose that they have something planned for us.'

'Does it frighten you?'

'Not really,' he said. 'Not until afterwards.'

'We might be going to Pietermaritzburg,' said Naomi. 'It's not far from Durban. There's a big hospital there and I was talking to an R.A.M.C. officer this afternoon who said that they needed more nurses out there. Do you think that it's going to be a long war?'

'I wish I knew,' said Ian. 'It shouldn't be; after all, there aren't many of them and there'll soon be a damned sight more of us.'

'So,' she said, 'tomorrow we go our separate ways. You to your masculine world and I to my feminine world.'

'Yes,' he replied.

'Why don't you stay the night?'

He tried to stem the desire that was rising within him, for Naomi Bruce was a very exciting woman. 'I can't,' he said.

'Why?'

'I'm a married man with a large family.'

'Would it be wrong?'

'It wouldn't be right.'

'But would it be wrong?'

'I don't know. Do you want to?'

'Yes.'

'So do I.'

'We wouldn't be hurting anyone,' she said. 'What have we to lose?'

'Honour.'

'Only if you take it too seriously. I am very fond of you, Ian. Once I was in love with you. I have known many men since those days we spent together. For me, it has always been an act of friendship, a way of finding comfort. If you like, a way of escaping from the realities and the hypocrisy of the world and society. Probably tonight is the last chance for either of us for a very long time. For me, it would be a comfort and a memory, no more than that. If it would be the same for you, then you are welcome in my bed.'

Now he couldn't answer. He tried to think of Victoria, but she was a vague, shadowy image, not real, part of another world.

'It doesn't matter,' she said. 'Not really. Neither of us is losing anything. Your coffee is getting cold.'

And then, just as she had done so many years ago, she held out her hand for his.

'Come, then,' she whispered. 'Tomorrow, it never happened.'

And he let her lead him out of the room.

4

'Behold the might of Empire.'

Private Maclaren looked balefully at Private Donaldson. He would like to have replied, but he could not match Donaldson in rhetoric. Besides, if he had opened his mouth, he would have got a throat full of fine brown dust.

'See,' said Donaldson, 'how Britain's might stretches from horizon to horizon.'

'Aye,' muttered young Maclaren, and snapped his mouth shut, totally unimpressed by a man who talked like an officer and neither drank nor smoked, and who knelt by his palliasse every night and said his prayers.

He should have been impressed, though. For as far as the eye could see, both in front of them and behind them as they plodded north, stretched the long khaki dust-strewn column. It moved slowly along, like a long straight animal with a million legs.

There were mounted men – the fortunate ones, the cavalry and the officers on their chargers, and squadrons of irregular mounted infantry from the Cape. It was mostly the horses that suffered for them. There were guns, wagons, teams of oxen which assured the men of a hot meal at least once every day and slowed down their progress in the process. Mile upon mile of them, ambulances, all the specialized services like cooks and farriers, doctors, but most of all the men, the poor bloody infantry. There were in all nearly eighteen thousand of them tramping slowly over the dust-strewn, rocky-outcropped veld as they headed north from Pietermaritzburg in the direction of a small shanty town called Colenso.

The word veld means field. If it was a field, it was the largest, the most arid field that any of the men now marching through it had ever seen. The thin, sparse topsoil barely covered the hard ancient rocks which lay at the most inches beneath its surface. Thousands upon thousands of square miles of vast nothingness. There was little to look at; it seemed that they existed on a world deserted by all living things except for the insects which, by day and night, fed upon their bodies. Occasionally there would be a patch of red grass, shrivelling and browning in the summer sun, or an area consisting almost entirely of small drought-resistant shrubs, acacias, and the like, with thorns inches long that would pierce a man's spats and hose if he did not watch carefully where he put his feet.

Man had lived on the veld for two million years at least. There were those who would refer to it as the birthplace of humanity, though to the soldiers whose boots pounded the hard earth for interminable miles, why humanity, with all of the world, should choose this God-forsaken hole, was a mystery. Every now and then the rocks broke through, forming *kopjes*, hillocks and rands, many of which were flat topped and capped with hard basaltic rock. Wherever the men looked, be it before them, to the side, or behind them, there was this vast, empty, unchanging horizon. Always above them, rising out of the uttermost limit of their vision, the deep blue of the unchanging South African sky.

The land through which they were trudging lay between two and four thousand feet above sea level. By day they sweated until their clothes were wringing wet. By night they shivered miserably when the sudden chill came with the setting of the sun.

If it was not the largest, it was certainly one of the largest armies that Britain had ever put into the field.

Buller had arrived at Pietermaritzburg, and with his usual caution and solicitude for the well-being of his men he had, before giving the order to march, seen to it that all the stores and baggage trains that they could possibly need were assembled and ready to move off with them. The men knew it, and in consequence Redvers Buller was probably the most loved soldier in the whole of the British army.

It was December, but not the sort of December that the Maclaren Highlanders had become accustomed to in their native glens and mountains. It was the height of the African summer on a latitude of twenty-five degrees south.

As Commander-in-Chief, Buller was, theoretically at least, not responsible for the tactical handling of the operation. That was General Clery's job. But Buller was a man who could not stay away when the troops under his command were marching into battle to fight and die because he had ordered it. There had been much talk during the voyage from Cape Town to Durban, and during the rail journey beyond Durban and into the interior. Everyone now knew that Ladysmith and Kimberley were besieged and there had been much speculation as to which of these towns was to be relieved. Of course, Ian Maclaren, commanding the Maclaren Highlanders which formed part of General Hart's brigade, had hoped that it might be Kimberley, where both Maud and Donald were. But now the answer was obvious to any of them who could read a map or who was privy to information from those in high places. Not that it mattered to people like Private Maclaren: there was going to be a fight and young Alasdair Maclaren, like most of the men marching with him, neither knew nor cared where it was. Their sole interest was to be alive at the end of it.

It was to be Ladysmith, where General White had been holding out, ringed in by the Boer forces.

Between them and Ladysmith itself must be the Boers, who were led by a man called Louis Botha. Botha, though he was not yet forty and was inexperienced in command, possessed a fine tactical brain. Also, he had the native knowledge of the Boer, and the terrain was the sort of land that he had known for most of his life.

In the British camp, so-called experts spent hours poring over maps which were not remarkable for their accuracy, and tried to decide where they were likely to encounter the main opposition. They had, after much deliberation, decided that the most probable place would be the Tugela, a river which ran in great looping curves near the small township of Colenso.

Colenso included a very few houses, all tin roofed, and a railway station, and precious little else.

Between the approaching British force and their objective, the country was flat. It consisted in the main of a huge open plain which undulated only slightly but sufficiently to give cover to a man, providing he was not mounted. *Kopjes*, small hills, were dotted around Colenso and offered excellent cover for small groups of men, and there was little doubt that the enemy would make full use of them. Buller had made no attempt at concealment. It would have been a waste of time with a force as large as he had under his command; but it was known to those in his confidence, and this included Ian Maclaren, that he was uncertain as to whether the best course would be a frontal attack or whether he should swing around out into the open veld where he would, hopefully, outflank his enemy and be able to continue on to Ladysmith with his force intact. On the face of it the second seemed to be the better alternative, but this would leave the enemy force intact to fight another day. If he took the first, he would, he believed, destroy the enemy in the field and thus hasten the end of hostilities.

It was the afternoon of the fourteenth of December 1899 when they bivouacked not more than five miles from Colenso. The whole force was spread out on either side of the railway line which ran from Durban, through Pietermaritzburg, to Ladysmith. Beyond them and to their right stood Hlangwene, a mountain which towered three thousand feet above the veld, commanding the whole of the plain around it. Before them, though not in view, lay the Tugela River, Colenso, and, twelve miles beyond that, Ladysmith itself.

For the men there was little respite. Weapons which had become dust encrusted had to be cleaned, ammunition checked, canteens filled, and so on. They did have good food, however, thanks to General Buller's foresight. Field kitchens were set up and soon the smoke from their fires was rising on the still air. The guns were brought in and then moved out again, most of them to the right flank in readiness for the morrow. As the short tropical twilight gave place to darkness, scouts went out to reconnoitre and returned with the information that Botha was lying in force just beyond the river.

The Maclarens were on the left of the line and among those

regiments which comprised their brigade were the Dublin Fusiliers, the Inniskillin Fusiliers, the First Connaught Rangers and the Border Regiment, two Scottish, two Irish, and one English battalion.

Sentries were posted as the darkness came and the flicker of campfires began to spread throughout the camp, fitfully revealing the drawn faces of the men who huddled in little groups fighting against the chill and the darkness. By one of those campfires sat a group of senior N.C.O.s of the Maclaren Highlanders, including Frankie Gibson and Colour-Sergeant Peter Leinie. They were finishing off their ration of mutton stew and bread and cheese. As soldiers have done throughout history, cocooned in their own little corner of the military machine and knowing nothing of the deliberations of the high-ranking officers who next day would send them into battle, and possibly to their deaths, they philosophized about the morrow.

'I can tell ye that tomorrow's the day,' said Leinie.

'I dinna think that there's a muckle o' doot aboot that,' said Frankie. 'They've been moving the guns up and there's a squadron o' dragoons as have just camped awa' oot there.' He made a sweeping motion with his left hand. 'Ye ken what that means, laddie?'

'What?'

'It means that we are the end o' the line and if yon Boers get roond us, then the Maclarens ha' lost the battle.'

Frankie was right, though he did not know it. For Buller had finally made up his mind and decided on a frontal assault. It would be costly now, but if he succeeded, then it would save many lives in the future.

'Ye ken what this minds me o'?' said Leinie.

'No, what?'

'It minds me o' that time in the Sudan. Being here wi' you.'

'Ye niver got as guid a supper as youse had tonight in the Sudan. What time are ye talkin' aboot, anyway?'

'No the first time. I mean the time when Captain Bruce saved ma life. Ye ken that I'm lucky tae be still alive. I learned sense that day. Anyhow, there's nae mair o' the damned squares. We'll all be crawlin' aboot the groond on oor bellies taemorrow.'

'I would nae be sae sure o' that,' replied Frankie. 'Dinna forget we've got General 'No Bobs' Hart.'

'Why dae they call him that?'

'Because in thirty-five years naebody has ever seen him bob doon when he was under fire.'

'Then he's a guid man.'

'A brave yin, there's nae doot aboot that. But that doesna make a guid general. I heard only the ither day that he was complaining aboot these new tactics.'

'What did he say?'

'He said that the infantry, that's us, should always be in square because it had always been done that way.'

'Ach, mannie,' said Leinie, 'I'm only a sergeant, but even I can see that ye canna bunch up taegether over country like this. Especially when the other fellow has at least as guid a rifle as you hae thanks to the bloody Germans.'

'Aye,' said Frankie, 'and he's got plenty o' them an' all. Mausers.'

'Are they as guid as the Lee-Metford?'

'Better,' said Frankie.

'Hoo mony o' them dae ye think there are?' asked Peter Leinie.

'Twa million.'

'Dinna be daft.'

'Weel, hoo the hell dae I know? I'll bet ye that there's mair o' us than there are o' them. We ought tae be able tae eat them up in aboot half an hour unless somebody does something bloody stupid.'

They were silent for a while.

'I wish I had a dram,' said Frankie.

'Aye,' said Peter Leinie, long and slow, as he conjured up the thought of the delicious amber liquid, 'I could dae wi' a woman, too.'

'No, you couldn't,' said Frankie. 'You're just a bittie scairt. Like me, like everybody. I would nae mind being hame and having ma wee Molly cooking me a fine venison stew on a chilly Highland night. Bugger Africa.'

'I wonder hoo Captain Bruce is getting on,' said Peter.

'Major Bruce, ye mean.'

'No, I dinna. I mean Captain Donald. He'll always be Captain Donald tae me. I heered that he was in Kimberley.'

'Aye,' replied Frankie. 'That's right. He's in Kimberley.'

The siege of Kimberley had begun on October the fifteenth. The population had been informed of its commencement by the banshee wail of the sirens and hooters of the mines. When this happened, the Boers could be seen on the horizon. Bands of horsemen. The railway which linked them with the Cape and the south had been cut. What livestock they possessed was mostly on the outskirts of the town where the enemy in a series of raids had either taken it, or, what they could not carry away, had slaughtered.

Kimberley was not defenceless; regular troops and volunteers amounted to a not inconsiderable force of nearly four thousand. The non-regulars consisted of a small number of Cape police, some mounted infantry, and a body of volunteers who called themselves the Kimberley Light Horse. The town itself was, of course, a great prize. Acre for acre, Kimberley was possibly the most valuable part of the whole British Empire.

The population, once the town had been besieged, steeled itself for the assault which they felt sure would come. It did not come. The Boers, always careful of their resources, had no intention of suffering the casualties which an assault would inevitably bring upon them. They were content to sit and wait until nature forced the surrender. The town was surrounded and cut off from all hope of relief; they were content to wait.

The inhabitants of Kimberley dug rifle pits and, sweating under the merciless summer sun, kept a perpetual watch for raiding parties. October gave way to November, and it was not until the seventh of that month that the civilian populace was subject to their first taste of the war.

The Boers brought up nine nine-pounder guns and commenced to bombard the town. For two whole weeks, until the twenty-first, they poured an average of fifty shells into the centre every day. Though this was naturally a most frightening experience, especially for the women and children, the amount of damage done was minimal and casualties were light. This was in the main due to the fact that the mines within the perimeter of the defences provided excellent and almost impregnable cover.

The main problem was not the shelling, which was more of a nuisance than a danger, but food. In the beginning everyone believed that relief could not be more than days, or, at the most, a week or two away. As a result, though rationing started almost immediately, it was by no means rigorous. The major problem was the almost complete absence of fresh milk. What little there was was reserved for the children. But there was very little even for them.

When the bombardment started, Brenda Bruce found this absence of milk for her three little ones more worrying than either the shelling or the proximity of the enemy.

Lieutenant-Colonel Robert Kekewich commanded the garrison. This was comprised of the non-regular and volunteer forces and a number of British regulars. The Northumberland Fusiliers, half of the North Lancashires of whom Colonel Kekewich was the commanding officer, a few Royal Engineers, the Munster Fusiliers, and the Ninth Lancers comprised Kekewich's force. Kekewich was a busy man; he was a good and very experienced soldier of some twenty-five years' service. He was of average height, bull necked and balding, with a drooping moustache and broad shoulders. Those shoulders of his had to carry not only the problems of the defence of Kimberley, but also the irritation of constant interference from Rhodes, who did not think much of soldiers. All of this made his job that much more difficult, and it was not without a feeling of irritation that he agreed to see two ladies, both by the name of Mrs Bruce, on the morning of the tenth of November.

Colonel Kekewich glanced up warily as the pair were ushered into his office by his orderly. He rose from behind his desk.

'Good morning, ladies.' The elder of the two, he estimated, would be about his own age, and the younger, well, she could be anything. She was one of those indeterminate young women. Still, they were probably related in some sort of way. 'Er – won't you sit down,' he added.

'Thank you, Colonel,' said Maud.

'Now then,' he said when they were all seated, 'what can I do for you?' He was well aware that most people wanted to see him in order to gain some sort of favour. He had declared the town under martial law, primarily to give himself power to deal with Rhodes, but it brought with it other responsibilities, as it made him the virtual ruler of everything; consequently many people came to him with odd little requests. But he was a fair-minded man and not in the habit of granting favours. He steeled himself for yet another 'No!'

'We have come,' said Maud, and she suddenly stopped as a shell whined overhead and landed with a 'crump' somewhere beyond them. 'It's about that, really,' she continued calmly. 'The shelling.' She waited. Brenda had agreed to let Maud do all the talking.

'Continue, madam.'

'This is my daughter-in-law, Mrs Donald Bruce, and we thought that it might be a good idea if we ladies – I include others apart from our two selves – were to form some sort of hospital or first-aid station in case the shelling might produce a sudden large number of casualties.'

'Ah, well,' thought the colonel. This was different, at any rate. They were not after something; they were actually trying to help.

'We have our own doctors, you know,' he said.

'Any large number of casualties may stretch their resources and we would be there to help if needed.'

'Have you any nursing experience?' he asked.

'Formally? No,' replied Maud. 'But my husband is a soldier.'

'Indeed, madam?'

'You may know him. General Bruce. He has retired now, o course.'

The colonel was impressed. 'General Willie Bruce, that would be?'

'The same.'

'I don't know him personally. But, of course, I know him by reputation.'

'So,' said Maud, 'at least I am an army wife and I have lived with the army long enough to realize some of their needs and some of the needs of people who are in action. After all, a casualty is a casualty whether or not he is wearing the Queen's uniform.'

'That is a very kind offer,' said Kekewich, 'but I think that I should have a little time to think this matter over.'

'I do not agree,' said Brenda, joining the conversation for the first time. 'A shell has just fallen in Kimberley. The next one could quite easily fall among a group of children. I think the sooner we get started, the better.'

'Indeed!' said the colonel. 'And what does your husband think about this? I suppose that he is in Kimberley.'

'Yes, he is in Kimberley.'

'Serving with one of the volunteer forces, I presume?'

Brenda looked a little embarrassed by that remark and Maud replied, 'No, he is not with one of the volunteer forces. My son does not believe in killing. He is a pacifist. Now, please don't tell me what you think about pacifists. I can guess. But I do know that if we were given permission to form our little hospital, my son would help in that to the utmost of his ability. As for ourselves, we would appreciate it if we could possibly have an immediate answer.'

'What about premises?'

'We would have room enough for fifteen beds in the offices below our apartment,' said Brenda.

'What offices are those?'

'Wilson and Bruce, diamond merchants. Obviously, we are not doing any diamond dealing at the moment. I also believe that the building next door could be used for the same purpose.'

'Yes, I know the place,' said the colonel, and he rubbed his jaw. 'And you want an immediate answer?'

'Of course,' said Maud.

'Would you be prepared to attend to Boers as well as our own people?'

'Naturally,' said Brenda.

'Stores? Linen and all the rest? Have you thought about that?' he asked.

'If you give us permission, we will organize a group of older children to collect whatever people can spare.'

'You seem to have thought of everything. Let me see if I have it right. You want to do this, you don't want any help, and you don't need anything from me?'

'That's right,' said Brenda.

'Well, don't sit there, ladies. Get on with it.' He rose to indicate that the interview was at an end.

'Thank you, Colonel,' said Maud, and they made their way to the door.

'Let me know when you're ready,' called the colonel as they reached the door, 'and thank you, ladies, thank you very much.'

He sat down again at his desk as his orderly brought in a cup of black coffee. 'Damned fine pair, don't you think?'

'Yes, sir,' said the uncomprehending orderly.

And Colonel Kekewich picked up a letter from Cecil Rhodes, grimaced, and got on with his work.

Things went well. The local hospital gave them the services of a trained nurse, and within two days, after a long and tiring series of house calls, they had managed to accumulate sufficient beds and bedding to deal with up to twelve patients. It was a case of getting a bed here, blankets there, a pillow, some pillow-cases, and sheets somewhere else. In a very short space of time they had sufficient to be able to say that they were ready to receive their first patient.

They were going to start the next morning, the sixteenth, training in simple basic nursing. Nurse Wickstead, a matronly woman in her forties, would be their mentor, and Maud and Brenda and the two ladies whom they had co-opted had scrubbed and polished until the company offices were immaculate.

All the heavy work had been done by Donald – Donald who, after wrestling with his conscience, had decided that he could not, under any circumstances, join the volunteer force. He was delighted to find that in this work of mercy, he had a way out. He found it quite reasonable that he should help the injured, if injured there were, for casualties had been extremely light, and do something other than face what was to him the appalling alternative of firing on his fellow men.

It was late in the afternoon of the fifteenth of November. Donald and Brenda went out to collect the last of their supplies. They had arrived at a stage when they were able to live with the shelling. The idea was that you waited for a shell to fall. After that, you knew that you had two hours at least before the next. The Boer had never fired at an interval of less than two hours, and so it was that, immediately after a shell had fallen, the town came to life and people appeared on the streets.

There were two houses to call on. They lay facing each other on opposite sides of a wide, dusty road leading off the market square. The ladies of those houses, though both had young families, were anxious to help and had offered to do the laundry. They had taken all of their linen to them the previous day and were now on their way to collect it.

Every horse had been commandeered by the military authorities, and Donald was pushing a handcart made out of rough wood upon which he had mounted a pair of wheels from an old perambulator. He left the cart outside one of the houses and started to cross the road to collect the linen from the other, leaving Brenda with the crude vehicle. He had almost reached the door of the house when he heard the rising scream of a shell.

'Down!' he screamed at the top of his voice and started to turn to run back to his wife.

He had barely gone a pace before the shell landed and the air between him and Brenda was filled with thick dust. For a moment he could see and hear nothing, and then he heard Brenda scream.

He ran through the dust, falling over the shattered remains of his cart, and almost on top of his wife who was lying beside it. A large jagged splinter of wood was protruding from her stomach. She was clutching it with frantic hands and moaning.

'Brenda! Brenda!' he called, crawling to her.

There was no recognition in her eyes. They were open and staring, but not seeing. He heaved the piece of wood out of her gut and tore the shirt from his back, stuffing it over the wound in an attempt to staunch the flow of blood. He heard someone running down the street towards him.

'Get a doctor!' he yelled, not looking up. 'I'll get her home.'

Gently he picked her up and stumbling, half running, half staggering, made his way to their house. He went in through the open door. He took her into the first room, the one which had held the safe and now held four beds. He laid her gently on the nearest of these and shouted for the nurse.

Nurse Wickstead hurried into the room and went straight to the figure on the bed.

'It's Brenda,' said Donald.

The nurse did not reply. She pulled Donald's blood-soaked shirt off the wound and started to cut away Brenda's clothes.

'Get the doctor,' she called.

'He's coming,' said Donald tonelessly, and he slumped on to

the next bed, feeling helpless and useless as he watched while the nurse tried to stop the bleeding.

Maud rushed into the room.

'Donald, what's happening? Oh, God!' She saw Brenda and went to her. 'Can I do anything?'

'Get your son out of here as soon as the doctor arrives,' Nurse Wickstead said. 'She's not conscious. There's nothing we can do.' She looked up. 'I think that is the doctor now.'

Through the window Maud could see a dogcart pulling up in front of the house.

'Try and get him away,' said the nurse.

'Come with me, Donald,' said Maud.

Donald did not reply. He just sat there staring at Brenda. Maud went over and stood in front of him, cutting off the vision of his wife.

'Donald,' she said.

She got him out just as the doctor entered the room. She took him upstairs into the little sitting room. As soon as she got there, Maud called Nambi.

'Nambi,' she said, 'I want you to keep the children in the playroom and stay with them there. Their mother has been injured and Mr Bruce is in a state of shock. I don't want him disturbed.'

'Yes, missie,' said Nambi. 'I look after Master Donald, if you like.'

'That will not be necessary. Just do as I say,' replied Maud, and Nambi went out.

Several times Maud tried to speak to Donald but there was no response. He just sat in his chair staring straight in front of him.

About half an hour later she heard the sounds of the doctor leaving.

'Donald,' she said, 'I'm going downstairs to try and find out what the doctor has said. Please stay here, I'll be up as soon as I know.' He did not even turn his head as she left him.

In the little ward Brenda now lay between clean sheets. There was a mound in the middle of the bed where some cagelike contraption had been erected to keep the weight of the sheets off her wounded stomach. She was very, very pale, and her eyes were now closed.

'She's not —?' said Maud, turning to the nurse.

'No, Mrs Bruce, she's still alive, but there's very little hope, I fear. Doctor will come back every two or three hours to administer sedatives and something to ease the pain, but he says that there is very little else that he can do. What about Mr Bruce?'

'I don't think that we should tell him,' said Maud. 'Not yet. anyway.'

A moment after Maud had finished speaking, Donald came back into the room.

'Donald,' said Maud, 'what are you doing here? I asked you to stay upstairs.'

He ignored them both and went and sat on the bed next to his wife. Very slowly and gently, he touched her forehead with his hand, but he did not speak.

It was dusk on the seventeenth when Brenda died. In all that time Donald had not moved from her side nor had he spoken to anyone. The doctor had left a bottle of some sort of medicine for him, but he ignored it. He just sat on staring at Brenda, refusing to be moved.

When the doctor came in and examined Brenda and then stood up shaking his head, and gently laid the sheet over Brenda's face, Donald neither spoke nor showed any emotion. He just got up from the bed he was sitting on and walked out the door.

It was beginning to get dark outside and the night sentries were being posted as Donald Bruce walked through Kimberley with two and a half days of stubble on his chin and the dust from the explosion which had killed his wife still clinging to him. He was unarmed apart from a hunting knife which he always carried in a sheath on his belt.

On he went. He got close to the forward pickets without being challenged. Then, summoning up the instincts of his Highland blood and the skills learned as a boy stalking the deer on the hills around his home, he started to creep through the picket lines.

Donald knew clearly, in spite of his confused state, exactly what he was going to do. Somewhere ahead of him would be the Boer pickets and they were the people who had killed Brenda and Donald Bruce was going to punish them.

Slowly he made his way across the flat land, taking advantage of every little hillock and tuft of sun-parched grass which he could use as cover. Ahead of him, in the light of the half moon, not more than ten yards away, he saw a hole in the ground. That was what he was looking for. He made a wide sweep to get behind it and then, silently, crept forward.

The Boer in the pit was called Pieter. Usually Jan was with him, but Jan had gone home for a few days to see to his farm, so Pieter was alone. Pieter was taking it easy. Night pickets were fairly safe. Nobody ever opened fire, and if they did not bother you, then you did not bother them. Like his comrades, he believed that as long as they could maintain the siege, Kimberley would have to fall eventually, and the less blood that was shed, the better.

So Pieter lolled in his pit, striking the occasional match to keep his pipe going, his Mauser lying against the side within reach. But he never reached for his rifle. Donald Bruce's arm wrapped itself around his nose and mouth, and Donald Bruce's hunting knife sliced a great gash across his throat. Donald felt the bubbling fountain of blood spurting from the wound as he waited until the body went limp and the life passed out of it.

As soon as Pieter was quite dead, Donald went through his pockets and found forty cartridges in clips of five. He took off the man's jacket and his slouch hat, picked them up with the Mauser, and headed out on to the open veld.

Two hours later he assumed that he was clear and found himself a place to rest by a small *kopje*. He had been there only a minute or two when a voice called his name.

'Master Donald. Master Donald.'

'Who's there?' he hissed, reaching for the Mauser.

'Nambi. I follow you.'

And suddenly in the moonlight, he saw her. She was standing, straight and black and beautiful with her full young breasts naked and silhouetted against the night sky. She was wearing nothing but a skirt, and she was carrying a bundle.

'I bring you blanket and some food, Master Donald. On the veld, it is cold at night.'

'How did you know what I was doing?' asked Donald.

'You are man,' she replied. 'In my tribe, if a man has his woman chopped, then he must chop man that did it. If he does not, he is not man. Was that the man that killed your woman?'

'That was only the first,' said Donald through tight lips.

'You eat now,' she said, producing a cold chicken from her bundle.

He suddenly realized that he was starving and ate ravenously for a while, tearing the carcass apart with his hands. He had the Boer's canteen with him and he took a little sip of the precious water and then offered her some. She refused.

'No,' she said, sitting down beside him. 'After tonight, I go back and look after Master Donald's children and his mammy.'

'Yes,' said Donald. 'You'll be safe, of course.'

He said it because the blacks were not part of this white man's war and they could pass unharmed.

'You can go now if you want to,' he said. 'Thank you, Nambi, for bringing this.'

'No, Master Donald,' she replied. 'Tonight I stay with you. I keep you warm.'

'No,' he said.

'Yes, Master Donald. Tonight you make me have child. All the girls in my village will have children now. I know it. I am old and ashamed for not having children. You give me child. I want your child, Master Donald. That will be a fine child.'

'It is not possible, Nambi,' he said. 'You had better just leave me.'

But he felt the warmth of her body close to him and when her breasts lightly brushed his face as she came closer to him on her knees, the passion rose within him and he obeyed her request. His desires, long restrained, were at last fulfilled.

It was the pleasant time when Donald awoke, that brief period between the chill of the night and the sweltering heat of the day, when the sun had just tipped above the horizon. He stretched out a hand to touch Nambi, but she was not there. He was wrapped in the blanket that she had brought with her. Donald sat up and looked around and could see nothing but the open and seemingly endless veld. She had gone. For a moment he let his thoughts dwell on the night that had passed and wondered if he had succeeded in giving her the child she wanted. He was never to know, for Nambi would leave the white man's world and go back to her people. Then he thought of his children, and his mother in Kimberley. They would be all right; at least, as all right as they would be anywhere in South Africa.

Then he recalled grimly the task which he had set himself. He tied up the blanket into a roll, put on the Boer's slouch hat, checked his Mauser, and started, a predatory animal, stalking across the lonely veld.

5

'The man is mad. Our esteemed General Hart seems to think that you can deal with this situation the way we handled the fuzzy-wuzzies at El Teb.'

Ian Maclaren was talking to Hugh Grant in his tent. It was about ten o'clock at night on the fourteenth of December. The camp had quietened down and the men were huddling together in their bivouacs against the chill night air. The briefing was over and all was supposed to be ready for the dawn attack. The campfires which had flickered merrily a short time ago were now little glowing spots of red, dying embers. In the near silence and to the left of the Maclarens could be heard the occasional whinny or stamp of a horse coming from the cavalry lines. Under the velvet black of the sky, the stars shining bright and clear, it should have been an atmosphere of utter peace, but it was not. The tension within the thousands who lay there that night was an almost tangible thing which could be felt, real and potent, on the still night air.

Hugh Grant sat looking at his old friend and comrade.

'What's the problem?' he asked.

'It's simply this,' said Ian. 'You know that there is a big loop in the river just in front of us. Well, we are supposed to ford it and attack the Boer on the other side.'

'It'll be expensive, but it makes sense,' said Grant.

'But he wants us to march into that loop, it's practically a bloody island, in column of eight – "shoulder to shoulder," he said.'

'You're not serious.'

'I wish to God that I wasn't.'

'Is it as bad as you say?'

'Frankly,' replied Ian, 'I don't trust the scouts we've got. So I sent Frankie Gibson out to recce the lie of the land. I'm not saying that we shouldn't do the job, but I'm damned sure that we shouldn't do it Hart's way. We need to be in open order and grabbing every bit of cover that we can find until we're across. Dammit, Hugh, there might be a thousand Boers on the other side and we can't do a blasted thing about them until that river is behind us. Can you imagine what a thousand Mausers will do to what is in effect an old-fashioned square? It'll be a bloody massacre.'

'What did Frankie say?'

'Apparently there's a path. It goes right down to the river, and must lead to a ford. We ought to be crossing there at night. The rest of the river is running pretty quickly and Frankie says that he thinks that it's quite deep.'

'You mean that the only place that we can get across is at the ford?'

'Exactly. We'll be sitting ducks.'

'Who goes in first?' asked Hugh.

'The Dubliners.'

'Poor bastards. But thank God it's not us.'

'I tell you, Hugh, I'm damned if I'm going to let my men go in pressed tight against each other and offer the Boer the fastest and easiest target that he could possibly dream of. We'd be cut to pieces before we're anywhere near the riverbank.'

'You're going to disobey orders?'

'Stretch them, Hugh, stretch them,' said Ian with a little smile. 'Well, I suppose that we ought to get some sleep.'

'What time's reveille?'

'Five thirty. I'll have a think about it and talk to the officers just before we move out. You are married, aren't you, Hugh?'

'Yes,' he replied. 'Anyhow, why do you ask? You know that I'm married.'

'Do me a favour. If anything happens to me tomorrow, go

and see Victoria. I feel a bit guilty about her.'

'Why?'

'I have reason. And if I should be wounded, ask them not to ship me to Pietermaritzburg.'

'Why ever not? It's the best hospital in the area.'

'It's part of the reason. Will you do it for me and not ask any questions?'

'I'll try,' said Hugh. 'But I don't suppose anything I say will have much effect.'

'Thanks. Well, good night, old boy, see you at dawn.'

Hugh Grant got up and left Ian's bivouac. Just as he came out of the tent, an orderly hurried up to him.

'Sir,' said the orderly, 'is the colonel in there?'

'He is. What do you want him for? Is it important?'

'I dinna ken, sir.'

'I don't think that you should disturb him. He's going to sleep now.'

'I'm sorry, sir, but the guard commander telt me tae gan and gi' him a message.'

'Can you tell me?'

'No, sir.'

'All right. If you've got to do it, I suppose you have to.'

The orderly got to Ian's tent just as Ian was taking off his khaki doublet.

'Yes, what is it?' said Ian in a resigned tone.

'Sir, the er – the captain of the guard told me to report tae you, sir.'

'Can't it wait?'

'It's a Boer, sir, we've captured one.'

'What the hell! Can't the captain interrogate him himself?'

'It's no that, sir. This yin says he kens you,' said the orderly.

'Knows me? That's ridiculous. I don't know any Boers.'

'Well, this yin talks like an Englishman and says that he kens you weel.'

'You saw him, then?'

'Och, aye, sir, he's like all the rest o' them. Dirty and smelly wi' a beard that looks as if it's never been washed.'

'And the captain told you that I ought to see him?'

'Aye, sir.'

'All right, orderly, wheel him in.'

A few moments later, accompanied by an armed guard, what must have been one of the most disreputable sights Ian had ever seen was ushered into his tent. He was tall, sunburnt, dust encrusted and he had an unkempt, straggly beard. His fingernails were black and there were sores on the backs of his hands. He wore ragged trousers, a torn, bloodstained bush jacket, and an ill-fitting slouch hat. The only thing that seemed strange about him was the way he stood, straight and firm, like a soldier.

'They tell me that you claim to know me,' said Ian.

'I know you well, Ian Maclaren,' was the reply. '*Si vis pacem para bellum*,' he quoted the regimental motto.

'My God,' said Ian. 'It can't be.'

'I'm afraid that it is, Ian.'

'Donald Bruce. Donald, how are you, and where the hell have you come from?'

'Kimberley.'

'How did you get here?'

'I walked,' he replied. 'I walked most of the way. I rode a little, then I shot the horse and ate some of it. It didn't matter, I stole it from a Boer.'

Ian suddenly became aware of the guard still standing there. 'It's all right,' he said, 'I do know this gentleman. Go and see what you can get him to eat. Are you hungry, Donald?'

'That's an understatement. I haven't eaten for three days.'

'Well, sit down, man, for God's sake. You look all in. What about your mother? She's in Kimberley, isn't she?'

'Yes, she's with the children.'

'And Brenda, of course.'

'Brenda is dead.'

'Donald – what can I say? Sorry seems a very inadequate word, but you know what I mean.'

'The Boers killed her.'

'That can't be true. The Boers don't make war on women.'

'It was a shell. They'd been shelling us for a week when I left.'

'I'm sorry, Donald. This must be a terrible thing for you to have to bear. I'll get you a meal and see if we can do anything about clothing. Then I'll have you taken to the rear. We've got a fight on our hands tomorrow.'

'No, thanks, Ian. I don't want that.'

'You don't want what?' asked Ian, puzzled.

'I don't want to go back to the rear.'

'But, Donald, you're a noncombatant. You are a civilian. You can't stay here.'

'I want back.' He almost spat out the words.

'You?' Ian could hardly believe what he was hearing.

'I want back,' repeated Donald. 'I want back into the regiment. I left Kimberley nearly a month ago. Just after Brenda. . . . I got out through the pickets. I slit a Boer's throat. I took his rifle and ammunition. This is his hat and jacket. Since then, I've killed eight of the bastards. Five men and three women, and all I want to do is to kill some more.'

'No, Donald, you can't expect me to believe that. Not you, of all men.'

Donald had hardly raised his voice. Practically everything he had said had been in the same flat monotone. He was simply stating facts and Ian knew it.

'You know that you cannot come back, Donald,' said Ian. 'You were cashiered. I can't go to the general and tell him that I have an officer here who was cashiered and now he wants his commission back. You know as well as I do what sort of reply I would get.'

'Ian, I don't care about a commission. You could take me on as the lowest private soldier in the regiment. As long as I have a gun, that is all I want.'

'Well, you can't have a gun. Not a Maclaren gun, anyway,' said Ian.

'But, Ian,' pleaded Donald, 'I want to kill Boers. Isn't that the whole purpose of the exercise?'

'No, Donald, you're wrong, that's not the whole purpose of the exercise. The whole purpose of what we are doing is to win this war with as little bloodshed as possible.'

'Once I might have believed that. So you are not going to help me?'

'Donald, for one thing, you are not fit. You can't be. You need rest, and for this engagement tomorrow, every man must be fit. You can't set yourself up as an avenging angel, no matter what has happened to you. You don't have to tell me how tragic it was for you when that happened to Brenda. But you cannot blame the whole Boer nation for it, and you can't go around killing their women. That is murder, Donald. You know that I ought to have you arrested for that?'

'I don't care if I'm arrested. I have been arrested before. Or had you forgotten?'

'I know that only too well,' replied Ian. 'Do you remember why you were arrested?'

Donald was silent.

'You were arrested because you refused to kill. I didn't agree with you, but I admired you as a man of principle. That was the reason. It started when you refused to kill Jimmy Grigor. Grigor had to do it for you himself.

'I'm going to tell you something, Donald. You're not going to like it, but I am going to tell you and you will bloody well listen. Grigor was shot because he bore grudges and because he was a violent man. You were kicked out of the army because you could not fight alongside your comrades, because you had too much feeling for the men you were shooting at. But now you are a different person from the Donald Bruce I knew and admired. You are like Jimmy Grigor.'

'I warn you, Ian, don't try me too much.'

'I'm not afraid of you, Donald, and I'm not going to have you in the regiment. Not even as a private soldier. Don't you understand? We do not want people like you in the army. The army is no place to work out a grudge. The army is no place for you to take your revenge. The army is a place where you do what you're told and you obey the rules.' There was no answer.

'Your food should be here any moment,' said Ian after a pause. 'Eat and then you are going back to the rear.'

'But —' said Donald.

'Don't argue with me,' said Ian. 'There is no place for you in the army.'

'I'll come back, you know.'

'Not to me you won't, not to the Maclarens.'

'Can I have my Mauser back?'

'No.'

'Then give me a safe conduct through the lines and turn me loose.'

'No,' said Ian. 'I just want you to remember, Donald, that the army uses its soldiers, but the soldiers do not use the army.'

'You won't stop me,' said Donald.

'That's as may be. But I'm not going to help you, and I'm damned if I'll let you use this regiment to work out your hatred. You'll have to find some other way.'

'I shall.'

An orderly came into the tent with a plate of stew. Donald ate ravenously. He did not speak and Ian sat and watched him in embarrassed silence. When he had finished his meal, Ian called for the orderly and told him to take Mr Bruce back to the R.A.M.C. lines at the rear.

As Donald left, Ian said, 'I'm sorry, Donald, but I had to do it this way. I promise you, though, that no one will hear about what you have told me tonight.'

Without a word, Donald left him.

Ian sat at the open flap of his tent gazing out at the black night sky. It had all been very upsetting, but there were other things to think of. He looked down the shadowy lines of tents. There were nearly a thousand of his men around him. A thousand men for whom he would have to devise some manner of safety from the gross stupidity of his commanders.

He had been sitting there some little while when he saw the orderly returning.

'You haven't been long,' he said.

'No, sir. Mr Bruce teld me that he kenned the way, so I left him.'

'You what?!'

'Sir?'

'It doesn't matter. You'd better get some sleep now.'

And Ian went back into his tent and tried not to think about Donald Bruce.

6

The first grey streaks of dawn were appearing in the eastern sky when the bugles sounded reveille. Private Alasdair Maclaren rolled himself out of his blanket and sat up rubbing his eyes. Naturally, no one had told him anything, but he was well aware that they were going into action that day. The signs were all there. However, Private Maclaren was not worried. He was still going to be among the living when the day ended. He was untouchable and he was safe. Had not Marhi Crow told him that he would see her again before he died, and Marhi Crow was thousands of miles away. Private Maclaren believed what Marhi Crow had told him because she was a witch and she had the sight. He could afford to be brave; he might even win himself a medal. That would be a grand thing to take back home to the glen and show to his family in Drumnadrochit. There was no risk, so there was no cause for fear.

Private Maclaren, as did all the other men in the battalion, got out his oil bottle and his pull-through. He put a smear of oil on a cotton square of two by four, slipped it through the loop in the end of the pull-through, and ran it a couple of times through the barrel of his rifle. He checked the action of the bolt and then, one at a time, he pressed five cartridges into the magazine. Ready now, he stepped out of the tent, which he shared with thirteen others, and blinked at the sun which was just beginning to show above the horizon. He shivered slightly in the chill of the morning, but knew that within minutes it would be warm and pleasant, and within an hour or so, hot and uncomfortable.

He poured a little water from his water bottle into his tin cup and sat on the ground outside his tent, dipping the corner of the five-inch square of rock-hard biscuit into the water in order to soften it sufficiently for him to be able to eat it. He thought wistfully of a cup of strong, black tea, looking at his breakfast with distaste and pondering on the possible use of it as a missile.

A little way down the lines Corporal Anderson was also loading his rifle, but before he inserted each cartridge, he carefully snipped off the end of the bullet. Having done that, he then got out the rest of his fifty rounds and did likewise. Corporal Anderson lacked Private Maclaren's feeling of immortality and he was not going to take any chances. If anyone came at him, the dum-dum would stop him dead, literally. Corporal Anderson had seen enough action to know that a good clean wound from a normal bullet would still leave the recipient able to function for a few seconds, and he had seen other men die in those few seconds. To allow such things as humanitarianism to affect his personal safety was completely foreign to Corporal Anderson.

Over by his tent Ian Maclaren had his company commanders grouped around him.

'Gentlemen,' he said, 'we are going to attack the Boer today, take Colenso, and clear the way to Ladysmith. The Boer is entrenched on the far side of the Tugela. Now, I did not trust the information which I received from H.Q., or at least, let me say that I wanted it to be confirmed. I sent Regimental Sergeant-Major Gibson to go out personally and do a recce. You will no doubt be aware that the R.S.M. has spent a lifetime moving unobserved on other people's property, not the least my own.'

There was a polite laugh which did not disguise the tension that they were all feeling.

'It appears,' continued Ian, 'that there is a ford at the corner of the loop in the river which we are facing. That loop, for those of you who do not know, is shaped like a large elongated U. From where we lie, the U is on its side. We have to go into that, a little way, in order to get across the river. The ford – by the way, they call them drifts out here – is not going to be easy as the enemy is no fool and will have it well covered. Unfortunately, as far as I can see, there is no other way we can cross that damned river, so we just have to accept the fact that there are going to be casualties and that they may be quite heavy.

'My orders are that the brigade will move out in about an hour's time in column of eight with the Dublin Fusiliers in the van and ourselves following. I have received instructions from the brigade commander that we are to march in close formation.

'Gentlemen, I do not like criticizing my superior officers but this command strikes me as somewhat foolish, to put it mildly. It will unquestionably offer the enemy an excellent target and result in major casualties. In view of this, I am now going to issue you with the following orders which I expect every one of you to obey. If I am wrong, then the responsibility is entirely mine. If I am right, there will be a lot of our men alive tonight who would otherwise have died.

'We will march out in column of eight, but no man will be less than two arms' lengths away from his neighbour or from the rank in front of him. We will follow close on the Dubliners and if they get stuck, we will not attempt the crossing, but take cover, and cover them as best we can from this bank. I don't envy them and I'm damned glad that it is not us. One other thing. For your own safety, gentlemen, I would suggest that you do not wear your Sam Brownes and that you endeavour to look as much as possible like a private soldier.'

'Why is that, sir?' asked Robert Maclaren.

'Because, Robert,' replied his brother, 'if you are faced with an advancing enemy, whom do you aim at? Who is your prime target?'

'The commander, of course.'

'Precisely. So obviously, any officer, especially a senior officer, makes a more desirable target than a private soldier. Therefore, gentlemen, I suggest that we do not try to look smart.' Ian turned to Hugh Grant. 'Are the ammo supplies to hand?'

'Yes, sir. We have half a platoon bringing up the boxes in the rear of the battalion and every man has been issued with fifty rounds.'

'Good,' said Ian. 'Well, there's not much else that I can tell you. We shall have to play it by ear. One last thing. If you are ever in doubt, make your own decisions. I'll back you in whatever you do. And make sure that, in the event of any of you becoming a casualty, the chain of command is clear and decisive within your own company. If you consider it necessary, you have my full authority to act independently.

'You had better get away now and see that your subalterns and senior N.C.O.s are well briefed. Good luck to you all. It's going to be a hard day.'

For the first three-quarters of an hour, nothing happened. They marched along a well-worn track in the direction of the Tugela. Away to their right and near the railway line, they could see the tents of Buller's headquarters, and shortly after that, maybe a mile further on, a couple of naval twelve-pounders with their crews standing idly around them. Away to the northwest they heard the sound of heavy guns as their artillery on the far side of the railway commenced their bombardment. The dragoons trotted past them, raising a cloud of dust, rattling and clanking and shouting well-meaning insults. Very shortly afterwards they passed the dragoons who had halted, apparently to await orders.

It had been downhill for most of the way and by this time the river itself, now only a mile away, was clearly discernible. The track which they were following led right down to the river bank and the drift which Frankie Gibson had spotted. It was at this moment that General Hart galloped past on his charger.

He glared at the Maclarens and shouted, 'Close those men up! Close those men up!'

Ian Maclaren tightened his lips and gave no orders. He turned to Hugh Grant.

'Did you hear what he was saying, Hugh?' he asked.

'Not a word of it,' replied Hugh, grinning.

A few minutes later Hart careered past them again, heading towards where the Dubliners led the column. He reined in his horse when he got level with Ian.

'Colonel,' he called, 'didn't you hear my orders?'

'What orders, sir?'

'I ordered you to get your men closed up, see to it.'

'Sorry, sir,' replied Ian, 'they must have drifted out a bit.'

'Well, see that they drift back!' shouted Hart, and then he galloped off.

'Very good, sir,' called Ian to the retreating figure.

He turned again to Hugh Grant who raised his eyebrows.

'I think I've lost my voice, Hugh,' said Ian, and Hugh grinned again.

They were about four hundred yards from the river when a young dragoon officer came up to the column at a full gallop. He spotted Ian at the head and called to him.

'Where's the general?'

'I'm not sure,' Ian shouted back. 'I think he's up at the head. If you see him, don't ask him to come back here. What is it?'

'Can you send a runner to tell him that we've spotted the Boer in strength on the other side of the river.'

'Where?'

'They're right along the banks but most of them seem to be covering the big loop.'

'All right, I'll get the message to him,' said Ian.

'Good luck to you, sir,' said the dragoon. 'You're heading right for them.' And he was away.

Ian turned to Frankie Gibson. 'Sergeant-Major, send a man up to the head of the column and give that message. You got it all right?'

'Aye, sirr. Corporal MacTavish, awa' oot and tell the general that the Boer's in strength on the other side and especially aroond the loop. Leave your rifle wi' yin o' the men and double up.'

'Yessir,' said MacTavish, and doubled away towards the head of the column.

'I'll just gan doon the column and dae a wee check, sirr,' said Frankie.

'Righto, Sergeant-Major, carry on.'

When he arrived at C Company, Frankie looked around and noticed that they were veering away to the right and leaving the path.

'What the hell's gannin' on?' he said to Sergeant Leinie, who was marching just behind Robert Maclaren, his company commander.

'What is it?' asked Robert. 'Something worrying you, Sergeant-Major?'

'The drift is right doon this path. There's a wee burn at the tail o' the loop and unless we're ganna cut right across tae there and join up wi' the brigade on oor right – och nae, ye canna be sich a lunatic.'

'What do you mean?' said Robert.

'Sir, if we get trapped in yon loop it'll be a massacre. We'll be cut tae ribbons.'

'How do you know this?'

'I was oot there last night. I had a guid look aroond. There's nae way ye can get across that river excepting right doon this path.'

'Thanks, Sergeant-Major,' said Robert. 'Will you hang on here with Sergeant Leinie while I go and have a word with the colonel.'

Robert hurried down the column but when he got to Ian, he didn't have to tell him anything.

'I think our dear general has gone off his head,' said Ian. 'Bob, pass the word quietly. Open order, keep spread out and keep your eyes open for cover for when the shooting starts.'

The word was passed throughout the ranks.

'You're taking a bit of a chance,' said Hugh Grant.

'Perhaps, but not with the lives of my men,' replied Ian.

They were very close to the Tugela now. They could see the river running straight away to their left, then behind back again to create the salient which was on all of their minds. It was half a mile wide and a mile deep and Hart was taking them right into it.

They were almost up to the first bend of the river when the shooting started. They heard the crackle of rifle fire but no whine of bullets and they certainly could not see any of the Boers.

'I think that the poor bloody Dubliners are getting it, sırr,' Sergeant Leinie said to Robert.

'Yes,' said Robert grimly. 'It'll be us next. Where the hell's that bloody fool taking us? You can't see any of them, can you?'

'No a one, sirr.'

It was just then that they got their first casualty. Private Alasdair Maclaren was marching alongside Jamie Ross. Jamie Ross was his marra, not much older than Alasdair but much more afraid. Alasdair was telling him that all he had to do was to stick close to him and he would be safe, sure that his own security would rub off on to his friend. Jamie was just about to say something. He opened his mouth, but instead of words, a big glob of blood came out. His eyes went glassy and he fell across Alasdair. Alasdair could not believe it.

'Jamie, Jamie, what are you saying!' he called, leaning over the body. 'Jamie, for God's sake, say sumthin' tae me.'

But Jamie was very dead, shot through the head. Alasdair looked at Jamie, horrified. He had never seen a man killed before. He had never even seen a corpse.

'Get up. Get up,' he said.

Then he got to his feet and stood transfixed as the battalion went on past him until he got a boot up his arse and Corporal Anderson said, 'Get on wi' it, sodjer, he'll fight nae mair battles.'

The rifle fire was becoming more persistent and more and more directed at the Maclarens and men were beginning to fall. Ian at the head of his column realized full well the trap that they were marching into.

'Look,' said Ian to Hugh Grant and Frankie Gibson, 'I'm going to try and get the men out of this. We'll take them across to the other side of this fucking salient. At least we'll be able to get out of it from there. Pass the word. Open order. Straight across as far as we can go. If there are Boers there, we'll fight them. If not, then we'll start to move out.'

'What about the general, sir?' said Hugh.

'To hell with the bloody general. Pass the word.' Ian was in a state of cold fury.

'Aye, sir,' said Frankie Gibson and he even allowed himself a smile. This was the kind of C.O. that a soldier could appreciate.

Within a matter of a minute the Maclarens were spread out in open order and were heading across the salient. Fifty yards from the bank a rapid fire opened up on to them from the far side.

'Take cover,' shouted Ian at the top of his voice.

Right then a big rock was just about the most precious thing that a man could find, but a little hillock or even a tuft of scrub grass would do.

The Boers were entrenched on the opposite bank, to all intents and purposes invisible. On their left they saw a sergeant from some other regiment shouting at the top of his lungs as he led a group of a dozen men straight into the river. Those that the Boers did not get, the river did; it must have been fifteen feet deep just there.

'There's a brave man,' said Sergeant Leinie.

'There's a bloody fool,' said Frankie Gibson.

General Hart, mounted on his charger, came galloping down the Maclaren section of the river bank.

'Where's your colonel? Where's your colonel?' he shouted.

Nobody knew, and if they had known, it is doubtful that they would have told him.

'I want this battalion closed up,' he raged.

'I want some Boer to put a bullet through yon bastard,' said Sergeant Leinie.

'Och, they wouldna dae that,' said Frankie. 'He's worth a couple o' brigades tae them.'

Peter Leinie raised his Lee-Metford and started to take careful aim.

Frankie Gibson realized what was in Leinie's mind. 'Dinna be a bloody fool, they'll hang you and yon's nae worth hangin' for.'

The Maclarens did not close up. They stayed where they were. Here and there one of them was hit, but they were so dispersed that no one knew quite who.

They stayed there, pinned down for two hours, under the scorching sun. The backs of their legs – that exposed portion between the bottom of the kilt and the top of the hose – was seared red and agonizing by the sun. All around them was the sound of firing. Somebody seemed to be having a battle.

Ian Maclaren was sharing the cover of a large rock with Gordon Bruce and two privates.

'Are we going to do anything, sir?' asked Gordon. 'We can't stay here forever.'

'We're not going to do anything if I can bloody well help it,' replied Ian. 'This is the stupidest thing that I have ever seen in the whole of my life. God preserve us from the generals.'

'Yes, sir, but what are we going to do?'

'If necessary, we'll stay here till dark; then we might have a chance of getting out of it. How are you two feeling – MacKay, isn't it?'

'Aye, sirr,' replied the soldier, a grizzled, stoical man of about thirty. 'I'm all right, sir, but I dinna want tae stand up.'

'I don't think that we've had many casualties, sir,' said Gordon.

'Thank God for that. I daren't think how many there would have been if we had obeyed orders,' replied Ian.

On another part of their little front, Private Donaldson was holding forth.

'You know this is a nonbattle,' he said to Corporal MacTavish. 'The idiots who control our lives and deaths seem to have decided that the Boer was in need of a spot of target practice. I really do think that they ought to be taught a lesson.'

'Who?' said MacTavish. 'The generals or the Boers?'

'The Boers, of course. You cannot teach generals anything. They are completely solid between the ears.'

'Aye? And are ye ganna be the yin tae dae it?'

'Perhaps,' said Donaldson. 'After all, I have less to lose than almost any man in the regiment. I have no home, no honour, no reason for living. Goodbye, Mister MacTavish, I shall probably see you in hell.'

He crawled out from behind the bit of scrub which was their cover, dragging his Lee-Metford with him.

'Come back, you bloody fool,' shouted MacTavish as he watched in horror.

There were a couple of little spurts of dust around Donaldson as somebody on the other side spotted the movement. Donaldson stopped and fired and a man rose from a trench on the opposite bank and fell.

'All right,' yelled MacTavish. 'You got yin. Noo, come ye back.'

Donaldson moved forward a little way and fired again.

'Twa,' shouted MacTavish. He half rose from the scrub and immediately took cover again as a volley of shots whistled round his ears.

By this time half of the battalion was watching Donaldson as he approached the water's edge. From the tenuous security of his rock, Ian turned to Gordon Bruce.

'Who is that bloody fool?' he demanded.

'It looks like Private Donaldson, sir,' replied Gordon.

'If he ever gets out of this, I'll have him court-martialled.'

In another part of the field Frankie Gibson saw what was happening.

'Cover me,' he yelled, 'I'm going tae get the stupid bastard oot o' this.'

'You'll stay right where you are, Sergeant-Major. That is an order,' called Hugh Grant who was nearby.

Frankie pretended not to have heard and started to crawl out towards the river, but he was too late. Donaldson had paused and then suddenly rose to his feet with his bayonet fixed.

'Charge!!' he yelled and started rushing towards and into the water.

He had barely got his feet wet before he was cut down. He must have been hit a dozen times. He was waist deep in the water when he fell. His body started to float downstream in the middle of a big red stain. He was floating face down, the flow of the water pushing his kilt up and revealing his bare buttocks. Frankie Gibson crawled back to his cover.

'Why does a man dae a thing like that?' he said to no one in particular.

General Buller, instead of remaining at his headquarters from which he could have directed the progress of the battle, had mounted his charger and was riding around different sections of the front. He discovered the plight into which Hart had inexplicably led his brigade, and at eleven o'clock in the morning he ordered that the battered remnants of Hart's brigade should retire. It fell to General Lyttelton to take his brigade in and cover their retreat.

They came out of the salient in dribs and drabs, each pathetic little group making its own way to the safety of the rear. Once they realized what was happening, the Maclarens provided what cover they could for the bloodied Dubliners who had been trapped on their left.

After the Dubliners had got out, Ian turned to Gordon.

'Right, Gordon,' he said. 'It's our turn now, let's try and get out of this hellhole.'

By one o'clock that afternoon the Maclaren Highlanders were back in their lines.

When he arrived at his bivouac, Ian Maclaren flung himself wearily down on his cot. But it was only for a moment. He was the commanding officer, there would be no pause for him;

there was work to do. He struggled out through the flap of his tent and called a passing soldier.

'Find the R.S.M. and tell him to report to me,' he said.

The soldier went off at a reluctant trot. A minute or so later Frankie Gibson arrived at Ian's bivouac. Somehow or other he had managed to look spruce and smart. Even his buttons seemed to be newly polished. Ian eyed him enviously.

'How are you feeling, Sergeant-Major?' he asked.

'I'm fine, sirr,' was the reply.

'We had better call the roll.'

'We're daeing it noo, sir.'

'Have you got the casualties yet?'

'Not yet, sir. But they're no heavy. Apart from Donaldson, there seems tae be only twa deed. There are some wounded, but nae many o' them bad. I dinna ken if anybody's missing. Not yet, anyway.'

'All right, Sergeant-Major,' said Ian. 'Let me know as soon as you have the figures.'

Frankie went off and Ian sat down on his cot. He was damned tired, though whether it was through exhaustion or fury, he could not tell. It had been such a criminal waste. It was the biggest nonbattle that he had ever heard of. Neither side had even tried to attack and the Boers, secure in their trenches, had dealt a crushing blow to a British force which must have outnumbered them by four to one, at least.

Five minutes later Frankie was back.

'Well, let's have it,' said Ian.

'Three deed; seventeen wounded, three serious, eight fit for duty and twa missing.'

'Do you know who?'

'Sergeant Leinie, sir, and I'm sorry tae have tae tell you, but the ither yin's Major Grant. What are we gannin' tae dae aboot them, sir?'

'I'll do it,' said Ian. 'Tell somebody to get my charger.'

Ian went into his bivouac and removed his kilt. He put on a pair of light serge breeches and a pair of leather riding boots. He checked his Webley to see that it was fully loaded and shoved it into his leather holster. He came out of his bivouac to find Frankie Gibson waiting for him with his charger.

'Where are you gannin', sir?' asked Frankie.

'I'm going back to the loop, Frankie,' said Ian. 'I'm going to see if I can find them. If anything happens to me, I want you to tell Major Bruce that he is in command. Do you understand?'

'Let me come wi' ye, sir.'

'You'll do no such thing, Sergeant-Major. I'm going alone. Can you rig me up a white flag or something?'

'A white flag?' said Frankie, horrified.

'Yes, Sergeant-Major,' said Ian impatiently. 'A white flag. The Boers are not animals, they'll respect it. They'll know that we are looking for wounded.'

'All right,' said Frankie, disapprovingly.

Soon Ian was riding out of the camp back towards the loop with a white handkerchief fluttering from a little stick.

He had been quite right; the Boers did respect the white flag. Moreover, he was not alone on the battlefield. There were several small groups of men moving around. There were stretcher bearers carrying out the wounded. Well, thought Ian, at least the Maclarens had got their own wounded out. And there were other little clusters of men who were digging shallow graves while a chaplain went from one to another and said a few words over each corpse.

Ian was back in the sector where they had been pinned down for two hours and he felt sick at the utter, useless waste of it all.

'Have you seen any Highlanders?' he called to a couple of stretcher bearers who were hurrying past.

'Naw, sir, 'aven't seen a sign of one,' one of the men replied in a thick Cockney accent. 'If any have been picked up, they'll be back at the dressing station if they're alive.'

'Thanks,' said Ian, and commenced his search.

He had been looking without success for a little while when he was interrupted.

'Englander,' said a voice.

Ian whipped around, startled. A tall bearded figure rose from the scrub. Ian started to tug at his revolver.

'All right, Englander,' said the Boer. 'No more shooting, the battle is over.'

'What battle?' said Ian bitterly.

'The one you just lost, Englander.'

'I'm not an Englander,' said Ian. 'I'm a Scot.'

'Where is your skirt, then? But it doesn't matter what you are. You all want our country. I have one of your men here. A Scot.'

Ian ran to where the Boer was standing. And there, lying in a shallow depression, he saw Hugh Grant. There was blood all around him, flowing from a massive wound in his stomach. Ian could even see bits of his gut through the remnants of his kilt.

Ian stopped, horrified at the sight of his old friend. 'Is he alive?' he demanded.

'Just,' replied the Boer. 'I gave him water but —'

Ian got down beside Hugh and cradled his head in his arms. Hugh's eyes flickered open.

'Hello, Ian,' he said. 'It's bloody sore.'

'Don't try and talk, Hugh.'

'Nice of you to come and see me,' murmured Hugh. He coughed and a little trickle of blood oozed from the corner of his mouth.

'We've got to get you back,' said Ian. He turned to the Boer. 'Can you get some stretcher bearers?'

The Boer shook his head. 'No use, Englander.'

'He's right,' said Hugh. 'This is it, you know.'

'It shouldn't be you, Hugh,' said Ian, and there was a catch in his voice. 'You should have had command.'

'No, Ian, I wasn't right. You're doing a great job. You're the finest Maclaren of them all.' He raised his head a little. 'It's such a pity, it's such a lovely day.' He coughed once and was silent.

'He was your friend?' said the Boer.

Ian nodded.

'I am sorry, Englander.'

'Thanks,' said Ian bitterly.

'You like I should help you to bury him?' asked the Boer.

'No,' said Ian, rising to his feet. 'There's someone else that I have to find.'

'I help you look.'

The area around them was clearing now. It seemed doubtful that anyone was within half a mile of them. They walked together among the few boulders and the bits of scrub that had meant the difference between life and death to his men only a couple of hours ago. They found Peter Leinie. He was sitting up, his back against a rock, smoking his pipe. He had been shot through the thigh and obviously could not walk, so, with Highland resignation, he had made himself as comfortable as he could until such time as somebody came and found him.

'Hello, sirr,' he said, 'I'm glad you've found me. It's getting bloody hot here.'

'All right, Sergeant,' said Ian. 'I've got a horse here. We'll be able to get you back to camp on that.' He turned to the Boer. 'Will you help me to get this man on to my horse?'

'Yes, I help,' said the Boer. 'We have sent many of your men back today, if you —' He stopped.

There was the crack of a rifle and a neat little hole appeared in the man's temple. He fell like a log.

Ian hit the ground trying to shield Peter Leinie, tugging at his Webley as he did so. He could see the man who had fired, another Boer it looked like, but this one was carrying a rifle. A tall, bearded figure in ragged clothes with a bandolier and a slouch hat.

'Don't draw your pistol, Ian. I wouldn't like to have to shoot you.'

Ian got to his feet, astonished. It was Donald Bruce. 'You murdering swine!' he said. 'That man was helping me with our wounded.'

'He was a Boer,' said Donald, his face expressionless.

'I'll see you hang for this,' said Ian coldly.

'I doubt it,' replied Donald. 'Is that your horse?'

'What of it?'

'I'm taking it.'

'Where?'

'I'm looking for Boers and I'll go on doing that until one of them finds me first. I'll take your Webley while I'm at it.'

Ian did not move.

'Just unbuckle your belt and let it fall.' Then as Ian hesitated, 'Ian, if you do not, I shall shoot you and then your sergeant. I don't want witnesses, but I'll make an exception in your case. Get on with it, and then step back.'

Slowly, Ian complied. 'How do you think you are going to get away with this?'

'Frankly, Ian, I don't care. Step back,' he said as Ian's belt fell to the ground.

Keeping Ian covered, Donald approached and slipped the revolver out of its holster and tucked it into his belt. He started to back away towards Ian's charger.

'Goodbye, Ian,' he said as he mounted. 'If you see my mother, give her my love.'

He rode off at a gallop in the direction of the Boer lines.

Ian realized that Peter Leinie had not known who was speaking to him. 'That was . . .' Then he stopped, knowing he would never repeat what he had seen, and his voice went quiet. 'That was one of the enemy.'

7

The twentieth century was only eleven days old when Willie Bruce burst into the library at Culbrech House. Of course it was not the library anymore. It was the War Room. Here Willie and Andrew played at generals, just as when they had been children together they had played at soldiers. The big desk had been completely cleared. On it could usually be found a large sheet of paper with a sketch map of the current battle and there they moved guns and men and fought the battle, much more efficiently in their estimation, than the general in command. The lower bookshelves had become a filing system for newspaper cuttings. They collected every piece of literature written about the war and decided what should have been done and what should not have been done. Of course they had the advantage of fantasy, they could conjure up a hundred field pieces as fast as a thought or move a battalion over a thousand miles with the same speed that it took to make the decision. The only thing which remained in the chaos which had replaced the former order of the library was the sideboard with its decanter of Glenlivet and two crystal glasses for the refreshment of the armchair warriors.

One wall had had a large board pinned against it covering the masses of leather-bound volumes. On to this had been pinned a large-scale map of South Africa.

On this map Willie, who spent a great deal of time at Culbrech House, together with Andrew moved little flags and pins about as they got news of what was happening. There were blue ones for the family. Maud and the children in Kimberley; Ian, Gordon, and Robert with the regiment, now withdrawn to Durban; and Naomi at Pietermaritzburg. There was one other single blue flag. It was stuck into the border of the map. That was for Donald, for no one knew where Donald was.

Little red-headed pins indicated casualties in the battalion; the smaller ones were for wounded and the larger ones for killed, or died on active service.

They had spent many long hours poring over this map and arguing about what was being done and what should be done. During the course of such discussions they had both come to the conclusion that territory did not matter and that the only way to end the war was to bring the Boer to action in a set-piece battle where they could destroy his forces in the field. But, as they both agreed, that would be no easy task.

Willie had written letter after letter to Sir Garnet Wolseley, the Commander-in-Chief Great Britain, begging him for a command. The only response that he got was the offer of a desk job in Whitehall and there was no way that Willie Bruce would be persuaded to spend a war polishing the seat of his pants behind a desk.

It had become apparent to them and to the rest of the nation that what they had imagined would be a short, swift campaign which would send the Boers scurrying back to their farms with their tails between their legs, was not going to be like that at all. They were in for a long, hard war against a courageous and tenacious foe. Willie blamed the generals and Andrew blamed the terrain, while the truth probably lay somewhere between the two.

Andrew heaved his pegleg off the stool in front of his arm-chair and got to his feet as Willie entered the room.

'You'll have a dram, Willie,' he said, stomping over to the sideboard.

'Thanks,' said Willie. 'Andrew, have you heard the news?' There was a ring of pleasure in his voice.

'What news?'

'They've arrived at Cape Town. They got there yesterday. Roberts and Kitchener. Now we'll be able to show the Boer a thing or two.'

'What about Buller? I suppose he'll resign his command now that he has been placed under Roberts's command.'

'Not Buller,' said Willie. 'He's always been a number twa and he kens it fine. Remember that he never wanted the job in the first place. He'll be happy tae serve under Little Bobs.'

'I don't know why you're so keen on Roberts,' said Andrew. 'He's an old man now, he's older than I am.'

'Aye, I ken that's true. But he's tough and he's got the right sort of mind for a general. Niver forget the march from Kabul tae Kandahar.'

'But,' said Andrew, 'this is a big war. That was an ordinary colonial campaign. And another thing, Wolseley doesn't like him. I can't understand how he got the appointment.'

'Wolseley had nae choice. It was the government and though, as you ken, I hae little time for the politicians, I think they did the right thing this time.'

'Kitchener, I can understand,' said Andrew. 'He was an obvious choice.'

'Aye. Though I canna say that I like the man; he's afu' cold. No a man's man. But he's a deep-thinking soldier and he did a good job in the Sudan. I have a wee feeling in ma bones that those twa will manage tae sort it oot between them.'

'I can only hope to God that you are right,' said Andrew. 'Have you had any other news?'

'No, I had that letter from Maud a few days ago. She and the bairns seem tae be doing all right in Kimberley. It's funny, is it no?'

'What?'

'Well, there's a toon under siege and yet they still get letters oot as if nothing had happened. They tell me that Cecil Rhodes is still conducting his business all over Africa even though he's cooped up there. You know, Andrew, I canna understand why the Boers dinna attack.'

'I suppose,' replied Andrew, 'it's because Kimberley is well garrisoned. They don't want a lot of casualties and they probably think that if they sit it out long enough . . . I mean, whatever food they have there cannot last forever, and there must come a time that they will just have to surrender.'

'Well, according to Maud, they dinna seem tae be doing too bad, and the bairns are fine, though I wish I had some word of Donald.'

They were silent for a little while, both of them wondering what had happened to Willie's son since the day his wife died and he had stolen out of Kimberley.

'Did you go and see Hugh Grant's folk?' asked Willie, changing the subject.

'Yes, I did. I went down the day before yesterday. They had the news, of course. It's a bloody shame, a pretty wife and four children. They'll not want for anything, of course.'

'Except for their father,' said Willie.

'Yes, I know. I suppose we've been lucky in a way, even with this.' He gazed ruefully at his wooden leg.

'And Brenda?' said Willie.

'None of us really knew her,' said Andrew. 'I often wonder what she would have been like if we had.'

'What aboot your mother?' asked Willie. 'How's she keeping?'

'Pretty much the same,' said Andrew. 'She's getting very frail. Doesn't come down often now, stays in her room most of the time.'

'Aye, we're all getting older.'

Just then the door opened and Victoria came into the room. The worry of having her husband away on campaign had shown on her, and there was a tenseness about her that had never been apparent before. However, she gave signs of genuine pleasure at seeing Willie.

'Hello, Uncle Willie,' she said. 'Will you be staying to lunch?'

'Well . . .' said Willie, hesitating.

'Of course he'll be staying to lunch,' said Andrew, 'and to dinner. I don't know why the devil you don't move over here. A five-mile trek every other day so that we can play at soldiers together. There's plenty of room here. You could shut up Cluny Cottage and move in. Doesn't that make sense to you?'

'Why don't you, Uncle Willie?' said Victoria.

'Och, no,' replied Willie. 'It's fine the way it is. After all, I want tae keep the place nice for Maud and I enjoy pottering aboot in the garden.'

Andrew glanced out of the window at the snow-covered landscape. 'I shouldn't think that you are getting much gardening done at the moment.'

'Well, not exactly,' said Willie. 'But there could be a thaw any time now and then I can get on wi' the digging.'

'I had a letter from Ian,' said Victoria. 'It was from Durban. They've been taken out of Buller's force and moved back there. I wish they'd send them home.'

'There's no much chance o' that, lassie,' said Willie. 'We're sending oot men as fast as we can get them half trained. Everybody's singing "Goodbye Dolly Gray" and then awa' they go tae the war. It was no like this in oor time, was it, Andrew? A wee bittie here and a wee bittie there. But now there's only one war, the big yin. And men like me and your father-in-law not allowed tae dae anything aboot it. We just sit here on our arses, sticking pins in a map while others mak' the mistakes. Sorry, Victoria, I should no have used such language in front of you.'

'It's all right,' said Victoria. 'I'm a soldier's wife, you know. I've heard it all before.'

'Aye,' said Willie. 'Did somebody say something aboot lunch? I'm afu' hungry.'

'Come on in, Uncle Willie,' said Victoria. 'It's all ready.'

In Kimberley their principal enemy was boredom. Maud Bruce had arranged her little hospital and in spite of her worries about Donald, she had continued her preparations with a group of ladies of the town. They had all received their course of instruction in first aid from Nurse Wickstead. Not that their little ward had had a single patient since Brenda died. Kimberley was fortunate in possessing a very well-equipped hospital which even boasted a primitive X-ray unit, and this had proved ample for all of the town's needs.

Food, however, was beginning to become a problem. Fresh milk was almost nonexistent and the child mortality rate had risen to alarming proportions, especially among the Bantu. Maud and her ladies did what they could to alleviate this, but the milk simply was not there. On the ninth of January, Maud tasted horse flesh for the first time in her life and had to confess, much to her own surprise, that she could barely distinguish it from good beef. Some of her friends were quite shocked at the thought of eating horse, but it was not many days before they too gave way. Cats had almost disappeared in the town. A kitten would bring as much as five shillings and sixpence, while a plump fully grown tom would bring seven shillings more. Things got to a stage where you never asked what it was that was on your plate for fear that the knowledge would spoil your appetite.

It was a month since the abortive battle of Magersfontein, when they had watched the smoke and heard the gunfire of Methuen's army which Buller had given the task of relieving them. Their hopes of an early relief were finally dashed on the eleventh of December when the Boers sent a message into the beleaguered town saying, 'We have smashed up your fine column.' Later that night they had the Boers' claim confirmed when Methuen's searchlight blinked a message to them: 'I am checked.'

Morale for the subsequent days was probably at its lowest ebb during the entire period of the siege, but by the turn of the year the new century was welcomed in with whatever festive fare they could scrape together. Apart from the shelling, which did little damage, the Boers made no offensive move, and strange though it may seem, spirits began to rise again.

Then there was Mr Labram. Maud found him a most charming and engaging young man, even though he was an American. He seemed to be possessed of two qualities in boundless excess, energy and mechanical knowledge. He was the chief engineer of the De Beers company and had applied himself to many tasks, including the fitting out of Maud's ward, since the siege had begun. On the twentieth of January he proudly showed off his latest piece of engineering to an admiring populace. It was a cannon which he had constructed in twenty-four days. It was a breech loader with a rifled bore of 4·1 inches, able to fire a shell weighing twenty-eight pounds. All of the town dignitaries including Rhodes, Colonel Kekewich, and many ladies, came to see Mrs Pickering, the wife of a De Beers executive, pull the lanyard to fire the first shell.

Maud, along with everyone else, was suitably impressed, even though she wondered at such a warlike act being performed by a lady.

Maud was, of course, completely unaware of the politics which were going on around her; of the intense hatred which had sprung up between Rhodes and Kekewich. She felt reasonably safe. The shelling was more tiresome than it was dangerous. She stayed close to her grandchildren, always ready to be called on in an emergency, and just waited for the siege to end. Perhaps with the raising of the siege she might get some news of Donald.

Naomi stood looking at the card which was hanging on the foot of the bed. The hospital at Pietermaritzburg was enormous and she was well aware that it would only be a matter of time before someone she knew was sent there. The wounded were now coming in by the hundreds, and every day she scanned the lists to see if they contained some familiar name.

It was a vast place; there were fourteen wards, long and pillared down the centre, with a long row of cots down either side, each with its burden of suffering humanity. It was a place of smells. The smell of carbolic was everywhere as the black orderlies scrubbed the wards from end to end every day. This mingled with the smell of festering flesh, and in the dysentery ward, where they laid the men on sloping boards so that their excrement would dribble down into the bucket of carbolic at the end, the stench was indescribable.

Outside on the well-cut and watered lawns ladies, mostly of the establishment, wearing what would pass at a distance for a senior nurse's uniform, pushed wheelchairs with convalescing patients and talked to them about the season in London and the delights of home.

Naomi was not one such as they. And it is only fair to say that many great ladies did as much as she. Naomi scrubbed, and changed filthy bandages and comforted the dying and never showed the nausea that often she felt within her. On one occasion – it was two o'clock in the morning – she made no protest when a dying soldier fondled her breasts.

He had looked up at her and said, 'Eeh, lass, that were just like the missus.' And then he died with a smile on his lips and

Naomi gently covered his face with the blanket.

She never wept. Not even in the solitude of her room. There was no time for tears. Whenever she did stop it was because she was so tired that there was nothing left but sleep.

That morning she had found a name she recognized. Lieutenant de Vere-Smith, Duke of Beverley, of the Duke of Lancaster's Imperial Yeomanry. The regiment was one of many which had been raised in the first months of the war and sent overseas with a minimum of training.

She had assumed that the duke must be the elder brother of Charles, whom she had not seen since that day, long ago, when he had given her the pearls and walked out of her life. Still she held him in deep affection and had resolved that she would make herself known to his brother and help in any way that was possible to provide him with little extras while he was in the hospital.

She looked from the card to the sleeping figure in the bed. It was Charles himself. There could be no doubt of that. It was not his brother, of that she was quite sure.

The man lying before her was not seriously wounded. A bullet in the shoulder had put his left arm out of action. It was nothing that should not clear up in a week or two. He had arrived at Pietermaritzburg that morning and been put in D ward, which was a ward reserved for junior officers. Exhausted after his long journey, he had gone straight to sleep and had been sleeping for about five hours when Naomi found him.

As if in answer to her presence, his eyes flickered and opened and puzzlement followed by recognition flooded his face. Naomi, for her part, did not speak. She observed the man who had been her lover and so much more for five years. He had not changed much. There were streaks of grey in his hair and his features were lined, giving them a maturity and a new attractiveness.

'I suppose I am awake,' he said.

She nodded, still smiling.

'Hello, Naomi. If I am not dreaming, then I should like to know what on earth you are doing here?'

'I might as well ask you the same,' she replied. 'You are not old, Charles, but surely you are a little too old to be playing at soldiers. Or is it "Your Grace," now?'

'It must be ten years,' he said.

'Yes, indeed,' she answered. 'Are you really the Duke?'

'Oh, that's true enough. I fear that my story since we parted is not a very happy one.'

'You lost your brother, that is obvious. I'm sorry about that.'

'Not only my brother, my wife also. She died in childbirth; it was her fourth. Life seemed very empty after that until this lot started. I joined a yeomanry regiment, spent about five minutes in action, and ended up here.' He smiled. 'Not a very distinguished military career. It's good to see you, though.'

'Thank you, Charles,' she said. 'But why didn't you come to me when all of this happened?'

'I spent the happiest time of my life with you. I was afraid of spoiling the memory.'

'I see.'

'Are you going to look after me?'

'Not really. This is not my ward. I look at the admission lists each day in case there's someone I know. That's how I found you. Just now I'm on nights, in B ward. So I'll be able to come and see you during the late afternoons. That is, if you'd like me to.'

'You know that I would.'

Strangely, she felt awkward in his presence. It was that awkwardness which comes when meeting someone with whom one has been intimate, after a long passage of time.

'I'm glad that you are not badly wounded,' she said.

'No, it's not really bad at all. It's not even enough to get me shipped off home. I'll be out of here in a couple of weeks and . . . back there, I suppose. Wherever "there" is. Naomi, do you mind if I tell you that I think you look as beautiful as ever?'

'In this?' she said, laughing at her plain linen blue-and-white hospital uniform.

'You could make a sack look like a ball gown.'

'You are very kind, Charles. And I am sure that after you have had a shave, you will look as handsome as ever. And now you must excuse me because I must get some sleep.'

'So soon?'

'I'll come and see you this afternoon at about half past four.

Perhaps if they let you out of bed, we might take tea together outside.'

'I promise to shave before then,' he said.

For the next two weeks they met every afternoon for tea on the hospital lawn. Their conversations were mainly light reminiscences, nothing serious. Though they were not as they had been, or so it seemed, they were still very good friends and fond of each other. The one thing that they never discussed was their last meeting in London, not until the day that Charles appeared without his arm in a sling and with the news that he was expecting to be discharged from hospital within the week.

'Do you still wear your pearls?' he asked.

She coloured slightly. 'I look at them every day,' she said. 'But I don't wear them very often.'

'You have them with you?'

'Yes.'

'Then you must wear them for me.'

Naomi laughed. 'Really, Charles. Can you imagine me being seen here wearing Marie Antoinette's pearls? Matron would . . . I'm not sure what she would do, but it would be something pretty awful.'

'Naomi, I . . . ' And he stopped.

'What is it, Charles?'

'I haven't asked you before, but, you're not married yet?'

'No, Charles.'

'But there have been other men.'

'Many.'

'Will you marry me?'

'But you admitted yourself, that is impossible.' She had not even paused after his question.

'Not any more.'

'What if there were children?'

'I hope that there would be.'

'Even if one of them was coloured?' She looked at him frankly as she spoke.

'It wouldn't matter much, not now.'

'Why?'

'I have an heir, and if anything happened to him, he has a younger brother.'

Naomi's face hardened. 'Charles, for a moment I almost said yes. But now . . .'

'I have been honest, Naomi.'

'Yes, Charles. And I thank you for that. I don't think that it would be right for me to let you take the risk. You would not want to soil the line; you would be haunted by the ghosts of your forefathers. They wouldn't approve.'

'But, my dear, it's you I want. Don't you understand?' He was pleading with her now.

'Come and see me when you get to London. You'll always be welcome. And now I really must go.'

He watched her as she disappeared into the main building, then angrily he kicked his chair over and strode off in the opposite direction.

8

The Maclarens were not destined to stay long in Durban. It was good while it lasted, but they had not been badly mauled at Colenso, and by the twelfth of January they were on the march again. This time over hundreds of miles of veld, twenty-four miles a day. They were heading for the Modder River in the Orange River Colony. There they had orders to search out and find General Methuen's force and place themselves under his orders.

The long march itself was a symphony of monotony and a triumph of endurance. Each day was exactly the same as the one before. The same blank horizon, the same dark-blue sky. The same shimmering heat rising from the dust. The same thorn bushes and the same patches of arid red grass. Day after day, week after week. There was so much of nothing that on one occasion Sergeant Smith assured Private Alasdair Maclaren that they were walking round in circles waiting for the war to be over and Maclaren almost believed what he was told. There were, however, few attempts at humour. It was long, it was hot, and devoid of any sort of diversion.

Once they spotted a group of black tribesmen, leaning on their hunting spears and watching them.

'I tell ye yin thing,' said MacTavish. 'That lot think that we are mad and they're no far wrong.'

But that little incident apart, they hardly saw a living soul. It was just one step after another. Backs aching from the weight of their packs. The metal of their rifles so hot that they could barely touch them. They carried everything with them. Two Maxim guns, all the stores that they needed for a month out in the open, drawn by mules on wooden carts which kept having to be repaired. They even had their own medical unit, Captain Gordon Mackintosh of the R.A.M.C. and three orderlies having been assigned to them in Durban. They for their part had accumulated vast quantities of gregory's powder and castor oil for the inevitable bouts of diarrhoea alternating with constipation with which the men were afflicted. Once on the move, there was no turning back. If a man was ill, he had to be dumped into a cart, and if he died, as three of their number did, he was buried by the wayside in a shallow grave with a few rocks piled upon it after Ian had read a passage from his Bible.

They had started gaily enough. Their piper, Angus McLeod, played as they marched out onto the open veld. Young voices rose in songs like 'Dolly Gray' and of course their own irreverent version of a popular hymn tune:

We are Maclaren's army,
The Highland Infantry,
We cannot fight, we cannot sing,
What bloody use are we?
And when we get to Cronje
We'll hear the bastard say,
Hoch, hoch, mein Gott,
What a bloody fine lot
To earn a bob a day.

But long before the end of the journey Ian and his officers were devoting all of their energies to keeping up the morale of the men they were leading.

For Gordon Bruce the long march was no hardship. They were heading in the direction of Kimberley where his mother and his niece and nephews were still under siege. He hoped and prayed that it might fall to the Maclarens to raise that siege. But Gordon was alone in his anxiety to press on. For the rest of them, it was a searing hot, eventless bore.

Every evening when they bivouacked for the night, Ian held

a conference with his officers, all armed with maps and compasses, to decide on the route for the following day. This was the most vital part of the entire exercise as they had to find water every few days, or horses, pack animals, and men would never survive. A decision having been made, forward pickets were sent out to look for hostile Boers and for signs that water was ahead for them. The pickets were mounted on what few saddle horses they possessed and would send a man back as soon as they knew the way was clear for the column, the balance of them bivouacking and waiting for the column to catch up.

It was on the morning of February the eighth that the forward picket sent word back to Ian that they had sighted Methuen's camp. It was Corporal Anderson who brought the news to Ian just as they were striking camp and preparing for another day's foot-slogging.

'I niver seed naethin' like it, sirr. It was like a great city. There was tents and campfires fer as far as ye could look.'

'How far are they, Corporal?' asked Ian, his face showing the relief he felt now that the long march was nearly ended.

'Aboot twelve miles, sirr. That's what Captain Maclaren said.'

'Thank you, Corporal. Tell the R.S.M. that I want to see him.'

'Sirr.' Corporal Anderson saluted and went off in search of Frankie Gibson.

'Well, Sergeant-Major,' said Ian as soon as Frankie had arrived, 'we're nearly there. How do you think the men would feel if we were to have a short march today and then bivvy in time for everyone to get cleaned up before we march into the camp?'

'How far would we have to march today, sir?' asked Frankie.

'Not more than ten miles. We'll head straight for the river and spend the afternoon bathing and cleaning up, and then tomorrow morning we'll march into that camp and show them what a Highland regiment looks like after four hundred miles.'

'I think that the men would appreciate it, sir. There'll be work tae dae as soon as we make camp, and it'll be mair like a wee holiday if we dae it as you suggest.'

'Right, Sergeant-Major, we'll move out in an hour. Send

Anderson back to recall the picket. We'll head straight for the Modder and camp there tonight.'

Methuen's camp came into sight briefly during the morning's march. It was a city of tents which spread as far as the eye could see. The hot sand on which it was based gave off shimmering waves of heat into the upper air. They were tired and they were foot weary. But in spite of all this they paused and looked and wondered. Never had any of them seen so much military might within the compass of a single glance. There were men, guns, mountain after mountain of supplies, little tents and big tents in the thousands, and hundreds and hundreds of horses and oxen in a vast, steaming menagerie. Beyond the camp lay the Modder, and beyond the Modder the Boers.

This was the force that had been assembled during the months since the war had started and rushed out to the Cape. This was the force that was going to crush the Boers and get them, the Maclarens, back home.

Ian looked with something approaching awe as the massive panorama unfolded before his eyes. He had brought nearly nine hundred men over four hundred miles of open veld. He had lost only three on the way, and, that apart, his battalion was intact. He looked back at his men, the long, straggling column, all khaki, all the same colour as the land they trod; even their kilts were hidden from view by the aprons which had been issued to them before they left Durban. But he looked back with swelling pride. These were the Maclarens, his men, his family, and if they could do what they had done in these last weeks, then they could do anything. A battle would be a pleasant divertissement after this.

Once the camp was in view, about five miles' distant, Ian took his column to the right and headed to the river. There they bivouacked. There they stripped naked and splashed about in the water. There they polished and cleaned and washed and shaved so that they were almost as neat and smart as if they had been going on parade at their home barracks.

They stayed there until the afternoon of the ninth and then, with pipes and drums playing, rifles at the slope, and marching at attention, they entered the camp and down the broad lines of tents. It was with shoulders squared and heads held high in the pride of their regiment that they looked with contempt at the listless, slow-moving troops as they passed them. They were the Maclarens, the right of the line, the terrors of the Punjab, the bloodsuckers of Burma, and the pride of the British Army. And they were proving it.

They had discarded their aprons and Ian at their head was wearing a pair of tartan breeches and mounted on his charger. He halted the battalion between the lines of tents, dismounted, and called a passing officer.

'I want to report to the C-in-C. Where will I find him?'

'His tent is about a hundred yards down this line on the right, sir,' said the man, looking curiously beyond Ian at the battalion as they stood strictly to attention, not one man moving a muscle. 'You might find him busy, though; he only got here yesterday.'

'But I thought General Methuen had been here for months,' said Ian.

The young officer smiled. 'General Methuen is not the C-in-C. Lord Roberts has arrived. He is taking charge of the whole operation.'

'Oh,' said Ian. 'Thank you. I had better report to him all the same. Sergeant-Major,' he called, 'stand the men easy.'

At last, Ian thought, he was going to meet him, that legendary figure, Field-Marshal Frederick Sleigh Roberts, Baron Roberts of Kandahar, and known throughout the army as 'Little Bobs'. He had been born in Cawnpore in 1832, long before the Mutiny in which he had served with great gallantry and distinction, being awarded the Victoria Cross.

Probably his most famous feat, and that which had captured the public imagination more than the feat of any other soldier since Wellington at Waterloo, was marching his army for three hundred miles across the barren wastes of northern India from Kabul to the relief of the besieged garrison at Kandahar.

Ian thought of these things, of the man who had become a legend in his own lifetime, as he walked down the lines to the field-marshal's tent. Outside the tent an A.D.C. was sitting at a trestle table dealing with some papers.

'Good afternoon,' said Ian.

The A.D.C. looked up. 'Oh, good afternoon, sir. Can I help you?'

'I would like to see the field-marshal,' replied Ian.

'I'm afraid he's very busy,' said the A.D.C. 'Is it something I can deal with?'

'I have just brought a battalion four hundred miles across Africa in order to join his force. I thought that it would be my duty to report to him personally.'

The young captain was impressed. 'If you'll just wait a moment, sir, I'll see if the C-in-C can spare you a few minutes.'

'Thank you,' said Ian.

The young man disappeared into the tent and returned within a matter of seconds. 'What battalion are you with, sir?' he asked.

'The Maclaren Highlanders,' replied Ian.

'He thought you might be; he says that he will see you immediately. If you care to go in now, sir?'

Ian walked into the tent and saluted. Before him sat a little man; tiny would probably be a more accurate description, for he was only five feet three inches tall, two inches below the minimum height for enlisted soldiers in the regular army. He was sitting behind a plain wooden table, wearing a khaki forage cap which covered a head of iron-grey hair. He had a large white moustache which drooped over and beyond his upper lip, and curled away upwards at the ends. He wore a plain khaki tunic which was rumpled and completely devoid of any adornment. It bore not even the ribbon of his V.C. His neck was scrawny and the skin of his face and hands was leathery and creased by a thousand wrinkles. The thing which struck Ian most was his eyes; they were pale and bright, and when he looked up seemed to bore right through the man standing before him.

He finished reading the document with which he was occupied when Ian entered, initialled it, and looked at Ian.

'You are the commanding officer of the Maclaren Highlanders,' he said in a thin, piping voice which in no way matched his reputation.

'Yes, sir.'

'Yes,' said Roberts, 'I believe I met your father once. How many men have you brought me?'

'Eight hundred and fifty, sir. And three Maxims,' replied Ian.

'Good, good,' was the reply. 'And your name?'

'Lieutenant-Colonel Maclaren, sir.'

'Family, eh?' said Roberts with approbation. 'Yes, it was your father I met.'

'Yes, sir,' said Ian, permitting himself a little smile in the awesome presence.

'Well, Colonel, if there is anything you need, tell my A.D.C., Captain Leslie. And tell him I told you that if he can give it to you, then he is to do so. How are your men? They must have taken a hammering on that march.'

'They're fit and well, sir. They could go into action this afternoon if you wished.'

'Hm,' said Roberts, raising his bushy eyebrows.

'My men are rested and ready for anything, sir.'

'I hope you mean that, Colonel; we have a long way to go,' said Roberts. 'Well, I'll send for you as soon as I can let you know our plans in detail.'

'Sir?' said Ian.

'Yes,' said the field-marshal a little testily. He had regarded his last remark as a dismissal. 'What is it?'

'Sir, might I be so bold as to ask, are we going to relieve Kimberley?'

'*You're* not,' said Roberts, 'but we are.'

'We, sir?'

'Yes. It will be mainly a cavalry action.' Then, seeing the look on Ian's face, 'Don't you agree with me, young man?'

'Oh no, sir, I would not presume to disagree, sir. It's just that . . .'

'Well, come on, out with it. I haven't got all day, you know.'

'Well, sir, it's one of my officers. His mother and three orphaned nephews and niece are in Kimberley.' Ian forgave himself the white lie for he could not bear to mention Donald at this juncture. 'He's been very excited about the fact that we are approaching Kimberley and is hoping desperately that he might be in the relief force.'

'Is he a good man?' asked Roberts.

'One of the best, sir,' answered Ian. 'He's a Maclaren Highlander.'

'What's the fellah's name?'

'Major Bruce, sir.'

'Any relation to Major-General Bruce?'

'His son, sir.'

'I see. Then those are General Bruce's grandchildren in Kimberley, eh?'

'That's right, sir.'

Roberts drew a deep breath. 'All right,' he said. 'You can tell your Major Bruce that he is to report to General French tomorrow evening. He can ride, I suppose?'

'Yes, sir, he's a good horseman.'

'Well, he'll need his charger. Tell him I'm attaching him to French's force; you can spare him, I suppose?'

'No one is indispensable, sir, not even a Maclaren.'

Roberts almost allowed himself a smile at that. 'You can tell him that I'm doing this for Willie Bruce. Not for him, not for his mother. Tell him it's for his father. I know him. He's a fine soldier.'

'Yes, sir, and thank you, sir.'

'All right, Colonel,' snapped Roberts, 'now will you please get out and let me get on with my work?'

'Sir,' said Ian. He saluted and left the great man's presence.

'All right?' asked the A.D.C. as Ian came out.

'Fine,' said Ian.

He went back to the battalion and arrangements were made for the bivouacking of the men. Then he sent for Gordon Bruce.

While he was waiting for Gordon, Ian started to think about the younger man. Gordon had always been self-effacing. He just got on with the job quietly and you barely knew that he was around. He had never stood out, but he had never failed in his duties. A first-class regimental officer was a fair assessment of Donald Bruce's younger brother. Not highly imaginative, but not easily fussed. In some ways he was the very best type of officer. The sort that would obey orders and not try to do the generals' staff work for them. He was dedicated to the regiment and to his men and no commander could ask for more than that. Ian did not want to lose him but, on the other hand, he had a great affection for his Aunt Maud and she must have suffered a lot. Her daughter-in-law dead and as for her eldest son, God alone knew what would become of Donald.

He looked up as Gordon came in.

'I want a word with you, Gordon,' said Ian.

'Yes, sir?'

'Gordon, you are going to leave us for a little while.'

'Oh, come off it, Ian,' protested Gordon, 'I don't want to leave the regiment.'

'I think you will when you've heard what I have to say. I'll be perfectly honest with you. I don't know what is happening, but I have talked with the field-marshal.'

'Field marshal?'

'Yes, "Bobs" is here. Do you want to go to Kimberley?'

'Of course I do, you know that.'

'All right, then, you are going.'

'How? Why?'

'Why? Because Roberts thinks that your father is a bloody good soldier and he seems to want to do him a favour.'

'I see, but how?'

'Details I cannot tell you because you can't ask a busy field-marshal for details when he wants to get rid of you,' said Ian, smiling. 'But I gather that General French is going to get the job of lifting the siege. The C-in-C has agreed that you can be attached to French's staff. I haven't the faintest idea what your job will be, so don't ask me. I think they are lying somewhere to the south of us. You're to make your own way there, with your charger, and report to the general tomorrow evening.'

'But I'm not a cavalryman,' said Gordon.

'You don't have to tell me that and I'm damned sure that you'll have corns on your arse by the time you get to Kimberley. Seriously, I cannot see you getting much of a job. But if, as I suspect, French is going into Kimberley, you'll be with him.'

'Thanks, Ian,' said Gordon.

'Give Aunt Maud my love when you see her and tell her . . .' He paused for a moment thinking of Donald. 'Tell her I hope that everything's all right,' he added lamely.

It was in the late afternoon of February tenth that Field-Marshal Roberts called his cavalry commanders together. They were briefed for what Roberts described as the greatest cavalry operation in history. He was going to send his entire cavalry division under the command of Major-General French to relieve Kimberley.

'But gentlemen,' he continued, 'Kimberley is not our final objective. I am going to take my entire command into the Orange Free State and I intend to take Bloemfontein.'

General French was a man of average height who had already won some little fame as a bold and dashing cavalry commander. He had dark hair and the fashionable full curling moustache. He had raised some slight objection to having a Highland infantryman attached to his force, but did not argue when Roberts insisted. He returned to his headquarters where he found the gentleman in question waiting for him.

'Who the devil are you, sir?' he demanded.

'Major Bruce, sir, Maclaren Highlanders. The field-marshal said that I was to report to you this evening.'

'Yes, I know,' said French abruptly. 'You're the fellow who wants to go to Kimberley. Is that right?'

'Yes, sir.'

'Can you ride?'

'Reasonably, sir.'

'Well, you're not going to be much damned good to me, but I suppose if the field-marshal wants it, you had better come along.'

'Thank you, sir.'

'Can't give you a command, you realize that.'

'Naturally, sir.'

'The youngest trooper in the division probably knows more about cavalry than you.'

'I'm not a cavalryman, sir.'

'Have you got a charger?'

'Yes, sir.'

'All right, then,' said French. 'Captain Westlake!' he called.

A young hussar officer came in, not in the glory of busby and braided tunic, but wearing the same drab khaki breeches and jacket that was the mark of them all. All, that is, except Gordon who was sporting a pair of breeches in Maclaren tartan.

'Sir?' said Captain Westlake.

'This is Major . . . er . . . what's your name again? Oh, yes, I remember, Bruce. Major Bruce is riding with us. Captain Westlake,' he added by way of explanation, 'is a member of my staff and will be in close touch with me throughout the entire operation.' Then, turning back to the captain, 'I want

Major Bruce to ride with you. Don't let him go wandering off. He isn't cavalry.' He made it sound like an insult.

'I understand, sir.'

'All right, Bruce,' said French, 'Captain Westlake will look after you. We are to be ready to ride out at two.'

'Tomorrow afternoon, sir?' asked Westlake.

'Tomorrow morning,' said French.

It was dark as they came out of the general's tent. Gordon had, in spite of his length of service, never been in a cavalry brigade. The smells on the darkening evening air were all so unfamiliar. The smell of horseflesh as the troopers groomed them, and the farmyard odours of their droppings, mingled with the smell of leather. The noises were different too. There was a constant chorus of horses whinnying and nickering, the stamp of a steel-shod hoof, and the rattle and clank of the harness of the draught animals which would draw the guns of the horse artillery.

'Best thing you can do,' said Westlake, 'is get some sleep. It's going to be a hard morning and a long one.'

'Where shall I go?' asked Gordon.

'Have you got a bivvy?'

'Not here.'

'Well, you don't want to go tramping all the way to your lines now. I'll send my servant to collect anything you need and you had better come and share with me. It'll be a bit of a squeeze, but we'll manage.'

'That's jolly decent of you,' said Gordon. He was beginning to like the young cavalryman.

'Shouldn't bother to undress, either. It'll be boots and saddles in about five hours.'

They crept into the tent together and Westlake handed Gordon a blanket. ''Fraid that's all I can offer,' he said. 'Tell you what, though, I have got the remains of a bottle of whisky if you feel like a nightcap.'

He produced a bottle of Johnnie Walker and Gordon eyed it enviously. He had not seen a dram for well over a month.

'Light the candle, will you?' said Westlake as he shared the last of his bottle into two equal portions in a pair of tin mugs. 'Here you are, a taste of home. Sorry I haven't got any soda.'

'I'm a Highlander,' said Gordon. 'Only an Englishman would

put soda into good whisky.' They smiled at each other.

'Well, that's the last of it,' said Westlake, draining his mug. 'It's a bloody awful war.'

'What's French like?' asked Gordon.

'He's all right. He's a bit gruff, but he knows his stuff all right. Well, we had better get some shut-eye.'

Gordon took off his Sam Browne and his sword. They helped each other off with their riding boots and lay down, Westlake on his cot and Gordon on the bare earth, wrapped in the blanket which Westlake had given him. Gordon lay there for a long time gazing at the blackness above him. He did not think that he had slept at all, but he must have because when the bugles sounded reveille at two o'clock, he woke up with a start, wondering for a moment where he was.

Westlake was yawning and stretching. 'Get your boots on,' he said. 'Then you had better find your horse.'

Within fifteen minutes, Gordon was mounted and in the company of his new-found friend.

'I shouldn't take that with you,' said Westlake.

'What?'

'Your sword. It's excess weight and you won't be using it.'

'It's rather important,' said Gordon. 'It belonged to my brother. He got it at Sandhurst.'

'By George,' said Westlake, 'Sword of Honour, what? What happened to your brother?'

'He . . . he resigned his commission and left the army. I don't know where he is now.'

'Ah, well, take it with you if you want to, or I'll ask my man to put it with my baggage. It'll be safe enough there, though you might have to wait till the war's over before you get it back.'

Gordon acquiesced, though it made him feel a little treacherous when Watkins, Westlake's servant, took it away.

In the bright moonlight Gordon could see the masses of cavalry as they moved out. He estimated that there could not be fewer than five thousand of them. He had never in his life seen so many horses and riders at the same time. As for himself, he rode along beside Westlake just to the rear of the general, saying little and trying as far as possible to keep out of everybody's way.

They were on the move at a gentle trot. There were men and horses ahead and on both sides of them stretching away until they were swallowed up in the darkness. There were the guns, too, clanking and bumping along with their limbers dragging behind them. It was an awesome sight, but Gordon could not feel part of it.

They met little opposition for the first four days. There were a few minor skirmishes on the flanks, but nothing that Gordon was able to see. The principal enemy was the country itself, and the heat, and the necessity of continually finding water for the thousands of horses and men. On the morning of the fifteenth of February, shortly after they had crossed the Modder at Klip Drift, a rider came galloping into General French's headquarters. They were within earshot of Gordon.

'Sir,' said the horseman, a subaltern in the lancers, 'there are Boers in strength just ahead of us. There are quite a lot of them, though we cannot be sure about numbers. They seem to have good defensive positions. They are in a sort of semi-circle of *kopjes* and pretty well hidden. Sir, the battalion commanders want to know what are your orders.'

French did not reply immediately. He knew that his decision at this point would make or break his military career. But his orders were plain, take Kimberley. French was a man of quick decision. It was a risk; he might be facing the main force of Cronje's army, but he made up his mind in a matter of seconds.

'Send out riders and tell the commanders that we are going straight through them,' he said to Westlake. 'I don't want them to stop. I don't want any battles. I want Kimberley. The lancers will go in first, and then the rest. Make it perfectly clear that not a man is to stop until we are through them.'

Westlake galloped off, leaving French with the rest of his staff looking ahead at the barren empty plain. He turned to Gordon with a smile and spoke to him for the first time since he had handed him over to Westlake.

'Well, Major,' he said, 'you're about to see a genuine cavalry charge, and if this comes off, you should be in Kimberley today.'

Within half an hour all commanders had been briefed, and standing mounted on a little rise, Gordon watched the lancers way far ahead of him looking for all the world like the toy soldiers he had played with as a child, as, with lances lowered, manes streaming, men rigid on the backs of their horses, they broke into a gallop. Then the hussars and the dragoons, and suddenly the whole five thousand of them were tearing across the plain. The dust was incredible; within half a minute it was impossible to see anything. His horse, shivering with excitement, joined in the chase, but though he could hear the sound of rifle fire and the shouting of men close to him, Gordon saw nothing else, not a Boer, not a man laid low. It was just a headlong rush through a cloud of yellow dust.

Suddenly Westlake appeared at his side.

'We're through them,' he shouted at the top of his voice.

Then they emerged from the dust and there was the division halted – horses covered with white steaming lather, men stooping in their saddles – and Gordon realized that he, too, was exhausted.

'What did you think of it?' cried the elated Westlake.

'I didn't see a bloody thing,' said Gordon. 'What happens now?'

'Now, my friend,' said Westlake, 'you dismount, rub your horse down, and we'll be in Kimberley in time for afternoon tea.'

Shortly after French had moved out, Lord Roberts, with almost twenty thousand infantry, eight thousand cavalry, and his artillery, with all their services and stores, started north from his encampment below the Modder, and what future generations would always call 'The Great Flank March' had begun.

9

The man lay among the stones and the pebbles of the almost dried-up river bed. He was asleep. Not the deep sleep of one who lay in his own bed, but the sleep of the predatory animal, ready to awaken fully in less than a second with all his senses functioning. Last night he had found water. The water that had evaded him for over two days, during which time the meagre supply of his water bottle had vanished to almost nothing.

For weeks now he had been trudging across the veld. Every day had been so like the one before, blank, barren, and sweltering. The heat of the sun had bleached his hair and his beard until they were almost white, and hardened and reddened his skin, save for the white lines at the corners of his eyes which he had kept screwed up as he peered across the limitless plain, searching. The metal of his Mauser in the heat of the day had burned his hands when he touched it. He had had a horse, but over a week ago it had thrown him and trotted off towards the horizon where doubtless it would fall victim to one of the big cats which roamed the plains in search of food.

The man had shot a springbok four days ago. He had eaten the raw flesh until his belly was bursting. Then he had slung a portion of the balance of the carcass over his shoulder and trudged off – to where? He did not know. The remains, over half the beast, had been left for the vultures.

The man travelled light. He carried with him only his Mauser which he had taken from a dead Boer, the Webley which he had taken from a British officer, a hunting knife, and a water bottle. In the weeks that he had spent out on the veld he had learned a lot and he had learned it quickly; that was why he was still alive. He had become accomplished in the art of the hunter. He hunted to live. He was the complete predator. And he also hunted for another reason. He hunted because he was a man consumed with a fierce, all-embracing hatred; not a blinding rage. There was nothing hot-blooded about his quest for revenge. His was a cold, calculating, icy lust for the blood of those who had taken the one he had lived for.

When he killed, be it man or beast, he killed quickly and he killed at dusk. He did this so that darkness would deny pursuit, or that light would give him time to find refuge for the night before other, even more accomplished killers should begin their nocturnal, never-ending quest for survival.

His mind, which had thought fine thoughts born of good reading and gentle surroundings in his youth, was now a dark, endless channel. It had narrowed until it was capable only of a single thought, and that, that they should pay. That a whole people should pay a bitter price for the loss of that one who had meant so much to him.

It had been dark when he had come upon the river, and he had hidden until dawn; until those creatures who were stronger than he had slaked their thirst and left, their night's work over, to sleep through the heat of the day. He waited until the sun was well over the horizon, until he knew that he could go and drink from the water and rest his aching body without the fear of anyone but man.

It was well into the afternoon. The man stirred in his sleep. Instinctively his hand reached for and clutched the small cloth package made from a corner of his bush jacket and tied with string around his neck. It was all right, it was still there; the man was still rich.

It had happened about a week ago, though the man could not

have told you that. Time had ceased to have meaning for him. But that was when he had found it. Found it in a river bed just like this one, except that that river had completely disappeared under the cracked, parched earth. With his knife he had dug away at the rock-hard mud, searching for the dampness which must lie below when, clawing out the bricky dust, his fingers had touched a pebble. It was smooth and cool to his touch and he felt his pulse increase as he rubbed his thumb over the soapy surface. It was translucent and white, and it was nearly as big as a hen's egg. He knew that he had found his fortune. He knew that he was rich, for he knew all about diamonds and this was the largest that he had ever seen though he had been looking at them for many years as they were dug from the mines at Kimberley. Now that diamond represented the rest of his life to him.

If he ever managed to satiate his overwhelming lust for vengeance, he would be able to leave this God forsaken land, live wherever he chose. He would be wealthy. And he could spend the rest of his life trying to forget.

Suddenly he was awake, alert and lethal. His reactions were automatic. The Mauser was in his hands, there was a cartridge in the breech; there was always a cartridge in the breech. He was lying in the regulation prone firing position, looking up the dried bank of the river towards the point from which the sound had come.

They came down towards him, down the bank towards the river. There were four of them and they were blacks. But they were not ordinary blacks – the man could tell that at a glance, for they were wearing neat white linen shorts. They were wearing nothing else, but the shorts themselves told him that there were whites in the neighbourhood. Though what the neighbourhood was and who the whites could be the man had no idea.

The blacks were unarmed and one of them waved a hand in his direction. Slowly the man got to his feet, keeping the muzzle of his Mauser pointed at them. The four men stopped. One of them, the man who had waved, spoke, and much to the man's surprise, he spoke in English.

'You Afrikaan?' he asked.

'No, I am not.' He almost spat the words.

'English?'

'It'll do.' He was not prepared to enter into a discussion about the Scots being a separate nation.

'Me Paul – Peter, John, Thomas,' the black man added, indicating the others.

Well, the names were British enough. They sounded like mission boys.

'You name?'

'Bruce.'

'I don't know Saint Bruce, do you?' he looked at his companions who responded by shaking their heads.

'Where do you come from?' demanded Donald.

'Over there,' said the black, pointing towards the river bank on his right. 'Not far. Maybe you need food?'

For a moment Donald did not reply. But the mention of food had made him aware of the gnawing hunger in his gut.

'Yes,' he said at length, 'I am very hungry.'

'Come with us then,' said the black cheerily.

'Why?' Donald said, suspicious. 'Why do you want to feed me?'

'Because Jesus say, "Feed the hungry." You are hungry, so we must feed you.' His tone was very matter of fact, as if the reason should be obvious to a child. 'You come with us now, Bruce. No need to point your gun. Look,' he spread his arms and opened his palms wide. 'We not kill anybody. Perhaps some day somebody kill us for Jesus. That will be very good for us.'

Wondering, Donald allowed himself to be led away over the opposite bank. When he got to the top he could scarcely believe what he saw. There in front of his eyes lay a neat wooden building, planked and painted white and looking cared for and cherished. There was a broad flight of wooden steps which led to the arched front door. Above this and rising from the gabled roof there was a little tower about three feet square, open sided and containing a bronze bell. Above the bell a tiny four-sided spire rose for about another five feet and this was surmounted by a cross. The paint on the building looked fresh and did not have any of the flaking and blistering which was so common in even the best-kept buildings in that part of the world. Around it the ground had been cleared and there was even a patch of green lawn and a few trees. It was of course a church. Set around it, in a circle, as if paying homage to the large building, were native huts. There was nothing unusual about them. They were the same as could have been found anywhere in the area, small, straw beehivelike structures about fourteen feet in diameter. He found it strange that he had spent nearly twenty-four hours within yards of this little village and been unaware of its presence.

'Father he feed you as soon as he see you and you have nice bath, take away bad smell,' said the one who had been introduced to him as John.

Apart from the wooden church it could have been a native village almost anywhere in Africa. The usual sights were in evidence, the women sitting outside their huts grinding corn or cooking over smoky wood fires, and a few milk cows foraging around the huts for whatever they could find. There were a lot of children around and they were having great sport dragging a cow away from a hut which it had decided was good to eat.

Paul led Donald to one of the huts; they were all identical. Paul stuck his head through the door and called inside.

'Father, I find a white man and he's hungry.'

'Ah, b'God, the poor fellow,' said a rich Irish voice from the dark interior.

'Shall I bring him to you, Father?' asked Paul.

'Well, of course you bring him in,' said the voice, and as it did so, the owner appeared. He was a rotund little man wearing a white soutane and with a greying fringe of hair around his balding pate.

'This man smell a lot,' said Paul. 'Perhaps he should have bath first.'

'That's no manner to be talking to a guest,' said the priest. 'Away wi' youse before I box your ears. I'm sorry, they take everything literally and I keep tellin' them that cleanliness is next to godliness. I'm sorry, Mr . . .?'

'Bruce, Donald Bruce,' he replied.

''Tis a Scotsman you are, then,' said the priest. 'I'm Father

Xavier O'Mally, and you won't be surprised to hear that I'm Irish. We'll get you something to eat in a few minutes.' He sniffed rather pointedly. 'You can be after having your bath while I get it ready for you, if you like.'

'That sounds a good idea, Father,' said Donald, who did not know how he was expected to deal with this situation.

'Well, me tin bath is right inside there and you can put all o' that stuff in me hut unless you're thinking of having a private war before your dinner,' he said, indicating Donald's weapons. 'And there's little game around here, and in any case we've got plenty of meat. When did you last eat?'

'A couple of days ago.'

'Ah, b'God, you must be starving and me keeping you talking here as if I had nothing else to do except pass the time of day.'

'I'm very grateful.'

'Ah, well, we'll feed you and then we'll be able to sit and have a talk. I think I might have a drop of the cr'ature left to loosen our tongues.' Then he shouted out something in a language which Donald did not understand. Two small boys rushed up, grabbed two large zinc buckets each, and ran off in the direction of the river.

'I have soap,' said Father O'Mally, 'so if you'd like to go in and take off your clothes, I'll not embarrass you by standing watching you. It's beside the tub. I hope you don't mind, it's carbolic. Away you go and give yourself a good rubdown while I get one of the women to cook a meal for you.'

As he was speaking, the two boys returned with their buckets brimful of water which they took to the priest's hut and poured into the zinc bath. Donald followed them into the dark interior. As he did so, Father O'Mally stuck his head through the door.

'There's a towel lying on the end of me cot. You'd better use that. It's the cleanest one I've got,' he called.

Donald stripped off and bent his long frame into the tin tub. He scrubbed and scrubbed until the air reeked of carbolic.

After his meal, which consisted mainly of hard, round, tasteless cakes of some sort of unleavened bread, and a piece of springbok which had been roasted and tasted very good, Donald sat with the priest outside his hut.

'Well now, young man,' said Father O'Mally, 'do you want to talk about yourself or would you rather not?'

Donald looked at him inquiringly.

'Oh, there's a lot o' people these days who don't want to talk about themselves. Sometimes because they're a little bit ashamed about what they've done. Sometimes because they're not quite sure what they've done, and sometimes because they don't really know why they've done it. There's a terrible war going on all around us, but here we try to ignore it, apart from helping people if they come our way. Are you a soldier?' He smiled. 'You don't have to answer that.'

'No,' said Donald, 'I'm not a soldier. I was one once, but that was a long time ago,' he added almost wistfully. Then he hesitated and added, 'I left the army. I was working in Kimberley when the war started.'

'Well, you haven't come very far, have you?'

'You mean I'm near Kimberley? Oh, my God.'

The priest looked at him for a moment as he put his hands over his face. 'Man,' he said, 'have you no idea of where you are?'

'None.'

'Well, if you went east for about forty-five miles, you'd find yourself in Kimberley. Of course, the Boers are in Kimberley. At least that's the last I heard.'

'In it?' said Donald, as thoughts of his children, Harry, Susan, and Johnny, flooded his mind.

'Well, all around it, anyway, what's the difference? But come now, I promised you a drop of the cr'ature.'

The priest went into his hut for a moment and then returned with a bottle of John Jameson. There was just about an inch left in the bottom of it. He carefully measured out the whiskey into two small glasses, making sure that the portions were equal, and that he got every last drop out of the bottle.

'I was saving this for Easter. It was me Christmas bottle, and I usually do. But as this is a special occasion, we'll drink it now. Good health to you, young man, and good luck, whoever you may be.'

'And to you, Father,' said Donald, and there was a catch in

his voice as he experienced emotions which he thought had left him forever.

'What would you be after wantin' to do with yourself now?'

'I don't know,' replied Donald. 'How exactly do you mean?'

'Where are you going from here?'

'I think that I would like to get out of Africa. I've done terrible things here.'

'Well, I won't ask you what they are, but in those clothes you won't get out of anywhere. I'll see if we can find you something decent to wear. We have quite a lot of clothes about the place. People send them out to us. Can you imagine somebody sending a heavy topcoat with an astrakhan collar to wear in this climate?'

Donald laughed for the first time in many weeks.

'Oh, 'tis true enough. They do it, God bless them, and we're grateful for it.'

'That's damned nice of you. I'd be very grateful if you could manage to fix me up with something to wear,' said Donald.

'I hear,' said Father O'Mally, 'that the railway is running practically up to Kimberley. If you were to head southeast from here . . . have you got a compass?'

'No.'

'Well, don't worry about that. I can let you have one. If you go southeast, you should be able to get onto a train. Have you got any money?'

Donald's hand went automatically to the little package around his neck. 'Nothing negotiable,' he said.

'Ah well, we might be able to find you a bit of that. Would you be all right after you got to the Cape?'

'Oh, yes,' said Donald. 'I'd be all right after I got to the Cape and I'd be able to return anything you lent me, if you'll tell me where to send it.'

'You don't have to, but if you do, just hand it in to any Jesuit house and tell them that it is for me.'

'I'll do that. You cannot imagine how much I want to get away from here.'

'Get away, or run away?'

Donald ignored the question because he knew that it was true: what he really wanted to do was to run and he wanted to run because he was ashamed. 'I think I've had enough,' he said.

'Is it home that you want?'

'Yes, but I don't think I shall ever be able to have it.'

Father O'Mally was silent for a while. He did not want to pry, but he knew that the man sitting with him was suffering and he wanted to help.

Donald sat there thinking. Of course he wanted home, but where was home? How could he ever face his children, or his mother, after all that he had done? He had deserted them, he had become a murderer; that was really what he was, not the avenging angel which he had claimed to be to justify his behaviour. He did not know that he had the right to see his family again. They were in Kimberley, besieged, but even if he could get to them, he would only be an added encumbrance to the beleaguered town. No, the priest was right; he wanted to run away because he was a coward. He was a coward even if he could ever manage to justify his actions. If it were possible, he would wipe his mind clear of the memories of what he had done, but it was not possible, and he would have to live with it for the rest of his life. He would go away, to London possibly; Scotland was not for his kind. He could try to start again, but he could never escape himself. The first thing was to get out of Africa. Perhaps some divine inspiration would come to him and tell him what to do.

'Now, me boyo' – the priest was speaking again – 'you'll stay with us until you are properly rested, and when you're ready, we'll start you off on your way towards the railway. With a little bit of money in your pocket to get you to the Cape, and God go with you.'

'Why do you do this?'

'Because you need it. A man who's spent as many years in the confessional as I have knows a soul in torment when he sees one.'

'Father, I —'

'No, don't say anything. Perhaps we'll talk again before you leave. When you've had a good night's sleep, I'll listen if you want me to. If you don't, that'll be all right as well. You know, somebody told me something once which was a great comfort to me and has been all my life, so I tell it to you now and hope it will be a comfort to you.'

'What is it, Father?'

'Always remember that every saint has a past and every sinner has a future. Now, away to your bed. God bless you, Donald.'

10

On the afternoon of the fifteenth of February, French and his staff rode into the town of Kimberley and the siege was at an end. Kekewich was not there to greet them. When he realized that relief was imminent, he had gone out with as many mounted men as he could still spare. They were attempting to capture Long Tom. Long Tom was the name that Kimberley had given to a huge Boer gun which had been shelling them continually during the last weeks. His mission was, however, to prove fruitless, as by the time they arrived at the emplacement, the Boers had gone, taking their gun with them.

French rode through the streets to a remarkably subdued welcome, stopping at the entrance of the Sanatorium Hotel. There they found the mayor and Cecil Rhodes waiting to greet them.

Maud Bruce's little hospital now had four occupants, women who had sustained minor injuries during the shelling; the more serious cases were naturally held at the town hospital itself. She had been busy in the ward when she heard the sound of horses. They knew, of course, that relief was at hand, and Maud and one of her volunteer nurses rushed to the front door to see French and his staff pass. They all looked dusty and saddle weary as they trotted down the main street. Suddenly Maud's heart leapt; she could hardly believe her eyes. Could it possibly be true? Was it really him? Yes, it was!

Riding just behind the general was her own son Gordon. She waved frantically, but he was already past and did not see her.

'That's Gordon,' she said, addressing the nurse beside her. 'That's my son. Please, look after things for me, I must find out where they go.'

Without pausing for an answer, she went flying down the street after the riders.

At the hotel French and his staff dismounted with that weary stiffness which comes after days in the saddle, and presented themselves to the mayor and Rhodes.

'Welcome, welcome,' said Rhodes, booming and magnanimous. 'Come in, come in, all is prepared, all is prepared.'

Good God, thought Gordon, does he say everything twice?

'I am sure that a good meal would not go amiss at this point,' Rhodes continued.

French glanced around at his aides. 'Well, gentlemen, shall we take advantage of this generous offer?' He was already starting to move into the hotel alongside Rhodes. 'I thank you, sir, but should we not bring our own rations? After all, we have not been under siege.'

'We have been prepared for today for a long time,' said Rhodes, and there was a note of censure in his voice. 'Come in, come in, all of you,' he boomed, 'and let us toast the victors.'

'I say, Westlake,' said Gordon, 'do you think I could disappear for a while? I want to see if I can find my mother.'

'Better come in for a little while,' replied Westlake. 'I'll have a word with the old man as soon as I can.'

So they trooped into the hotel dining room. Gordon, all of them, were amazed at the sight which met their eyes. A buffet had been laid out. It contained every conceivable kind of meat, game, and poultry, bottles of wine without number, and sweets, and so on and on; if you could think of it, it was there.

Major Douglas Haig, French's chief of staff, looked quizzically at the magnificent spread. 'Hardly think they can have suffered much privation,' he murmured.

'No, sir,' said Rhodes who had overheard the remark. 'We have been saving this for this very moment of this day. Come and enjoy yourself. There is champagne and any other sort of wine you care to mention. Anything you do not see, just ask one of the waiters.'

Gordon, like all the men who had ridden with him, was hungry. So he decided to get some of the food inside him before he set out in search of his mother. He was busy eating a cold chicken leg when the door to the banqueting hall opened and a member of the hotel staff came into the room. The man went to Major Haig and had a short whispered conversation, after which Haig came over to Gordon.

'Bruce,' he said, 'there's a lady outside and she's asking for you.'

'That will be my mother,' said Gordon, putting his plate down on a convenient table. 'Do you think that I can get away?'

'The devil with that,' said Haig. 'If that's your mother out there, bring her in.'

'Thanks, Douglas,' said Gordon.

He went out of the room and there she was; standing, looking smaller than he expected, waiting for him. She was wearing a plain blue linen dress over which she still had her hospital apron. Their eyes met, and for a moment, neither of them moved, each savouring the sight of the other.

'Mother,' said Gordon, swallowing hard. 'It's good to see you.'

'Oh, Gordon,' she said, a catch in her voice. 'Gordon.'

He put his arms around her as she sobbed her joy at their reunion. She stepped back to look at him, wiping her eyes with the hem of her apron.

'Oh, Gordon,' she said, 'this is too wonderful. However did you manage to get here?'

'It was Ian's doing, really. He managed to swing it with the C-in-C. I was detached to General French's staff. I didn't really do anything. I was just a passenger. Apparently father's name still carries some influence in the army. Are the children all right?'

'Oh, they're fine,' said Maud. 'They've been down a mine shaft for the last two days but we got them home this morning. Of course they don't know that you're here, but they'll be overjoyed to see you.' And then she added in a more sombre tone, 'Did you hear about Brenda?'

'Yes.'

'And do you know that Donald has disappeared?'

'He's alive, Ian saw him.'

'Saw him? But where is he? Is he all right?'

'I don't know where he is now. But I do know that a few weeks ago he was safe.'

'Thank God for that. It was Brenda's death that did it. He took it very badly. I have never seen such a change in anyone. It just didn't seem like Donald.'

'I know what you mean. He's still taking it badly.'

They were silent for a moment, each thinking their own thoughts about Donald. When Gordon spoke again, he raised a more immediate matter.

'Mother,' he said, 'I haven't got permission to leave here yet. I have to go back into this reception but the chief of staff says that I am to bring you in.'

'Gordon, I can't possibly go in looking like this.' Maud became very feminine and very agitated.

'Of course you can,' he replied. 'There's the mayor and Rhodes in there looking as if they were all dressed up for a city luncheon, but the rest of us are pretty scruffy. At least let the general see that somebody has been doing some work around here. Come on, mother, and I'll ask the general, as soon as I can get in a word, and maybe we can get away.'

Gordon led a reluctant Maud, smoothing down her greying hair, into the dining room. There Cecil Rhodes was giving forth in a very loud voice about the deficiencies of Kekewich's handling of the siege.

'That man,' hissed Maud, 'I could strangle him. Colonel Kekewich has been absolutely superb. He has done everything that any man could do, and he's had to put up with that. Only a few days ago Rhodes tried to get all the townsfolk together to insist on a surrender. I suppose that he was running out of champagne. Kekewich wouldn't hear of it. He's had a dreadful time. He's been fighting the Boers and Cecil Rhodes ever since the war started.'

'Where is he now?' said Gordon. 'Why isn't he here? He ought to be.'

'I heard that he had gone out on a patrol this morning,' replied Maud. 'It's funny, though. It all seems such an anti-climax. I mean, the Boers have been around us for so long. We've got so used to the shelling and now it's all over. But nothing seems to have changed.' She stopped and her eyes widened as she saw the buffet which had been laid out. 'My goodness, look at all that food.'

'Yes, I know,' said Gordon. 'You don't seem to have been short of food.'

'Not short of food!' exclaimed Maud. 'We haven't been able to get milk for the babies and I know people who have been eating cats and worse. Really, that man is disgusting!'

Gordon was getting a little worried at his mother's tirade and he was just about to say something when the door at the opposite end of the room opened and Colonel Kekewich came in.

The colonel walked straight over to General French and saluted. 'Colonel Kekewich, sir,' he said.

'I will not have that man in my house,' shouted Rhodes.

French gave the 'great man' a baleful glance.

'I thought that this was a hotel,' said French.

'It is,' said Rhodes, 'and I own it.'

'Very well,' replied French. 'Perhaps we had better have our discussion somewhere else?' And with that, he put his arm around Kekewich's shoulder and led him from the room.

There was an awkward pause until Douglas Haig turned to the rest of the officers and said, 'Stay here, gentlemen. I'll find out if the general has any instructions.' Then he, too, left the room.

'Can we go now?' asked Maud.

'Honestly, I don't know,' replied Gordon. 'Look, I've got a friend here, I'll go and have a word with him.'

He sought out Westlake, and asked, 'I say, Tom, would it be all right for me to go off with my mother now?'

'Well,' said Westlake, 'there's nobody here who outranks you. If I were in your position, I should just shove off. Where will you be if you're wanted?'

'I'll introduce you to my mother, she'll tell you.' And they went to Maud. 'Mother, this is Tom Westlake; he's on the general's staff.'

'How do you do, Captain Westlake,' said Maud.

'Mrs Bruce. I just want to know where you'll be in case I need to get hold of Gordon,' said Westlake.

'We're going to my house,' said Maud. 'It's not far.' She told him how to find the place. 'And if you don't find it, anyone will tell you where I live. If you can get away, please come and call on us.'

'I shall certainly try. Now off you go before somebody gets back and you get trapped. I'll find out what the form is and come and let you know.'

'Thanks a lot,' said Gordon. And together they left the hotel.

Gordon had never seen Donald's children before and when Maud took him into the upstairs room where they were waiting for her, they huddled quietly into a corner as children do in the presence of a stranger.

'This is your Uncle Gordon,' said Maud.

There was no response.

'Aren't you even going to say hello?' asked Maud. 'Uncle Gordon chased the Boers away.'

'Did you?' said Harry.

'Well, I had some help,' said Gordon, smiling slightly. 'You must be Harry.' He was feeling every bit as awkward as the children.

'You look like my daddy,' said Susan, 'but he didn't wear funny trousers.'

Gordon glanced self-consciously at his tartan breeches. 'He used to, a long time ago,' he said. 'He had a pair just like this for riding a horse.'

'My daddy's coming back soon,' said Susan. 'Do you know him?'

'I know him well. I've known him all my life, ever since I was born.'

'That must be an awful long time,' said Harry. 'Daddy is very old. But he is away and Grandma is looking after us.'

'I'm hungry,' said little Johnny.

'All right, darlings,' replied Maud. 'You stay here with Uncle Gordon while I get you something to eat.'

Harry, recovering somewhat from his shyness, approached Gordon. 'Are you a soldier?' he asked.

'Yes, I'm a soldier.'

'Daddy doesn't like soldiers.'

'I know he doesn't,' said Gordon. 'But I have to be a soldier.'

'Why do you have to be a soldier?' lisped Johnny.

'Because . . .' Then he thought. Why the hell did he have

to be a soldier? 'Because – it's the regiment, you see. It is ours. It is like a family.'

'Whose family?' asked Susan. 'Do you have girls?'

'No, we don't have girls. But there's me and your daddy, he used to be in the regiment. And then there's Grandpa and Uncle Robert. Have you ever met Uncle Robert or Uncle Ian?'

'Who are they?' asked Harry.

'They're my cousins and your daddy is my brother.'

'Harry's my brother,' said Johnny. 'Have you got a sister?'

'Oh, yes, that's your Aunt Naomi.'

'Is she in the regiment?' said Harry.

'No.'

'There you are,' said Susan. 'It's not a proper family.'

'But she's a nurse. She takes care of us if anything goes wrong.'

'Where do they all live?' asked Harry.

'In Scotland.'

'Why don't we all go to Scotland? Then we could all be together,' said Harry.

'Except for Mummy. She's gone to see Jesus and I don't think that she will want to come back,' said Susan.

Gordon was beginning to wilt under this cross-examination. He felt awkward at the prospect of being drawn into a discussion about Brenda. But Scotland? He realized that he was really longing to get back there, to see the mountains and the glens again, and most of all to get away from this bloody land and the heat and the killing. Right then he could feel a certain sympathy with the Donald he had known before Brenda's death. But Scotland seemed a very long way away, and, at that distance, a very desirable place to be.

'Perhaps we will soon be able to go to Scotland. At least you and Grandma. She might be able to take you very soon.'

He was saved from further prolonging the discussion by the return of Maud.

'There you are, then,' she said. 'Tea's nearly ready. How about you, Gordon?'

'No, thanks, I had plenty at the hotel. Supplies should be easier now. We should have the railway open within a day or so. So you can let yourself go a bit.'

'Yes,' said Maud bitterly, 'like Mr Rhodes.'

Tea was ready and they took the children into the little dining room where there were tea and scones waiting for them. Gordon noted that the tea was without milk and that the scones were without butter, a great contrast to the luxurious feast which had greeted him at the Sanatorium Hotel. The children seemed to accept all of this as a matter of course and were soon tucking in to their meal and arguing as to how alike, or unlike, Daddy Gordon was.

Maud smiled at this and caught Gordon's eye, indicating that they should leave the children to it. So they went back into the sitting room.

'I can offer you a glass of sherry,' said Maud, 'but I fear that there is nothing else.'

'No, thanks,' replied Gordon, 'I really don't want anything. You'd better save what you have.'

Before they had a chance to get into conversation, there was a tap on the door.

'Come in,' said Maud.

It was one of the nurses from downstairs. 'There is a Captain Westlake here. He says he's looking for Major Bruce.'

'Ask him to come up,' said Maud.

'That's torn it,' said Gordon. 'It looks as if I have work to do.'

Tom Westlake came into the room. 'Hello, Gordon, Mrs Bruce.'

'Would you care to take a glass of sherry?' asked Maud.

'Thank you, no.'

'All right,' said Gordon. 'Tell me the worst.'

'No, it's not like that at all. It may be a little insulting but I wish somebody would insult me the same way. I've seen French.'

'And?'

'Well, to quote him verbatim, he said that you are no damned use to him. You'll never make a cavalry officer, so you might as well take your mother to the Cape.'

'But that's wonderful,' said Maud.

'Oughtn't I rejoin my unit?'

'I mentioned that to him as well. He said that he hadn't the faintest idea where your unit was and that if you go to the Cape you can find somebody to report to there. If you want my advice, I wouldn't find anybody and just ship off home. I'll see that your battalion is informed if and when we make contact, which we must do sooner or later.'

Gordon's heart leapt at the prospect of going home. 'How soon would we be able to start?' he asked. 'The railway must be in pretty bad shape.'

'Surprisingly it's not. They reckon that there will be a train out of here tomorrow. We are sending our wounded on it,' said Westlake. 'If you like, I'll see the transport wallah and get a compartment for you. How many will you be?'

'There's my mother and three children.'

'Children?' said Westlake. 'That should make it easier. They'll want them out of here. We might be pushing on fairly soon and there's no guarantee that the Boers won't be back. And now, if you'll excuse me, I have to get back. The brass wants me in attendance. Oh, another thing, what about your charger?'

'What about him?' asked Gordon, who could not have cared less about a horse at that moment. 'Haven't you got anybody who has lost his horse?'

'Plenty,' replied Westlake.

'Well, give it to him.'

'I think the general was right, you're not a cavalry man,' said Westlake smiling. 'But thanks a lot, I will do that. Now I really must go.'

'Won't you stay for a meal?' said Gordon, not seeing the worried expression which crossed his mother's face.

'We've only got horsemeat,' said Maud. 'But you're welcome to stay.'

'I'd love to, but I can't. We've got a staff meeting.' And then with a fair imitation of General French's voice: 'And now, gentlemen, these are my orders. I would like your suggestions of how we are to proceed.' He resumed his normal tone. 'We'll argue for an hour, he'll take no notice of us, and then tell us what we are going to do.' They all laughed and Westlake continued, 'It has been a rare pleasure to meet you, Mrs Bruce. Are you sure you're not his sister?'

'You're very charming, Mr Westlake.'

'It's the cavalry, you know. Goodbye. Goodbye, Gordon.'

'Perhaps we'll meet again,' said Gordon. 'But anyhow, I

want you to know how grateful I am for all you have done for us.'

'Think nothing of it, old boy,' said Westlake, and then he was gone.

'Gordon,' said Maud, and her face was serious, 'this is wonderful news, but do you think that we really ought to go until we know what has happened to your brother?'

Gordon thought for a moment. It was not possible for him to tell his mother the truth, not even the little Ian had told him. 'I don't think,' he said, 'that staying here will do any good. Donald could be anywhere and we can leave messages. I'm sure that he'll end up in Scotland. He'll know where to find us.'

'And what about Naomi?'

Gordon smiled. In a way Naomi was the most capable of them all, but he said, 'We'll write to her at Pietermaritzburg and let her know what is happening. I don't think that we have any need to worry about her.'

In the end Maud allowed herself to be persuaded, primarily on account of the children. But she did point out that if and when they got to Britain, they would have to see Mr Wilson in London and allow him some voice in his grandchildren's future.

'Well,' she said, brightening once the decision had been made. 'At least we have not got much to pack. Do you think I should tell the children now?'

'Oh, yes,' said Gordon. 'We don't want to spring it on them just before we get onto the train, and you heard what Tom Westlake said; it could be tomorrow.'

Gordon watched her as she left the room. His mother was still a very trim and attractive woman. The door closed and he was alone with his thoughts.

His thoughts were of Scotland. It was all right. Everything was all right. He would never catch up with the battalion now. So, unless somebody found him a job to do at the Cape, he was going home.

But there was no time for daydreaming. 'Possibly tomorrow,' Westlake had said. Well, there was the business, he would need to hand that over to somebody, and the packing and the official paperwork and money to get for their journey and . . . He grinned. No use sitting around, better get on with it.

11

It had been a bitter January. The snow had fallen thick upon the glen and the northeasterly wind had piled it up in ten-foot drifts. Culbrech House was to all intents and purposes marooned in its white sea. It had not worried Andrew. After the death of his mother, just before Christmas, he had become if anything even more sedentary than he had been previously. His pegleg bothered him quite a lot and he moved around with increasing difficulty. He spent most of his days in the library gazing, frustrated, at the map on the wall, unable to move his pins and flags because they were so cut off from the outside world. Even the new telephone was useless. During the first days of the blizzard the lines had come down and the workmen could not get out on to the hills to repair them.

A more serious matter was the fate of the sheep. People, Andrew knew, would probably be all right. They all laid in large quantities of provisions against just such a winter, and unless they were in urgent need of medical attention, they just sat it out in their cottages until it was possible to dig themselves out and get on to the hills to find and rescue what stock they could find still alive.

Andrew had been very much estranged from the world after his mother's death; for a while, at any rate. It had not been for the obvious reason, but because on the morning before she died, she had been lying in her bed looking very frail and had asked to see him. When he had arrived at her bedside, she had clutched spasmodically at his hand.

'Andrew,' she had said, 'I want you to forgive me.'

'Forgive you?'

'I want Maud to forgive me, too. When you see her, will you tell her that I asked?'

'Of course, but what is there to forgive?'

'No, Andrew, there is little time left and I have something to tell you before it is too late.'

'Whatever it is, you know that you have my forgiveness, and I am sure that I can say the same for Maud.'

'It was the letters, Andrew.'

'What letters? They don't matter. You must not exhaust yourself so.'

'I burned them, Andrew. Your letters to Maud. She never got them.'

He remembered then. It was forty years ago. Letters he had written to her from China and New Zealand. Letters to which she had never replied. 'Why did you?' he had asked. 'There was nothing in them.'

'I know. But I was afraid. I was afraid that you might want to marry her and I knew what that would do to you. I was very wrong, and it has been on my conscience all these years. My son, I beg you to say you forgive me.'

'Of course I forgive you,' he said, 'and I know that Maud, too, will understand.' What else could he have said, his mother dying. He had no option.

He never saw her alive again, and for some little time afterwards the thought of what she had said had rancoured him; but by now he had got over it. After all, it did not matter any more. Or did it? He had been pretty short with Willie for a while, and Willie had stopped coming round. Of course, he had told him nothing about what his mother had said and, after a little thought, he decided that Maud also should never know.

Now, on the twentieth of February, the thaw having set in, Andrew was sitting alone in the library and thinking about Willie and wishing that he would call, and wishing that he could get some news. The business about Maud was so much in the past that it really did not matter any more. His mother was dead; let the secret die with her.

It was almost as if in answer to his thoughts that Willie Bruce at that moment strode into the room. Willie was seventy, but his back was as straight as it had been when he was twenty, and he still strode like a soldier, marching rather than walking.

'Hope you dinna mind me bustin' in on you like this, Andrew,' he said.

'I'm delighted,' replied Andrew, struggling to get out of his chair.

'Dinna fash yourself,' said Willie. 'Is the bottle in its usual place? I'll get the drams.' Without waiting for a reply, he went to the sideboard and poured out two generous measures of the Glenlivet. 'Here, you'd better read that while I pour them.' He tossed a copy of that day's edition of the *Inverness Courier* on to Andrew's lap.

'How the devil did you get this?' demanded Andrew. 'And how the devil did you get over from Cluny?'

'I didna. I've been in Inverness. I was trapped there and couldna get hame. I've been livin' it up at the Station Hotel. I still canna get tae Cluny.'

'Then you'll stay with us, of course,' said Andrew.

'Stop blathering. Of course I'll stay here. Read, mon, read.'

Andrew opened the paper at where he knew that he would find the war news, and the first thing that caught his eye was a column headed *Kimberley Relieved.* It started:

> The cheering news was received on Friday morning that Kimberley had been relieved. Owing to the interruption of telegraphic communication, the information was not known in Scotland until Friday night or indeed generally until Saturday morning. The exploit of General French and his Cavalry Division seems to have been one of the most brilliantly executed in the annals of our mounted troops, and affords another proof of the enormous advantage of a force possessed of great mobility. Let us note General French's movements from official telegrams.

Tuesday morning 11:30 A.M. – Left the Reit River.

Tuesday afternoon at 5:35 reported that he had forced the passage of Klip Drift on Modder River after marching twenty-five miles.

Wednesday – Left Modder River.

Thursday evening – Reached and relieved Kimberley . . .

Andrew read quickly through the rest of the article but could find no mention of the Maclarens. Finally he put the paper down.

'Willie, this is wonderful news.'

'Och, man, you've heard nothing yet. I've been on the telephone tae Whitehall and Maud and the bairns are safe.'

'Thank the Lord for that. Where are they?'

'I can tell you that, too. You canna whack auld Willie when it comes tae gettin' information. They arrived at the Cape yesterday. They're coming hame on the *Majestic*.'

'I'm really very happy for you, Willie,' said Andrew. 'Any word of Donald?'

'No. Of course, I have nae way of knowing if Maud has news.'

'Of course not.'

'But stop interrupting. I havena finished.'

'What else could there be?'

'Gordon.'

'Gordon?'

'Aye, he's wi' Maud. Somehow he got into Kimberley wi' French and he's wi' them at the Cape. Well, ye ken I hae a wee bittie influence in high places.'

'Go on, Willie, what have you done?'

Willie was acting like a naughty schoolboy who had just put one over on his teacher.

'Man,' said Willie, 'I persuaded them tae let Gordon come hame. I told them that he'd be verra useful here.'

'How the devil would he manage to be that?'

'Why, raising a volunteer battalion, o' course.'

'But,' said Andrew, 'there's hardly anybody around here who could have gone who hasn't gone already.'

'You ken that, I ken that, but they dinna ken that in London, and I didna want Maud and the bairns coming all that way by themselves.'

'What about the regiment?'

'They're up country wi' Kitchener. Roberts is ill. Nae doot we'll hear aboot them soon.'

12

The idea was to march east along the Modder River and then bear slightly south and into Bloemfontein. That way Roberts's huge army would always be able to get water for men and draught animals, and though it would undoubtedly make their intentions obvious to the Boers, Roberts had decided that the convenience afforded by never being away from water was worth the added dangers that were involved.

What they were not totally aware of was just where the masses of the Boer forces lay. The largest of these was under the command of Cronje and it did in fact lie between them and their target, albeit on the north side of the Modder.

It was on the night of the seventeenth of February, just over two days before Willie Bruce and Andrew Maclaren got the news of the relief of Kimberley, that the Maclarens marched eighteen miles, making a grand total of thirty-one miles in the preceding twenty-four hours. They arrived, just before dawn, on the south bank of the Modder opposite a hill which went by the name of Paardeberg. It was there that, footsore and weary, they slipped out of their packs and prepared to bivouac for a few hours. It was now the eighteenth of February and the grey line of dawn was just appearing in the night sky.

As the light improved, a sight they had never expected met their eyes. On the other side of the river lay what looked like a sprawling village with oxen, horses, wagons, and literally thousands of people moving about and looking from that distance like a colony of ants. It was Cronje's laager.

Field-Marshal Roberts was not with his troops. Illness had detained him and the command had fallen upon General Kitchener. The Maclarens were in the sixth division under the command of an officer, General Kelly-Kenny, who was senior to Kitchener, but who accepted his orders because Kitchener also held the post of second-in-command to Roberts.

It was therefore Kitchener as chief of staff who took command of the operation. He realized that he had been presented with an excellent opportunity to smash Cronje's force in the field. So far as he was able to ascertain, no other sizeable Boer contingent lay between him and Roberts's avowed objective, Bloemfontein. Kitchener was a good, if ruthless, soldier and he knew that the task would not be an easy one. Along the banks of the river were lots of trees and vegetation which would afford the enemy good cover and make any attack upon his position a highly costly operation, so far as casualties were concerned. To counter this advantage, Kitchener detailed an entire division for this phase of the battle.

Kelly-Kenny hastily convened a conference of his battalion commanders in order to explain his plans. There was a drift about three miles upstream from Cronje's force. It would be necessary to cross the Modder at this point. It fell to Ian Maclaren and his battalion to cross, force if necessary, the river at that point. There they were to establish a bridgehead for the rest of the division or, if there was little or no opposition at that point, to proceed on towards the laager and take the first line of entrenchments. They were to move out within half an hour.

So, just when the sun had risen fully above the horizon, the Maclarens moved out. They had not even had time for breakfast. A quick swill of coffee and they were on their way.

They arrived at the drift without incident. There they halted and viewed the muddy, brown, fast-flowing water with extreme distaste. Sergeant Leinie waded into the water and before he was halfway across, it was up to his chest. He returned and reported to Robert Maclaren.

'It's no going tae be easy, sirr. Yon watter's bloody fast.'

'I'll talk to the colonel,' replied Robert and went to seek out Ian Maclaren. 'I think we'll have to get a line across,' he said to Ian. 'It's running pretty fast and my guess is that it must be over four feet, which is going to make it pretty tough on the small fellows.'

Ian tried to sum up the situation. He studied carefully the problem which confronted him. The river curved gently and they were inside a small arc. Climatically it was almost pleasant; the fast-moving water was no breeding ground for mosquitoes and the river itself kept the temperature down within bearable limits. The ground shelved quite gently towards their side of the river, but on the opposite side the natural erosion had produced a pretty stiff climb – not very high, a matter of ten or twelve feet, but very steep. It would mean quite a stiff scramble on the far bank. There was vegetation along the banks and even a few trees. All of this was good, for, as they had no precise idea of how far along the far bank the Boer lay, they might need the cover. However he did not seem to be too close, as no one had opened fire on them yet. They would certainly be lucky to get the men across without being spotted and that was the immediate task.

Robert was quite right. If that water was four feet deep, then the smaller men with their equipment and their weapons were going to find it very difficult and casualties would be a near certainty.

Ian turned to Robert. 'I see what you mean,' he said. 'The obvious thing to do is to get a rope across and then the men will be able to use it as a hand rail.'

'Agreed,' said Robert. 'Who's going to do it?'

'Who do you suggest?'

'There's no choice. I'm the tallest man in the battalion and the toughest.'

'We'll let that pass,' said Ian with a smile. 'But I take your point. There's another thing. All the gear will be soaked when we get across. We'll need time to dry out rifles and ammunition. I tell you what we'll do. Send a runner back to the general and tell him the form. Ask him for cover from this bank if we find any opposition. All right?'

'As you say,' said Robert.

'We're right under the hill and as far as we can see there are no Boers there; we shouldn't need the cover. But just in case . . .'

The runner was sent off and then, with a light cord around his waist, Robert stepped into the brown muddy water and started across. It was not easy to maintain a foothold, but after about ten minutes he managed it and crawled out on to the opposite bank. The battalion had taken up position along the bank just in case there was any attempt to stop Robert, but he managed to get across without a single shot being fired. Ian felt that his luck was in. If only it would hold for the next couple of hours . . .

Robert hauled away at the heaving line which was attached to the rope which would form the handhold to get them across. He made the rope fast to a tree after getting it across, a feat which took all of his strength, and then under the command of the R.S.M., four men took up the slack and made it tight, attaching it to a convenient tree on their side. Robert, his task finished, for the moment at any rate, sat down with his back to the tree to which he had attached his end of the rope. For the smaller of them it was difficult, though it would have proved impossible had they not had that handhold. On they came, all eight hundred of them, slithering and slipping, sometimes helping the weaker as they almost lost their grip.

All had gone smoothly and the majority of them were across when Alasdair Maclaren stepped into the water followed by Corporal MacTavish. Maclaren was almost in midstream when he suddenly stopped. A gap widened in front of him and other men started to bunch up behind him. It seemed to Corporal MacTavish that young Alasdair had his eyes firmly fixed on some object downstream, though MacTavish himself could see nothing.

'Get on wi' it, you daft bugger,' yelled MacTavish. 'You're ho'din' us a' up.'

There was no reply from Maclaren, none that was audible anyway, for his lips moved soundlessly.

Corporal MacTavish was a big man but even he could feel the drag from the current as he stood there hanging on to the rope. He knew that if he released his hold and tried to get around Alasdair, he would not stand a chance. The scudding water was up to his armpits. 'Move, damn ye, move,' he shouted.

Maclaren looked at him. MacTavish had seen that sort of look before. It was the look that a man gets when the sun has got to him or when he is half crazed with drink.

'Dae ye no see her?' said Maclaren.

'Shut up and get on,' hollered back MacTavish, trying to push the young soldier into motion; but Maclaren seemed to be oblivious to what was going on around him.

'I can see you, Marhi Crow,' he called. 'I mind you were coming for me! Here I come, Marhi Crow.'

And with that he let go of the rope and took a step downstream where, in an instant, the pace of the current and the weight of his equipment had sucked him under and into fifteen feet of water. For a moment MacTavish and the men behind him stared horrified at what had happened, and then, without thinking, MacTavish started to let go of the rope to try and save Maclaren.

'Hald on tae that rope, sodger. Let him go!' It was the voice of authority. Frankie Gibson, who was bringing up the rear, had seen it all and knew that any attempt to rescue Maclaren would only result in further loss.

With an instinct born of long service and instant obedience to orders, MacTavish grabbed back at the rope just in time and continued across. Maclaren's body was recovered several days later, and when they found it, his tightly corked water bottle smelled of methylated spirit; might that have been the explanation?

It had been a scary experience for MacTavish. Like most of the men from the glen, the name Marhi Crow was not unknown to him. Nor were some of the stories about her. He would, however, never know what it was, or who it was that Private Maclaren had been looking at there in the middle of the river, before the muddy water had swallowed him up. He got to the far bank and scrambled ashore. Robert, who had watched the whole incident, was waiting for him.

'What the hell happened out there?' demanded Robert. 'What was that fool doing?'

'I dinna ken, sirr,' replied MacTavish. 'He stopped all o' a sudden. I yelled tae him tae keep movin', but he dinna seem tae see me. Then he said something about Marhi Crow, she's the yin wi' the sight. And then he was gone.'

'All right, Corporal,' said Robert. 'It was not your fault. You were right not to go after him.'

By this time all the battalion was across and busy with oil bottles and pull-throughs, cleaning and drying their weapons.

'What dae we dae aboot the rope, sir?' Frankie Gibson asked Ian.

Ian thought for a moment. 'There are more men of ours over there. They'll need it to back us up. The Gordons and the Canadians should be close behind us.'

And indeed the first of those two battalions was already approaching the south bank.

'Now, Sergeant-Major, as soon as the men have made sure that their weapons are fit for use, we fix bayonets and we'll start for the laager as soon as they are ready.'

'Dae ye mind tellin' me what we'se are supposed tae be doing?' asked Frankie.

'You saw the laager this morning?' said Ian.

'Aye, sirr.'

'Cronje's there. We're going to attack.'

Frankie's weatherbeaten face assumed a sober expression. 'That'll no be easy,' he said. 'It'll cost us mony a man. They hae plenty o' cover.'

'Dammit,' said Ian, 'I know that it's not going to be easy. But I've got my orders.'

'Aye, sirr,' said Frankie.

The sun was well up now and it took them very little time to dry out their rifles and ammunition. Then Ian ordered the advance in open order by companies and they started towards the laager.

They moved up a little way from the river which brought them a little north of Cronje. This gave them the advantage of high ground. Within half an hour the whole Boer position was within their view and consequently they knew that they must also be quite visible to the Boers. They could see the trenches between themselves and the laager. They advanced slowly and cautiously, conserving their energies for the charge which must come. Each man had five rounds in the magazine of his Lee-Metford and he was well aware that, when the fighting started, there would be no time for reloading. Each and every one of those rounds had to tell; after that, it would be the bayonet.

Ian knew that Frankie Gibson's fears were well founded and that he would lose a lot of men that day. He tried hard not to think about that as he moved forward straining to keep his mind on the objective and not on the price that he would have to pay.

Robert Maclaren, leading his company, had no such thoughts. He casually relit his cigar which had gone out when young Alasdair had been lost in the Modder, and strolled forward as if he were taking a Sunday afternoon walk in the park. Only when someone in the ranks behind him started singing 'Dolly Gray' and their pace quickened so that he was getting ahead of the battalion which stretched out on either side of him, did he seem to be aware of the purpose of this stroll. He ordered the men to stop singing and slowed them down so as to keep level with the other companies.

As they moved they saw lyddite shells starting to burst inside the laager.

'The poor bastards,' said Corporal MacTavish.

'Aye,' said Sergeant Leinie, who was just behind him. 'There'll be women and bairns in there; they always take them wi' them.'

'Mair bloody fools them,' said Corporal Anderson unfeelingly.

They were less than a thousand yards from the first of the trenches when the firing started. Each and every one of them had a compelling urge to shoot back.

'Don't fire,' shouted Ian, 'unless you are sure of your target. Maintain open order.' He was fighting against the instinct of the men to bunch together.

By the time they were within two or three hundred yards of the Boer lines, several of their men had fallen and Ian decided that the moment had come to take stock of the situation.

'Take cover,' he called.

Within a couple of seconds the whole battalion was lying prone. At that moment, the most valuable thing that any man could find was a tuft of dried grass or a large rock, anything which could give him concealment while he got his breath back, waiting for the next order.

Ian dragged his field glasses from their case and looked carefully along the dark line of the Boer trenches. Suddenly he stopped scanning and concentrated on a point on his right near the river.

'Sergeant-Major,' he called.

Frankie Gibson was at his side. 'What is it, sir?'

'Take these and have a look at that,' he said pointing to the Boers' left flank.

Frankie took the glasses and did as he was bid. 'It's a Maxim, sir,' he announced.

'We'll have to do something about that before we go in,' said Ian. 'Get Captain Maclaren over here.'

Frankie snaked away across the brown dusty earth and returned with Robert.

'There's a —'

'There's a machine gun on their left flank,' said Robert. 'I've seen it.'

'Well?'

'Let me take half a dozen men and we'll knock it out. They don't know that we know that it's there or they would have used it before now. They must be waiting for a point blank target.'

Ian looked up at his brother. Not the gay young cavalier, the man about town, that was not what he saw; not the debutantes' delight, not the indolent, well-dressed young officer who would lounge in the anteroom of the mess with his feet impudently placed on the C.O.'s favourite leather armchair. That wasn't the real Robert; the real Robert was a real soldier. As good a soldier as Gordon Bruce, but in Robert's case flamboyant with it. Robert had little time for the petty restrictions of army life and showed his contempt for them by flouting most of them. But when it came to the job, when it came to real soldiering and doing the work for which they existed, Ian believed that there was none better than Robert Maclaren. Ian knew all this and Ian knew that what Robert had said was right and Ian knew the risks which Robert would be taking and Ian loved his brother.

'I don't want you to go, Robert.'

'Because I'm your brother or because I'm not good enough?'

'Because you're a company commander,' replied Ian, but he knew that that was not true.

'No, Ian. It's got to be me. I've seen it and I'm as good as the next man and you know it.'

'What's the matter? Are you after a bloody medal?' snapped Ian.

'Yes,' said Robert smiling, though that was not true, either.

'All right, go, damn you. We can't spend all day arguing about it.'

'I'll go, too, sir,' said Frankie Gibson.

The brothers looked at him. There was no doubt about Frankie's ability. If any man could get close to that gun unobserved, it had to be him.

'I'll get three mair men,' he continued. 'Wi' Captain Maclaren and meself, we'll dae it.'

Ian could not argue. 'Very well, Sergeant-Major,' he said, and then added, 'Would my revolver be more use to you than your rifle?'

'They're daft wee things,' replied Frankie, 'but this time it could be. And dinna worry, Master Ian, I'll look after yon.'

'Thanks, Frankie.' He passed him his Webley. 'Leave me your rifle. We'll go in as soon as you engage them.'

'We're no going tae engage them, sirr, we're going tae slit their throats.'

'Thanks anyway, Frankie,' said Ian. 'Good luck, Bob.'

They crept away and picked up their three 'volunteers'. Corporal Anderson was one, not because anybody liked him, but because he was fearless and brutal and he would enjoy the killing. Two other men from Strathglass, Privates Robertson and Fraser, both of B Company, made up their number.

They backtracked a little away from the battalion and then scrambled down the sandy bank until they were almost at the water's edge. There was more cover here. Quite a lot of tall grass, shrubs, rocks and one or two trees. They turned towards their objective. Only twelve feet above them there were a thousand of their comrades waiting to do battle, yet the five of them seemed isolated and alone. It was silent and they could smell the damp earth by the water's edge. Now and then the silence was broken by the crump of a shell as it landed in the laager, as if to remind them of the task in hand.

They moved slowly forward, locating the next bush or rock large enough to give them shelter before they abandoned the present cover. If they spoke they spoke in whispers and each man felt the tension building within him as they drew nearer to the target.

Robert and Frankie led with the others bringing up the rear.

'How many do you think there will be?' whispered Robert.

'Four, five at the most, sirr,' replied Frankie.

They moved on. They were still at the riverside when Frankie whispered again, 'Stop them noo, sirr.'

'Where are we?' asked Robert, waving the others down into the tall grass and reeds.

'Yon gun,' said Frankie, 'is just up there.' He pointed up the bank on their left. 'If you'll all wait here, I'll tak' a wee lookie.'

Robert watched as Frankie crawled away, full of admiration for the man. He seemed to turn into a khaki snake as he slithered away.

Frankie did not hurry. A man does not hurry when he's out on the hill stalking a fine stag, and this was the same game. He examined every piece of ground before he put his weight on it, removing any twig or loose stone gently in case it would make a noise as he passed over it. At the top of the bank he carefully eased himself up by a small shrub, peered over for less than a second, and then allowed his body weight to take him back out of sight. As slowly as he had gone up there, he started his return.

'Well?' asked Robert.

'We outnumber them,' replied Frankie with a grin. 'There's only four o' them. It's a Maxim, all reight. I coonted three rifles in there as weel.'

'How do you suggest we go about it?' said Robert, accepting without question a subordinate role.

'Weel, sirr, we're all reight until we get tae the top o' the bank. But at the top o' the bank, there's aboot ten yards and nae cover before we get tae the pit. Yon pit's only aboot another ten yards frae a trench, but they'll be there, all reight.'

'They'll be keeping their heads down,' said Robert.

'They're nae lookin' towards us,' continued Frankie, 'so we'll awa' up tae the top o' the bank and then it's a matter o' gettin' tae them before they spot us and dealing wi' them before they can grab their rifles and open fire.'

'Right,' said Robert. 'We'll do it your way.' He knew better than to argue with the expert. 'This is it. Come on, lads, and good luck.'

'Listen,' said Frankie addressing the other three, 'this is no game. When we get in there, we've got tae kill the lot o' them. We're in nae position tae tak' prisoners. Then we use their gun to cover oor lads as they come in.'

Corporal Anderson replied with an evil grin through his blackened teeth.

It seemed to Robert that it took hours, though it was only a couple of minutes, before they reached the top of the bank. They were all watching Frankie, who had taken upon himself the mantle of leadership as easily and as naturally as if he had been born to it.

They peered over the top and there they could see the four Boers alert and watching, but looking the wrong way, towards the ground where they knew the battalion lay.

It seemed incredible to Robert that his little band was still unobserved, but it was. Frankie slipped a vicious-looking dirk from its sheath; he was wearing this in preference to the R.S.M.'s sword to which he was entitled. With Ian's Webley in his left hand and the dirk in his right, he looked around to assure himself for the last time that they were all ready. The three soldiers lay waiting, with bayonets fixed, as the tension mounted. Robert cocked his revolver and glanced towards Frankie. Frankie nodded.

'Now,' said Robert, rising to his feet.

They rose from the bank and hurled themselves across the ten yards which separated them from the Boer machine-gun emplacement. They had only gone a couple of paces when a hoarse shout from the pit signalled that they had been seen.

They opened fire as they ran forward, but at the speed they were travelling it was impossible to take aim, and they scored no hits. Four of them made it to the emplacement. Private Robertson fell on the way there. One Boer had his rifle in his hands; he must have been the one that got Robertson. One was trying to swing the Maxim around and the other two were grabbing for their rifles. Frankie Gibson sprinted around to the side of the pit and slid into it with the wall at his back, grabbed the nearest Boer around the throat, and all but sliced his head off with his dirk.

Robert gave forth an almighty yell and jumped into the pit, firing as he went straight on to the bayonet of one of the Boers. Corporal Anderson shot the man as he was trying to free his weapon from Robert's body, and then died himself, a dumdum through his kidneys which splattered his entrails all over the pit. Frankie, using the body of the dead Boer as a shield, calmly picked off the two remaining.

By now they could hear the clatter of men and weaponry coming from the trench which was only yards away, and there were only Frankie Gibson and Private Fraser left standing in the pit.

The Maxim was ready cocked with a full belt of ammunition. Frankie grabbed it and swung the unwieldy weapon around to bear on the trench. Fraser, who had been picked for his knowledge of machine guns, knelt at the side of the gun and fed the belt into it as Frankie opened fire.

The Boers in the trench scuttled back behind a bend leaving several of their number writhing on the ground. Every time a head popped up, Frankie fired a burst and soon the Maxim was steaming.

'It's boiling!' yelled Fraser.

'Then piss on it, man!' Frankie shouted back.

Fraser did as he had been bid, and while he was at it, Frankie shouted to him.

'Here they come!' he yelled.

Up from the yellow-brown earth the Maclaren Highlanders rose as a man, like a moving wave of khaki. For a moment there was silence, and in it Frankie was sure that he heard Ian Maclaren.

'Maclaaaaarens CHAAAAAARGE!!!' shouted the voice.

As one man they started running for the trenches, and the charge and the killing had begun.

Frankie kept up a stream of bullets low over the top of the trench, but it was still a horrifying spectacle. The Highlanders were swatted down in their dozens long before they were within fighting range of the trench. But at last they were there, leaping in on top of the Boers, stabbing and jabbing the guts out of one another with their bayonets, and within five minutes the trench was taken. Already the Gordons were tearing across the open ground. They leapt across the trench, now occupied by the Maclarens, and on to the Boers' second line of defence. A bloody hand-to-hand struggle ensued in which quarter was neither asked nor given. But it could not last. The Maclarens had been decimated. The Gordons had suffered heavily, and Kelly-Kenny knew that he could not commit his Canadians without the risk of losing his entire force.

In a lull in the fighting the plaintive notes of the bugle could be heard calling the retire.

'What dae we dae noo, sirr?' asked Fraser.

'We get tae hell oot of here,' said Frankie. 'We gan back.'

'What aboot yon?' Fraser indicated the Maxim. 'We canna carry it.'

'Awa' you go, I'll deal wi' it,' said Frankie.

'Sir, you've been hit,' said Fraser, seeing blood oozing down Frankie's leg.

'Aye,' said Frankie, 'I got a wee nick in the arse. Noo awa' wi' ye.'

Fraser climbed out of the pit and headed back the same way that they had come. Frankie found a large stone in the pit and smashed the Maxim's breech mechanism.

He was just about to leave the pit when a sound made him whip around. It was Robert. He was not dead, not yet, though with a bayonet wound which had entered him around the navel and come out of his back through his lungs, he had not long to go. Frankie knew a dead man when he saw one and there was no mistaking the pallor on Robert's face. He went over to him.

'I'll bide wi' ye, sir,' said Frankie.

Robert managed a negative motion of his head, and then, 'Please —' He barely breathed the word, and a stream of blood oozed out of his mouth. 'End it, ahaaah —'

Frankie lifted up Ian's Webley. 'Ye mean?'

There was no word but the head nodded ever so slightly.

Frankie knew what Robert was asking him to do, and he knew that he would do it, but it did not stop the tears welling in his eyes. 'Guidbye, sirr,' he murmured and pressed the trigger.

After one last look around the carnage, he slipped out of the pit and headed for the rear of his own lines.

Once in the rear he sought out what was left of the battalion, who were exhaustedly trudging into reserve, leaving the

Canadians to hold the forward positions. Almost the first man Frankie encountered was Corporal MacTavish.

'Are you all right, jock?' he called. MacTavish had a crude bandage around his head.

'Och, I'm fine, sirr. But no many on them made it,' was the reply.

'Is the colonel —?'

'He's all right, I've seen him. He's been hit but it doesna look tae bad. He got one in the arm or the shoulder or something.'

'I've got tae find him,' said Frankie. 'His brother's deed.'

'Captain Robert?' said MacTavish.

'Aye.'

'It's a fuckin' awfu' war.'

Frankie continued in his search for Ian and eventually found him propped against a rock with a medical orderly binding up his shoulder.

'Where's Bob?' said Ian as soon as their eyes met, but the look on Frankie's face gave him the answer.

'There's only me and Fraser left,' he said. 'Captain Maclaren's no coming back, sir.'

'You're sure he's dead?'

'Aye, sir, he's deed.' Frankie could not tell him the rest.

Ian's lips trembled, but only for a moment. This was all part of the game. This was all part of being a soldier. Robert had gone. Robert was his brother whom he loved. But so far as he knew, most of his men had gone, and nearly all his officers. It seemed to Ian unfair that he should still be alive.

'Call the roll, Sergeant-Major,' he said.

'De ye mind if I get ma bum fixed up first, sir?' asked Frankie.

'I beg your pardon?' said Ian.

'Och, I got a wee nick in it and it's bleedin' a bittie.'

'Of course, Sergeant-Major,' replied Ian, smiling in spite of his feelings. And as Frankie was about to go: 'Mr Gibson, that was a magnificent job you did today. You will hear more of it.'

'I'd rather forget it, sir,' said Frankie grimly, and he moved on in search of a medic.

Kitchener was determined that he would take Cronje's laager by a frontal assault, but it was proving extremely costly in the lives of the men under his command. The Maclarens' four companies had been reduced to only two companies of fit men. The rest were casualties, dead or wounded.

When he heard of the situation at Paardeberg, Lord Roberts left his sickbed and came straight up to the front to take personal command of the operation. Without criticizing him, he gave Kitchener another job and decided to pound Cronje into submission with his artillery. It came as a shock to Roberts when he discovered that there were many women and children in the laager and he promptly offered the Boers the chance to send them out to a place of safety. Cronje refused this out of hand, and so the slow process of shelling him into submission continued.

It was not until the twenty-seventh of February that General Cronje finally surrendered. This was a most significant day as it was the anniversary of the defeat which the Boers had inflicted on the British many years before at Majuba.

During the time of the shelling an increasing danger made itself felt, more deadly than the bullets of the Boers. The water of the Modder River, which was their only supply, was becoming increasingly polluted. Dysentery was rife throughout the British camp and, in its own insidious way, the water caused many more casualties than Kitchener's attempt to storm the laager.

When Roberts moved on towards Bloemfontein, the Maclarens did not go with him. The remnants of the battalion were transferred to Kimberley for garrison duties. There, with the approval of Kelly-Kenny, Ian submitted a written report to Lord Roberts telling him of the part played by his brother and R.S.M. Gibson in that first attack on the laager at Paardeberg. Of course, communication being what it was, it took some time for Ian to receive a reply, but when it did come in the middle of March, Ian had a conversation with his R.S.M.

'Sergeant-Major,' he said, 'I have no doubt that you will be delighted to hear that you have been awarded the Victoria Cross.'

'Aye,' said Frankie, as imperturbable as ever, and ever the practical Scot, 'I believe there's a wee pension goes wi' it.'

'Yes,' said Ian, smiling. 'As a matter of fact there is. I'm not sure what it is, about ten pounds a year, I think. And I believe that only noncommissioned ranks get the money.'

'Weel,' replied Frankie, 'I'll no be sayin' no tae that.'

'The other thing is that you and I are going home. My shoulder, it seems, will still be quite a while mending, and as for you, you are to receive your medal from the Prince of Wales at Buckingham Palace.'

'Why do I get tae go hame, sir?' asked Frankie.

'That's easy. The second battalion is coming out from Australia. They will take over what men we have left. As for you and me, well, we've got to put a regiment together again. I'm not going to be fit for active service for quite a while, and our first V.C. will be quite an attraction.'

'It'll be nice to get back to the glen,' said Frankie.

'I haven't finished yet. There's something else. I have suggested that you be recommended for a commission.'

'What, me, sir?' said Frankie, sounding surprised for the first time.

'Yes. We're going to need a first-class quartermaster. That could be you.'

Frankie stroked his chin reflectively. 'I have nae doobt that this is a great honour that you are offering me, sir. But would it be all right if I was tae say no? I dinna want tae appear ungrateful, but I dinna want tae be an officer, either.' He paused. 'Of course, I do thank you for the kind thought, sir.'

Ian raised his eyebrows. 'You don't want a commission?'

'Well, sir,' said Frankie. 'The Victoria Cross, that's fine. It doesna mak' any difference. But, sir, I am the regimental-sergeant-major. That's something. Lieutenant Frankie Gibson? He'd be a nothing and I'd hate the man that got ma job. Besides, sir, there's another thing. If I became an officer, you and the Bruces, you'd a' be ma brother officers. Now if that happened, how would I feel aboot takin' a salmon frae the Glass. Or a wee stag from the hill. I couldna dae it, sir. I have no got long tae go afore I retire and after that, weel, you ken hoo it is.'

'Yes, Frankie,' said Ian, smiling again, 'I ken how it is.'

'Thank you, sir.'

'Well, you had better see that your kit is packed. We go to the Cape tomorrow and then it will be home for both of us.'

13

It was the way of things, the way that they always happen, that after their arrival in Cape Town, though Frankie Gibson was shipped home almost immediately, Ian found himself landed with a series of dull administrative posts. He was shunted from one desk to another and seemed to be achieving nothing. He wished that he could have rejoined his battalion, but that was not possible. It would have been very awkward for Colonel MacKay, who commanded the second battalion, had Ian attempted to do any such thing. However, he did succeed in convincing the authorities that his presence in Cape Town was contributing nothing to the war effort, and in August he was given a berth on a ship out of the Cape to Tilbury.

It was a mild, warm September evening when his ship docked in London. Ian had already made up his mind that he would stay in town for a day or two. There he intended to contact Mr Wilson and see if there was any news at all about Donald. Not that he had any desire to see Donald, but he felt that he had a duty to Willie and Maud to find out anything that was known.

He stayed the first night at the Great Eastern Hotel, from where he telephoned Culbrech House. Victoria was, of course, delighted to hear his voice and she quite agreed that it would be a kindness if he tried to get word of Donald before coming home. When she had assured him that the children were all well, Andrew came on the line. Ian suggested that he should spend the next couple of nights at the house in Charlotte Street, but Andrew told him that it was temporarily shut.

'Why don't you,' said Andrew, 'go along and stay at Naomi's house at 182 Park Lane?'

'I could, I suppose,' replied Ian.

'Her housekeeper is still there and I know it would be all right.'

Ian felt, as always, guilty at the mention of Naomi, but it was the obvious thing to do, and so, the next morning, he called a hansom and set out for Park Lane after sending his chest on to Scotland by rail.

He got to the house and Barker answered the door. They had never met before, but when Ian introduced himself, Barker recognized the name.

'Won't you come in, sir?' she said. 'I am sure that madam will be delighted to see you.'

'Madam?' Ian was surprised.

'Yes, sir,' replied Barker, 'Mrs Bruce returned home four months ago.'

'But that's not possible,' said Ian. 'I was talking to Scotland only last night, they would have told me.'

'No, sir. Mrs Bruce has informed no one of her return to this country.'

Ian had certainly not expected to see Naomi and did not really know how he felt at the prospect. He had been certain that she was still nursing in South Africa.

Barker led him into the softly furnished, airy sitting room. She left him standing, looking out of the tall windows on to the traffic jostling its way up and down Park Lane. It was just the same as it had always been except that there were now quite a few of the new horseless carriages rattling and smelling their way around the streets of London.

He had only been standing there a moment or two when he heard the click of the door behind him and he turned. She was wearing a tight-waisted skirt of deep green, and a brocade bodice-cum-jacket from which a mass of white lace flowed from her throat rather like an ornate jabot, and she was as beautiful as ever. Graceful were her movements and she greeted him with that little smile which he had come to know so well.

'Hello, Ian.'

'I didn't expect to find you here.'

'I hardly expected to see you,' she replied.

'I was going to stay here for a couple of nights,' he said haltingly.

'Oh.'

'Yes, I docked yesterday and I'm on my way up to Scotland. I thought that I should like to contact Donald's father-in-law before I went home.'

'I see,' said Naomi. 'Why do you want to see him?'

'I thought that I might be able to get some news of Donald. I am sure that your father is worried about him.'

'Donald is all right,' replied Naomi. 'He is in London. As a matter of fact, he is living with his father-in-law. As it happens, he is coming here to dine with me this evening.'

'Oh,' said Ian. 'Well, I'm glad he's safe.' Then he continued awkwardly, 'Well . . . that is really all I wanted to find out. So I suppose that I could go up on the night train tonight.'

'You could,' said Naomi. 'But why not stay and see him?'

'No,' Ian said quickly. How could he? What was there that he could say to Donald? He was probably the only one who knew the real story about him.

Something in his expression must have betrayed his thoughts.

'He's changed, Ian,' said Naomi.

'How do you mean, changed?'

'I mean that he has told me everything. I think that he has gone back. I think he is now again like the brother I knew.'

That was all very well, thought Ian, but he doubted even so that he would be able to face Donald, whichever Donald it was; the gentle man who could not kill or the predator who had stalked the veld lusting for vengeance. He looked worried.

'You need not decide right away,' said Naomi. 'He won't be here until seven o'clock. I have asked Barker to make us some coffee. You will have some, won't you?'

'Yes, of course, thank you.' Funny, he thought, how awkward he felt in her presence. He had really almost forgotten her. His mind had been so filled with the imminent prospect of reunion with his family, Victoria and the children. Yet somehow, there was always Naomi. Well, he would have to learn to live with it.

As they sipped their coffee, he asked her, 'Why did you come back?'

She studied him with great solemnity. 'Yes,' she replied at length, 'I think that perhaps you should know. I was never going to tell you, but perhaps that would be unjust and you should know the truth.'

She got up and he rose with her. 'Come with me, Ian,' she said.

She led him into the hallway and to the foot of the stairs. She smiled as he hesitated.

'Don't worry, Ian,' she said softly. 'It's not that way. It can never be like that again.'

She led him up the stairs to a room on the first floor. It was all pinks and blues and golds. It overlooked the tiny patch of garden at the back of the house. In the centre of the room, canopied in lace and ribbons, white lace and blue ribbons, stood a cot.

'Go on, Ian, look.'

He leaned over the cot and saw the baby within. There was something he wanted to ask but was afraid to.

'It looks like a Bruce,' he said.

'He, Ian, not it. He is mine,' said Naomi. 'I thought that I was past it. I thought that I had been barren all my life and that I had reached that age when a woman can no longer have a child. When I knew that he was on the way, I was happy, I mean really happy for the first time in my life. I knew that that was the only thing that I had been searching for all these years. And Ian —'

'Yes?' He could barely whisper the word.

'He's not a Bruce. He's a Maclaren.'

Ian just looked at her as the implication of her words became clear.

'Yes,' she said. 'Your son. I called him Robert. I thought that you would like that.'

'Naomi,' he said, and stepped towards her.

'No, Ian,' she replied very calmly, 'don't touch me. That is all over now. I have got what I wanted. You are his father, Ian, but he is all mine and he is mine alone. I hope that this does not distress you. I feel that you have a right to know and then a duty to forget. No one else will ever know.'

'But —' started Ian.

'There are no buts. You must go back to Scotland. You must go back to Victoria and you must tell her nothing of this because this is my secret and my fulfilment – and I shall share him with no one. Not even you.'

14

It was the twenty-second of January, 1901. That date was the ninety-fifth anniversary of the raising of the 148th Regiment of Foot which in 1881 had been given the name of the Maclaren Highlanders.

The great Boer War was won but not over. There was still skirmishing going on in South Africa, and a smouldering resentment still burned among the Boer farmers against the imperialism of Britain. It was a resentment that would never die, just as, when a brush fire starts on the high veld and the flames are beaten out, the fire remains. It lies smouldering under the sod waiting for the moment when the flames can break through again. Always that resentment would lie there, just beneath the surface, waiting for the time when they would again be able to claim that which they regarded as their heritage.

Field Marshal Roberts had returned earlier that month in triumph, to resume the retirement which at the call of the Empire he had so readily abandoned. He had been met and greeted by the Prince of Wales and driven through the crowded streets of London, cheered to the echo, the hero of the hour.

At Osborne on the Isle of Wight, the reign of Queen Victoria was drawing to its close. The great matriarch of the dynasties of Europe was dying.

At Culbrech House they were having lunch, the Maclarens and the Bruces. They were nearly all there, for Andrew had decreed that it should be a special occasion for the children. Sir Andrew sat at the head of the table. He was slimmer now. He had managed to shed some of the weight he had accumulated during the years of inactivity which had been forced on him by the loss of half a leg. He was surrounded by his families, both of them. Of the Maclarens, there were Ian and Victoria, reunited and settling down to the humdrum of approaching middle age. Their children were there: Emma, the eldest, now nine, shy and retiring; Henry, now eight, and showing something of the ebullient characteristics of his great-grandfather after whom he was named; Albert, at six, endowed with all the charm that Andrew had possessed as a child, and also with some of the gentleness which had made soldiering so difficult for his grandfather; Phillipa, who was only five, had, after grave consultation, in which she displayed a maturity beyond that of her brothers, also been allowed to be present. Only little James, now approaching his third year, was still confined to the nursery.

Willie and Maud were there, of course. Maud had not changed much, but Willie was beginning to show his years. Somehow he seemed to have got smaller of late, and his pace had slowed somewhat. Naomi had come up, but just for the day. She would leave on the early morning train on the twenty-third. She had still not told any of them about the existence of little Robert, whom she had left in London in the capable hands of a now rather aged Barker. Donald and Brenda's children were firmly ensconced in Cluny Cottage where they regarded Maud and Willie as their parents. Harry, Susan, and Johnny all regarded themselves as a cut above the Maclaren children. After all, they had been through the war, while the Maclarens had been taking life easy up here in Scotland. The table was completed by the presence of Gordon, the only one who was still serving in the regiment.

Andrew had intended that the meal should be somewhat in the way of a celebration, but unfortunately it did not work out that way. The children were overawed by the presence of the adults, and the adults were restricted in conversation by the presence of the children. Victoria had chosen the menu with care, hoping that the young, unsophisticated palates might find a soup, mutton pie, and jelly to their liking. In fact they did, to which the clean plates at the end of each course bore witness. But it took place in near silence in spite of a few half-hearted attempts on Andrew's part to get the conversation going.

It was the first time that Andrew had managed to have the entire brood around him. He had looked forward to it, but sadly it just did not seem to have come off. However, there was another purpose in this luncheon. Before he and Willie and Gordon changed into mess kit and went off to dine in the officers' mess at the barracks in Beauly, there was something that he wanted to say to the young.

When the last jelly plate had been cleared and the last sticky face had been thoroughly wiped on its napkin, Andrew got to his feet.

'Children,' he said, 'before you go off to play, there is something I want to say to you. I do not know whether you all realize it, but today is the birthday of our regiment. This is the regiment that all of us grown-ups have served in one way or another for most of our lives. It was founded by your great-great-great grandfather – I hope that I have got the right number of greats.' There was a titter. 'It was founded when our country was fighting a man called Napoleon who wanted to rule the world, but we did not let him. Since then, the regiment has served our nation all over the world, and it has become a proud thing to be a Maclaren Highlander. When you boys have to decide what you are going to do with your lives, I would like you to remember that, and at least consider serving in the regiment which gave you your fathers and mothers.

'There is another thing I want to tell you, and that is that before the next batch of recruits take the oath of allegiance, we will probably no longer have a Queen, and probably the greatest chapter in the history of the greatest Empire that the world has ever seen will have ended. But whatever happens, the regiment will go on. It will always be the Maclarens and it will always be your family.'

Andrew sat down. He looked around the blank uninterested faces at the table. It had not worked. Ah well, he thought, it probably takes a much wiser head than mine to be able to talk to children.

While he had been speaking, James, the footman, had come into the dining room carrying a silver salver.

'Yes, what is it?' demanded Andrew.

'If I might have a word with General Bruce, sir.'

'Go ahead then.'

James went over to Willie. 'Sir, Mrs Buchannan has just come over from Cluny. She fears that the house has been broken into.'

'What?' Willie said, rising.

'Sir, she says that she cannot find anything missing, but when she went into your bedroom just after you and Mrs Bruce had left, she found this.' He offered Willie the salver.

'What is all of this?' asked Maud, coming over to join her husband.

On the salver was an envelope addressed to Willie and a small parcel wrapped in a dirty piece of tattered linen. Willie seized the envelope and tore it open. He read the note inside and then looked up gravely.

'What does it say?' asked Maud.

'I think,' said Willie, 'that you had better all hear this. It says:

> I really cannot face you so I have left this by your bedside while you were still asleep. Please try and forgive me for things that I cannot tell you. I am returning to Africa. Please look after my children and try not to remind them of their father. The package should take care of them until they are grown up.

'It's from Donald.'

'Let me see that parcel,' said Maud.

She opened the package and a whitish-grey pebble fell out. 'It's just a stone,' she said.

Gordon came across and picked it up. 'Mother,' he said, 'you've seen stones like this before. Not so big, but similar.' He held the stone up between his thumb and forefinger. 'You've seen them in Kimberley and this is the biggest diamond I have ever seen in my life. It must be worth a king's ransom.'

In the mess that evening there were a lot of familiar names and a lot of unfamiliar faces. The regiment was re-forming.

They had a Chisholm, a Grant, two Farquhars, and among the ranks there were a young MacTavish and three young Gibsons. The family was becoming one again.

As colonel-in-chief, Willie had been accorded the place of honour beneath the colours; colours which that year would be renewed, emblazoned with a host of new battle honours. Andrew sat on the right of the mess president. While they were still at dinner, the head steward handed a note to the president, who glanced at it and folded it. While the port and Madeira were going around for the first time, the president leaned over to Andrew.

'As the senior Maclaren present, will you propose the loyal toast?'

'Thank you, Mr President,' replied Andrew.

'You had better have this and tell them first,' replied the president, and he slipped the note to Andrew.

Andrew rose to his feet. 'Gentlemen,' he said, 'at six thirty this evening, Her Majesty the Queen died peacefully in the arms of her grandson Kaiser Wilhelm the Second of Germany.'

There was a long silence before Andrew spoke again:

'Gentlemen,' he said, raising his glass, 'the King.'